# Also by Douglas Stewart:

## FICTION
*Hard Place*
*Late Bet*
*Undercurrent*
*The Dallas Dilemma*
*Cellars' Market*
*The Scaffold*
*Villa Plot, Counterplot*
*Case for Compensation*

*Capital Crimes* (contribution to thriller short stories)

*M.O* (contribution to crime short stories)

## NON-FICTION
*Terror at Sea*
*Insult to Injury*
*The Brutal Seas*
*Piraten* (German Edition)
*Roulette—Playing to Win* (under pen name Brett Morton)
*Shipping at Risk* (Contributor)
*A Family at Law* (with Gavin Campbell)

# TABLES TURNED

## DOUGLAS STEWART

MP Publishing

# TABLES TURNED

First published in 2016 by
MP Publishing
12 Strathallan Crescent, Douglas, Isle of Man IM2 4NR British Isles
mppublishingusa.com



Cover design by Alison Graihagh Crellin

ISBN 978-1-84982-337-1
10 9 8 7 6 5 4 3 2 1
Will also be available in eBook.

To everyone who shares the excitement
of a white ball slowing on a rotating wheel.

# CHAPTER ONE

*Avoid stress!*

That had been the advice.

Dex scowled at the phone's noisy intrusion. He could guess who was phoning and why. "Sod off," he muttered as he killed the ring-tone. Dawn was breaking and he was alone, fishing for big carp. The silvery surface of the pond spread over a couple of acres. It lay just south of the Thames, between the bridges at Putney and Hammersmith. Far away over Docklands, the sun was just rising.

Before the intrusion, Finlay Dexter had felt chilled. Night fishing was an escape—secreted away from the noise, fumes, and stress of Londoners going about their business. Here, he could savour the smell of unkempt grass and the sweet fragrance of the wild flowers. But night fishing meant more than that—he avoided waking up screaming from the nightmares.

*Give it more time, Mr Dexter. Try fishing!*

That had been Dr Wilfred Grierson's advice two years ago. If the psychiatrist was right, *a big if*, recovery would be another twelve months.

Recently, he had started working some evenings at the Black Sheep pub off the Fulham Palace Road, a brisk walk away from *Who Cares*, the red and green barge on which he lived. It was a forty-five-foot Cheshire narrow boat, moored upstream from Hammersmith Bridge, his own island in the stream.

Occasionally, he thought back to a life now lost. Most often, the reminders came at two or three in the morning, when he awoke screaming with his sheets soaked in sweat.

But never here by the placid waters as dawn broke around him. Here was peace and solitude.

Unless Beth phoned to whine about losing at roulette.

Grierson's words lingered: *Imagine your brain as a badly bruised tomato. Mistreat it and it won't just be a bruise. Keep taking the tablets.*

Grierson were big on tablets.

After the two deaths and his mental breakdown, he had exchanged the rat race for vodka and red wine. Now, medication had replaced the booze.

Being perched on a small stool gave him the simple pleasures he needed. He looked across the still depths beyond the motionless rod tip and watched a pair of moorhens and a white duck glide toward the reeds. He just knew the caller had been his much-loved sister Beth.

He checked his watch: 5:17 a.m.

He had no interest in bling, and he cherished the Cartier only because Beth had given it to him. For someone so intelligent, what she saw in chucking money at roulette wheels was beyond him. As a currency trader at Canary Wharf, she could gamble *other people's* millions—far more sensible.

*Ding!*

Her text arrived. *Dukes Casino tonight. Dinner first at the Wolseley. Urgent. Very. Beth. xxx.*

An hour later, with not the slightest sign that a twenty-pounder fancied the sweet, sticky dough he used as bait, he packed up and swung into his powerful stride along the dusty towpath to Hammersmith. Later would come his four-mile jog and then the smell of sizzling bacon and brown sauce.

After that? More research into the death of Diana, Princess of Wales—murder, as he saw it.

Oh yes. And he'd ring Beth.

It was nearly eleven before he even considered calling her. Sitting at his desk surrounded by cuttings about the Paris tunnel, he stared at his phone, torn between his love of Beth and his hatred of the world in which she moved.

In the narrow confines of the barge, there was no room for a desk as big as he needed. Stacked around him were motor-racing magazines. On the wall was a photo of him in an anti-Iraq War march. A cutout from a newspaper pinned to a corkboard proclaimed CAPITALISM SUCKS. Beside it was a newspaper cutting reading PRINCESS D—IT WAS MURDER.

On the TV, a twenty-four-hour news programme was running.

A summery-looking journalist ended her piece to camera. "This is Tiffany Richmond from the Euston Road for BTC-TV."

Dex had always fancied her in a long-distance way. There had been some great reviews of her book about child starvation and corruption in African foreign aid. He empathised with that big time.

He looked at his phone as it challenged him for a decision. For a moment, he imagined Beth at her smoked-glass desk, high up in a glitzy tower with dozens of colleagues under her command—her team all lined up like battery hens. At thirty-one, Beth was two years his junior. He had always loved her rotten. For his little sis, he would usually do anything—but revisiting Dukes Casino was a leap too far.

But her text sounded desperate.

In his darkest hours, Beth had been there for him. More recently, her attitude had been brusque: *time you put the past behind you.* "You're wasted in that pub pulling pints."

"Pulling the occasional customer too," he had reminded her with a cheeky grin that others found engaging. With his dark hair flopping across his forehead, he had retained a boyish charm that even the tragedy of the murderous fire had failed to age. His looks had survived unblemished. His eyes were wide-set and blue-green, his nose strong and his chin square and prominent. At thirty-three, he still kept in good shape with jogging and regular sessions at the gym near Turnham Green.

At Radley College in Oxfordshire, Dex had been a good athlete, standing just over six feet tall with a lean, muscular build. He had been keen on most sports but had not continued after leaving school.

"Dex, you're wasting your life away. Snap out of it," Beth had persisted. "All your business skills. Your success. Don't waste it." And then had come her big mistake. "And after everything Father did for you."

"Don't you ever come the father bit again," he had angrily snapped back. That had ended their convivial lunch a week or so back. Except for an exchange of apologetic text messages, they had not communicated since.


Decision time.

Tonight?

Chatting up the drinkers at the Black Sheep? Or rubbing shoulders with oil-rich and oily gamblers being fawned over by Dukes' obsequious staff?

He reached her voicemail and listened to her beguilingly soft tone inviting callers to leave a message. "Hi, Beth. Got your message. Sorry I can't make it tonight. Big job on. I'm washing an elephant's testicles. Love you!"

Twenty minutes later, Beth picked up the message and laughed at her brother's typical irreverence. She was still smiling when a friendly colleague, Jason Rodway, stuck his head round the door. "You wanted a word?"

"I'm leaving for Vegas tomorrow, so I need you to read these." Beth pointed to a bunch of reports she had just printed off. "How about coming to Dukes tonight? I need someone there with me. I can explain why over dinner."

Rodway saw the concern on her face. "Sorry. My folk are over from France. Their anniversary."

Disappointed, Beth looked down and then through the window over Docklands before turning to Rodway as if about to say something important. But then she stopped, rounded mouth slightly open.

"Go on," Rodway encouraged.

Beth shook her head, nibbling her lip as she did so. "Another time. Jason, I'm really worried. Dukes Casino is bent. And I've got a lead taking me to Vegas."

"That why you're going?"

"I'll play the tables, of course…but yes, that is precisely why I'm going."

"Sure you don't want to tell me more?"

Her routinely calm look changed as she agonised. Rodway knew that whatever the crisis on the markets, his boss was never flustered. Her razor-like brain made quick decisions, and usually correctly. But something had really shaken her usual confidence. "No, Jason. Not fair to involve you. Maybe when I get back. That's if I can't get Dex interested."

"Your brother's such an idle bastard these days."

Beth's tone was suddenly sharp, quick to defend her brother. "He's under doctor's orders. He's been to hell with no return ticket."

Rodway shrugged. "You know best. But anyway," he grabbed the reading matter, "you take care. Didn't you say Dukes is tied up with that new Space City project on the Strip?" He saw her agree. "Those Vegas guys won't be pussycats. Don't tread on the wrong toes."

Beth fingered a silver picture frame showing her at the Cheltenham Gold Cup with Pepe Carmino, Dukes' London boss. It had been a gift following a hospitality day for their biggest players. "You're right. Space City's a five-billion-dollar super-casino. It should have opened seven months back." She put down the photo. "It's way behind schedule due to strikes and cost overruns. It'll maybe launch in about two months." She turned the picture frame away as if shutting out Pepe Carmino. "Dukes has a big stake and has been digging deep to keep Space City alive."

Rodway looked concerned. "I always reckoned Carmino was less sincere than a whore's squeals of ecstasy."

"Didn't realise you were an expert in that area, Jason." Beth's grin was similar to her brother's as she returned to her screen.

# CHAPTER TWO

The small ball landed on 33 black. "Sonovabitch, I'm quitting." The Texan thumped the roulette table as he spoke to no one in particular. "Your magnet under the table is working overtime, pal." Neither of the staff said anything. The Asian dealer was inscrutable and the inspector seemed to be busy inspecting his fingernails.

Beth nodded in sympathy. She had been a regular at Dukes for nearly a year. The casino operated in an impressive building approached up a flight of stone steps. It stood not far from Scott's restaurant in fashionable Mount Street, Mayfair. Members and guests knew at once from the sight of the doorman in his black and burgundy top hat and matching frock coat that this was something rather special. No Chinese waiters had ever trod down the sweep of the thickly carpeted staircase. They gambled away their tips in the mass-market casinos centered around Leicester Square.

Dukes had been part of the establishment scene for over forty years, and Pepe Carmino, CEO, had owned it for nearly five.

Beth looked at the Texan. "You've had a wild ride." And she knew why—if she could only prove it. But now was not the time for anything beyond soothing words. The American left the table, leaving Beth alone with Jeb Miller, who was the inspector, and the Asian dealer. His name badge said he was Wun Yee but regulars knew him as One-Eye.

The inspector, Miller, was a portly, self-important little man with a tiny mouth beneath a thick black moustache. His beady black eyes watched everything from his high stool. Above him and watching the table from at least four different angles were cameras tucked in behind smoked-glass bowls.

The captured images were watched by staff constantly on a bank of monitors tucked away in some obscure part of the casino. Known colloquially as the *Man-in-the-Sky*, they were designed to prevent fraud by casino staff or cheating players or collusion between players and staff. Beth had always regarded the cameras as her friend when other players had claimed ownership of winning bets she had placed. The cameras had always resolved such disputes quickly and correctly.

A dealer had once told her that they spotted the tiniest detail, like a player having a broken fingernail. "Nothing escapes the boys up there for long,"

"There's got to be a red number soon," said Beth, muttering to herself. Around the Leicester Square casinos, sometimes ten or twelve players would be pushing and jostling to place a two-pound bet on the layout. Dukes was different. Occasionally there were more, but very often, there might be just one or two players when oligarch wealth squelched its way across thick carpet under the discreet lighting of the ornately classical room.

From her seat midway alongside the roulette table, Beth could see fifteen or maybe eighteen players scattered around the baccarat, blackjack, and other roulette tables. Most would leave by dawn having lost hundreds of thousands, if not millions. Most would return hoping for better luck later the same day.

Right now, she could see an Iraqi playing blackjack. He often lost millions for the pleasure of the occasional win. Gobsmacked, she had watched an Indian mogul lose over twelve million at baccarat in a single session—and still come back for more. Beth knew that in comparison, her play was kitty litter, but even so, her own stakes kept Carmino purring.

"Gotta be a red soon," she repeated, more to herself this time. As she spoke, she pushed a mountain of chips onto the box for bets backing any of the eighteen red numbers to come good. As the ball slowed, she gripped the table to watch its dying moments as it skittered across the metal frets that divided each number. And then it dropped, settling in 22 black.

She slumped back in her seat and looked at her remaining chips as One-Eye cleared away her losses. For just a moment, she debated what to do before impulsively pushing out all her chips, once again backing red. Never before had she suffered such a long run of black numbers. Never before had she got down to being cleaned out if she lost.

Without being aware that she had done so, Beth stood up to watch the ball more closely, a vein on her forehead throbbing, her palms slightly moist as she leaned on the green baize. The ball was moving fast, tight beneath the wheel's rim. She could scarcely breathe, her heart pounding, her eyes locked on the ball as it raced above the numbers.

A win now would pull back everything lost and give her nearly eighty thousand in profit.

Beth relished this love-it, hate-it time. This was the kick, the buzz. As the ball slowed, it was like torture by waterboarding, a relentless drip-drip. It was like stepping into thin air tied to a bungee, knowing it was too late to change your mind. It was like free-fall parachuting before the chute opens.

The die was cast. No turning back now. No time to say *sorry, mister, I want my bet back. I've changed my mind.* Suddenly her bet seemed crazy, risking everything on a bouncy white ball. In agony, she watched it dance erratically as it hit the strikers. Reality, the outside world— everything disappeared. Nothing mattered but a white ball and a red number as it skated around the polished steel beside the numbers.

*30 Red.*
*Bounce on.*
*11 Black.*
*Still got legs.*
*36 Red.*
*Teasing me.*
*13 Black.*
*Faltering.*
*Barely moving now. Stopped.*
*But no!*
*There was just enough energy.*
*The ball trickled over the metal fret.*
*27 Red.*
*I've won. Yes, yes, yes!*
*Thank Christ for that!*

A flood of relief coursed through her. Nearly eight hundred thousand smackeroos! Nearly eighty thousand profit! Distantly, Beth heard Jeb Miller's voice. From his stool behind the wheel, the inspector had spoken, but whatever the voice was saying never registered. Beth was still emerging from her trance-like bubble. She felt breathless, drained yet exhilarated all at once. She stared, almost hypnotised as the ball slowly circled on number 27.

Miller's tone was sharper now. What was he saying? She looked up. "Ms D., I am sorry but that was a late bet, a no-bet. I had to get it taken off. You must get your bets on earlier. The ball had dropped before you placed your bet."

Even as she heard the words, Beth saw that One-Eye had pushed her chips off the layout. Beth spoke sharply but in total control of her emotions. "That is so-o-o wrong! I bet long before the dealer said *no more bets*. What's the problem?"

"Not so, I'm afraid. I ordered the dealer to remove the bet. You obviously didn't hear."

With a sinking sensation in her stomach, Beth realised the futility of her position and her tone changed to one of anger. "And I'm telling you my bet was on in plenty of time. And I won."

As Miller edged his fat bottom from the stool to carry on the conversation, Nigel Forster-Brown, the casino manager approached, with a Maltese pit boss and a shift manager. Noisy scenes in an exclusive Mayfair casino were an embarrassment. FB, as he was known to everyone, waved his arms soothingly. "Ms D. Please keep your voice down. If there's a problem, a slight misunderstanding, I'm sure we can sort it."

Beth looked at the tall, stooping figure with contempt. "Come off it, FB! This place stinks! Mr Miller called my bet *late*. In his dreams! I had £790,000 on red and it won. I saw the ball circle the wheel many times after my bet was on. No way had it dropped."

FB spoke quietly, trying to defuse the position. "Please, now please be quiet. Our cameras will resolve it." Forster-Brown moved away to a telephone out of Beth's earshot as Miller struggled back onto his stool, the seams of his dinner jacket straining at every movement. "Do you want to carry on or wait?" He puffed. "Normally, we'd carry on, but as you're the only person at the table, it's your choice."

"I'll wait," Beth snapped back. Then she saw FB answer the phone, nod his head once or twice and then walk across, his eyes looking at some distant horizon. Beth knew this meant nothing. FB only rarely met anyone's gaze. He stood beside Miller. "I'm sorry, Ms D. I'm afraid the inspector was right. The cameras caught it all. After that American left and with nobody else playing, the dealer spun rather sooner than before. Perhaps it caught you unawares. You started to put out all your chips but then you hesitated. After the dealer said *no more bets*, you finally pushed the whole lot on. But the ball had dropped. Not onto number 27 at that point, you understand. But it had reached that slow speed where no casino allows any more bets. You didn't lose, but unfortunately you didn't win."

"This is unbelievable!" Beth wanted to let rip with a torrent of words last used when she had been aged eighteen and a pupil at Roedean. But something held her back "This is one big unfunny joke. Who writes your scripts? Ben Elton? I insist on watching the recordings."

By his gentle and almost effeminate standards, FB's tone was frosty as he stared at the thick pile carpet. "Not possible. House rules. We are not running the Odeon Cinema."

Beth thought for a moment. "I want to see Pepe." But even as she spoke, she knew this was a lost cause, just another indication that Dukes was crooked as hell. *Damn Jason! Damn Dex! If either had been with me, Miller could never have pulled this trick.*

FB looked at the wheel as he replied. "Mr Carmino is having din-ner. He'll talk to you later." He turned to One-Eye. "Carry on. Spin the wheel."

"Hold it," commanded Beth. Her voice was taut and her tone clipped as rage continued to rip through her. "*I* will decide when *I* am ready to bet. You will then spin the wheel when my bet is on. If I decide to bet. Understood?"

FB nodded okay and then scuttled away, exiting through a door marked PRIVATE. Seconds later, after climbing a flight of stairs, he tapped in the code and was admitted to the Surveillance Room, where three employees were studying several banks of monitors with ever-changing views.

"Wipe all recordings of Roulette Table Three and any other one in that area. Technical problems." The listeners laughed as one of them set to work.

Downstairs by Roulette Table Three, Beth was still moving her chips from one pile to another as she debated what to do. At that moment, Pepe Carmino appeared, gliding across the carpet as smoothly as a snake. He was probably just over six foot with dark, Latinate features. If his movements were smooth as silk, his tongue had been designed to match. The only blemish to his mid-forties matinée-idol looks was an old and faded scar down one cheek, but even that only added an air of attractive mystery.

"Ah, Pepe," Beth volunteered at once on seeing him in his dinner jacket and immaculate white shirt. "I've a serious…"

He patted her arm. She had always felt uncomfortable when he touched her, but most of the women members fawned around him and seemed flattered by his attention. However, Beth did enjoy listening to his pseudo posh accent.

To the majority of the non-Brit clientele, he probably sounded like aristocracy, one of the braying masses who come out to play at Glyndebourne, the Royal Enclosure at Ascot, or to watch polo in Windsor Great Park. But on Dex's only visit to Dukes, he had spotted the occasional mistake and had convinced her that Pepe was either an East-Ender or an Essex boy who had paid for elocution. Now she enjoyed listening out for lapses into estuary English.

"I know. I've been informed. I've just viewed the recording. It was indeed a late bet. We was…were perfectly in our rights to take it off."

"Let me see the recording, then."

"Club rules. Nobody gets into our Surveillance Room. I wish it were otherwise, as I would far rather have you convinced. But I cannot make exceptions. The cameras don't lie."

Beth stood silent for a moment. "No. Not the cameras." She glared at Carmino, who got the unspoken message.

"But Ms D, you didn't lose. You just didn't win."

Beth turned to Jeb Miller as she pushed out every single chip betting on red again. "Spin the wheel." Then she faced Carmino again. "And if I lose, you've just made the biggest mistake in your life bar none. I never forget. I never forgive."

The ball trickled to a stop.

"Ten, black, even," said One-Eye.

# CHAPTER THREE

From the canned music system, the strains of Adele could be heard above the mid-evening chatter of the under-thirty-five drinkers who sat at chrome tables or stood in cliques, toes tapping as they chatted. Behind the bar of the Black Sheep pub, Dex was just adding the tonic to a blonde's vodka when Beth appeared. On seeing her, Dex waved cheerfully and moved to an empty part of the counter so that he could lean across and kiss her. In her expensive outfit of cream jacket, red blouse, and shortish black skirt, she oozed class and style as she shimmied between the other drinkers to cross the room. For a moment, Dex suddenly felt very guilty at ignoring her request for help.

She stretched across the bar to add a hug to his kiss. "Where's the elephant?"

"Out the back, drying off. Tomorrow I'm on rota for washing a skunk's scrotum. Can life get any better?" As he spoke, he poured her a diet Coke and nothing for himself.

"Probably not unless you're talking Formula One, cricket, Princess Diana theories, or chatting up blondes."

"Guilty as charged, but don't forget the fishing."

"But no time to help your little sis."

"I'd be no help at Dukes."

"Wrong." Beth's stare penetrated deep. "I needed you there. It cost me over eight hundred thousand tonight."

Dex whistled. "You're mad. Crazy. Risking money like that on roulette. But didn't you say you always won at Dukes? Your system?"

She nodded. "All my winnings these past eleven months. All gone, just like that." She snapped her fingers to highlight the speed. "That is not the point."

"Eight hundred grand could have fed a load of orphans." Dex picked up a couple of bottles and started to juggle them, much to Beth's irritation. "Anyway," he continued as he deftly caught a falling bottle behind his back, "how in hell could I have stopped you losing all that dosh?"

"By being there." Quickly, she explained how, on her previous visit a week or two back, she had been suspicious of a *late bet* call and how she wanted a witness to prevent a repetition.

"More fool you for risking it."

Beth made no admission, though her eyes conceded her mistake. "I still need your help."

She watched as Dex opened his wallet and pulled out a couple of fivers, which he offered to her. "Will that get you through the weekend?"

"Be serious, Dex. I'm onto something big, seriously big."

"Look, you know what old Doc Grierson advised."

"Lifestyle gurus, psychiatrists, quacks. Mumbo-jumbo and psycho-babble. Dex—you're better! You know it. I know it. So get a life again."

"I'm ill and I have a ton of pills to prove it. Besides which, perhaps I now enjoy just being a bum." He waved cheerily at two new arrivals who had seated themselves along the bar. "Back in a mo. The brunette, Molly, is, well, one of my specials. I've been chatting her up for weeks. I think I'm winning."

He went to serve the two women. The process turned into animated chat and raucous laughter from the customers, much to Beth's irritation as she seethed on her own, tapping at the keys on her iPad. When Dex came back, she moved straight into overdrive.

"Listen, Dex. This is not just about me. I know they're cheating the members."

"Casinos don't need to cheat. They get rich off mugs like you."

"Remember Pepe Carmino?" Dex nodded as he dried and polished glasses still hot from the dishwasher below the counter. "I've been given a contact in Vegas—a dealer over there called Tavio. Apparently, he can give me the whole nine yards on motive for cheating. Better still, Tavio knows about a skeleton rattling around Dukes. I'm told it's bigger than the *Angel-of-the-North*."

Dex was more interested now than he appeared. "So what do you want? Me to go to Vegas?"

Beth fingered the gold brooch that dominated her lapel. "Come with me. I fly in the morning. Two nights there and back to Heathrow." She saw that she had his attention now. Then she paused, knowing the next bit was tricky. "On the return flight, I change planes in Chicago and Father gets on there. He's doing a deal on some property by the lake."

"Then it's a no. It would be no even without Father. With him, it's no, no, no…not bloody likely." He leaned across the bar and held her hand. "You must understand that? I'll never forgive him."

"But to help me? Couldn't you? Wouldn't you?"

"No."

She looked across at him, a hint of tears welling up in her eyes. "Dad's knocking on a bit and feels very alone."

"Walking out was the best thing Mother ever did. And even with all his riches, he's never found anybody else. Does that tell you something or what?" The bitterness showed in Dex's eyes and in his mouth, which had turned mean and narrow. His voice had taken on a throaty edge like a dog's deep growl.

"If Tavio comes good, I'll hold the nuts on Pepe's corruption. If you refuse to come, at least when I get back, I'll need your help twenty-four-seven till we sort this out. I can't handle this alone."

"*He never got to Vegas.* That's what I want on my tombstone. You know my views on America after being at Harvard…too full of Americans."

"You're big on conspiracies like Princess Di and JFK, yet you won't take me seriously."

Dex shrugged. "So far I'm underwhelmed."

"Please come. I'm scared."

"Don't go, then. It's not your problem. Forget gambling. Forget casinos. Forget Pepe Carmino. Find yourself a husband, have a couple of kids. Get yourself a life."

Beth's knuckles whitened and the colour rose to her cheeks. "That's rich coming from you! I will *never* surrender to cheats like Dukes." As he looked at her and thought back to their childhood, Dex knew her comment was on the button. She never would give in.

"Maybe if you uncover something positive, I might help a little. But I'm not fit to be a bodyguard. Or a wet-nurse, come to that. You're playing with fire. You realise that?"

"Calling *late bet* a few times a week could save Dukes twenty million a year. Blackjack scams could add another ten mill."

"Dukes doesn't need the money."

"You're wrong. They do. They're bankrolling Space City like crazy." Beth scowled as Dex returned to his juggling—this time with three bottles, much to the delight of the brunette with a skirt that had ridden high up her thighs as she perched on a barstool. "This Tavio guy has something about Pepe and Panama."

"Must be a hat, Beth." Dex chuckled.

Beth drained her Coke angrily, but then her face softened and she stretched out to give him a hug. "Think about it, Dex. I'm scared."

He went round the end of the bar to stand close to her. He pulled her next to him and was shocked to find her trembling. He held her tighter. "Don't go, but if you really must, then take care. If you poke a bear with a stick…well, you know the rest."

"I can't let go. There's something in me tells me I must."

"That's why you've done so well down in the City. Love you, Sis." Dex watched her exit. Somehow she seemed smaller, more careworn than the eye-catching person that had made her entrance just thirty minutes earlier. As she disappeared from sight, he felt queasy and then deeply wretched at what he had done. He slipped through the door behind the bar and downed another three of his prescribed pills with a gulp of water.

When he returned to the bar, he looked lovingly at the line of optics, any one of which used to give him temporary solace. But not now. By working in a pub, he had proved he still had enough of that inner steel he feared had been lost ever since…. He shut out the thought and turned to the two women at the bar. They both seemed ready for top-ups, *and perhaps more.* He moved toward them and grabbed their attention by juggling with three bottles, finishing his routine with a flourish. "Same again?"

"We're leaving."

"Come on, Molly. You too, Zoe. How about we meet at that Thai place round the corner when I finish?"

The two women laughed and Zoe, the younger one, flashed a ring. "I'm married."

"Never let a ring get between inclination and opportunity." The two women laughed again.

"Another time."

"We'd make a great threesome."

"Dream on, chancer!" Molly's words were far from dismissive, at least to Dex's ears.

With a blown kiss from Zoe, the women slipped off their stools and were gone, leaving Dex to his thoughts of Beth. But at just before 11 p.m., Molly was back, this time on her own.

"Thai place?" Dex enquired, having quickly moved to serve her an appletini.

"Sounds good. Zoe needed to get back to Wandsworth, so I thought maybe I'd enjoy a Pad Thai."

"My pad or yours, then?" The grin was infectious.


The digital clock by the bed showed just after 2 a.m. Molly and Dex lay entwined on his queen-sized in the otherwise dark confines of his bedroom. As she stroked his ear, Molly purred sleepily with contentment, "Where have you been all my life?"

"Sex on a boat. The earth always moves." He continued to run his fingers down her cheek and was about to offer more of the same when he realised she was already asleep. Moments later, he joined her, arm still cradled around her neck.

But under an hour later, Molly awoke terrified. The shouting seemed to be right in her ear.

"Fire! Fire!"

Beside her, Dex was half-raised on one elbow. He was screaming, the sweat pouring off him and soaking her. His entire body was twitching and shaking out of control.

Now fully alert, Molly leaped out of bed. She stood naked looking at Dex's contorted face, which scared her in the greenish light from the clock's face.

"Call 999. Fire! Fire!"

Molly looked around the narrow room and knew at once that there was no fire. "Wake up, Dex. You're dreaming. F'Chrissake, wake up!" She switched on the bedside light, and after a few seconds, she saw his eyes flicker open. Gradually the world according to Dex came into focus and he too rose from the bed, his body glistening all over with rivulets of sweat.

"Christ, Molly! I'm sorry. I'm okay now."

Molly was already pulling up her crimson panties and hastening to get away. "You scared the hell out of me, Dex."

"I'm sorry. I sometimes get these vivid, terrible nightmares. Not often, mind. Always the same. But don't go. Please. Let me get you a coffee, water. Whatever."

Molly sat on the corner of the bed. She shook her head as she adjusted her short, tight skirt and then started to pull on her tall black boots. "I'm out of here. That was too weird for me."

Dex grabbed his dressing gown and wrapped it around him as he followed her into the confines of the sitting area and galley. "Let me walk you to your car."

"No. I don't want you anywhere near me."

When she was out of sight, Dex returned to the cabin and headed for the bathroom, where he kept his tablets for his *psychotic disorder*, as Grierson loved to call it. He took two with a glass of water and then flopped onto the rumpled and sweat- soaked sheets, his hands clenching and unclenching. The room smelled stale, and he opened the small porthole to let in the chilly night air. That had been the first nightmare for days, maybe even two weeks. He held his head in his hands and tried to shut out the fear that kept hitting him with the force of a steam hammer.

*Maybe I never ever will be cured.*

*Maybe I just have to accept nights like this.*

*Maybe those memories will always haunt me.*

"Damn you, Father."

# CHAPTER FOUR

Just under a mile off the Las Vegas Strip on West Sahara, Enzo Letizione emerged from the Nevada & General Bank. It was nearing noon and the heat shimmered off the sidewalk and the roof of his black BMW sedan. The sky was cloudless except over the Spring Mountains to the west. It was too soon for the Vegas monsoon season, but the exceptional heat even by Nevada standards suggested that there could be a storm by late afternoon.

Letizione was wearing a lightweight pale blue suit with a striped shirt and no tie. Beneath his wavy, thinning hair, there was a hint of moisture he owed to the meeting with the bank rather than the heat that now beat down on him.

As he walked the few yards to his car, his heavy jowls were unusually taut and his eyes flashed hatred. There was a frown on his forehead as he wrestled with the aftermath of the uncomfortable meeting. It was a relief when he swung his bulky figure into the car, slammed shut the door, and set the air conditioning to full blast.

Before pulling away, he reset the radio station from the heavy beat of the blues channel which he had been listening to on the way to the bank. Now he needed something different, and he chose a cool jazz station as background for his drive to the Venetian Hotel a few minutes away. Letizione, a youngster in Vegas during the bad old days of mob rule, phoned Pepe Carmino, who confirmed he would be waiting for him under the canopy.

Letizione spotted him at once. The Englishman was talking on his phone. Kitted out in a lime-green shirt and yellow slacks, he reminded the American of a golfer. They greeted each other with mutual profuse but false sincerity and then headed south toward the towering edifice of Space City. As they rounded the curve on the Strip just before reaching Caesars Palace, Space City could fleetingly be glimpsed beyond the MGM, but then it was obscured. By the time they were backed up by the lights at Flamingo, the banal pleasantries had been concluded.

"Enzo—we're in this shit because you screwed up." As he spoke, Pepe lean slightly toward the driver, who could smell the type of expensive aftershave for which he had no time at all.

"We been unlucky."

"Bullshit! I put you in charge. You're the boss over here. Due to your lousy management, London's being bled white. We're working our backsides off to throw money at your bankers. Till the strikes, the cost overruns, Dukes was legit. Life was sweet."

"Don't blame me for the unions."

"But I do." Pepe's retort was instant, and Enzo looked ahead to avoid the steadiness of Pepe's stare. "Your job is to fix problems. Your job is to deliver." Pepe unwrapped a piece of chewing gum and started to chew vigorously as at last they crossed the busy junction at Flamingo and saw the crowds gathering to watch the sway of the fountains outside Bellagio. "We okay for the Grand Opening? On time, is it?"

"You got it."

"And those leeches at the bank? You got them tranquil yet? If not, you've got to fix them."

"Purring. That extra moola you're sending, they're pussycats." Enzo could see from the corner of his eye that Carmino was not buying into this. "Believe me," he added, making the disbelief mount further.

Pepe tugged Enzo's sleeve. "I don't buy that shit. I can smell your sweat. There's more. There's *a but*, isn't there?"

"Okay, so they just told me they called in another slug of capital. Fifty mill, pronto."

"Fifty million dollars!" Pepe thumped the dashboard. "You think my name is David Copperfield and I can produce that kind of money from a rabbit's backside? Where the hell do I find another fifty?" Neither had an answer to the rhetorical question, and there was silence except for the strains of Brubeck from the surround sound. "Going bust is not an option. Firing you is."

A security guard in a peaked cap and navy-blue uniform recognised Letizione and waved the car through the security and into the nearly finished Grand Entrance. No sooner had they got out than Letizione's gofer appeared offering bottles of water, hard hats, and the opportunity to stare upward at the nearly complete building. It was truly magnificent, and from the outside, looked ready to open. It towered over the Strip—sixty-three floors of shimmering metallic blue in a gentle curved design.

Inside, however, they watched dozens of electricians, electronics engineers, carpenters, and supervisors scurrying in every direction. Everywhere, there was movement. Overhead, there were still multi-coloured cables awaiting the ceiling tiles to complete the finished look. The floor was still uncarpeted so that the sounds of jackhammers, cutters, welding equipment, and circular saws surrounded them and made talking impossible.

They walked up the long staircase to Letizione's office. It was spacious and comfortable to a fault. Modern artwork adorned the walls and figurines on plinths nestled between fronds of greenery that softened the box shape. From a drinks cabinet with sink unit, he poured Bombay Sapphire gin with generous slugs slopped over ice and lime and low on the tonic. Here in his own domain, the American felt more at ease, and was pleased that at last Pepe had mellowed after seeing the progress.

"Look, Enzo. I've sweated most of the players at Dukes dry—used up all the usual, old-time scams. But I'm concerned. If just a few members get suspicious, then gossip could spread. There's a woman. She's a ball-breaker. The word *feisty* would undersell her. She was rolled over the other day and she knew it. She couldn't prove it, of course. No witnesses."

"And so?"

"There's only one option left. The one we discussed before. Last-chance time. And I'm not doing that for free. If my balls is on the line, some of the cash being shifted will never reach Vegas. We top up our offshores, you and me both. Ninety-five percent skim to me, five percent to your account."

Carmino was in no mood to negotiate. Letizione saw the dead-eyed look and decided to be grateful for what was on offer. "So you doing a deal with that tight-assed Geneva lawyer? The guy you said was so mean he even cuts his own hair?"

Pepe laughed for the first time since his arrival. "That's him. Pudding-bowl look. But he's smart. His clients is bent politicians, Brussels insiders on the take, industrialists, people-smugglers. They all got the same problem. Untaxed wealth, maybe bribes, maybe stolen money. And now Swiss Banks and their secrecy—that's gone, dead like the dodo. The panic word is *transparency* – tax havens sharing information and whistleblowers getting pay-offs for snitching to Government about bank customers. The Feds can open up Swiss Bank accounts quicker than a can of beans. So this lawyer, he's also got a shed-load of funny money from Europe, Russia and the Japanese Yakuza. It's all hidden behind anonymous foundations and companies in remote islands but they is…are all run through this lawyer's office. And he needs to shift it quick."

"Piggybanks ain't no fun till they're empty." Letizione pressed a switch and a floor-to-ceiling mirror suddenly became two-way. From his office on the mezzanine level, the two men stared across the atrium, which was dominated by a mockup of a Space Shuttle on a launch pad.

"We done some good stuff back in London. Like Boy Scouts—well prepped with a second set of books, new bank accounts. Last month, I fixed the inspector from the Gambling Commission."

"What's the deal then for laundering?"

"Like I said, pudding-bowl is a mean bastard and wants a cut, but his clients are desperate." Carmino's smile was greedy, showing a lot of whitened teeth. "Dukes won't be over-generous. So, wiv everything else we got running at the tables, I reckon to keep your cocksuckers at the bank happy."

"That's cool then," Letizione commented, thinking more about the question he had been putting off asking. "You ever work in Panama?" The American tried to make the question sound casual.

"Never been there. Why do you ask?"

"I was playing Texas Hold 'Em, low stakes stuff, down at the Golden Nugget. I met an off-duty dealer there. Name was Tavio. He'd had a few drinks, I could tell. The guy was playing loose. He works in that joint by the Trop, deals blackjack."

Pepe swirled the tonic with a swizzle-stick and then sipped. "So?"

"Reckons he and a friend came across you down south in Panama. Years ago."

"Guy's mistaken. Like I say. I've never been there."

Enzo Letizione shrugged dismissively, though he was sure Carmino was lying. He wanted to ask several follow-on questions but decided to keep them for another time. "Ain't no big deal. I guess the guy was even drunker than he seemed." He sat down at his U-shaped desk and pulled out a slim folder from a locked drawer. "Here's the schedule till launch. That's the ongoing work; those are the celebs to be invited and the high rollers we're flying in." He turned the final page. "And that's the plan for the soft opening. You got it all there."

Carmino looked distracted, as if lost in the details of the documents. He grabbed a handful of peanuts and washed them down with the remains of his drink. "I'll take this with me. We can talk over dinner tonight."


That evening, as Letizione and Carmino settled down for dinner in the Picasso Restaurant at Bellagio, Beth was seated in the Nine Fine Irishmen bar in the New York, New York Casino barely eight hundred metres away. She hadn't moved for twenty minutes, but her eyes had been watching everybody who had stayed, left, or arrived. Satisfied that nobody was tracking her, she emptied her glass of Merlot and then swapped the convivial atmosphere of the bar for the sprawl of the main floor of the casino. She was taking no chances, and decided not to return directly to her hotel. Instead, she headed for the escalator to the footbridge across the Strip to take her into the MGM-Grand Casino.

As she walked with short, bustling steps, a maroon bag slung over her shoulder, a solitary man who had been seated by the slots, watching the bar entrance, stood up and slipped into the throng so that he was five behind her as she rode the escalator. As she turned at the top to gaze back down, he kept his face obscure and then mingled with the crowd behind her, all crossing over the Strip in the hot night air.

Still not totally at ease, Beth used a small side exit from the MGM. She crossed a dingy street and hurried through the racks of souvenirs and toys in a gift emporium and then hastened north along the busy sidewalk until she could cross back to the Mandarin Oriental. And all the while, the solitary man was in the kaleidoscope throng of pedestrians who were heading in both directions. He kept pace with her, not too close but never letting her out of sight, never so obvious that Beth had the slightest reason to be suspicious.

By the time she had reached her room and locked the door, she was feeling sheepish at her paranoia. Her bag and its contents she locked in the safe. It was nearly 10 p.m., so she decided on room service before going down to hit the roulette table in the glitter of the Cosmopolitan next door.

It was pushing toward noon when Dex returned from the supermarket and settled down to read a novel called *Family Legacy*, written by an American who seemed to have a pretty strong insight into how and why JFK was murdered in Dallas. He had just reached a chapter about the sighting of Lee Harvey Oswald in New Orleans when his phone rang.

"Beth! How's Vegas?" He checked the time. "God! It must be around 3 a.m. over there. You had a big win?"

"It's just gone four—but listen, Dex." He heard what sounded very like a sob at the other end of the line.

"Beth? You okay?" Her voice sounded strained and her breathing seemed noisily uneven.

"I'm leaving today. That guy I came to interview. Tavio Sanches? Y'know from Panama?"

"How did it go?"

"I just heard. He's dead. Gunned down."

# CHAPTER FIVE

Dex spent an anxious afternoon trying to concentrate on the JFK book while his mind kept replaying the conversation, full of images of his petrified sister. On several occasions he looked wistfully at the bottle of Glenlivet that he kept beside the TV to remind himself that he was still fighting his demons. Somehow, he resisted, instead taking 100mg of his pills for what the men in white coats called his *acute depression and personality disorder.*

In his head, he could still hear her frightened voice. "It was on the local news. Las Vegas Homicide reckoned a contract killing. No known motive. I'm scared, terrified."

Dex wanted to say he had warned her not to get involved but he did not. *Now* was not the time. *Now*, she needed him. *Now*, his little sister was alone in a city of two million people, one of whom was a gunman whom she obviously feared might want to kill her too. Stunned at the implications, Dex simply whistled while he gathered his thoughts. "Where's Pepe Carmino?"

"Dex—I'm scared to death." Her voice was breaking with emotion.

"Does Carmino know you are in Vegas?"

"I told FB—Forster-Brown, so I guess, yes, Pepe could know.

Where he is, I have no idea."

"Get the next flight to Chicago. That's where you're meeting Father, isn't it?"

"Correct. We land at Heathrow at 7:15 a.m. Father's limo will meet us there." There was a brief pause and he heard rustling paper. "Take down my computer username. It is GADECH714538. And my password—ZAYBXCWB. It's backed up on the Cloud."

"Beth, chill out a little. Nobody is coming to get you." Dex found he was wrestling to find the right words. He knew, they *both* knew, that his soothing words were meaningless.

Dex heard another sob and a sniff and he imagined his little sister in a foetal position on a bed, clutching her phone. "Dex, write down this name too. Maria-Elena Sanches. Panama. Got it? Okay. Let's meet tomorrow. Drinks in the Rivoli Bar at the Ritz. 7 p.m. There's nobody else I can trust. Dukes and Space City must be destroyed."

"Father?"

"Confide in him? You know that's plumb crazy." The old Beth shone through for a moment.

"Love you, Beth. Safe flight."

"And if…" Again Dex heard terrified sobs. "…and if I don't make it, promise me you'll never rest till you get back my losses and destroy…" Her voice gave out completely.

"You'll be just fine, Beth. But if it makes you feel better, then yes, I promise. I'll never rest. Drinks at 7 p.m."

Now, as he looked at his scribbled notes of her username and password, it all seemed unreal. He wished he could take the call all over again and explore why she was so terrified. He needed to be briefed on what she had actually done, what she had achieved to put her at such risk. The day dragged, and it was a relief when it was time to head for the Black Sheep. He needed to be busy to stop his imagination running wild.

Pulling pints and mixing absurd yellow or pink cocktails helped Dex through the evening, and he was just ending his stint when his phone rang. It was Beth, sounding much better. "I got out of Vegas pdq. But I'm fine now."

"Where are you, then?"

"I'm with Father at O'Hare, Chicago. He's in the bar downing a double Jamesons. We're boarding in two minutes."

"I told you. See? You'll be just fine. Love you, Beths."

"Love you, Dex. See you at the Ritz."

Unseen by Beth as she had cleared Immigration at McCarran in Vegas, someone had been watching, intent on making sure that she was boarding—a solitary figure who then spoke rapidly into his cell phone. In London, Arnie Fisher, a right little weasel of a man, took the call that Pepe Carmino had said he should expect.

He and Pepe went back to schooldays in Essex, but ever since, their careers had taken very different routes. To Pepe, Arnie Fisher was indispensable, his go-to man *par excellence.*

With Beth safely away from Vegas, Dex slept remarkably well. On awakening, he looked out to take in the picture-perfect scene—the blue sky beyond the river with a rowing-four skimming by, the cox bellowing instructions. It was a wonderful summer morning in a year when days like this had been too rare. As he stood in the galley scrambling eggs and turning the sizzling smoked bacon, he was planning the day ahead. Beside him, the TV was on. After a jog down beyond Fulham Football Ground at Craven Cottage, he wanted to track down that lawyer who had been close to the Alma Underpass when Princess Diana's car had crashed into the pillar. It would be another piece of the jigsaw.

Whether he would ever publish his research as a book, Dex was still undecided. It would not make him popular with the Establishment. For sure, he had gathered an impressive list of unexplained questions - the answers to which did not fit comfortably with an accident. But the market had become crowded. Anyone who catalogued the long list of unexplained facts and downright contradictions risked being painted as a subversive or crank. *Do I care?* The media had largely closed ranks to ring-fence the outcome of the investigation.

As he settled down at the small table to enjoy the eggs and bacon, he heard the wail of sirens from emergency vehicles. With the busy Great West Road close by, it was a sound he was well used to.

He munched contentedly on the toast, remembering that he had to be at the Ritz in Piccadilly at seven. He saw the scribbled note with Beth's username and password to get onto her computer data through the Cloud. He tucked it into the JFK book and returned to planning the afternoon. *Maybe some trout fishing over at Brentford?* As he devoured the last of the smoky bacon, his mind was not really attuned to the talking heads on the TV until the words *Hogarth Roundabout* grabbed his attention.

# CHAPTER SIX

"…for drivers in West London. There are reports of a major accident on the eastbound carriageway of the A4 on the approach to Hammersmith. First reports are of at least two vehicles involved, with one of them on fire. Both carriageways are now closed, and drivers are advised to take an alternative route. We will update this shortly, but expect severe delays in the Hammersmith and Chiswick area during the morning rush hour."

Traffic warnings always made him feel smug that he was out of the madness of daily commuting. He glanced out of the small window to the north and saw that the blue of the sky was now tainted by a rising plume of thick black smoke that paled gradually as it rose and spread, darkening the horizon as far as he could see.

He imagined his father's face, puce with rage that even with all his wealth, traffic jams left him snarled up and helpless. His money could fix most things, but short of using a helicopter into Battersea, this was beyond his power. Thoughts of Father prompted him to phone Beth, just to check in. He dialed her number but it rang unanswered.

He had no number for his father, an arrangement that suited them both equally well. As he settled down again to the pot of Kenyan coffee and wheat toast, he found himself wondering if just maybe the limo had been involved. He checked Heathrow Arrivals and established that Beth's flight had landed ahead of schedule at 7:05 a.m. It was odd for her not to switch on her phone as soon as permitted.

With none of the usual enjoyment from his hot toast and Oxford marmalade, he hurriedly pushed the plate to one side. He turned on LBC radio and at the end of an interview with a Labour politician, they cut to Hammersmith. "Traffic in West London is at a standstill within the entire network surrounding the Great West Road between Hogarth Roundabout and the Hammersmith Flyover. Eyewitness reports as yet unconfirmed say that an HGV loaded with aggregate has mounted an executive saloon car on the eastbound carriageway. One vehicle caught fire, but reports suggest that perhaps four vehicles are now ablaze. So far, there is no word about casualties. Our reporter…"

Dex had heard enough. Like a man possessed, he was away, striding through the galley and out to the deck before leaping onto the steps up to Chiswick Mall, a street full of classy homes looking across the Thames. From there, he ran into Eyot Gardens, his speed increasing to a pavement-pounding flat-out as he headed directly toward the lingering black smoke. When he reached the dual carriageway with every lane of traffic at a standstill, he looked westward and saw, less than a quarter of a mile distant, the blue flashing lights of police, fire, and ambulances.

Fists pumping furiously, he raced beside the jammed cars that had been trying to head west for Heathrow and beyond, but was soon faced with the blue and white tape that blocked any further access. Both arms held high, he waved at a WPC who was standing just beyond the central barrier, and although she saw him, she turned away to talk into her phone. From as near as he could get, Dex could see swirling black smoke and steam rising from where the fire crew had been hosing down several vehicles.

The air was flecked with burning particles, and there was no escaping the acrid pungency given off from the destroyed vehicles. It filled his mouth and lungs and his eyes were stinging. He could hear the whine of cutting equipment, but details of what or who were involved were zilch except for the very obvious burned-out cab of a truck. Its chassis was at an angle of some forty-five degrees to the road surface, the remains of the cab pointing skyward like a giant praying mantis. What remained of the door on the driver's side was wide open.

Dex turned to a West Indian driver of a hemmed-in flatbed truck, intending to ask if he could clamber onto it for a better view. However, at that moment, he saw a TV crew packing up and crossing the central barrier toward him. With the cameraman was the reporter he recognised as Tiffany Richmond. She was wearing a pale blue blouse under a black jacket with a simple silver chain around her neck. She looked smaller than when on the news, maybe five foot six and daintily built. Her two-tone chestnut hair was cut short but with distinctive highlights.

"Hey, Tiffany!" he yelled at the top of his voice against the hub-bub of noise from the crash scene. He tried again, and then the West Indian beside him tooted to catch her attention and she turned to see Dex waving furiously. For a moment she hesitated, but then changed direction and approached him, phone clamped to her ear. Her elfish face asked him what he wanted without words.

"Heh! Thanks! I need your help. What did you see? Is there a limo involved?" As she ended her call, he continued, the words tumbling out. "My sister. My father, they were in his limo heading into London. Is it a limo? Anything you can give me?" He barely took in that she needed scarcely any makeup, her pale skin being smooth, her eyes almond-shaped and watchful. Her sympathetic look came more from her eyes than the small mouth, which had the slightest hint of pink lipstick.

"You tried phoning them?"

"No answer." From his height, he looked slightly down to her uptilted face.

She answered at once, her voice quiet and sensitive. "No names have been released. I doubt they're even known yet. There was a limo involved and it had three occupants—all taken to the Charing Cross Hospital, Fulham Palace Road."

"And their condition? I mean, were they…?" Dex could not bring himself to finish the sentence.

"We were given no details beyond *serious condition*. They had been removed just before I arrived."

"Did you get the registration of the limo?" Dex spotted from the flinch that she knew the answer, but there was a delay while she decided whether to tell him. He was vaguely aware of her perfume as he hovered close to her,

"Your name is?"

"Dexter. Finlay Dexter. Known as Dex." He saw the immediate shocked reaction and her oval face puckered, her jaw tightening. "The limo would have had a personalised number-plate. He owned CHAS 111 and DEX 911."

"The two main vehicles were burned out. The truck appears to have struck the limo from behind. It rode up and onto the roof. That's what a witness told me." She paused. "And the car's front number plate was partially destroyed." She lowered her eyes. "Look. I mean…I'm sorry."

Dex saw a slight hint of tears in her eyes as she glanced up at him. He found himself amazed that reporters who saw and heard so much suffering could get emotionally hung up. Especially someone like Tiffany Richmond, who had watched countless children dying in Africa. "Dex, I'm sorry, but…the registration of the limo was DE something. The rest was unreadable." For a moment, he felt faint and swayed alarmingly. Instinctively, she grabbed his bare arm to steady him. "Would you like a lift? You don't look too good."

Dex clenched his fists, took a deep breath, and forced himself to stay calm when every nerve end was sending messages of despair. *Was fire about to destroy his life again?* He tried to appear stoic and stiff-upper-lip as he fought to meet her gaze, but his voice was strangulated and his brain was pretty much scrambled. "Thanks. I mean yes. But no. I can walk back…so yes. I'll be fine. I only live just over there." He pointed vaguely toward the river. "I'll head for the hospital. The Chelsea & Westminster, you said. Right?"

Tiffany corrected him gently. "The Charing Cross. Much nearer." As she spoke, she pressed her card into his hand. "If I can help, let me know. Sometimes we can find out more than the public—and that includes family members. But we don't always report it. Or not at once, anyway." She squeezed his arm. "And I hope you get some good news at the hospital." Her face told Dex that he should be prepared for the worst. "And maybe I can chat with you when the dust settles. By the way—your sister's name and your father's?"

Dex was in no mood to tell her where to stuff her question. She had helped him, and so without hesitation he told her it was Beth Dexter and Sir Charles Dexter CBE. But instantly he regretted his cooperation as she followed up.

"When I get further ID confirmation, of course I will mention their identities. On an *unconfirmed reports suggest*, you understand. And I'll mention that you raced to the scene."

"You're a reporter." He gave her a feeble despairing smile. "As a breed, I despise you. But yes, go on—say what you like." She looked puzzled at the strength of his animosity but said nothing as he turned away and headed back to the towpath toward the Fulham Palace Road.

That number-plate. The chauffeur plus two occupants. Three in all. Not good … heh…but… he thought back to Beth's fears for her life. *Perhaps it had not been an accident.*


It was over seven hours later when a weary-looking surgeon entered the small room where Dex had been waiting for hours. He was a distinguished-looking man. "I believe you're Sir Charles Dexter's son?"

"Correct."

"I'm sorry. You've had quite a wait. Simon Morrison. I'm a neuro-surgeon. We're alone in here, so let's just stay put, shall we? Take a pew."

As Dex seated himself on the utility chair, he wondered how many times Morrison had brought bad news to families in this windowless green-painted room. There was a NO SMOKING sign on the wall, yet there was a cheap tin ashtray and the air was fusty. Dex placed Morrison at about fifty-four, as slim as his delicate fingers, greying at the temples and with small eyes. The face was watchful, the beard neat and well-trimmed. "Your father is alive but in a coma. He suffered a severe head injury. There were also three leg fractures and several cracked ribs, but his spine is intact."

"But he'll come round okay?" Dex was surprised at how concerned he felt about the man he had grown to despise beyond measure.

"Oh yes. I'd say so, yes. But it was quite a bang, so it may be some while before we can assess the long-term effects." He raised his hands defensively.

Dex stood up and circled the small room. "You heard that my sister and the chauffeur were both killed?" Dex spoke without emotion, as if he were passing on news about strangers, yet inside he was being ripped apart.

"Oh God, no! I am sorry. I had no idea. My team was working in its own bubble." He stretched out a consoling arm. "They were travelling together, were they? Do you want to talk about it?"

"Thanks, but no. So—a long haul for Father? Months, years?"

"Not necessarily. For now, caution is the word."

# CHAPTER SEVEN

Had it been Father's funeral, no doubt Sir Charles's pinstriped solicitors would have had instructions for a big send-off with choirs, processions, and a string of eulogies, London's fat cats filling every pew. But Beth had hated pomp, and so Dex had fixed a private ceremony by invitation only.

This sunny but unusually chilly morning, just fifteen people had passed through the lychgate and walked along the flagstones into St Martin's Church in Bladon, a small Oxfordshire village. Six were aunts and uncles. Their mother had flown in from her Italian villa near Sorrento and had arrived on the arm of her twin sister.

Adam Yarbury was an old family friend and had been godfather to both Dex and Beth. He was semi-retired from banking in the City, but had always been comfortably off without needing to work. His preferred newspaper was *The Racing Post* and his haunts were London casinos where occasionally he had met up with Beth. The other mourners were four of Beth's school friends and two colleagues from work. Still in hospital, Sir Charles was out of the coma but had yet to be told of Beth's death.

The small Oxfordshire village of Bladon was nearly two hours northwest of London and had become famous because Sir Winston Churchill and others from his family had been buried there. The Churchill ancestral home at Blenheim Palace was close by. Dex and Beth's childhood had also been spent in the village, and besides this link, the Reverend Hillyer, whom they had known from childhood, was still the local priest. With his gold-rimmed spectacles, silvery hair tufting out around his ears, and a cheerfully rounded face, he had the jolly look of someone more suited to weddings than funerals.

As they exited the small church, Dex spotted an absurdly lavish wreath. Among the array of floral tributes, it stood out. It was nearly a metre across and was a tasteful blend of chrysanthemums, carnations, and pink and white roses. He bent down and opened the message.

Shocked onlookers saw his face harden and his eyes flash with rage. In a sudden move, he ripped the card from the wreath and tore it into small pieces. Then, to the jaw-dropping looks of the bystanders, he stooped again, picked up the wreath, and after taking a few steps, hurled it Frisbee style over the wall and into the meadow beyond.

Dex could see that some sort of explanation was expected, but he said nothing, simply joining the vicar on the short walk to the waiting grave. Hillyer too gave him a quizzical look but said nothing before intoning the final internment formalities. Before the service, Dex had taken a double dose of his medication. Now, as he threw a scoop of earth onto the maple coffin, he doubted that the pills had helped. He still felt shaky, tearful, and above all saw the red mist of anger at finding a wreath *"from Pepe Carmino and the team at Dukes—with deepest sympathy."* To add to his torment, just a handful of paces away were the graves of Carole and tiny Jamie, his wife and infant son, who had been buried here just two years before.

The service concluded, Hillyer led the mourners though the churchyard toward the wooden lychgate. The churchyard was lined with evergreens and hawthorns. All around was the cheerful chatter of sparrows and swooping swallows, grabbing the summer flies. Their carefree movements somehow made Dex more aware of the burdens he now faced.

Only the Reverend Hugh Hillyer knew anything of his inner torment. Decisions had to be made—his promise to Beth had to be kept or broken. Pepe Carmino's wreath had been a sharp reminder that since Beth had died, he had shut out the future. Besides that, he had ducked even thinking of the little he knew and what he now feared.

As the mourners drifted toward their cars, Hillyer tapped Dex on the arm and stopped him beside Sir Winston's grave. For a moment or two, they both stood in respectful silence. "Winnie stood alone. Defiant." The slate-grey eyes turned to Dex. "But you cannot emulate that great man. Nor should you try. Not with your health problems. You've told me your fears. Or some of them. I think there's more you have not explained." The words were accompanied by a hurt look, the eyes delivering the message. "I remember your courage as you grew up. Don't be ashamed to do nothing." He pointed back toward the three graves. "Beth would understand. After the tragedy with Carole and Jamie, you have your own life to lead. And getting you better is a priority."

"But," Dex faltered. "Isn't that selfish? I made promises."

"Dex—if Beth had *known* what lay ahead, she would never have burdened you. If she had truly known of the dangers, then yes, *that* would have been selfish. But of her. So do nothing hasty. But if you must do something, then never try to carry it alone. I know what you went through when Carole and little Jamie died."

"When they were murdered," Dex interrupted sharply. "When they were murdered *by persons unknown*."

Hillyer acknowledged his hurtful understatement by an immediate apology. "And now this…" Hillyer struggled for words "…this horrendous outrage." He shook his head slowly, his voice fruity and mellow. "We cannot know precisely what Beth had got herself into, but you know enough to understand my warning—don't you go standing alone." He turned to Sir Winston's grave. "Even he needed the Americans. And he knew it."

As Hillyer finished and Dex was about to comment, he spotted one of his aunts approaching. She was whispering to her husband rather louder than she thought. He caught the words *that hell would freeze over before she would ever look after her brother.* The husband's grunt and nod of agreement said it all. Dex knew that his father had been loved by nobody.

All the family had sided with his mother when at last he had knocked her about once too often and she had fled the family home. The aunt's remark was an untimely reminder of another decision to be taken—that of his father's welfare on leaving hospital.

Dex stood with Hillyer's comforting arm across his shoulders as the last of the mourners headed to the wake at The Bear at Woodstock. At that moment, he became aware of a solitary figure standing just beyond the gate. His mind was racing with so many confused and unwelcome thoughts that for a moment he did not take in what he was seeing. As the vicar shook his hand and declined the invite to the wake, Dex left the churchyard and saw that it was Tiffany Richmond.

"This was strictly private. No media." Dex regretted sounding quite so severe. He took in that she was dressed entirely in black, a colour she wore well.

"Look, I'm not here as a reporter. I came here…" She sounded embarrassed. "…as a mark of solidarity. But…" She nodded to the security man who stood bolt upright a few paces away. "No access."

"Solidarity?"

"Explanations can come later."

Dex was intrigued yet wrong-footed by her arrival and by what she had said. He scuffed the gravel with his highly polished black shoe as he debated. "The wake is not the place. Come to the boat. Maybe Thursday? Around 7 p.m. I could rustle up pasta."

For the first time, Dex saw her give the faintest of smiles. "Can we say 8 p.m.? By then I'll have finished my book signing in Leadenhall Market." Her smile had gone, to be replaced by a quiet sincerity in her gentle voice, so unlike the matter-of-fact style she used on screen.

For a second, Dex thought she was fighting back tears, but that seemed unlikely and he decided he had been mistaken. "Truly, I did not want to intrude. But ever since breaking the news to you about Beth—oh, it's strange, but I've felt a bond." She walked beside him as he went to his VW Golf. "Now is not the time to go into why."

His look was puzzled but friendly as he twisted into the driving seat. For a moment, he stared at her as if trying to read her mind but decided to let her remark pass. *She was right—now was not the time.* "I'm sorry they wouldn't let you in. If I had known…"

"And, Dex—I've picked up something else that may interest you too. But again…now is not the time."

Dex nodded goodbye and slowly pulled away. His thoughts as he drove toward Woodstock were uncomfortable. Were carefree days of fishing, juggling beer bottles, and slopping around the boat now over? Or should he ride roughshod over his promise to Beth and continue with the comfortable old shoe that was his daily routine?

# CHAPTER EIGHT

Being unable to sleep after the funeral, his mind still in torment, Dex gave up trying. He made a bacon buttie with oodles of brown sauce, leaving the bacon to grill while he dressed in his waterproof jacket and trousers. Lastly, he grabbed his fishing tackle and walked briskly along the darkened towpath, hoping as always to lure one of the big carp. He had no fear of darkness. He had trodden the lonely towpath many times before, never considering there to be any danger.

Tonight was no different, even though he had been lying awake wondering what Beth had discovered and whether it was enough to have her murdered. It seemed incredible—but then, this Tavio guy's death had been a cold-blooded execution. Had Beth spoken to him before he was murdered? Who knew, if anyone, that she had been sniffing around?

As he padded along, not another soul around, the familiar but distant sounds of London at night surrounded him—the hum of traffic on the A4, barking dogs, the yelp of an urban fox and a church clock striking four. Ahead of him, the first hint of dawn was appearing across the generally sleeping city. As he walked, he chomped on the last of his bacon roll and tried to unwind by listening to the pleasing hiss and swish of the Thames flowing by.

Usually, when he went fishing, he shut out the world by pitching his stool in a damp, chilly, and muddy place where all that mattered was the bait, the rod tip and that mighty tug. Water dripping on him from overhanging branches, strange unexplained noises and fish that got away were all part of the pleasurable bubble, made even better by the solitude and scalding coffee.

But not now. Every moment, as he watched the rod tip, his thoughts were tormented by images of his father and the irony of the developing situation. Two years ago, he had vowed to cut him out of his life. But now? Could he really do that? And then there was Beth. For the umpteenth time, he imagined the final cruel seconds.

He could almost see her sitting in the leather comfort of the rear seat, a cup of Starbucks in one hand and her fingers working feverishly on a keyboard as she checked for news about the yen, the euro, and the dollar for the day ahead.

Rarely a moment seemed to pass without recurring images of the huge DAF tipper-truck rearing up over the limo like a stallion about to service a mare. Now, she lay in Bladon churchyard next to Carole and Jamie, all three of those closest and dearest to him savagely cut down. But Father had survived. The old curmudgeon had never worn a seatbelt and had been thrown clear in the collision.

Beth's laptop? The police said it had never been found, presumably destroyed in the conflagration. But like eternal life, what she had learned in Vegas was there for him to read, nestling safely in some cloud somewhere.

*But am I ready to read it?*

*Or shall I take the path marked* Easy Life?

As dawn turned to first light, he was well settled on his collapsible stool, waiting for something that might never happen at all. And while he sat, eager for that tug-tug, that knock-knock of a carp's lips playing with the bait, he found himself replaying his discussions with Reverend Hillyer.

Though Dex had no time for religion, Hillyer had always been someone to whom he could chatter. In his teens, Dex had often opened up about life at home—the violence, Father's drunken abuse, the shouting, the beatings, the stony silences and the constant destruction of his self-esteem. The advice had usually been the same—that Hillyer was counselling them both to work harder at the relationship—advice Father had never once put into practice.

As he poured coffee from the thermos, Dex found himself listening to the vicar. "I can't explain why God chose to take Carole, Jamie, and now Beth. I could say that God moves in mysterious ways. I could say that God wanted them for his own. You would say God would never want your father." He said those words with a wry smile. "Try to forgive your father. He needs you now."

And his promises to Beth? Get back her losses? Doable? He had no idea. Destroy Carmino, Dukes, and Space City? It seemed unreal. Yet Beth had been convinced she could do it.

He thought of Carole, the diminutive waif-like girl that he had married and loved so much, and of Jamie, his life cut down before barely walking and talking. *Damn you for that, Father.* Suddenly the rod trembled in his hand. Then came the tug-tug of a suspicious carp nosing around the honeyed bread. Would it swim away with a contemptuous swish of its mighty tail, or would its thick bulbous lips finally grasp the bread? Now was the time to do nothing. Now was the moment to be ready. Now was the moment to grip the rod firmly and to hope for the almighty pull. Two, three, five seconds passed before, with an explosion of movement, the fish seized the bait and raced away, only to realise it had been duped.

Dex was now on his feet, the rod bent and straining as the powerful fish made a bolt across the pond toward the reeds almost fifty yards away. The surge of its path across the previously still water created a spreading bow wave that raced in both directions like a power-boat cutting its way through the flat calm of the Mediterranean.

Somehow Dex managed to slow the dark silvery grey and brown fish before it had dived deep into the reeds and weeds, where his line would almost inevitably break. Then the fish was turning, racing sideways across the pond before turning straight back toward the place of its hooking. Frantically Dex reeled in the line, but never as fast as the fish was approaching. He could see its back breaking the surface and knew that this one would weigh in at eleven pounds or maybe a little more.

He knew he had to get his line tight on that powerful jaw. But he could not, so fast had been the fish's approach. Suddenly the line went limp and the carp's back disappeared as it dived, free of the hook, deep into the dark muddy green of the bottom. Slowly, he reeled in his line and saw that the bait had gone and the barbed hook was bare. With a sigh, he dismantled the reel and line and packed to go home.

And that was the moment he knew.

Pepe Carmino was not going to get away like the carp. Nothing was going to stop him.

Life had to have a purpose, and he knew he had found his. Beth deserved nothing less.

That morning, after the rush-hour lemmings had sworn and cursed their way into work on the buses, in their cars, or crammed shoulder to armpit into the Underground, he headed for Holborn, where Beth used to visit a gambling bookshop run by an eccentric Scotsman called Gus McKay. Chatting to him seemed the right place to start. If he had understood Beth correctly, the old boy had been part of a team that had cleaned out a casino playing roulette.

"You ought to read this book." The dapper little Scot, resplendent in his tartan trousers, headed toward the fifty or more books on roulette that lined a shelf. His small shop was tucked into a back street of Dickensian London not far from the London School of Economics and behind the Aldwych.

McKay returned from the crammed shelves clutching *Gambling Scams* by Darwin Ortiz. "Essential reading, that one. Here's another—*Thirteen Against the Bank* by Norman Leigh. He organized a coup against the casino in Nice. For all I know, Norman's probably dead now. With three pals of mine from Glasgow, I used his system. It's called Reverse Labouchère. We visited a casino in Germany and took them for so much we were banned."

"Banned? Just for winning?"

McKay's watery blue eyes above an aquiline nose showed his astonishment at the ignorance of his customer. "You've a lot to learn, son."

Dex stood beside the counter and looked at the little man with his lined face and saw the mocking smile. "I intend to bring down a casino."

McKay's laugh was throaty and the right side of his face twitched. "I've heard that often enough. True…casinos have gone bust. But not because players have won all their money. They go belly up from financial mismanagement or by fabricating losses to cheat the tax authorities."

He looked at a half-hunter watch on a gold chain that was draped across his tartan waistcoat. "Look, pal. It's about time for a pie and a pint. We need to talk. Your sister was a daft gambler herself. I'm sorry to say so, but it's true. You see, she played the Martingale system." He shook his head. "I warned her that one day it would bite. But," he shook his head sadly, "she never did believe me."

"She lost because the casino cheated. Otherwise, she would have won." Dex regretted that he sounded too defensive, too pleading.

"So you said, so you said. But playing the Martingale—doubling up after every lost bet till you win or hit the table limit—a mug's game. No disrespect, mind. Your sister was a bonny lass who got lucky for months."

Dex said nothing as McKay double-locked the door and pocketed the key. Then the Scot's eyes narrowed as he wagged a finger. "If you want to end up a millionaire in a casino, start with two million."

Dex laughed as the small but spritely figure took off down the narrow street, leading him to a poky Dickensian pub round the corner that was filling with students.

As they waited for the barman, Dex decided to ask a question that had been puzzling him. "But you became a millionaire. Beth told me. So it *can* be done. So if you broke a casino and won big time, surely you wouldn't be flogging books from a Holborn back street?"

McKay looked at Dex with renewed respect. "Fair point. I lost it all in Vegas—playing poker, a cash game it was. I was out of my league."

Dex was suspicious. "So you and your Glaswegian pals just go play somewhere else—France, Holland, Australia, wherever. Use this reverse thingie. Win another fortune and then don't lose it at the poker tables." Dex saw from the bored amusement on the listener's face that he was not the first person to probe with this line of questions.

Having ordered, they sat down in a booth made from former church pews. "I'm banned. I'm in the Griffin List subscribed to by the Vegas casinos. My mug shot is known globally."

"Griffin?"

"Griffin Investigations. They gather the names and details of anyone who is a known cheat or who is regarded as bad for casino business. Card-counters can beat the casino, and so once caught, they are blacklisted and labelled as *advantage players*. Besides identifying them from the way they play and how they wager, casinos now counter them by using continuous shuffling machines and so on. But their ace is the Griffin List, with details of the player, the style of play used, and of course their appearance."

"So wear a wig and a false moustache."

As they waited for their steak pies with peas and mash, McKay downed a generous slurp of his Guinness while Dex sipped from a pint of orange juice. "You've a lot to learn, especially if you intend to break a casino." The words were accompanied by a war-weary expression and a shake of the head. "Casinos increasingly use face-recognition software that can see through a disguise."

"Were you cheating?"

McKay's grey hair shook with the vehemence of the denial. "I was card-counting at blackjack. Pure skill. But casinos regard it as unfair to their profits."

"So card-counting? Legal or illegal?"

"Legal…but you get caught card-counting, then expect to be banned globally, with your mug shot in Griffin."

Dex found himself warming to the man by the second. There was so much of life's experience in the eccentricity of the tartan-clad body. There was an easy air about him. The expression *comfortable in his own skin* seemed apt. There was a weary resignation about him that *shit happens* and that at seventy-two he had finally lost the will to fight it.

Dex watched the Scot adjust his low-slung brown woollen tie that was tucked off-centre under his waistcoat. Even the brown brogues looked more suited to tramping through the heather than pounding the pavements of London WC1. But there was still a crackle of electricity about him that made every word seem valuable. "So you want to break the bank. Want to tell me why?"

Dex made clear that he was not ready for that explanation, and McKay shrugged as if it was of no concern "Not why, no, but yes—I promised Beth that I would continue her plan. She intended to destroy two casinos, one in London, the other in Vegas."

"Impossible. Even if you win big, you'd be as effective as a flea biting an elephant's bum." For a man who stood less than five foot four, he had a rich, resonant voice. He wiped a watering eye. "Look, laddie, casinos are too experienced, too rich to be broken. They're run by mean bastards." McKay spat out the last word with surprising vehemence. "They're not good losers, ye ken. A smile from a casino boss is another man's porkie." He looked across the narrow table and his eyes held a warning. "If you're a big loser, casinos smarm and grease you until they've bled you dry. If you're a big winner, they red-carpet you to keep your business—to win back what they see as *their money*. Once you've been cleaned out, they drop you. The smiles, the handshakes, the freebies disappear." He peered watchfully at Dex from over the rim of his pint. "Which casinos?"

"I'd rather not say."

"Good answer. Take care. And not just what you do but *who you confide in*. Casinos are all ears. To revisit that WW2 expression, careless talk costs lives." His eyes narrowed. "Don't get me wrong, but you've the hands of an accountant, not a street fighter."

"I want your help, not your opinion," Dex intervened sharpish, stung at the accusation.

McKay looked at him as if appraising a prize bull. "Well…surprise me! Maybe you have balls of steel after all! You'll need them, especially when they get to work with the wire cutters or pincers."

Dex blinked, uncertain how seriously to heed the words. "Are you kidding?"

"You're going all in." He pointed his fork toward Dex. "And all in means you're staking your life."

"But you did it, you broke the bank." Dex's tone was over-strident. "And what about that song—*The Man who Broke the Bank at Monte Carlo*."

"Charles Wells. Back in 1891." McKay shook his head ruefully. "He won a fortune but died broke, so they say. But the casino wasn't bust. Not even close. When Charlie boy had won all the chips *at his table*, they simply placed a black cloth over it like a shroud. The casino was never busted. These days, they would keep the table open, topping up with more chips."

Dex's face showed disappointment. "So the Monte Carlo casino never did go belly up?"

McKay laughed, but not unkindly. "Not even close. Nobody has ever won enough to break a casino." He wiped the froth of the Guinness from his mouth. "If you want to destroy a casino, you need to find out what they're hiding, their dirty little secrets."

Dex liked that advice. "But your system was infallible?"

"Reverse Labouchère? Yes…and no! You could win a fortune, but you need deep, deep pooches to get through the bad times. You could run out of money first."

"Could I do what you did—but on my own?"

"In theory. But I'd say you need at least two of you. You can win big, but the key word is *eventually*."

"I'm listening. Explain Reverse Labouchère."

"At the roulette table, you bet on both red and black. One bet will always lose, and if zero hits, you both lose. Sounds crazy?" The Scotsman winked a watery eye and started to explain. "The secret is in the staking system—what you bet."

For the next thirty minutes and while sinking another Guinness, McKay waltzed through the explanation, scribbling ever larger numbers on Dex's notepad.

"Try tossing a coin one hundred times. It should come down fifty heads and fifty tails. But it won't. It might be forty-six heads and fifty-four tails. But occasionally it could be thirty-seven heads and sixty-three tails or even seventy-three to twenty-seven. Roulette is the same. That is the type of imbalance that lets you win big."

"Terrific! But how long could that take?"

"Till you get a run of far more reds than blacks…or vice versa?" He shrugged. "It could happen in the first hour. It could be ten days. In my case, we waited and played for seven days. Near cleaned out we were, too."

"And this is not cheating?" Dex saw the emphatic denial before continuing. "Know someone who can help me?"

McKay's already twitchy face went into twitch overdrive and ignored the question. "In London, they might say they don't like your style of play and withdraw membership."

"Ban me? For winning?"

McKay laughed. "Why not? Or they might close the table or lower the maximum bet limits once you started winning serious loot. In Vegas, it's different. If they don't like you, a pair of gorillas will encourage your departure. It's shit-yourself time, believe me. Those Vegas heavies have voices like they gargle with gravel."

"Happened to you?"

"My gorilla moment? Aye! In Vegas. That's when I was put in the Griffin and became the casino equivalent of *America's Most Wanted*. You can run but you cannot hide." He looked wistful for a moment, and Dex noticed that McKay's hands were shaking at the recollections.

Dex went to the counter and returned with two coffees. "You actually counted the cards at blackjack?"

"Forget winning big at blackjack. You card-count, you'll be caught.

Your play gives you away. Besides, they shuffle up more often now or use continuous automated shufflers. That or cut the deck with such a generous slice that even the inventor of card-counting, Edward Thorp, could never win today. If you change your stakes big-time, as you must if the count is favourable, alarm bells ring and you are dead meat. So, sonny, forget blackjack."

Dex stared at the empty plates. "Besides Reverse Labouchère, is there no other positive?"

McKay nodded thoughtfully. "I've stopped your pipe dreams. That's a positive." He beckoned Dex to lean forward, although nobody could hear them in their secluded booth. "You want to destroy them? Strike them where they are vulnerable." He leaned forward to whisper. "It's Dukes, isn't it? And Space City?" His face suddenly looked young again, the wrinkles almost fading for a fleeting moment.

Dex had no need to say anything. The shocked look was a clear admission.

"Elementary, son! You mentioned London and Vegas. Dukes is opening Space City. Your sister played in Dukes." He paused to stir the coffee. "Anyroads, I never did trust Pepe Carmino. Dukes is a private company. Means they have a better chance of financial manipulation."

"And Carmino?"

"A magnet for women. Oozes daytime soap charm. He's got the tongue of a lizard—fast and smooth. To me, he's a total shit. I certainly wouldn't trust him or his casino. But don't quote me!" He produced an artificial cigarette and sucked on it thoughtfully. "There's a rumour, a story behind Pepe's scar, but what it is, I've no idea."

Dex was unsure whether the Scot was withholding something but let it pass. Instead, he went close to mentioning Panama and volunteering about Beth's late bet experience, but something held him back. Perhaps it was McKay's earlier warning about careless talk. "So Dukes could be bent?"

"I'm not saying it is. But it could be. And that's the way to destroy a casino. Prove cheating. Prove serious breaches of the Gambling Commission's rules. If they lose their licence, they're dead, buried, kaput!" He leaned forward and grasped Dex's sleeve. "No Dukes, no cash flow to Vegas. No Space City. Job done. Destruction."

"You make it sound so easy."

"Uh-ho. No way! Watch your back. Careless talk, remember?" The Scot drained his Guinness, and as he put down his glass, his face lit up but twitched once again. "Come to the shop tomorrow. I'll show you some tricks used by bent casinos or bent dealers."

"Tomorrow works. Thanks. And someone to help me—a real expert who isn't banned? You never answered that."

"There is someone—a good card-counter. He's low profile. He loves beating the casino at anything, and he might help at Reverse Labouchère. His name is Billy."

"How do I find him?"

"He used to play at the Victoria Sporting Club, the Palm Beach, Russell Square, the Golden Orb, and some place in Bayswater. Even saw him once in the Ritz, though that was a bit posh for him. Generally, he worked the middle-market places. But he never used to count cards in London. Or so he said to me."

Dex was desperate to take away something more positive. "Surname?"

"Edwards?" He sniffed the air as if it would give inspiration. "Billy Edwards. No. That's not right. Evans. Aye! Billy Evans, right enough. As clever a guy as I've ever met in a casino."

"I can sense a *but* in your voice…a big but. Right?"

"Billy got himself hooked on the white stuff." McKay rose from the bench seat and brushed the crumbs from the tartan trousers. "It's time to open up."

Dex stood to join him and motioned McKay to wait a moment as he opened his back-pack. From it, he removed a brown envelope and showed the Scot a photo of Enzo Letizione at the topping-out ceremony for Space City. "Know him?"

Dex knew the answer even before the reply came. McKay's face said it all. "Letizione. Enzo Letizione. Looking older, fatter, bigger jowls than when I used to come across him."

"A gorilla?"

McKay shook his head. "No. But casinos where he cut his teeth gave a fair few beatings. Now, he's a Vegas insider, big time. In a city that runs on juice, he has plenty enough. But the unions—they've outflanked him. They have juice too."

"Form? Violence? Convictions?"

"I doubt it. He wouldn't be approved to run Space City without a robust CV. But I remember him. It must be thirty-five years gone. He worked Downtown in the days of mob rule. He'd have seen or heard most things. Executions, torture, beatings. Like the car bomb attack on Lefty Rosenthal. Aye, Enzo would have been taught never to cross Tony Spilotro. Someone would have warned him to show respect to the made men. He survived." McKay looked deadly serious. "So he obviously followed mob rules."

"But he's not a mobster?"

"I never heard that. But don't underestimate him. Not all sharks live in the sea."

# CHAPTER NINE

Five thousand miles away, as Dex left the Holborn pub, Enzo Letizione changed his position in his deep recliner. He was seated in Pepe Carmino's suite at the Venetian Hotel, just north of the midpoint of The Strip. It had been a difficult evening involving a long debriefing about the problems. Throughout, Pepe had been at pains to keep Letizione firmly on the defensive. "I gotta be going." The American tapped his watch. "I'll hardly get my head down before them dumb fucks from the union are banging on my door."

Carmino swirled a large glass of seventy-year-old Champagne Cognac. Normally, by the second glass, he felt chilled out, but the late-night dinner and then hours chewing the fat with Letizione had failed to calm his anger at the shit flying about. "You be sure that nobody delays us or shits on us again. Do whatever it takes! Got it?" He saw the American's face show resentment at the topic, but Letizione simply nodded. "You got the message, Enzo? *Do whatever it takes.*"

Enzo Letizione rose stiffly from his chair to stare out at the neon lights far below on the Strip. "You still with that Hungarian blonde? Irenke, was it?"

"Ever porked a corpse?" Carmino fingered the scar on his cheek as if in recollection of something and then continued. "Forget opening her legs. Now, she opens the blackjack tables. That's all she's good for. Know what I mean?"

"Sure I do. But heck…what about your Gambling Commission? Smart guys, huh? You pulling their chain?"

Carmino smiled, but it was not the smile he used when greeting wealthy Arabs or Far Eastern high rollers. There was both satisfaction and contempt in the way his cheeks sucked in and his lips curled. "I got the inspector…" He pressed his thumb hard onto the tabletop and rotated it slowly. "Exactly where I want him. Set him up a treat. Now he's mine."

Enzo looked less impressed than he was. He had no intention of letting the Londoner know that. But he knew his own position was way beyond the crappier side of crap following the cost overruns. Yet as he watched the flashing lights of a cop car weave a path toward Downtown, he reckoned to have pocket aces. The problem was when to play them. When to milk the biggest pot? Not now, for sure. "Extracting the dough from this Swiss lawyer's clients? Give."

"Their hot money?"

"Sure, the red-hot money." Letizione chomped on his cigar. "You gotta keep shifting it from Dukes to the Caymans and on to our bankers here." The American sounded as hesitant as he was. Shifting big bucks around the globe without questions being asked was increasingly difficult. "You reckon you can shift enough to raise fifty mill, plus the sticky bits for me and you?"

The Englishman looked and sounded smug. "Two hundred million. That's what I reckon. Like I said, the inspector's our man now. And being a private company, we're running a second set of books okay, no sweat. We can say *go fuck yourself* to making large or suspicious transaction reports like we should." He drained the last dregs from his glass. "We'll get the hot money, you'll see. I've someone in mind. She can help relax these guys. Make their dicks rule their brains."

"Nobody I've met?"

Carmino shook his head, yawned and stretched before standing. "She's an Aussie. Worked in a Sydney hospital. She headed to London a couple of years back. She's been hanging out in the best bars, the top hotels."

"A hooker?"

"Jude? No. She's more of a good-time girl. Greedy for the high life, with the body to get her there. He glanced across to Letizione. "She'll go down a treat with these rich bastards, if you get my drift."

The dirty chuckle brought a rare smile to Enzo's heavy face, which was in need of a shave. "Seems you got all bases covered." The words carried no conviction, and both men knew the compliment was meaningless. The American resented being relegated to junior partner status, but short of playing his pocket aces, he could not resist Carmino's insistence on a golden share when Space City was close to going belly up.

Letizione waddled toward the door still uncertain whether Carmino was being straight with him about the money or about *anything*,
come to that. "Sounds all good." Again the meaningless words hung
between them as the American exited.

Once he was alone, Carmino immediately phoned the Geneva
lawyer. He knew there was no time to lose.

# CHAPTER TEN

After returning from the wake in Woodstock, Dex had quit his job at the Black Sheep with mixed feelings. Then, after meeting Gus McKay, he had phoned Adam Yarbury. They hadn't spoken since the usual banal pleasantries, platitudes, and shared recollections in Woodstock. But his godfather had been a regular at Dukes. They agreed to meet for dinner in Motcombs.

Back aboard *Who Cares*, Dex sprawled out on the sofa, one end piled with cushions for comfort. Beside him on the floor and stacked several inches high were the books he had bought from McKay. He turned to Norman Leigh's *Thirteen Against the Bank*, about the team who had cleaned up in a French casino playing Reverse Labouchère. A quick reader, he had devoured nearly fifty pages before lack of sleep and the heaviness of his steak pie caught up with him and the book slumped onto his chest as he drifted off into a deep sleep.

It was turning 17:40 p.m. when he awoke, screaming, his clothes soaked with sweat. He sat up, arms flailing. "Fire! Fire! Help! Help!" But then the narrow strip of the cabin came into focus and he flopped back, his chest heaving, his hands shaking. He lay silently for a few minutes, wondering if the nightmares would ever end. The flashbacks were always the same and he inevitably awoke at the same moment of utter helplessness, the flames devouring everything he loved.

Slowly, the terrifying moments faded and he rolled off the sofa, desperately needing to wash away the dank stickiness that had soaked him from head to foot.

In the bathroom, he saw the rows of pill bottles. For a moment, he was tempted to take one or even two, but then came the recollection of this morning's vow to himself when the carp had got away. Had the pills and potions ever done any good? Had they been *causing* the nightmares? Was he just making Grierson rich? Okay, the heavy drinking *had* been destructive. But in moderation? Was drink such a crime? One by one, he removed every bottle and tipped the pills, hundreds of them, some white, some red, some pink through the window. It was deeply satisfying to watch them being swept away in the fast-flowing current.

*Get a life, Dex.*

*Live normally.*

*Wind back the clock to how it used to be.*

*And remember your promise to Beth.*

He turned on the shower and relished the thundering hot water. As it beat around his head and doused his body, the water seemed to be swooshing away the past torment as well as the clammy sweat. But then, as he reached for a fluffy white towel, he thought of his father. Forgetting the past was going to be harder than simply turning off a tap. Father would need to return home to St John's Wood. No way could he live there alone. Someone had to care for him.

*Maybe Father could go into a special unit somewhere?*

*You mean dump him?*

*Put him away, out of sight, out of mind.*

He finished dressing, and despite knowing that Adam Yarbury would probably wish even to be buried in a pinstriped suit with his old-school tie, he selected a charcoal open-neck shirt to wear with a fawn sports coat. When he descended the steps into the restaurant, he saw Adam at once, or rather saw someone sitting behind *The Racing Post.* "Hello, Adam."

The paper was dropped at once. Yarbury's face beamed enthusiasm. "Just planning my selections for the 3-45 at Newbury tomorrow. A trainer reckoned Sentosa Serenade is coming good. Seven-to-one. Good odds in a mixed field."

"I'll think about it. I never seem to get the luck you do."

"Horse racing, dear boy? Not luck. It's knowledge. Who you know, what you hear, and from whom you hear it. Otherwise, pick with a pin. I'm on G&T. Can I tempt you?"

"You can. As of today, I'm going to drink again—in moderation."

Adam nodded approvingly. He summoned the waiter and ordered doubles. "Moderation. Good word in everything. Women, horses, blackjack. Never been too hot at it myself, though."

Yarbury's laugh was self-deprecating, very much his normal style. Dex knew his godfather was pushing seventy, but he looked years younger, despite having lost most of his hair and what remained was silvery-grey. His face had a freshly innocent look, and in contrast to the ravaged wreck that had been Gus McKay, Adam Yarbury looked as if he had sailed through life with never a care.

And that was pretty much true. He had never married—but women who had passed through his revolving doors had always parted with a smile and on good terms. In the private bank where he had risen to be chairman, the philosophy had been *take no risks, have no worries.* "I only take risks in my personal life, never in the office," he had once told Beth and Dex while strolling in the garden of his Notting Hill home.

After they had ordered soup and rare steaks, Yarbury selected Chambertin from a good year. "No point dying rich is there, old chap," he volunteered. "Oh God! Sorry! Not a time to be mentioning death!"

Dex waved his arm dismissively. "I'm here with one agenda only, and that is to talk about Beth and Dukes, so whatever pain that causes, we must stay focussed."

"You? Talking about casinos? My dear chap. So out of character." He removed his heavy black spectacles and huffed on them, his rosy cheeks swelling out like bellows. "I thought we'd be talking fishing or your crackpot theories on Princess Diana in Paris."

"Another time, perhaps." Dex grinned. He knew that Yarbury was far too Establishment to contemplate that death in the Alma Tunnel had been anything other than an accident. "Still doing a bit of banking?"

"Not so you would notice. I'm non-exec now. I just drop in for board meetings. Most days, I toddle down to the club—that's Dukes, of course—and have a spot of lunch with some decent claret, lose money at blackjack or watch the nags on their big screens."

As their soup arrived, Dex waited till they were alone again. "You sound very cheerful about losing. Or are you being modest?"

"Winning?" Dex was rewarded with a look of incredulity. "My dear boy, blackjack's my vice—a legacy of pontoon played in the dorm at school. Winning is not the point. I don't play to *win.* I play for the *fun* of it, for the gamble. I don't expect to win and never do."

"So you never got into card-counting? Basic Strategy?"

"Don't laugh! I may be a banker by profession, but adding up numbers is not my strong suit." He selected a brown roll with olives. "Of course, I've heard you can work out whether the deck is still rich in tens and aces." He sighed. "Doing all that baloney would take the fun out of it. Anyway, don't they shoot you if you get caught? Bit like a fallen horse, what?"

"Casinos don't approve of card-counting, no." Dex spoke with all the authority of an expert despite having never heard of card- counting before meeting McKay. "Did Beth ever play blackjack with you?"

Yarbury gazed at the large oil painting on the wall beside them as if that would jog his memory. "No. She only played roulette. And that was never my game. Too slow, multicoloured chips being placed everywhere. I like more action—the turn of a card. Shit or bust. Usually bust in my case!" Again, the look was self-deprecating. "If I'd been paid out for every time my cards added up to 22 or 23, I'd be a rich man."

Dex nearly chipped in that Yarbury *was* a rich man, but refrained. "I'm joining Dukes. There's a shock for you."

"Lordy, lord! Well, bless my soul!" He swirled the burgundy in his glass and sniffed approvingly. "Chambertin! The king of red wines, truly noble. But you, joining Dukes? Splendid! We can dine there another time. They have a pretty decent Richebourg."

"Maybe." Dex was thinking of McKay's warning that anywhere in Dukes, including the bars, dining room and cloakrooms, were probably bugged. "Tell me, did Beth ever talk about Pepe Carmino?"

"Can't say she did." He paused. "No. I'm wrong. She did once volunteer that he made her flesh creep. She found him too unctuous. Yes. Unctuous. That was the word she used."

Dex was disappointed but not surprised. "And you? Your opinion?"

"Of Pepe? Works his favourites like Lothario at a tea dance. And his hands—soft and smooth but always ice cold. If you'll excuse the expression, shaking his hand is like caressing a corpse."

Dex admired his fillet steak and mixed salad. "Dukes ever cheat you?"

Yarbury's head rocked back with laughter. "Cheat me? Good heavens, no. Why would they? Casinos always win anyway—especially with mugs like me around."

"But you do win? I mean, you were joking when you said you always lose?" But even as Dex said it, he saw that same shocked look on the listener's face, so he continued. "I mean, not always win…but…well, quite often." He finished lamely on seeing Yarbury's bemused look.

"You really don't understand casinos, my dear chap!" The tone of voice was very much that of godfather to godchild, except that reading the Bible had never featured in what Yarbury preached. "I've been playing for damned near forty years, so I dare say I might have won once or twice but," he rolled his eyes "I can't say I can actually *remember* winning."

"But you must have had the occasional good day?"

"My dear Dex, you have a lot to learn if you're going gambling." He topped up Dex's glass. "Stick to good wine and bad women. And if I may say so, never drink more than half a bottle of wine. Now where was I? Oh yes. Of course I sometimes win a few hands, but in the end I'll always lose. So to answer you, no, I don't have the *occasional good day*. I might have the occasional good hand, but I don't stop after ten minutes just because I'm up a grand or two. Where's the fun in that? What would I do for the next couple of hours? I play for the pleasure; for the gamble, for the heat of the chase. When my last chip has gone, I stop."

"You enjoy losing?" Incredulity was evident from tone of voice and the penetrating look.

"I enjoy *gambling*. Losing is the price of my pleasure. Some folk lose money on pretty young things and fast cars. Me? Can life get better than splitting a pair of tens when the dealer has an ace and then beating him twice over? I know you should never split tens but I love the excitement. Sometimes, I'll even take a card on 18 just for the sheer hell of it. Because once in a while I'll get a 3 and hit 21."

"Dukes must love you."

"They do. I get a load of freebies—trips to Silverstone, Ascot, Cheltenham. Even Longchamps in Paris. Last week Pepe had a dozen of us up at Wembley to watch England v Germany."

"I watched it. Two nil to us for a change."

"Mick Glenn scored them both. He's a regular in Dukes. Plays big." Yarbury's lip curled in disdain. "He's a good footballer, but the man's an oik, a noisy oaf. A bad loser. A table thumper, what? I'm sure Pepe only tolerates him because he drops such big money."

"What does he play?"

"Always roulette. Usually with some popsy wearing what we old fogeys call a pussy-pelmet. And when he's losing, his effing and blinding carries round the room." He shook his head so that the silvery-grey hair rose and fell. "I'm darned if I know what women see in him."

"Maybe his income of £300,000 a week? The bling? The Armani suits, his Lamborghini, his huge pad in North London, the villa in Florida."

"Put like that…but call me old-fashioned—to me he's still a boorish yobbo who ought to stick to greyhound tracks."

"You ever chatted to Pepe about his past? His background?"

Yarbury was still on a roll about the footballer. "Sort of chap who swigs beer from a bottle. Vulgar tattoos on his arms."

Dex laughed. "Adam—my generation does that. You've got to loosen up."

"Fashion and trends pass me by." Yarbury grinned hugely. "But no, I never questioned Pepe about his past. Whatever it is or was, he would have a smooth explanation."

"Ever hear the word Panama mentioned?"

"Can't say I have, not in Dukes."

"Rumours of how Pepe Carmino got his scar?"

"Someone suggested it was over a woman. There again, I also heard he was in a car accident on the M25." Yarbury pushed the remains of his salad to one side. "But you said this was about *Beth* and Dukes."

"It is. Top confidentiality?"

Dex saw the slight hurt on his godfather's face at the suggestion that any conversation would be anything else. "Mum's the word, old chap. Anything you say is strictly *entre nous*. Chatham House Rules, of course."

"Beth was sure Dukes had deliberately cheated her—the best part of a million. But she never understood why a casino would cheat when they win nearly all the time. But through her job, she discovered from an American banker that Dukes has had to pony up on its investment in Space City to prevent the project going into Chapter 11."

"Go on, dear boy!"

"Then a poker player just back from Vegas suggested she meet a dealer with dirt on Pepe Carmino." As Dex rattled through the summary of what Beth had told him, he found Yarbury to be a good listener. "She had just returned from Vegas when…when she was killed." He choked on the words and wiped a tear from his eyes. "Was that sheer coincidence? Or was she silenced for finding out too much?"

Yarbury said nothing, but his eye movements signalled that his mind was in overdrive. They closed tightly shut, then opened briefly before closing again. "Dex, I don't like the sound of this. Not one little bit." He suggested they attack the ripe stilton before he continued. "A late bet call, eh? That may be right. I'd back her on that if there was no witness. But poking her nose into Pepe Carmino's past?" He shook his head in resignation. "And then asking questions in Vegas of all places. Bad place to be. Inviting trouble." His eyes fixed on Dex. "Did she meet this Tavio fella?"

"I don't know. She was very distressed by his murder, so the call was less coherent than it might have been. My guess? Yes, she did, which would explain why she was so worried after he was murdered." Dex selected a crunchy piece of celery to add to the stilton that lay on his plate.

"Who knew she was in Vegas? Carmino?"

"Maybe. FB did."

"Nigel Forster-Brown?" The way Yarbury said the name showed his disdain. "Pepe's poodle."

"There's something else. Beth gave me password access to all her computerised data, but I can't get in."

"You got her laptop back from the police?"

He shook his head. "Presumed destroyed in the inferno but she had everything backed up in the Cloud."

"The Cloud? Quite beyond me, dear chap. Foreign lingo. I can't even work a TV remote."

Dex laughed. "Anyway, the password doesn't work."

Yarbury positioned his arms in front of his lips as if in prayer. "If I get your drift, you think that…?"

"Beth was another Diana? Murder disguised as an accident?" Dex spoke slowly and his voice was lowered. "I've no evidence. But it was one helluva coincidence, don't you think?" He saw Yarbury was not instantly dismissive, so he continued. "The police are still investigating. Possibly the trucker was blinded by the sun and then slammed into Father's limo."

"Has the driver been charged? He survived, didn't he?"

"He's alive, yes, but I'm not aware of any prosecution. Early days, I guess."

Yarbury frowned, a rare sight. "So, I mean, what's this all about?"

"I promised Beth. She *made* me promise that if anything happened to her, I would not let it rest."

"Let what rest?"

"What she was working on."

"Meaning?"

"She had two aims—the first was to win back the million. Secondly, bring down Dukes and Space City. Her research on Pepe Carmino's background was the start."

Yarbury gulped and reached for his schooner of port. "And so… your intentions?"

Dex's response came quickly, but each word was spoken with such vehemence that he surprised even himself. "The same as hers…but more. As you might say—with knobs on!" He marshalled the crumbs on his plate into lines as he spoke. "I'm going to win back Beth's losses with more on top. Much, much more. Call it damages. That's phase one."

He thought back to McKay's advice. "I can never win enough to destroy a casino. So, to bring down Pepe Carmino's empire, I must find his soft underbelly." He glanced across the table and saw Yarbury's concern. His normally placid face, the pink and well-scrubbed cheeks and cheerful mouth were narrowed and oozed angst. "And of course, I want to know if Beth was murdered."

Yarbury exhaled a long sigh. "I wish you would leave it but you made this promise. I respect that. You've always been a man of your word. But I don't like it. Not one little bit." His tone turned from sorrowful to sharp. "Did you want any help from me? I'm not sure I can assist…but if I can?"

"I don't know yet."

"Do you have a plan?"

"Yes. Listen to this."

# CHAPTER ELEVEN

The following morning Dex was seated in the gloomy surroundings of a stock room at the back of McKay's shop. The Scot was seated beside a roulette wheel with the familiar green baize layout where players would place their bets. There was barely room to sit down due to unsold books lying everywhere or stacked high in boxes on metal racks on all sides. The air was stale and there was no window, the only light coming from a naked bulb that hung from the ceiling.

Most books were in boxes but some were wrapped in brown paper parcels and looked distinctly dusty. "Roulette books used to sell well," McKay explained as he saw Dex taking in the surroundings. "But suddenly poker on TV became the rage. I can't keep pace with demand for how-to-win or how-to-play poker books. Add to that the e-book revolution and I am stuck with enough unsellable books on roulette to feed every camel in a Khartoum zoo."

Dex shared McKay's resigned laugh as he seated himself on a typist's chair beside the layout, several stacks of green, red, orange and cash chips in front of him. The cash chips had a nominal value of one hundred or one thousand pounds each.

"I'll be the dealer," McKay prompted. "I want you to bet ten one-hundred-cash chips on black—a thousand pounds in total." He then dropped the ball on 17, a black number on the wheel. "You have just won! That's an even chance bet and you're paid out equal money. So how much?"

"I staked a grand, so I win a grand." Dex replied but with some hesitation in his voice but he saw from the reaction that he had been correct.

"So the dealer pays you ten chips like this." McKay grabbed a stack of one-hundred-pound chips from his side of the layout and pushed them across the green baize. "I now match the height of your pile with mine to pay you out ten chips. The casinos call this *sizing into the bet*. So watch." Dex did so and saw his single pile of ten chips get matched. "So you have two grand in front of you now—the two equal stacks. Correct?"

"Agreed."

"Count them." Dex looked at the two stacks of equal height and counted them down. He stopped at nine and stared across at the dealer. "There are only nine chips in each pile. I've only got eighteen hundred quid instead of two grand. But I had staked ten chips?"

McKay tilted his head back and laughed, his tic working overtime. "I've just robbed you of two hundred pounds and you never noticed." He grinned with obvious satisfaction that his sleight of hand had not been spotted. "You get a busy table, lots of players chatting, laughing, drinking, they're not obsessed with counting their win. Most would spot if the casino paid them *one* short because the two piles would not match. That's called a *short stack*. But this cheating technique I used—it's called *bumping*, is harder to spot and very profitable."

"What did you do? I'm staggered." Dex watched as Gus restored one of his stacks to total ten chips. He then withdrew the other eight to join the casino's float of chips.

"So this is a replay. What I should do is get ten, maybe even eleven or twelve chips and slide them across the layout to stand next to your staked bet." He winked. "What I should do is *to size into* your stake running my finger across both stacks to level them and take away any in excess of ten. Got that?"

He saw Dex's frown of concentration before carrying on. "What I actually did was to judge your stake at ten chips and then grabbed a stack of only eight chips which I slid across the table. Done lawfully, I should push your winnings across touching the green baize. But when I am cheating you I deliver the eight chips holding them slightly raised above the layout—like this."

He showed the gap between the bottom chip and the table surface. "This is called *going in high*. When my eight chips are beside your ten, with my hand positioned over the stacks, I bump the two stacks together so that the bottom one from your stack slides under my eight—and *voila*—both stacks are equal but with only nine in each. Result: the casino saves two hundred quid and carefully selected players will never notice."

"I suppose if he does count them, he assumes he put out less chips than he thought."

"Precisely. Now here's an even more profitable trick." He pointed to Dex's stack of cash chips each worth one-thousand pounds. "Put eight of those on top of the number 11 on the layout." When Dex had carefully counted out the chips and positioned them, McKay looked satisfied. "You have bet eight grand and if the ball lands on 11, you win 35 times your stake. That's a cool £280,000." He dropped the ball onto 11 on the wheel. "You win! Time for me to pay out £280,000." His grin was sly as he placed a small glass ornament on top of Dex's stake. "That's called *the dolly*. Casinos always place this on the winning number before paying out."

Dex nodded and watched intently hoping to spot whatever trick was about to be performed. "Go on."

"Remember that on a busy table, several players may have bet differing amounts backing 11 to win. So you wouldn't necessarily be the only player being paid out. But for this demo, it makes no difference." He deftly lifted the dolly and counted the chips staked and then proceeded to gather and count out several stacks of chips as winnings before pushing them across toward Dex.

Dex grinned confidently. "So because there's so many chips in these stacks, you're banking on me not bothering to count them. I'm too lazy to do the maths multiplying 35 times eight thousand. I just accept the winnings without thinking about it."

Dex grinned at McKay. "But I'm not falling for that." With a cocky look, he continued. "I'm going to count the winnings." With pedantic care, he did so and ended with a triumphant "Yeah! Caught you! You only paid me £245,000. You owe me another £35,000. You've underpaid me on my eight grand stake."

Gus McKay, sparrow-like, cocked his head to one side. "Aye, even honest casinos make mistakes. Usually the inspector spots them and sorts it." It was now McKay's turn to smirk across the layout. "So go on. What do you do now?"

"I say—hey! You've underpaid me. You owe me another £35,000. The payout should have been £280,000. There's only £245,000 here."

"Let me check again, sir." McKay lifted the dolly again and then counted out the chips staked. "I'm sorry, sir. You only staked seven chips, so I paid you thirty-five times seven thousand equals £245,000. The payout is correct."

"Hey, but I staked eight chips."

"I'm sorry, sir. You *thought* you staked eight but it was only seven." McKay wiped a watery eye. "At this point, the inspector will become involved with soothing words and you will be kicking yourself that you put out one less chip than you thought."

"But I *know* I placed eight chips. So what did you do?"

McKay grinned. "As I raised the dolly to count your chips staked, I palmed off the top chip from your stake. That is, I secreted it out of sight in my palm as I pulled away and then surreptitiously dropped it among the casino chips on my side of the layout. Net profit by under-payment £35,000."

"I'm not satisfied." Dex looked indignant. "I'm sure I bet eight chips."

McKay nodded. "So the inspector says, let's check the cameras, shall we?"

Dex groaned. "Don't tell me. I can guess. Minutes later, the message comes back that I only staked seven." He saw McKay's head nod. "So I ask to see the video recording—and am told that this is not permitted. In short, like Beth discovered, I am…"

"…well and truly shafted." McKay stood up and moved to his black-jack layout. "Want to learn some more tricks?"


Pepe Carmino showed no signs of jet lag after his private jet flight from Vegas via Geneva. Indeed, he was feeling exhilarated as he bounded into Dukes. True, the Swiss lawyer's terms had been fierce but Carmino had pointed out the urgency to shift hot money now that the US Government regarded once secret Swiss accounts as piggybanks to be raided. Almost daily, undeclared cash was getting harder to shift or hide. Within hours now, the first cash would be flowing through the tables at Dukes.

Carmino locked his office door and slid aside a large original painting of a racehorse by George Stubbs. He tapped in the code for the safe and from inside removed a box of tricks that controlled his own personal surveillance system. This operated independently of the official cameras that caught every angle on the casino floor. Every room in the building and every table in the dining room could be secretly bugged and filmed. Only his old mate Arnie Fisher and two overpaid technicians knew of the installation.

The wizardry had served him well. He had overheard card-counters boasting over dinner; had listened in as Nigel Forster- Brown moaned to Terry O'Keefe, the Finance Director about their boss. He had heard FB moaning again but on this occasion, the moan had been rather different. He had watched O'Keefe lock his office door and engage in a sudden and frenetic act of sodomy across the end of his desk, FB's fingers scratching helplessly on its polished wood surface.

*And both of them married men too. Tut-tut!*

The knowledge had been invaluable. Ever since, both men had preferred full cooperation in Carmino's plans to the threatened alternative.

When not on other special duties, Arnie Fisher and his assistant would spend long hours every day checking the recordings and reporting anything of particular significance. Today, Carmino noticed with a wolfish smile of satisfaction that yet again One-Eye and Jeb Miller had pulled the late-bet trick on a wealthy Nigerian diplomat. The call had saved the casino just under two million on the Nigerian's winning bet and he had lost on the following spin.

No witness.

No complaint.

Carmino sucked in his cheeks and laughed as he watched Miller commiserate with the drunken player who shrugged away his bad luck and left the table, swaying slightly as he walked.

He put away his wizardry and called FB. "Mick Glenn in tonight?"

"He's in the restaurant with a woman, another new face. He told me with a big nudge-nudge wink-wink that he won't be playing tonight. He's back tomorrow to play *roully*, as he calls it."

"Make sure that Jeb Miller and One-Eye look after him well." Carmino laughed unpleasantly. After ending the call, Carmino reached deep into the back of the safe and removed a framed photo of himself as a young man dressed in flip-flops, garish T-shirt and green shorts. Next to him stood a smiling young woman aged about twenty-two.

In the background was an ornate church and perched around the roof were several vultures, their backs bent as they watched the scene below. He gazed at the photo, reliving memories of his time dealing blackjack at the Casino Sienna where the young woman also worked. Scrawled across the foot of the photo in thick blue ink was his caption *Spot the Vulture!*

Looking at the old photo, he could almost smell the sultry heat rising from the Panamanian street and imagine the unforgettable toucans in the foetid jungle with their vivid beaks. Gently, he stroked the woman's face as he recalled their animal passion in a small hotel overlooking the Panama Canal at Colon. Slowly, and with obvious reluctance, he removed the photo from its frame. "Time for you to go, Maria." He then raised it to his lips and kissed the smiling face before slowly feeding it into the shredder beside his desk.


About six miles away from Dukes, Tiffany Richmond parked her two-seater Mercedes close to *Who Cares*. Having locked the car and grabbed a bottle of Tuscan red wine, she approached the barge, admiring the clean well-painted look. Before she had time to clamber aboard, Dex appeared on deck. "Saw you arrive," he explained needlessly. In his hands were two glasses and beside a small table and chairs was a bottle of Tuscan red which was already open. Tiffany recognised the label at once as she stood beside him and handed her bottle to him.

Dex laughed at seeing the same bottle. "Great minds, eh?"

"Or maybe coals to Newcastle?"

"Thanks, anyway. I thought we'd eat up here as it's such a beautiful evening. The food's actually ready now."

"My fault. Sorry to be a bit late." She sat down. "The book signing overran."

"Good crowd, then?"

"Above average. You never know what to expect. Leadenhall Market was great. Earlier, Chiswick High Street was good but the one in Hampstead, where I expected a big turnout, there was a cloudburst and only six turned up, including a cocker spaniel with a bandaged leg." They caught each other's eyes and laughed.

"Excuse me while I dish up." Dex reappeared moments later with smoked chicken pasta and mixed salad. They settled down and chinked glasses. Beside her, Tiffany had laid out her phone and she immediately apologised explaining that twenty-four-seven contact went with the territory. Overhead as the sun set, a few swallows soared and swooped endlessly and along the towpath, there was a steady flow of joggers or couples strolling in the warm evening air, perhaps going to one of the riverside pubs.

Deliberately, Dex had set their chairs so that their view was across the river to avoid passers-by gawping and pointing out the well-known face. As usual, rowing twos, fours and eights zipped by heading upstream toward Mortlake or back down to the boathouses by Putney Bridge. A police patrol chugged by ready to prevent any-one exceeding the river's speed limits and the barge rocked gently from its wake. "So do people come because you're a TV personality or because they really do want the book?"

"Good question. Probably a bit of both."

"Your name on the cover helps?"

Tiffany accepted the fact with a smile. "Look, not everyone is that interested in the plight of the starving Africans."

"I bought the book—funnily enough, a signed copy from your visit to Piccadilly. I'd read the reviews. They were compelling. You brought the smell of hot African dust and the wails of crying kids into our living rooms. It was very forceful. Opened my eyes too."

Tiffany did not look embarrassed at the compliment and acknowledged as much with the wave of her fork. "The royalties are all pledged to the cause, so you did your bit."

"It's being described as the number one bestseller."

"True, but to be able to give big money to feed the kids, the publishers need to sell overseas rights and help me make it big in the USA."

"You're not known over there. The book will have to sell on its merits."

"Hype too. I've a good PR machine."

Dex saw she had been about to add something. "Go on. There's more, isn't there?"

"I'm to share a platform with former President Bill Clinton in New York during my US tour. He's big on African tragedies."

Dex raised his glass. "I'm impressed. Here's to more success." Even as he toasted her, Dex was contrasting the shallowness of his own existence. Her success was a sharp reminder of his long period of self-pity. "I'd love to support your cause."

"But we're not here to talk about me. Or at least, not about my book."

"Let's finish the food and wine first. A full stomach and some more red may be a good idea before you…"

"Agreed." Already her sad-eyed look showed a hint of her inner thoughts. For the next twenty minutes they chatted about fishing, Africa and occasional amusing incidents from life in front of the camera. It was only after Dex had cleared the plates away and sat gazing at the dark water rushing beside the barge that he prompted her to explain her remark at Bladon. "You mentioned solidarity?"

Tiffany stood up and took a few slow steps to the rail on the far side of the barge. She motioned him to follow as if standing looking across the murky opaque surface would somehow make it easier. For a moment they stood in silence watching the moorhens' black heads bobbing around. "Remember the Bromley rail crash?"

Dex recalled the headlines well—thirty-one deaths and countless more injured "Must have been six years ago."

"Six years next December 15th." Tiffany stared even harder at the water below. "I lost both parents and my husband Chris." Her voice was barely audible but Dex heard clearly enough.

"I'm sorry. So…"

"I've been to hell and back, yes." She turned to him as she used her hand to wipe away a tear. "But the important point *for you* is that *I came back* from that dark place."

"But the ache, the pain?"

She shook her head sadly, her chestnut hair cut short so that it barely moved even with the breeze that had just sprung up. She shivered. "Black holes never turn white. For weeks, months even, I was like a zombie, trying to find a purpose in life. Trying to work out why such dear people should be oh, God, just hacked down when they had so much good in them."

"And the answer?"

"There is none. It's sod's law. Wrong place, wrong time."

"Before … y'know. I used to laugh a lot. What got you through it?"

"I took a complete break from TV journalism and went to Africa. Swamped myself in other people's struggle to survive." She closed her eyes as if locked into memories of famine and the cries of dying children in makeshift hospitals. "Watching starving orphans eating goats' dung." She sighed painfully. "When I came back, I started writing the book. But I returned to the day job too, filled every waking moment."

"Is that the solution for me too? To disappear? A change of scene. To write a book?"

"Only you can answer that." She looked him squarely in the eye. "But whatever you do, immerse yourself in it. No brooding time."

They fell silent as Dex weighed up his determination to destroy Dukes but before he could volunteer anything, it was Tiffany who continued, this time with her cool left hand placed on his wrist on the railing.

"Dex, I haven't been entirely straight with you." She saw a look of irritation as if he expected her to say she had recorded their time together.

"This is off the record?" Dex looked concerned.

"Of course. No, it's nothing like that. It's just that I know far more about you than you might expect."

"Oh?"

"The journalist in me, I suppose. I googled your father. I read Wikipedia and found plenty about his success in property development. But there was no mention of you or your sister in anything about him and so I was curious. I dug deeper. I tried the newspaper archives." She saw the wary look on Dex's face. "Dex—I know it all, or at least think I do. Beth was not your first tragedy, was she? Sorry, but as I kept digging, I found a goldmine." She stopped. "I can leave it there if you like."

Dex stood up straight, changing position from leaning on the railing. Contrary to her reluctance to continue, he wanted her to go on. "Talking to you, listening to you, could be part of the healing process. You're unlocking a box that has had the lid firmly shut." Dex looked at her with his eyes locked onto hers. It was sufficient encouragement.

Tiffany hit it with him straight. "You despise your father. That's brutally frank, but true. Right?"

"His greed destroyed my life."

"I read the planning documents."

"Father wanted to build a superstore in Camberley. All that stood in the way was land belonging to my company. I was the CEO. I had built it to over four hundred men and women manufacturing autospares. To grow the company, I'd made a big mistake. I brought in venture capitalists from the City. Foolishly, I became a minority shareholder dancing to their tune. I resisted Father's plans because they were going to destroy everything I had strived for."

He fell silent, looking at her in the half-light but other than a slight sign that he should go on, she said nothing. "I hated him for our childhood and what he had done to mother. When I refused to move the company elsewhere, he made a takeover bid—an offer that the venture capitalists found irresistible."

"Your father bought the company?"

"And immediately closed it down paying off everybody with generous redundancy. Plus I got a hefty—well, huge, actually—sum for my shares. But the factory-floor workers were outraged. Redundancy money is not a job. Most struggled to find employment. They called me Judas. Feelings ran high."

"But surely you were the least to blame?"

"The employees didn't see it that way. Lurid and defamatory stories swirled everywhere."

"Like what?"

"Like I was getting top-dog status in father's property company. Like father had bribed me with a million pound backhander into a secret offshore bank account. All rubbish." He shivered at the recollections. "There was a herd mentality. Nobody wanted to believe my version."

He faltered, struggling wiith his emotions. "Carole, me, and baby Jamie were living down a quiet lane, rather remote. One day the word *Judas* was spray-painted across the front of our home. I confronted Father—pleaded with him to publish something to stop the hate campaign." Dex ran his fingers through his hair. "He refused. In the end, after having enquiry agents working on it, we proved it had been Father feeding the poison into the community."

"Because you had not supported him." Tiffany looked at him enquiringly. She had read what had happened, but wanted to hear it from him. "So?"

"One night, I returned from a meeting with London lawyers about the defamation, about everything. I got back at just after 11 p.m. As I drove down our lane, I saw the house was ablaze—top to bottom. The fire brigade had not arrived but a neighbour who lived a few hundred yards away had seen the flames across the fields and had dialled 999." He fell silent and scuffed his foot on the deck.

"You must go on." She squeezed his wrist.

"Despite the flames, I forced my way in but it was hopeless. I couldn't get upstairs. It was an inferno. There was no sign or sound of Caroline or Jamie inside or out. The roar of the flames and the thick evil smoke masked everything. I was frantic." He gripped the rail and Tiffany could feel him shaking as frustration ripped through him. "It was impossible." Dex shuddered not even noticing Tiffany's consoling arm wrapped across his back.

"Obviously arson."

"They smashed the windows with rocks and then had lobbed in Molotov cocktails both upstairs and down."

"They?"

"Persons unknown. There were at least 150 suspects. Every one of them had an alibi. The police never charged anyone." He turned toward her, his eyes moist. "To my shame, I never did anything to track them down."

"And now Beth."

He nodded. "If you put me on the spot and wanted a straight answer, I'd have to say that Beth too *was* murdered."

Dex knew at once by her reaction, head rocking back, mouth dropping open, that his words had done more than shock her. For some reason, they seemed to have struck home. She removed her arm from across the small of his back. "Dex, you may just be right." She took in his stunned look at receiving support. "It's getting chilly. Can we go inside? Have a coffee, perhaps? I'll explain."

# CHAPTER TWELVE

In the cabin of the barge, the air was scented by a pair of vanilla spice candles that flickered as they entered. The twin table lights were dimmed and Tiffany was quick to take in the atmosphere of cosy seduction. The door to his bedroom was open, revealing the double bed and a small nightlight that burned from floor level. Feeling sheepish at his earlier thoughts, Dex shut the bedroom door, closed the burnished gold curtains in the galley, and motioned her to sit on the sofa.

"Getting a bit ahead of yourself, were you?" It was the sharp directness of the professional journalist but the pointed dig was said with amusement. Dex's flustered eye movement revealed his guilt at being caught with his hand in the cookie jar. The hands-up denial was accompanied by a sickly grin. Tiffany laughed. "You're not the first optimist! But after what I've been through and fending off rutting stags at the studios, I'm in no hurry. I need to know if a book is as good as its cover."

"Me? These days, I'm a well-thumbed library book—always returned within fourteen days." He enjoyed seeing Tiffany laugh. "Anyway, how do take your coffee?" Dex was keen to change the drift of the conversation.

She wanted it black. He watched as she prowled around the confined spaces taking in everything with the keen eye of a journalist and bestselling author. He knew she was taking in a load of stuff about him but when her comment came, it was not what he expected.

"For someone on the *Sunday Times* Rich List, you live a pretty simplistic lifestyle. Why?"

Dex battled to sum up the complexities in an accurate sound bite. He watched the percolator erupting with satisfying plops before speaking. "To Father, making money is everything. Or was. For him, winning every deal was his only goal." Dex looked across at Tiffany, his eyes showing his contempt. "After becoming a billionaire, he never needed more but always wanted it." He offered her crackers and cheese but she declined. "I kicked back at the nastiness in everything he stood for." He poured out two cups. "So yes, I'm on the Rich List from the private family trusts that Father set up years ago. I never needed to work but I started the autospares business, just me and Carole. That was life, not living off his wealth. To me, looking after the workforce and expanding our markets was worth far more."

"You've been very ill? Right?"

He handed her a chunky red and white mug before seating himself about as far along the sofa as he could, something Tiffany noticed with a broad grin as she edged nearer. In return, Dex looked uncomfortable and wriggled uneasily as he wondered just what she did not know about him. "It's been tough."

"Your two whiteboards. One is full of JFK's assassination and the other all about the Alma Tunnel. Do I sense a conspiracy theorist?" The heavy sarcasm was not lost on Dex.

"I hate being duped by the Establishment. You don't buy into conspiracies?"

"Like Elvis is alive and well and living in London?" As she laughed, she revealed her beautifully white teeth that seemed almost too perfect to be natural. "No. But I accept no facts till proven or corroborated." Tiffany's tone suddenly turned sharper. "Beth's death? A conspiracy theory there too then?"

Dex saw that she was not mocking him but the directness caught him unprepared. "I'm sorry, Tiffany but I'm not quite ready to bare everything to you."

"Look Dex. You're an enigma. I'm intrigued. The more I surfed, the more layers of a very large onion I unpeeled. So I do understand your hatred of the media and of the police." She speared him with an intense yet supportive look. "The local newspaper press cuttings after the fire were unsympathetic, almost hostile—but carefully crafted and never defamatory. Not in my opinion, anyway."

"That's what the QC advised too."

"But the media did a pretty good hatchet job on you." She clasped the mug and sipped.

"For sure, they stoked up hatred in the community." Dex looked away at the photo of the wrecked Mercedes in the tunnel. Then he eyeballed her, his venom piercing the gap between them. "After the fire the journalists changed sides. That made it worse. Scum, that's what I think—present company excepted," he concluded with a big grin.

"Look, if you don't want to, don't tell me why you think Beth was murdered. I'm here as a friend, not a TV journalist hunting for a scoop."

As he listened, Dex's thoughts had been racing back to his meeting with Gus McKay and the warning about careless talk. If he confided in Tiffany, that would be three people he had opened up to including Adam. "Tiffany, I do trust you but firstly, you've something for me. *You* thought I might be right about Beth's murder?"

She twisted her neat frame on the sofa so that she was half-facing him. Her phone bleeped as yet another text arrived and she glanced briefly at the screen, plainly irritated at being interrupted. She turned back to him. "I've been monitoring the accident. My sources suggest the driver of the truck gave a false name, a nonexistent address and produced a fake driving licence. Currently, he is untraceable." She was rewarded with a low whistle as the implications sank in. "Of course, he might have been an illegal immigrant. That *might* explain it."

Dex stared at the thick pile of the black carpet with its deep red piping. Neither said a word as Dex adjusted to the stunning news. Except for the ticking clock and the swish of the river outside, the silence was total. "You know, in a strange sort of way, I didn't want to hear that. This time I'd rather have been proved to be paranoid."

She leaned across and touched his knee in a manner that was supportive without being remotely suggestive. "Scary, isn't it?"

"So, the next thing will be the police results on the truck's tachograph—y'know to get the black box data on the driver's movements, his hours and the speed changes during the last few seconds."

Tiffany looked doubtful. "If the driver used a false ID, I'd bet he would have nobbled the tacho too." She saw her logic hit Dex as the enthusiasm in his look drained away. "The chart went away for analysis."

"You get to know far more from the cops than me." Dex sounded resentful—and was.

"That's my job. Despite the Leveson fuss, I help them. They help me. Always off-the-record and no money involved. Mutual back- scratching."

Had the cabin been larger, Dex would have paced around it but there was no space for that and he felt hemmed in, like a caged lion.

When he spoke, it was softly but with conviction as if he were thinking aloud. "Pepe Carmino, I'm coming to get you."

It was Tiffany's turn to look puzzled. "Pepe Carmino? *Who* is that?"

"It's a long story. Top, top secret."

She laughed. "I'm a journalist. Trust me." She saw Dex's angular face slowly break into a rueful grin. "I might even prove helpful."

His mind was made up. "Another coffee? This could take some while."

# CHAPTER THIRTEEN

Dex had been awake since five, and a glance outside had convinced him that sitting beside a windswept pond under an umbrella had little to commend it.

After a tasty fry-up, he cleared the table and set up a roulette wheel and layout, chips in front of him, his notes about Reverse Labouchère beside him. On his laptop, he saved a page as CASINO but then changed it to ONISAC. For the next two hours, he placed chips on red and black in ever differing amounts with the outcome faithfully recorded on his laptop.

At last when he had stopped, he checked the totals on screen and with a look of disappointment recorded that he had lost a nominal twenty-three thousand pounds. Yet he knew that the system had to work sooner or later. Today it was going to be later. And if McKay was right, later might be a long time.

He sat down to watch Sky News but his mind was barely focussed on problems about US health reforms. He reached for another book bought from McKay and after checking the index, quickly became engrossed in what he was reading. He flicked through several pages about roulette and then reread them with obvious care. For a moment, he was poised to record a summary of what he had learned but then with a muttered no, he rose to pour another coffee from the percolator.

As he went to the fridge for the milk, his attention was caught by a report on the football from the previous evening. "And in the friendly international in Paris, England striker Mick Glenn was sent off for throwing a punch at the French goalie." A clip of the ugly moment was shown and Dex thought of Adam Yarbury's opinion on Glenn being permitted inside Dukes at all.

Dex had no plans for the evening ahead. Tiffany had shown no immediate interest in getting together because she was tied up with book promotion, planning her US tour and winding down her self-employed deal with the TV station. Her departure the previous evening, long after midnight, had been sealed with a quick peck on both cheeks and a promise to do anything she could to help.

He picked up his mobile. "Adam? Good morning. It's Dex. Fancy dinner tonight at Dukes? Excellent. I want to become a member. You'll book? Okay. See you there. Oh and remember what I said—not a loose word."

He then returned to his laptop, and after finding his scribbled notes from his call with Beth, once again accessed her Cloud backup programme. That was easy enough. He typed in her username, GADECH714538. Then he added her password, ZAYBXCWB. He wondered why she bothered with such complex passwords. He had *dexdexter* as a username and *who-cares* for his password, though often he never even bothered to shut down the system at all.

As before, access was refused. By email he had tried to persuade the company to assist but they wanted proof of death, proof he was next of kin and a Grant of Probate before even considering helping. Given the speed that solicitors moved, he'd be collecting his pension before probate was granted.

He was still scowling at the access denied message when his phone rang. "Yes? Oh thanks." His face brightened. It was international enquiry agents he had hired. "Is that right? You've traced her in Panama? Maria-Elena Sanchez? Correct?"

When the call ended he felt elated, as if the positive news was a real step forward. But seconds later, the euphoria was drowned by a cold douche of reality. Was she really Tavio's sister? Apparently, she dealt blackjack in the Casino Sienna, so she sounded likely. There was also a home address. He sat at his desk, coffee in front of him, and drummed his fingers endlessly.

*Am I ready to step into the unknown? What am I getting into? Who ordered the contract-killing? What would Tavio's sister know?*

Well, she must know something because Beth wanted him to meet her. Would she talk if she knew her brother had been murdered? Did she even know he was dead? Two bullets. One in the head, one in the chest.

How did this link with Carmino? Where did she fit into Pepe Carmino's life? Did she know him? Worse still, was she still in touch with him? He looked angrily at the screen. All the answers could be locked behind the access denied words.

After downing a second cup of coffee, he reached for the phone and after another moment's hesitation, dialled a travel agent on King Street.

This was the point of no return.


At shortly before 7:30 p.m., Dex stepped out of the taxi in Mount Street. He looked up at the five-storey imposing red-brick building. It dated back to the eighteenth century and no doubt had once been the home for a lord and lady with the servants crammed into the basement below street level.

He had been there just once as a guest when Beth had signed him in. Tonight was different. Adam Yarbury had already sorted membership and he was arriving as a member, having paid the joining fee of £25,000.00 and having transferred one million sterling as evidence of commitment to playing the tables. Less eminent casinos welcomed all-comers with their minimum-wage pay packets and no membership formalities. Dukes wanted quality, not quantity of members.

The doorman at the top of a short but wide flight of paved steps greeted him with respect. He was kitted out in a black top hat with a burgundy band around it. The frock coat was to match. As he opened the door, he touched the rim of his hat respectfully. No doubt the regulars also got a cheery and more personalised word of welcome.

Inside, the building smelled of sandalwood and the sweet, sickly smell of newly laid thick-pile carpeting. As he walked down the sweeping curve of the stairs, paintings of rural scenes on the walls, he could sense the unlimited oil wealth that must have been lost at the tables. Everything was immaculate, classic in style and opulent to a fault. The décor was French but morphed by a touch of Arabesque styling. As he entered the main reception at the foot of the stairs, he was impressed with the array of valuable objets d'art, the giant gilt mirrors, the tasteful mix of original paintings and the thickness of the drapes that shut out the noise of the city and any glimpse of life beyond the grasp of seriously big-time gambling.

After being provided with his new membership card and declining an offer of being led to the bar, Dex continued alone, taking a peek into the gaming floor where about a dozen members were playing roulette, blackjack or baccarat. Adam Yarbury had explained that any of the big players could lose ten million in a couple of hours with no more pain than when mere mortals lost a five-pence coin.

As if on cue, a brilliantined Saudi prince in his oh-so-western Ravazzolo suit strolled from the roulette, cracking his knuckles as he walked. He entered the dining room and almost instantly, Dex saw a tall- slightly stooped figure slip effortlessly between the tables, shooting his cuffs as he did so. With a deferential smile and a slight bow, the casino employee walked with the prince to a discreet corner table where he joined another Middle Eastern colleague. The three men shared some banter before Dex moved on. It had not been Carmino, of that he was sure.

Incongruous in the eighteenth-century surroundings but essential in the casino, everywhere he looked were smoky-black bulbous protrusions fixed to the ceilings and walls. Behind each one was a camera monitoring every small detail and sending live images to the team watching screens in the secured back-office.

As Gus had warned him, these cameras could spot whether a player had clipped his nails since a previous visit. But of more concern was McKay's warning that there could be other bugs and cameras totally unseen but positioned to capture any tidbits of data that management could twist to advantage. *Where were they?* Dex spotted nothing but then he had never expected to do so.

He entered the book-lined bar which was designed like a room in the Palace of Versailles. The Spanish bartender expertly mixed him a spicy Virgin Mary which he placed on a small occasional table. Then on a silver tray, he delivered smoked-salmon canapés, a dish of large green and black olives, a pot of crispy biscuits and a side dish of caviar with a tiny silver spoon. Dex had barely sipped his drink before Adam Yarbury entered with the tall but slightly stooped figure he had seen earlier.He introduced himself as Nigel Forster-Brown. FB was wearing the inevitable black bow tie and dinner jacket. With difficulty, Dex forced a smile as he stood up to shake hands.

"FB, this is Finlay Dexter, brother to dear Beth. I'm his godfather."

Dex gave a very self-assured nod. "Generally I'm called Dex."

FB looked at the floor as he almost invariably did. Dex wondered if he was henpecked at home and bullied at work because there was an air of weary resignation about the man. He was tall, almost bald with a pale pink complexion and a nondescript, forgettable face. It was neither ugly nor handsome, just plain forgettable because it had no features that made any impression at all.

"Mr. Dexter, I am so very sorry. We all *adored* your sister. She was a real charmer and enriched our lives." FB flicked an eye upward but then quickly returned to staring at the carpet. "A true delight, that's what she was."

Dex nodded appreciation as Adam intervened. "FB, if you don't mind me saying so, you're looking rather tired, a trifle jaded."

"Overwork, the usual. I'm feeling pretty good but like any business, we always have to work harder for the next buck than the one before."

"How long till you retire? Not that I'm trying to get rid of you, what!" Adam's trademark laugh was always toothy and this was no exception.

FB looked thoughtful, twisting his hands in front of him before replying. "Two years. Since the recession, the fun seems to have disappeared. Two more years seems like a life sentence."

Yarbury nodded in sympathy. "But when you retire? Devon you once mentioned."

"Correct. A cottage near Dartmouth."

"Sea fishing or sailing?"prompted Dex.

FB managed a weak smile. "Mr. D. I'm a Capricorn—a landlubber." He examined his immaculate black shoes. "When I retire, I'll continue playing around with laptops, writing programmes, y'know the sort of thing."

Dex could now see *nerd* written big across FB. "Ah! You're a computer geek! That must be fun," he said thinking quite the reverse.

"Love it, Mr. D. Microchips beat casino chips any day."

"FB," Yarbury changed the subject. "Dukes used to invite Beth to the theatre or maybe Ascot or Silverstone for the Formula One Grand Prix. Maybe that could be switched to Dex?"

FB looked at the ceiling and then his eyes returned to the carpet somewhere behind Dex. "I'll have a word with Mr. Carmino. I saw you had a table booked for dinner. And after that?" The question seemed to be aimed at Dex but their eyes never met.

"I may play roulette," responded Dex. "Unlike Beth, I'm a novice, so maybe I'll just watch for a while."

FB thought of the one million just deposited with the casino. "Not a problem, not a problem. Play whenever you feel, er, comfortable. Well…enjoy your evening."

Over dinner, and as forewarned, Dex chatted about everything except gambling and Dukes. "So you see, I'm going to have to give up *Who Cares* and return to the family home to look after father."

"Back to St John's Wood? At least you'll be near Lord's Cricket Ground." Then Adam's tone turned serious. "But you and your father?"

"I can't bring myself to dump him in a care home, not without trying to do the decent thing first."

Yarbury looked doubtful. "Charles doesn't deserve any decency. He was and will always be a nasty bastard. But it's your call. How will you look after him?"

"If his consultant is right, Father will be almost immobile and scarcely able to communicate. But he will have insight into his surroundings, an awareness of life if you like. I'll need a carer, maybe more than one. I've placed an advert in a couple of places like *The Lady* magazine."

"They're discharging pretty quickly, then?"

"Morrison doesn't think Father is going to improve. It's all to do with something called the Glasgow Scale. It measures the severity of the trauma and guides consultants about the path to recovery."

"I never thought you had it in you to forgive. Not after what he did."

"I'll never forget." The words were snapped out with such bitterness that Adam flinched. Dex then thought of Tiffany's words of advice. "I will never forgive." He shrugged his shoulders. "Immersing myself in other people's troubles … well, that may help."

"Shall we?" Yarbury rose from the table, flicking a few crumbs from his three-piece city suit as he did so. Dex followed him toward the gaming floor while upstairs, Pepe Carmino switched off the feed from the microphone. He had focused on the new member finding it puzzling that someone Beth had described as risk averse would now plan to gamble, especially with a million pounds.

Surely Dexter wasn't suspicious about Dukes? He went over to his walk-in dressing room where he changed from his slacks and open-neck shirt into his dinner jacket to go downstairs. By the time he had adjusted his bow-tie, he had a plan and knew just the person to help. If she would.

He summoned FB to his office and briefed him to keep a particularly close watch on Finlay Dexter.

Adam Yarbury bought in at a blackjack table leaving Dex to watch the roulette. There were three roulette players, one being a loud-mouthed American from Houston. The others, Dex could not pigeonhole but were seemingly from somewhere around the Far East. They were quiet and respectful to the dealer they called One-Eye. None of them were playing the even chance bets of red/black, high/low or odd/even numbers. All were stacking mini-skyscrapers of chips all over the layout and between them backing almost every number between 1 and 36 plus the green zero.

After watching eight or nine spins, Dex had spotted nothing suspicious. He had tried to monitor One-Eye's fast-moving delicate hands as he placed the dolly, counted out the staked winning chips and paid out huge sums at thirty-five times the total staked.

Just like McKay had said, none of the players was obsessively interested in the winning payout. All three were busily placing their next bets on numbers not adjacent to the dolly while One-Eye sorted the winnings. Whenever One-Eye pushed across a wall of chips as winnings, each player glanced briefly only at the high-value cash chips that topped the pile and seemed satisfied without counting.

To Dex it was no different to shoppers never checking their change. The difference in Dukes was that some of these cash chips were worth £100,000 each so that errors could be costly. *But it's all relative*, he told himself realising he had already watched well over three million go back and forth across the table.

"It's Finlay Dexter, isn't it?" The voice from over his shoulder startled Dex from his thoughts. Though the tone was cream-egg smooth, Dex spotted a trace of Essex hidden beneath the urbane charm. Dex twisted to find himself confronted by Pepe Carmino. It was a shock seeing the man in the flesh. "I'm Pepe Carmino, the CEO and owner of Dukes. Welcome." Carmino extended a hand in greeting.

# CHAPTER FOURTEEN

Dex grasped Carmino's slim hand, uncomfortable at showing any sign of civility He was too aware that this could be the man who had wanted Tavio silenced and his sister murdered. As their hands met, he noticed the cold silkiness of the grip.

Hypocrisy was not Dex's style. Pangs of guilt raced through him but for now the charade of civility had to continue. "We met a while back. My sister brought me."

"So we did. But I think you never played the tables?"

"Just a voyeur, I guess." Dex laughed. "And again tonight. I need to get the hang of this scene."

"I'm sure FB has said this but everyone here, we was just devastated at the tragedy. The floral tribute was just a small token of our feelings." Dex relived the moment when the wreath had skimmed the churchyard wall and dropped out of sight. *That* had been just a small token of his own feelings. *Say nothing controversial. Stay on message,* he told himself.

"Thanks for your concern. Beth had so much to live for."

"May I lay on something to drink? Some Dom Perignon? Krug? Whatever."

"Thanks, but no. I'm interested just watching and learning for now. I might fancy blackjack. Beth was learning something called Reverse Labouchère." The lie came easily.

Carmino thoughtfully stroked the jagged scar that ran down his cheek. "Interesting system. Deep pockets is needed. Your late sister liked the Martingale. Of course, players can win most of the time by doubling up losing bets like she did, but when it goes wrong." He shook his head. "It bites big time."

"A good system changes the odds." Dex knew from McKay that this was bollocks but he wanted to play the village idiot as long as possible.

Carmino waggled his slender fingers, suggesting that the jury was out on that. "Every system works sometimes. None of them work all the time." He turned to leave, but then added, "FB spoke to me. Please join us for our special events. I can't always attend. I'm busy with Space City."

"Beth reckoned it was a millstone with problems during construction." Dex fixed Carmino with full-on eye contact.

Carmino's smile was patronising. "Scarcely a millstone. We was, were, seeing it as more of a *gemstone*. Believe me, the jewel in our crown."

As he listened, Dex was enjoying the pseudo posh accent with the grammatical errors. He wanted to retort but resisted, saying only that he was going to learn blackjack by watching Adam Yarbury. Carmino slipped away, a smirk on his face at the thought that *anyone* could learn blackjack from that old buffer.

Dex positioned himself behind Adam's stool and watched as he took a card on 16 against the dealer's 5—and promptly went bust with a 10, giving him 26. From his short time swotting up on Basic Strategy, Dex could spot that Adam's play was blackjack suicide.

The dealer was just shuffling up when Dex felt his phone vibrating in his pocket. His face lit up when he heard Tiffany's voice. "I'm back in town early. Fancy a drink?"

"I'm in Dukes. There's a bar here. I'll sign you in."

"Do I have to play? Remember, I'm a convent girl. Losing money on a ball landing on red or black is my idea of madness."

Dex laughed. "Madness is not compulsory."

It was barely forty minutes later when he signed her in. He led her into the bar. The Spaniard suggested specialty cocktails but both went for soft drinks, Dex feeling pretty smug at his continued moderation. Moments later, Pepe Carmino appeared as if by chance. Dex forced himself to make an introduction. "Mr. Carmino. This is Tiffany Richmond, a good friend." He liked adding those words—essential if she were not to be regarded as a journalist.

"And I am Pepe Carmino. Of course I recognize you. I'm a great fan. I finished *Pain at the Sharp End* on a flight to Vegas the other day. Very moving. Punchy stuff."

Dex resented that Carmino had charmed her almost instantly but took pleasure in spotting that the CEO must have had some Botox work on his forehead, because compared to the photos on the Web, his wrinkles had disappeared. But the scar on his right cheek remained. Keeping it must have been deliberate. No question, it added an aura of hard centre and mystery to his image.

As Carmino small-talked Tiffany about her work, he was standing very erect, hands at ease, utterly relaxed and exuding tea-matinée playboy. Dex sourly reckoned his sultry looks would have worked in a daytime soap set in Southend. He couldn't wait to get away. "Come on, Tiffany. We can take the drinks. Let's go to the roulette."

"Have a pleasant evening, and I do so hope you will visit us again, Ms. Richmond. Perhaps come for dinner as my guest?"

"I'd like that. Thank you." Tiffany watched him as he slithered to another table to chat to an Indian couple, the man wearing a turban. "Sexy bastard, isn't he? There's something edgy about him. Perhaps it's that scar. Is he married?"

Dex flushed, feeling more than a tad jealous at her readiness to accept dinner. "I don't know. Beth reckoned he often charmed the wives while their husbands gambled. Gallant to a fault." His sarcasm was not lost on Tiffany. They left the bar pausing to look at the artwork and the figurines.

"Too grand for my liking," Tiffany volunteered. "Reminds me of the Louvre—awesome, but after a couple of nights there, I'd run screaming to find a cave. I prefer art to be simpler, like pen and ink or etchings. And these frames—so ornate. But I suppose it works well enough down here."

In the gaming room, the tables were comfortably busy and soft chatter greeted them with the hypnotic hiss of the ball as it circled the wheels. "Our TV station is littered with Carmino clones. I could see precisely where he was coming from."

"And where he was trying to get!"

Tiffany pursed her lips by way of answer. "I'd love to question him, put him on the spot. Sincere he is not."

"He's an Essex boy," Dex prompted, as if that explained everything. He felt uneasy, on edge and irritated that she was chitchatting as if they were alone. She seemed to have forgotten his warning about hidden cameras and mikes. Her arrival without a reminder was endangering his agenda. He leaned over and whispered in her ear. "Remember what I said—no loose talk."

She smiled a response as Dex headed to the roulette tables. "You'll recognize the four at the roulette. FB told me—the two women are in that dreadful *Crawley Girls Abroad* programme. They are with Mick

Glenn, the footballer and Scotty Brannigan the American Formula One driver."

"I could spot Amber Murray a mile off. She's the blonde Mick's stroking. He should take care. She's shacked up with Creole Henry."

Dex looked shocked. Through the media, Creole Henry was well known to Londoners as a Jamaican reputed to be a dangerous Yardie. "Then Mick's an even bigger tosser than Adam Yarbury suggested."

He looked at the rack of chips behind the wheel. "Mick's bought in his orange chips at one hundred pounds each. He's plastering them everywhere—over ten thousand quid just on this spin. Five hundred on zero alone. Brannigan's just playing on red or black—the outside bets. Like Beth did."

Glenn tossed the two B-List celebs a few cash chips. "Here you are, Amber, Chloe. Have some fun with these."

"No more bets." One-Eye waved his hands above the layout.

Dex pointed to the man perched on a high stool at the head of the table. "That slob is Jeb Miller. He watches that nobody adds to their stakes or places bets after *no more bets* is called."

"18. Red. Even." One-Eye swept away the losing chips. Despite having covered almost every number, Mick Glenn had lost. Brannigan, using blue colour chips each worth a thousand, had backed black and lost three grand.

Glenn glared at the thin Chinese figure with the big black-framed glasses. "Give over, mate!" One-Eye ignored the comment. "Only backed thirty-three bleedin' numbers, didn't I? Last spin was 22. Now 18. Next door. Only four numbers could lose. That's the second time you've done me over. That is seriously out of order. Big time. Shake it up a bit. This place spooks me. Bleedin' magnets in the wheel. 'S all rigged."

One-Eye shrugged at the loser's typical rant. "The wheel has no memory, Mistah G."

"And we don't use magnets," chortled Miller, trying to add some frivolity.

Brannigan leaned over to his pal. "Don't shoot the messenger, buddy." He was laughing at Glenn's mounting frustration but the footballer's part-shaved face just scowled. "Look at me, Mick! I couldn't hit a dead fly with a banjo—let alone place a winning bet! It'll change. It always does if you don't go bust first."

Dex watched the lean and fit-looking American double up his previous lost stake and switch to backing red—playing small beer compared to the thousands that Mick was scattering across the layout using rapid jabbing movements.

The footballer had again covered thirty-three numbers but this time the stacks of his orange chips were even higher. "Mick's betting over twenty grand. Looks like a Manhattan skyline out there, doesn't it?" he whispered. Tiffany responded with a shrug of despair and a raised eyebrow.

"No more bets." The ball slowed and dropped. It appeared to land on 22 Black before slowly edging next door. One-Eye spoke like a metronome. "Nine. Red. Odd." He swept away every one of Glenn's towers.

"Shit! Bloody 9—22, 18, and now 9 again. All next to each other. You bastard! You fixed this. I'm down thirty-five grand." He scowled at Miller. "Get this dealer changed. Send him back to China for all I care. A slow boat." He didn't expect a reply. Miller simply fingered his moustache. "Yeah, yeah." Glenn burbled on. "Don't say nothing. Your smug face tells me you'll be getting a big Christmas bonus."

Scotty Brannigan scooped up his winnings and glared at his friend. "Shut the fuck up, Mick! Big boys don't gripe. What you've lost—just an hour's work for you anyway. A few throw-ins, two free kicks, an' you're there. So quit the shit, big fella."

Mick was unreceptive. "When I'm losin, if I want to, I'll fuckin' gripe until my bollocks fall off. Hey! You! One-Eye! Don't spin yet. I ain't ready. Gotta get more cash."

When Mick returned from the casino's cage, he had another one hundred thousand pounds in chunky plaques, which he changed into chips. Dex and Tiffany exchanged glances as their excitement mounted. Dex found himself intrigued by the pounding vein on the footballer's temple as he now gambled forty thousand across the layout. "Spin me up an' watch me clean you out!" He glared at One- Eye and then winked at Amber, the younger of the two women.

Tiffany was craning forward to watch the ball. The only sound now was the relentless hiss while it circled the wheel. The ball teased 22 again before skittering like a stone across the waves. "1. Red. Odd." It was not that far from the previous clutch of numbers.

"Done it! I've done it!" Mick's relief was obvious. There was sweat dripping down his neck, his eyes stood out and he snorted in excitement like a racehorse first past the winning post. He was as breathless as if he'd just played ninety minutes at Wembley. In contrast, Scotty Brannigan, who had staked £20,000 using twenty chips on red, showed all the coolness needed to corner at 160 mph on a wet track.

"How much will Mick win?" Tiffany looked at Dex.

"Thirty-five times his stake. With fifteen chips on that number, he wins, er, £52,500. But it won't see him right. That spin, he lost £38,500 on the other numbers. So his net profit is only £14,000. He needs to win another two or three spins to recover just what he'd lost before." He silently watched the dealer pay out Scotty's even-chance win. One-Eye assembled a single stack of blue chips, which Dex was sure he raised slightly above the green baize and moved to beside Scotty's bet.

The American was busily chatting with Mick, who was back into noisy swagger mode. The two stacks came together and Dex did a double take as he saw a small, sharp but definite movement. Coming in high over the baize and then bumping had moved the bottom chip from Scotty's stake into the bottom of the winnings. In his imagination, Dex replayed McKay's demonstration and knew at once that One-Eye must have delivered eighteen chips, evening out the two stacks by bumping across one chip from Brannigan's stake.

In a flash, One-Eye's forefinger ran across the two stacks. They were now of equal height—as they should be. Trying not to look obsessive as he stood behind the two players, Dex counted the two stacks. *McKay's trick had just been pulled by One-Eye!* There were nineteen in each stack. There should have been twenty.

Trying not to look shocked, Dex turned away as if he had spotted nothing and pointed out a laughing Adam Yarbury to Tiffany. Amazingly, his godfather had a large pile of chips in front of him. But Tiffany had spotted something in Dex's body language, a question in her face. "What's up?" Her mouth was deliciously close to his ear as she whispered, but the pleasure was lost on him.

"Say nothing. Remember!" His voice was a whisper, but the tone was acid as he faked a friendly smile. Dex looked back at the layout. The dolly was sitting on top of Mick's fifteen orange chips, but Glenn was not watching. He was busily chugging down a beer from the bottle while patting Amber's backside. Then, after roughly pulling her close to him for a smooch and snog, he returned to his beer, followed by a noisy belch. "Better up than down," he joked.

One-Eye broke the orange chips into a tower of three offset groups of five. Cameras all round could now verify the stake. He then rebuilt the tower. "Five-Twenty-Five orange."

"Yes." Miller nodded approval and gazed down as One-Eye prepared to pay out £52,500.

"What would you like, Mistah. G?" enquired the dealer in his robotic style as if he were taking orders in a Chinese takeaway. "Four purples, some golds, a few pinks, and the rest in orange?" The suggestion mixing different value cash chips and some colour was routine.

"No. Give us all cash chips. No orange." Mick turned to Amber. "This is where I win big using them golds. They're one thousand each. The purples is ten thousand. The pinks is one hundred. Shove a coupla pinks on your birthday, love. Even if you lose, remember, today's your lucky day—know what I mean, darlin'." Dex heard the dirty chuckle as she poked him in the ribs.

Dex murmured to Tiffany. "Like that, he'll cover just twenty-two numbers, plus his winning stake left on number one. That still leaves him fourteen losing numbers." He watched One-Eye count out the winning chips, breaking them down so that the cameras all around could check he was not overpaying an accomplice. With difficulty, Dex checked the value of the piles put together. They were correct. Miller nodded consent. One-Eye then restacked the winnings as Dex overheard Mick whispering to Amber what he was going to do to her later.

He just caught her saying *you beast but I like you* followed by a noisy giggle as the dealer stretched out, moving the winnings across. One-Eye pushed with his left hand and steadied with his right over the top of the stacks. Then he let go, withdrawing his hands leaving the winnings in front of Glenn.

*Christ! I saw that flash of colour.*

Under One-Eye's right hand as he drew away, Dex had glimpsed a gold chip—one thousand pounds that should have reached Mick had been palmed and slipped back beside others on One-Eye's side of the table.

Dex counted the new bets placed—only twenty-one gold chips on the layout—definitely one short, but Glenn had never noticed as he scattered them across his array of numbers.

The wheel spun and the ball rolled to a halt on 14 Red—a losing number for Mick and Amber. Glenn thumped the table angrily. "Heh! Chinky! You're getting on me tits! 'Ere. Change these for gold." He pushed the three purples across the table.

"Well I'm doin' jus' great now," Scotty volunteered, not altogether helpfully. "These kind folk keep givin' me money."

"Let's go and sit down," Dex suggested to Tiffany as he resolved he had to return but with a hidden camera.

They passed Pepe Carmino, who had paused to watch them from a few paces away. In particular, he had been admiring Tiffany's black stockings and the tasseled purple dress cut above her knees, so different from her television image. Whenever Tiffany had moved to watch the wheel, standing tiptoed as the ball was spinning, she had provided him with a tantalizing profile. "Not risking your money tonight then, Mr. D?" He fell into step with them as they left the room.

"Too much to learn still."

"Be our guests for some drinks," Carmino suggested, adjusting his dress shirt, flashing his teeth and his cufflinks simultaneously. "I'll show you to an excellent table." He walked them into the bar and settled them at a thick-cushioned settee for two. "Some champagne cocktails perhaps?" After he had organized the drinks, Carmino excused himself and headed for his office.

"Want to stay a bit longer?" Dex draped an arm across the back of the settee and offered her a choice of Belgian chocolates or savoury nibbles that had now appeared. "Adam won't leave for a couple more hours."

"Pure theatre in there, but that was enough!" She helped herself to a dark chocolate. "So when are you off to Pa…"

Dex jumped in quickly, horrified that the word Panama might be mentioned. He tried to sound less flustered than he felt. "To Park Royal? Checking out that care home for Father?" he improvised, hoping that any listener would be fooled. "Maybe tomorrow, but the advert in *The Lady* magazine has produced a few live-in applicants. I'll keep all options open. There's another place up in Northampton too, prob-ably the best but less convenient."

"You're sure he wouldn't be better off in a special unit?"

Dex looked serious. "I'm not sure of anything. But the consultant likes the idea of home environment and daily stimulation, y'know, see how it goes."

Tiffany's face turned sharply toward him but she lowered her voice. "What was the matter in there?"

"I saw…" His voice trailed away as he tried to recover from what he was about to blurt out. "Mick Glenn chucking away money like he was playing Monopoly. I was shocked."

"I'll tell you what surprised me. Everything the dealer did, the fat guy with the moustache checked. Not much trust around, is there?"

"Adam explained about that. It's a bit spooky, everybody watching everybody."

"I guess with so much money flying about," Tiffany pushed the chocolates further away from her, "it's not quite like nicking a can of soup from a corner shop."


Upstairs in his office, Carmino had locked his door and produced his box of tricks from the safe. From an array of settings, he selected one. At once, the conversation from the settee was live, picked up from microphones in the armrests. The hidden lens, built into the wall fabric, missed nothing either.

The dimmed wall lights and comfy chairs encouraged intimate exchanges, not least from guests relaxing on the settee. Carmino played back the video. She was asking about him going to Pa…no question, there was something in his facial behaviour before he witttered on about Park Royal. It looked as if he was shutting her up.

Carmino continued listening to the chatter. "What was the matter in there?"

Then came Dexter's reply. "I saw…" Then there was a pause. To Carmino, it sounded a tad too long before Dexter had continued about Mick Glenn. Wondering if he were becoming paranoid, Carmino poured himself a Baron Otard brandy, larger than normal for this stage of the evening. Then he selected a Padron cigar from his humidor. The cameras and recordings continued. *What's that she's saying about going to the USA?*

"So please don't get too close, Dex. Don't build any hopes or plans round me." She patted his hand as an act of kindness but not love. "It's a long tour." The mikes fell silent. Carmino saw disappointment on Dexter's face. Then he saw they were draining their drinks to leave.

"Let's go. I'll say goodbye to Adam."

Carmino switched off and stretched out on his easy chair. He tapped off the cigar ash. Like everything he did, even this simple act was delicate so that the dollop fell with precision and unbroken. Care in everything was his creed. Leave nothing to chance. He narrowed his eyes as he thought of the important call he had made earlier in the evening. A quiet smile of satisfaction crossed his face, but it was not caused by the cigar or brandy.

As their taxi splashed its route westwards, Dex made sure the driver could not overhear their conversation. "So I saw it—deliberate cheating, just like they cheated Beth. What I saw tonight, even without late bets call, could easily save Dukes one-hundred and fifty million a year - even without the blackjack."

"You're joking. One-fifty million! I didn't notice anything."

"Most players are trusting, off-guard."

"My God!" She wiped the condensation off the window as she gathered her thoughts. "I had no idea. Such huge figures make cheating worthwhile. Now, it makes sense after all."

"Extrapolate like this: from just one spin, One-Eye stole two thousand from Scotty—that's peanuts. But in a typical evening, on just one table, there could be three hundred spins just between 8 p.m. and 4 a.m. If they can steal on just fifty of them, that's one hundred thousand. Multiply that by four working roulette tables and you're looking at four hundred thousand a day, or nearly three million a week."

"Equals one-fifty million." Tiffany's enthusiasm seemed to be growing. Her nostrils twitched as she thought it through. "That's beside calling late bets."

"A lawyer told me that to prove adultery, it used to be essential to establish inclination plus opportunity. Dukes needs urgent big money for Space City—equals *inclination*. They have the *opportunity* to pick on players who don't check their winnings. Spot on, M'Lud."

"Different sort of shafting, perhaps?" Tiffany winked but in the gloom of the cab, Dex never noticed. By now they were passing the Natural History Museum in Kensington. Dex grinned and encouraged her to continue. She thought for a moment. "But they got it wrong with Beth."

Dex thought for a moment. "They got away with it, though. Nearly a million."

"Dex, they must be very desperate to take these risks."

"There was more in there. More cheating." He turned to her again in emphasis as he explained how Mick Glenn had been robbed.

"You spotted that?"

Dex made it sound easy. "I knew what to look for. Earlier on, I also saw a dealer called Andy palm a chip off a South African's winning stake. He saved the casino thirty-five thousand. Just one spin. So one-fifty million in a year is left for dead."

"What had Beth proved about Dukes bankrolling the building works?"

"I'm locked out of her data, but Beth knew."

"You'll need to work on that."

He looked serious as he agreed. "The dealers must know which tight-arses always check their winnings. Most don't."

"Could this just be the dealers stealing? Nothing to do with Carmino."

"One-Eye didn't palm the gold cash chip for himself. He discreetly returned it to the pile in front of him." He shook his head. "This is organised fraud coming from the top."

Tiffany moved closer and felt for his hand. "I meant what I said in there. I'm in no hurry. I'm still getting my head around life without Chris. Before him, handsome men like you fooled me. My fault—rushing in, not using my head." She squeezed his hand. "With you, your strength of purpose…intrigues me. It makes me feel close to you."

Dex patted her wrist softly, loving her assessment. At their next consultation, Dr. Wilfred Grierson would no doubt agree to differ. "I won't be deflected."

"I believe you. So what next? The Gaming Authorities? The Police?"

"Panama." The taxi was slowing up outside Tiffany's pad by World's End. "And I'm going to film Carmino's dirty tricks."

"Don't underestimate him, Dex. I'll bet he's from a tough background,."

"Yeah! Point taken but I've got to go on." The taxi stopped and as she unbuckled, he grasped her shoulders so that they faced each other at close quarters in the half-light. "But Dukes? They're weak." He recalled Gus McKay's words. "They're pygmies."

"Go on."

"Weak because they have guilty secrets; weak because they need to cheat. A successful casino has no need to cheat."

"But you're cornering a rat.."

"Do me one favour before you fly. I need the contacts for Scotty and Mick Glenn. Your sports editor will know."

"No promises." She sounded concerned. "Don't get involved with Mick Glenn. Scotty's different. Glenn's a loose cannon. And if Creole Henry finds out about tonight." She ran her finger across her throat.

"Maybe a loose cannon's just what I need. Since the fire, I've seen every ladder as a snake in disguise. Now, I need to take risks."

Tiffany opened the cab door, kissing him on both cheeks, arms around his shoulders. "Cornered rats. Remember?"

"Good luck with the US tour."

"Let's keep in touch."

# CHAPTER FIFTEEN

As Dex was poring over pages of figures while he practiced Reverse Labouchère, a swarthy Jamaican with a barrel chest and shaven head presented his passport at Heathrow Airport. It showed his name as Leroy Creole Henry. He was nodded through.

Dex meanwhile tried to lift his spirits with a bacon buttie and HP sauce. The roulette system had been dispiriting. By his calculations, he had played for over thirty hours in total and had never once got into a winning streak. And every day passing was one day closer to the launch of Space City.

That must never happen.

His phone rang and it was Tiffany. After a few pleasantries, she confirmed that getting anywhere close to Scotty was impossible. All approaches had to be through his management company in Scottsdale, Arizona but she had a couple of numbers for Glenn, who lived in grand style on the Bishop's Avenue in north London. "I was tempted to tell you I couldn't get Glenn's contacts. You need better allies than him. But it's your call."

After wishing her a safe flight, he went for a jog hoping to get rid of the depressing roulette experiment and wishing that he could contact Scotty Brannigan. Probably he was away somewhere prepping for the next race.

And Glenn? Maybe he was just the guy to stir things up. By the time, he had showered after completing his six miles, his mind was made up. He dialed Glenn's number, making sure that Glenn could not use callback to identify him.

The footballer was lying next to Amber on a giant sun-bed by his indoor pool. He removed his muscular arm from around her neck and answered with casual indifference. "Yeah?"

"Hi, Mick! You don't know me. Name's Johnny. I was watching you and Scotty at Dukes last night."

"So? I lost an effin' packet, didn't I?"

"Dukes cheated you both. I saw what happened. We need to meet."

"Them magnets. Bleedin' Dukes! Always said they used magnets."

"I don't know about that."

"I'll fucking do Carmino, know what I mean?"

"No—don't, Mick. You've no evidence. I have. We must meet, with Scotty too. Plan carefully."

"Fuck evidence. I knew I was stitched up by that Chinaman. I'll do it my way." Dex could take no more of the boorish oaf's stupidity and ended the call, wishing now he had listened to Tiffany.

The footballer looked at the dead phone for a moment and then ranted to Amber, who seemed too spaced out behind her headphones to give a damn.

"Bleeding Dukes. I'll fucking sort them wankers. Sod 'em. Anyway, enough of that. When's Creole back from Jamaica?"

"Lands tonight." Amber did not sound enthused at the prospect.

"We got hours yet, then." He leaned across her tanned body and started to remove her bikini top.


Dex drove over to the family home in St John's Wood where he had spent his final teenage years. Porcupine House held no happy memories—which was a shame, because it was magnificent to the last detail. Father's wealth had ensured that the interior décor was the finest throughout each spacious room of its three floors. The local estate agents would have drooled over their prose when describing the attention to perfection.

But Dex hated the place.

The bad vibes were over-powering.

It had been from here that his mother had walked out, never to return.

It had been here in the sitting-room that he had blackened his father's eye and broken his nose with a real haymaker of a punch. He could take no more. His father had refused to quash rumours that Dex was secretly in favour of selling his company.

Just days later, his home had been torched.

He peered into Beth's bedroom. It looked just the same as ever. Now, as he wiped back tears for Carole and Jamie, in here, he could almost see his sister. As a vibrant seventeen-year-old, Beth used to do her yoga in her red leotards, classical music playing softly. He rested his head against the wall and sobbed – for how long he had no idea. Eventually, he forced himself to control the powerful shakes that had gripped him. He bit his lip and turned to go downstairs.

After Dex had married and Beth had moved into a place overlooking the river at Greenwich, Sir Charles had continued to live there alone. No other woman appeared to have entered his life. Despite all his wealth, except for his renowned wine cellar, he had seemingly lived a simple existence of work and more work with a cleaner dropping by with basics and to clean and dust.

*Can I really be giving up life on Who Cares to live here again? Surrounded by a past I'd rather forget? To look after Father, rather than send him away?*

The thought reminded him of his last discussion with Simon Morrison at the hospital. He had accelerated the discharge date—pressure on hospital beds. "To be blunt, your father will never do anything meaningful again. I took in a second opinion, and we both agreed. He will never walk, talk, wash or clean himself." As they had spoken, they were standing just outside the room, where they had looked at the broken figure, his head lolling down toward his chest.

"He's not in a coma, though?"

"Oh no! He responds to stimuli. His eyelids fluttered when shown a photo of Beth."

"He's a prisoner, then? In his own body." Dex had been surprised at how moved he felt by the old man's plight. His voice was shaky. Nobody deserved that type of living death.

"The carer needs to provide stimulation. A good carer plus you will be better than sending him to somewhere like Northampton, wonderful though that unit is."

Shortly the first of the four hopefuls would arrive for interview. He opened the curtains and windows letting the gentle summer breeze blow away the stale air. He had just settled down to plan the interviews when his phone rang again. It was another applicant, so he slotted her in last of all at 5 p.m., even though officially the deadline had been the previous day.

Interviewing the hopefuls proved to be dispiriting. Two had no relevant experience, the third was well-qualified but if you asked her the time she'd tell you how to build a clock. She would have driven him crazy within minutes. The fourth was very experienced but had only recently recovered from a low-level spinal fusion and could never have coped with shifting the old man in and out of bed to the chair in which he would sit.

Dex steeled himself for the final applicant who had just rung the bell. Aged twenty-seven with deep copper hair, Jude Tuson had a bottle-brown skin and an attractively strong but slightly horsey face. She had the physique of a sportswoman and her lean frame and leaner face suggested that she worked out a great deal or took care with her diet. Or both. Her eyebrows were a prominent feature over green eyes, and jointly they exuded both confidence and a cynically street-smart awareness of life.

She oozed strength of body and mind, her eyes telling the world that she had been there, done that. After the opening questions, Dex had warmed to her, though he knew there was precious little competition anyway. There was an arrogant cockiness never far beneath the surface. Subservient she was not, but her answers seemed to tick every box.

Jude Tuson was pure Aussie, from her Sydney accent and Bondi sweatshirt right down to her Earl's Court address. The open-toed shoes revealed well-manicured toenails with green varnish. She wore little make-up but she still appeared well-groomed. In every answer, she exuded confidence—in her ability, her looks, and her flippant wit.

*Just like Aussie cricketers*, Dex had thought. *It must be an Aussie thing.* He reckoned that with her deep voice, Jude could easily make herself heard calling for lager across the throng in the Rat & Parrot. Her hair was well groomed and slightly bouffant adding further to her height, which Dex judged at a good five eleven, with hands suitable for wrestling crocodiles in the Northern Territories. After she had left him to consider his decision, he looked at his notes: tough, blunt, cynical, ambitious, sexy, grasping, "efficient, not loving"—her own description. His notes reminded him of the conversation about her experience.

"Yeah. Started in Sydney. Full nurse's training including geriatrics. I worked at Westmead Hospital. Brain-damaged victims. Then I went to Saudi. Couldn't stand that. No drink allowed and randy Arabs wanting to sodomize you. Turned my back on that, I can tell you. Well, so to speak." Her laugh revealed good teeth, well cared for. Dex guessed she had cracked that joke in London's Kangaroo Valley many times before.

Jude's eyes were deep-set but darting and there was something of the adventurer in her face; the brazen recklessness of a streaker in her look. Perhaps it was the way she stood—chest thrust forward and shoulders back that emphasized her figure and epitomized her character. He'd seen her sort clutching pints of lager heading for Twickenham to support the Wallabies.

"I've nursed everything from koalas to kinkies, babies to baldies. Yeah! Put me down as experienced. Your old man? Piece of cake. He's an in-and-outer, right? Shove it in, clean it out." Her appraisal was startlingly robust.

Dex was taken aback by the summary. "He'll need stimulating too."

"Right on! Course he does. Stimulating! That's essential." She looked at him slyly over the rim of a can of Coke she had brought with her. "Who gave you all that stuff about needing two carers? Is he a big fella?"

She saw him nod. "He was. Not now. Looks to have lost weight in hospital."

"No sweat. I could throw a sumo wrestler over the Eiffel Tower."

"What about the law? Working hours, lifting weights?"

"Aw, c'mon! Health and Safety crap. Politically correct bollocks. I want the money. I've one aim in life—to get rich quick. That's why I went to Saudi and now London. I'm up for the main chance. Bed baths in five years? Give me a break! I want to meet some rich layabout to keep me in Gucci and champagne. Meantime, don't hire two. Just pay me more and hire in cover for my evening off."

After she'd left, her personality had lingered with a smell of the Gitanes she had asked to smoke and the Gaultier perfume that she had applied as she was leaving. He went down to his father's cellar and found a bottle of 1990 Jean-Louis Chave Hermitage. It was in a section labelled READY FOR DRINKING.

His father had been obsessed with investing in wine. Now, the sad fact was that he would never get to enjoy it. Dex decided to drink just one glass while devouring a couple of Scotch Eggs he had brought in from Sainsbury's. It worked well while he munched, weighing up the decision. At five-hundred-and-eighty pounds a bottle, Dex was not used to drinking such great wine even though he could afford it by the truck-load.

In reality, there were only two choices. *Go for the Brummie woman with verbal diarrhoea or the headstrong Aussie with great tits*, while trying to keep her attractive shape out of the equation. But something niggled about Jude Tuson. She seemed to have the right answer for everything. Her references were coming and according to her would be impressive *if not sensational, mate.*

Was she as good as she had made out? Did she really tick every box? *Or was I seduced by those fluttering eyelashes and flirty smiles?* Each mention of the word *stimulation* had prompted a suggestive glance.

It took a second glass of the deep red Hermitage before he phoned her. "Jude. Subject to references, you're hired. Get those scanned through. Father will be discharged in a few days. Move in the night before. I'll give you a call." He replaced the cork in the bottle and slipped it into his grip.

No sooner had Dex ended the call than Jude made her own call. "Great news! I got the job."

# CHAPTER SIXTEEN

Dex had told nobody other than Tiffany of his plan to go to Panama. Even Adam Yarbury thought Dex was now in Vienna with a friend from Harvard. Gus McKay, for all his eccentricity, was a wily old sod and had earned Dex's total respect. His advice to keep everything close had weighed heavily, especially after Mick Glenn's crass reaction on the phone.

Tiffany had been right. Talking to him had been disastrous. The best hope was that Glenn would do nothing. *Don't kid yourself, Dex.* Bulls, china shops, and loose cannons all seemed apposite. But at least Glenn had no idea who had tipped him off.

*Poor consolation.*

It was early evening and sub-tropically hot as the air-conditioned taxi sped him from Tocumen Airport through the city outskirts and onto the dual carriageway behind the curving seafront of Panama Bay. It stopped at the Intercontinental Miramar Hotel.

While reclining in the balmy air on the balcony, he had room service, looking out at the perpetually moving lights of vessels approaching or leaving the canal somewhere in the darkness, away to his right.

It had been a long day involving a change of flights and the usual hassle of security at Miami International Airport. It was too late to start tracking down Maria-Elena Sanchez but his plans were ready for the following day. He slept badly, partly due to the time difference but more because of mounting fears at the irrevocable and dangerous steps he was now taking.

*Was Maria-Elena aware of her brother's murder? Had she been in touch with him? Worse still, was she still connected to Pepe Carmino? Would she warn him that Mr Finlay Dexter had been sniffing around?* The jumble of thoughts ensured that by dawn he felt as if he had never slept. Even the thundering water from the shower followed by a light breakfast looking over the deep blue of the ocean did little to restore him.

*Face it, Dex.*
*You're scared.*
*That's no crime.*
*Give up*
*Support Tiffany's work in Africa.*
*Tip off the Fraud Squad.*
*But Beth's money?*
*My promise?*
*Was Beth murdered?*
*Like Carole and Jamie?*
*Well…probably.*
*And yet you're walking away again?*

Finding the Casino Sienna looked easy on the map but first he wanted to catch Maria Elena at home. That was in the Old Town, a goodish distance from the hotel. He spent the morning being a tourist by visiting the Miraflores Lock on the Panama Canal just outside the city. At the Visitor Centre, he watched a giant container ship change levels on its route to the Pacific Ocean.

After watching a couple more ships get towed through, he got the driver to take him to the Old Town, the *Casco Viejo*, where Maria-Elena apparently lived. If the enquiry agent were right, she was unmarried with a widowed mother and three brothers. The taxi dropped him by the twin turrets of the impressive Metropolitan Cathedral, which had stood for hundreds of years in the heart of the mass of narrow streets that surrounded it.

Overhead, the sky was clear blue but the air was humid and he was glad he had not worn even a lightweight jacket. As it was, in his short-sleeved shirt and jeans, his skin felt clammy.

Thunderstorms were forecast before 2 p.m. but at present, as he spotted the vultures peering down from the cathedral's parapets, rain seemed a distant prospect. As they hoped for dead vermin, their curved backs reminded Dex of Forster-Brown in Dukes though anyone less like a vulture than him was hard to imagine.

He turned his map around until he had sorted his bearings and then headed into the shady back streets behind the Avenida Balboa.

The streets were clean with less litter than he would have expected, but there were a few scavenging mongrels making use of the ornate wrought-iron streetlamps.

From somewhere, came the sound of salsa music and occasional guttural shouts from open windows. An old man in a shapeless black suit chewed on a cigarette. He raised a feeble arm in greeting as he sat on a chair outside his front door. No doubt he had done the same thing yesterday and would be there again tomorrow. And every day until one day he would no longer be around. It was a chastening thought.

In these side streets, time seemed to have stood still. The stone houses, just two storeys high were poorly painted with the stone crumbling after centuries of weathering. The area spoke of folk living in homes where they had spent their childhoods, as had generations of their ancestors. Certainly when he knocked on the door that had faded blue paint and no bell or knocker, the old lady who answered did so without any sign of fear. No doubt it was a close-knit community and she had no expectation of a stranger dropping by.

Dex judged her to be late seventies, with her iron-grey hair tied tightly into a bun at the back of her head. She was wearing a grey smock that almost reached her clumpy black sandals. Her face was deeply lined and her narrowed mouth and cheeks suggested she had lost most of her teeth.

He gave her an exaggerated friendly smile to allay any fears but her face showed none anyway, just a quizzical puzzlement at seeing a stranger towering over her. Using the halting Spanish he had learned at school and employed occasionally on business trips to Madrid and Chile, he asked if Maria-Elena was at home. She shook her head and then responded with a few rapid words of Spanish, which were too fast for Dex. But he got the impression she could be at work. "Casino Sienna?" he asked.

"Si, señor. Si."

"Muchas gracias, Señora Sanchez."

He was rewarded with a toothless smile of pleasure as she closed the door. *Did she know one of her sons had recently been murdered?* She had not given the impression of someone grieving a lost son.

So now he had to beard Maria-Elena in the casino. It was not what he had wanted.

*I've got a plan.*

*If it works.*

He picked up a taxi from the square in front of the cathedral and headed for downtown. He saw the gaudy glittery façade of the casino with the name lit by flashing neon. As he was paying off the taxi, the entire street was illuminated by searing shards of lightning, instantly followed by a mighty crack of thunder that was nature at its most extreme.

At the same moment, the rain started, falling like a wall, bouncing off the roof of the taxi—and worse still, off of him. His head and shoulders were soaked even before he got under the canopy over the casino entrance. For a few moments, he stood there, awestruck at the intensity of the storm.

The street was now like a river, the water rushing by almost up to sidewalk level. He wiped down his face, entered the plush jazziness of the casino and dived into the men's room, where he used a paper towel to absorb the worst of the wet from his clothes. His hair he dried under a wall hand-drier, so that when he entered the atmospheric gaming-area, with the jangling music coming from rows of slot machines, he looked less like something dredged up from the deep.

It was not a busy time. A few tourists—four at the most, probably from a cruise ship—were playing the slots. He strolled between the tables most of which were unmanned. At the only open roulette table, the dealer was a man. Dex noted with relief that he was wearing a nametag. That was going to make it rather easier to find Maria-Elena without asking questions.

There were four craps table lying idle but two blackjack tables were in operation and he approached them. Both dealers were female. One was only mid-twenties, so he ruled her out. The other was an attractive woman with tight black curls topping her olive-skinned face. Her broad mouth was emphasized by red lipstick. Not wanting to peer obsessively at the nametag, he joined her table where there was a bored looking tourist. His multicoloured shirt had a map of Maui across the back.

As he hovered a few paces from the half-moon table, the dealer turned her head, offering a profile that made a nametag irrelevant.

He drew breath because of her eerie similarity to the photo of Tavio in *El Mundo*, a Spanish-language Las Vegas paper. No question, they were brother and sister—indeed, on looking at her face on, they could even be twins. As he sat down, he saw the words *Maria-Elena*. Just the sight of them was a stark reminder that he was at the tipping point.

*Stay strong, Dex.*

He bought in for one hundred dollars as the other player wished him luck because *he'd had his butt kicked by her*. "If she beats me again, I'm quitting," he concluded looking at his solitary chip. Dex muttered a few words of commiseration as the cards were dealt. Dex had 19, the tourist 20, and the dealer's up-card was a 4.

"Looking good," Dex volunteered.

"With any other dealer, I'd agree. You watch." The American with an accent from the Deep South sounded war-weary. They watched as she turned over her hole card, which was a 7. "See what I mean? The way she's been playing, she'll hit a 10." He was right. Her next card was a King of Hearts, giving her the winning hand of 21. She swept away their bets with neither pleasure nor regret. The tourist swung round off his stool. "Good luck, pal."

"Better luck." Dex then slapped out chips worth fifty dollars and waited for Maria-Elena to deal.

She looked at him for a moment. "Ingles?"

"You can tell?"

"After twenty-three years, señor." She shrugged with a smile. "It is easy." She dealt the cards and this time Dex cleaned up as he had blackjack. She paid him out, and as it was the end of the shoe, she prepared to shuffle.

This was the perfect moment.

*Just do it, Dex.*

"I have a message from an old friend of yours in London. Pepe Carmino. I'm his lawyer, his abogado." He saw her look of shock change to concern and then to fear all in a flash. "We need to talk. When do you finish?"

"Pepe? He here?" She saw Dex signal no.

"10 p.m. Meet me in *El Cuervo.* - a bar in the next street." Her English was good, but spoken with a Spanish-American accent so that Dex had to listen carefully. "*El Cuervo.* Tonight. About 10 p.m." He saw her nod at his understanding. "I'll quit while I'm ahead," he volunteered more loudly as he gathered up his chips and took them to the casino cage to be changed into US dollar bills. Outside, the storm had quickly passed and steam was rising from the sidewalk. He decided to dummy-run *El Cuervo* and afterwards to cure the rumble in his stomach with a paella.

In fact, he found the bar with no problem in a street with a very different character. It was traffic-free, and even in daylight the strip-club on the corner spoke of sleaze and late-night drunks. Sodden trash littered the cobbles over its length of about two-fifty metres. It was barely five metres wide and was deserted by day and appeared to have little going for it except for *El Cuervo* and the solitary girlie joint.

He walked hurriedly along it, feeling uneasy even in the heat of the afternoon. For the most part, it seemed to be a back street that one day might be up-and-coming. For now, it had a long way to go. Most of the buildings had once been lockup facilities or warehouses and were now shuttered and empty.

Perhaps a property-developer tycoon, a Panamanian version of his father, had already bought the entire street with plans to rip everything down to add yet another skyscraper to the horizon. He walked its entire length. In almost any big city, after dark, he would have avoided it.

Tonight there was no choice.

He was glad to get out of the narrow oppressiveness as he entered the small adjacent square. The contrast was immediate. Beneath the abundant trees and purple, pink and red flowering shrubs were bars and restaurants, many having shady terraces that were steaming dry under the thirty-degree heat. He stopped at one, with freshly painted wrought ironwork around the terrace. The tables looked cheerfully informal. Better still, it was offering paella and seafood specialties. After climbing a few wobbly steps, Dex settled down on the shady terrace with a Miller Lite, wondering what Maria-Elena was thinking.

Had he known that she was speaking in hushed tones on her mobile phone, his paella might not have been quite so enjoyable.

And that was not the only ticking time-bomb.

# CHAPTER SEVENTEEN

Mick Glenn ignored the respectful *good evening* from Tom the door-man as he entered Dukes and bounded down the curve of the white marble stairs. Normally he would have greeted Tom with a one-liner or even a chat about the most recent match.

Not tonight.

Only once at the Reception Desk did he stop. The young woman in her black evening-gown, recognised him but greeted him only with the same courtesy she gave every visitor. She swiped his membership card but he showed no interest in moving away to the bar or the tables.

"Where's Pepe Carmino? Tell him I want to see him here, now." Every word was barked out in his strong London accent that told of his upbringing on a Wandsworth council estate. The woman's face showed her surprise at the outburst. She recoiled from the smell of alcohol and wondered what his manager would say if he knew the condition of one of his star players.

"I'm sorry, Mr. Glenn. Mr. Carmino will not be in tonight. I'll tell Mr. Forster-Brown."

"That bald-headed softie! Okay! He'll do for starters." He paced the room, ignoring her invitation to sit on one of the Regency-style chairs. She spoke softly on the phone and a few moments later, FB appeared trying to look more confident than he felt. His body seemed to turn to jelly as he saw the snarl on Glenn's face. That same look had intimidated many a referee or opposing defender. FB was scarcely small but he swallowed hard and his eyes blinked behind the thick lenses as he took in all six foot four inches of packed muscle looking ready to explode.

"Mr. Glenn. Delighted to see you again. Mr. Carmino is traveling. He'll be in on Thursday. But I'm sure I can help. What seems to be the problem?" He tried to sound calming as his eyes avoided the listener.

"Fu-uckin' disgrace this place." Mick's voice was raised and slurred.

"Full of shits in penguin suits. You lot—oh, yes, all so la-di-dah—but you're only out to bleedin' cheat us. Rob us blind."

"Do please keep your voice down. You are talking nonsense, if I may say so. This is really most…unwelcome." FB's accent was far from posh, but compared to the uncouth star, he spoke like the Queen's equerry. His own career experience in top-end casinos hadn't trained him for dealing with an uncouth giant like Mick Glenn, whose eyes were now wild like a copulating stallion.

"Now you listen to me, rabbit-ears." Glenn moved closer so that his chin hovered close to FB's bald head. He rapped the acting boss on the shoulder. "Listenin', little man?"

FB, despite his own height, felt very small indeed. "I really think we should go into the office. Let's talk about your issues like civilised gentlemen in a calm way."

"Ain't no gentlemen round here. You'd be unsold as a used pisspot at a car boot sale, an' that's a fact. And we ain't goin' nowhere. Got it? Anyone mug enough to gamble at Dukes needs to hear this. You tell Carmino I know this place is fuckin' crooked. Your dealers cheat us, that's what. Last time I was in, you shits rolled me over. So just watch it. You lot was seen. Caught in the bleedin' act."

"You must be mistaken."

"Listen, you bald-headed bunny. You tell that ponce Pepe: I'm not leavin' next time without all me money back—all £210,000 I lost. Otherwise, I'm goin' to Scotland bleedin' Yard. I know the fuckin' works on you lot. An' I'm goin' to tell every fuckin' member the way it is. Got it, you carrot cruncher? I'll be in next Thursday evening. 10:30. You tell him."

Overhead, the security cameras captured the scene and the mikes were picking up every word. "Please go now. You're talking nonsense, but of course Mr. Carmino will wish to discuss your concern."

Above Glenn's shoulder, Forster-Brown could see Adam Yarbury faltering as he descended the stairs. He had stopped on hearing the commotion and was looking embarrassed. FB held his breath as Glenn spun around on his Cuban heels and then ran up the stairs. Halfway up, he glared back down. "The game's up, mate. You're all goin' to jail."

Yarbury stepped aside for Glenn to rush by before he continued his descent.

"I'm so sorry about that outburst, Mr. Yarbury. Most…unseemly."

"What a bore! Methinks Mr. Glenn needs some lessons in how chaps behave. Maybe I'll have a word to Pepe. He already knows my views about oafs like him being members. A red card, perhaps." Yarbury chuckled at his joke.

# CHAPTER EIGHTEEN

Dex had hours to kill till his 10 p.m. rendezvous with Maria, so he returned to his hotel and booted up his laptop. There was an email from his shrink Dr. Wilfred Grierson about his appointment at Harley Street with a reminder to *pay cash or debit card, Amex Cards not accepted.*

*That'll be fun—telling the miserable sod about the pills.*

He quickly moved on to an email from Tiffany. "Where are you? Let's Skype this evening. I'm on a train from NYC to Washington." Her email had arrived two hours before, so he responded confirming he would call later. Seconds after pressing the send button, his eyelids drooped and he fell asleep, stuffed from the generous portion of paella. The rice had been brimming with chicken, lobster, shrimp, squid, sausage, mussels, and onions. After a glass of chilled Chardonnay and a complimentary glass of the local Seco Herrerano with his coffee, he slept deeply until nearly eight.

He showered quickly, eager to discover how Tiffany had been getting on with her tour. A few clicks on his laptop and her radiant face filled the screen. It was almost like seeing her reporting on TV, except now it was interactive. "So you're in Washington now?"

"The Four Seasons, just where Washington becomes Georgetown and only a brisk walk to the White House. I'm here for two days—doing more of the same, and of course the seminar involving President Clinton. Odd they keep the title forever."

"How was NYC?"

"Tough! Seven TV and press interviews each day plus four signings."

"You're getting real traction, then?"

"The publishers say sales are shooting up the graph."

"That's great! And after DC?"

"Atlanta, New Orleans, Dallas, Houston, Los Angeles, San Francisco, Seattle and back to Los Angeles. Anyway, enough about me. You're… not on the boat?"

Dex hesitated. Skype was reckoned to be pretty secure but he decided to play it safe. "No. I'm travelling. Adam wants me to bring back a Sachertorte from Vienna."

Tiffany's face showed she had caught on at once. "Save some for me. Is it easy to find?"

"Not a problem. If I don't get time after seeing the Schönbrunn Palace and the Spanish Riding School, there's always a place in Knightsbridge that makes the real thing."

She laughed but quickly turned serious. "During a jet-lagged night after reading an article in the flight magazine, I revisited your problem. Y'know—access to Beth's stuff."

"Go on."

"I'll scan it through if you like."

"Please." His face revealed his boyish excitement at her news.

"Dex, there's no magic bullet, but this hacker was quoted as saying that nearly everyone uses passwords that are obvious—somehow linked to their life pattern. Kid's name. Family pet's name, place of birth."

"Beth's was more complicated. Random letters. And her username had no obvious link to her life—just a load of letters and numbers."

"This hacker would say that random is best but rare."

"Beth was smart enough to do random." He grinned at her. "Sorry if I sound a bit negative. I don't mean to. I'll take another look after I've read the article."

"It's coming through any time." She leaned across and Dex heard the scanner working and he saw her do a couple of clicks and nod in satisfaction. "It's gone. But Dex, how are you? Where's your father?"

"Father's returning to Porcupine House next week. I've hired an Aussie carer to look after him." He felt a tad uneasy even mentioning Jude Tuson, even though Tiffany had made clear that she and Dex were not an item or even close to it.

"And you? Now you're off the pills and back on the booze?"

"Best thing I ever did, chucking the pills in the river. They were frying my brain."

"No more nightmares?"

"Not one. And the drinking? I've been a good boy. Nothing excessive."

"I must rush. I'm doing a press conference in under an hour. You take care, Dex." Her face showed a moment of concern before the link was cut.

The article arrived seconds later and for the next hour, he read it before looking yet again at the details Beth had given him: user name—GADECH714538 and password ZAYBXCWB. He knew that if either were just a digit wrong, it would doom him to the *access denied* message.

*Why had she chosen GADECH? Why 714538? Had Beth been too smart and this was random, or was there some hidden logic? Had she fluffed the details on the phone? Or did I mishear?* The numbers bore no resemblance to any phone number she had used, not even close. He tried thinking of her school friends, business colleagues but nothing gelled that was not trite. He jotted down *GADECH equals Georgina, Angela, Dex, Edie, Chrissie and Harriet.* Okay, she knew someone with all those names. But even as he scribbled, he knew it was inconclusive and utterly speculative.

It was time to go. With a resigned look, he shut down his laptop wondering if he too should switch to a more complex and random name and password. He was just waiting for the elevator when he had another thought. *Hire a hacker*—maybe even the guy who had written the article. The thought was with him as he walked the short distance through the city until he reached the corner of the back street.

By night, it had not improved. Not enough had changed. A neon arrow was now lit, pointing to the distant lights of *El Cuervo*, some two hundred metres down the darkened street. As he paused taking in the emptiness ahead, a hustler for the girlie club pointed inside the door. "You Americano? Sexy girls. You make friends. Have good time."

Dex laughed away the opportunity though watching Latino beauties bumping and grinding seemed attractive compared to setting off into a darkened alley that smelled of rotting vegetation and drains.


Back in Mayfair, Pepe Carmino strolled through the bar toward the gaming tables. As he did so, a leggy blonde with a damson designer outfit rose from her stool where she had been perched, slinging back vermouth. She approached him with an exaggerated and provocative wiggle. As they came face to face, she pouted. Pepe gave her a dismissive glance and made as if to ignore her. "I miss you, Pepe," she said in her throaty Hungarian accent. "Couldn't we…maybe get together again."

He did not want a scene. In the casino, she was useful. In bed she was a bore. He was irritated that his discarded mistress still refused to get the message. On top of everything else, she was a distraction too many. "Irenke, darling, we are done, finished. Accept it. That's the way it is. Just be grateful for the generous pocket-money you get for opening the blackjack tables." He turned briskly away with no further formality and walked on, leaving her looking very alone before she returned to her stool and ordered another vermouth with an olive.

The previous evening, FB had phoned to give him the headlines about Mick Glenn's outburst. It had been graphic enough for him to advance his second meeting with the Swiss lawyer and a shifty-looking banker. He had jetted home early after leaving the mountain enclave of Liechtenstein. Back in his office, he had watched the silent images of the footballer confronting an obviously shit-scared FB. But the voice recordings showed that FB had done pretty well in the face of Glenn's outburst.

He replayed the recording. *You lot was seen.* What did Glenn mean by that? Was that the way Glenn spoke about himself, or had someone else spotted something? *I know the fuckin' works on you lot.* Now that sounded as if Glenn himself knew. But was that from what he had spotted, or had someone told him?

He decided to watch the recordings of the night when Glenn had lost his wad. He wondered if a sober Glenn had now calmed down and might not turn up at all. Might he chicken out? No. Not a bloke who headbutts opponents and swears at referees. Some careful planning would be needed. Carmino decided he needed help from Arnie Fisher. Extra security staff were required.

At about the same time, from Creole Henry's place off Upper Street in Islington, a distressed Amber Murray was on the phone to Mick Glenn. "He knows, Mick."

"What you mean he knows?"

"Creole knows." There was more sobbing and she dabbed a cold flannel on her swollen cheek. "Someone he knew saw us going into Dukes." There was more sobbing. "He hit me, kicked me, punched me."

"The bastard." Glenn threw down his snooker cue. He had been practising alone before going to bed. He often relaxed like this after a big match or if the boss had said no booze or partying. Like tonight.

True, it had been a so-called *friendly* but he had missed a sitter and the England manager's blue-language fury was still ringing in his ears after the no-goal draw. "Amber, love, Creole is so out of order. Big time. I'm sorry." He paused. "Where is he now? Want him sorted out? I know some heavies. He won't father no kids after they've done with him."

"He's out somewhere. Didn't say where. But I'm scared, Mick."

"Get out then. Go to a hotel. I'll pay."

"He said if I wasn't here when he got back, he'd hunt me down… anywhere." She shifted position and caught sight of her face in a mirror and burst into more tears.

"Tell the law then, love. He can't go knocking you about."

"No, Mick. He said if I went to the cops, he'd kill me."

Neither of them said a word as they weighed up whether it was an empty threat. Creole Henry's reputation for violence went before him. But murder? Was that a real threat? Mick grabbed the blue ball and jettisoned it round the full-size table. It cannoned off a couple of cushions before smashing into the bunched-up reds scattering them every which way.

Eventually, it was Amber who spoke. "Mick, he said he was gonna get you. Gonna do you. Them was his words. Do you."

"Creole? I'm not scared of him." But even as he said it, he was walking to the front door to set the alarm system, just in case the big Jamaican could somehow beat the security gates at the foot of the drive.

"I'm scared, Mick. For us both."

Mick slammed the bolt across the door and fixed the chain. "I'll think of something. Call me tomorrow when you can."

# CHAPTER NINETEEN

Hoping he looked more confident than he felt, Dex took large strides along the cobbled street. The walls of the old warehouses and abandoned lockups bore down on him, adding to the oppressive air of menace. Nobody seemed to be coming from or going to *El Cuervo*. There was no sign of movement anywhere between him and the bar. The smell of cheap scent from the clip joint was now gone, and now it was just him and the distant pool of light outside the bar ahead.

He had gone nearly halfway when he heard footsteps behind him. He flicked a quick look over his shoulder and saw that someone must have been concealed in one of the doorways. The shadowy figure was no more than twenty paces behind him. Dex quickened his pace but the footsteps seemed to accelerate and to be closing on him. He broke into a run. Whoever was behind him did the same.

At that moment, another figure appeared ahead from the left side of the alley. The man must also have been skulking in the shadows just beyond the lights of the bar in case Dex arrived from the other direction. Now the man ahead was accelerating toward him so that Dex was the meat in the sandwich.

His route to the door of the bar was blocked. In a flash, he knew he had but one chance and that was to keep going, using his bulk and momentum to crash the local out of his way. Making it to the bright lights of the little square was essential. It was so near and yet so far away.

From behind, he could hear the closing footsteps and the sound of the man breathing just a few strides behind him. It had been a mistake to falter even fractionally when he had seen the second figure appear. Barely twenty metres covered the three men as Dex jinked slightly to sidestep the man ahead of him. But he had none of the subtlety of an England rugby three-quarter and the local moved left and then stopped.

Dex had no choice but to steamroller his way through. Turning his left shoulder slightly, he used his thirteen stone to barge aside the much smaller man. For a fleeting moment, he saw a glint of steel as the light from the bar caught the knife that flew from the man's hand. The force of the impact caused Dex to lose his own momentum and he stumbled, his speed dropping.

It was enough for the figure behind him to launch at him, the diving impact on his hip knocking him off-balance. He lurched forward another pace or two before sprawling to the ground. As he tried to get up, he was sent crashing back onto the cobbles as one of the men dived onto him. He was far lighter than Dex, that much was obvious but he was joined by his accomplice who turned Dex over and knelt on his chest. The combined weight pinioned him to the ground and he cringed as he awaited the vicious plunge of a knife into his guts.

It never came. Instead, one of the men spoke in halting English. "What you want our sister?"

"I must talk to her."

"You no from Pepe. Bullshit."

Dex's mind raced as fast as was possible with two strangers pinning him to the cobbles. "I have information."

"From Pepe? You lie."

Dex assessed what was least likely to provoke them. At least they seemed more interested in talking than killing. "About Tavio. I have message about your brother."

Neither assailant said a word for a moment having been surprised at hearing something unexpected. "Tavio? He America. What you mean, message him?"

The other man, his face close now to Dex's and his minty breath still coming fitfully, then spoke. "You speak Tavio?"

That was a question Dex did not want to be asked. *Did they know he was dead? Murdered? Or should I be the first to tell them?* He thought of his brief chat with the mother this morning. She had not seemed distressed. Perhaps they did not know. "No. I no speak to Tavio." He found himself mirroring their broken English. "Tavio is dead. Murdered in Las Vegas." He paused to assess their reaction. Both men eased their pressure on him. Plainly, they knew nothing. *But why not?* "I must tell you everything. *Comprendo?*"

"Tavio no dead. He where? In Las Vegas?"

Dex managed a shake of his head. "Sorry, *amigos*. He is dead. I explain." He lay still as the two men spoke to each other in rapid-fire

Spanish. "Take me to Maria," he said commandingly, sensing that he had them rattled. He listened to more debate before the two men eased themselves off him and permitted him to stand. He stood several inches taller than them both as he awaited their next move.

The older man picked up his knife and jabbed it toward Dex's face. "We go Maria. No shit, gringo."

Dex raised both hands in emphasis. "No problems. Me…*amigo*. Friend."

The Panamanians did not seem convinced as they walked close to him into the bar. The barely concealed knife was still too close to Dex's left side for him to relax. Inside, the bar was poorly air-conditioned and it smelled of stale sweat but even more of garlic sausage and cured hams that hung from the ceiling.

The wall lights were low-watt bulbs set in wrought-iron fittings. On one wall was a mural of a giant crow seated on a branch with the words *El Cuervo* beneath it. There were under twenty people inside the surprisingly large room. In the background was piped music, and Dex guessed it was probably Ricky Martin mixing Spanish and English.

Dex was led to a green-leather booth in which a sultry-looking Maria-Elena was seated alone, a glass of red wine and tapas in front of her. Away from the casino, she was wearing a low-slung turquoise blouse and a pair of white figure-hugging jeans. Her perfume was heavy, as was the clumpy gold jewellery that highlighted her ears and neck. She ignored him, instead looking at her brothers with a question on her face.

Dex sat down opposite her without being invited and one man slid in next to him, the other opposite and next to Maria. He waited while with lots of arm-waving and animated discussion, Maria was seemingly given the entire history of everything that had happened outside. Dex judged that she was the eldest of the three by a good few years, and she seemed to be in command of the situation. Then he saw her look of shock as her mouth dropped open. Dex guessed they had reported Tavio's death but she looked in no way distressed, let alone close to tears. He watched her hands open and close, her knuckles turning white. She then gave him a quick and puzzled glance before firing off another question in Spanish. The two men looked at each other and then shrugged.

"You no from Pepe." It was a statement of fact and, as such, left Dex wondering if she had checked with Carmino during the past few hours—his worst nightmare.

"I know Pepe. He owns a London casino. My message is not from him."

"You say my brothers—Tavio…murdered? Las Vegas? He there?"

"He *was* there. Till he was murdered." Dex looked at the brothers in turn. They were both late thirties with swept-back crinkly black hair, slightly messed up by their exertions. Both were lean and fit with stubble lining their cheeks. Each had a moustache, one of them rather bushier than the other. They had similar brown eyes to their sister, though hers were mellow and warmly inviting in contrast.

"Please ask your brother to put the knife away," he invited, trying not to sound pleading. He waited while she spoke to the older man and he withdrew the blade of the flick-knife and stashed it away in an ornate leather holder. But he let it lie on the table.

Dex nodded his thanks, and as a waiter appeared, he suggested they have a jug of wine and cold meats. "We have much to talk about." Having ordered, Dex continued. "Are you in touch with Pepe?" It was a blunt question and her response was not immediate. He guessed the wording might be confusing. "You still speak with Pepe?" Jargon like being *in touch* was liable to be confusing. "You write to him? See him here? Maybe this year?"

He could see she understood and this time the response was immediate. "No." But then her eyes flashed a warning message. "Why you speak Pepe? You here talk Tavio or Pepe?"

Dex ducked the honest answer and explained that he would tell them about Tavio.

"Tavio, he go USA long time." She clapped her hands decisively in front of her as if to say he had disappeared in a puff of smoke like an illusionist's assistant. From his hip pocket Dex produced a copy of an extract from *El Mundo*, a Spanish language newspaper circulating in Las Vegas. It showed a mug shot of Tavio and reported his murder, describing him as Puerto Rican. There was a quote from his live-in girlfriend confirming he was originally from San Juan, having arrived twenty years before. "That is Tavio? Your brother?"

All three listeners studied the picture, which, like all mug shots, was scarcely flattering. They pointed and nodded between themselves until Maria responded. "*Si, si.* Yes. We not see Tavio long time He older. Different. Is Tavio but…" She turned to her brothers and spoke in Spanish again "…we not understand why say he Puerto Rican."

"Maybe he crossed into the USA illegally?" Dex was unsure whether they understood or whether they were just not going to admit that Dex might be correct. He spoke slowly. "The cops in Vegas maybe did not know he was from Panama.." The conversation was paused while a large oval dish was placed between them. It was brimming with a wide variety of sliced sausages and wafer-thin pieces of air-cured ham and cheese.

The younger brother then topped up his sister's glass and poured them all red wine from a large earthenware jug. "Why Tavio killed? Who kill him?"

"That…is a good question. Let's eat, shall we?"

It was impossible to ignore the burning question just because there was food. Anyway, it was no time for small talk. So while he munched away at a portion of chorizo, he let them read the long report in *El Mundo*, which once again loosened their tongues. For several minutes, he was surrounded by more rapid-fire Spanish, spoken in such a strong local accent that he had no clue as to what was being said.

"You know who kill Tavio?" It was Maria-Elena who had downed her cutlery to ask the question.

Dex was not ready to volunteer what little he knew, or *thought* he knew. There was more groundwork to be cleared first. "I will explain, but first tell me about Pepe Carmino."

"He kill Tavio?" prompted the younger brother angrily, spitting a piece of bread onto the table as he did so.

*Don't go there yet, Dex.* "Nobody knows. Maybe yes. But Pepe. When was he here?"

It was Maria-Elena who placed her elbows onto the maroon tablecloth and while clutching her glass, responded having silenced her brothers with a fierce stare. Her eyes had flashed a clear warning—*this is my territory* was the message. Dex was on full alert and he spotted her wariness as if megaphoned round the room. "Pepe work here twenty years ago. More."

"In a casino?"

"*Si!* Yes. I see him there."

"You worked with him?"

She nodded agreement using only the slightest possible head movement.

"He was a dealer? Roulette? Blackjack?"

"Blackjack."

"And he left here?" Dex saw the same warning look from the brothers before she nodded yes. "Why did he leave?"

Maria-Elena looked discomforted as she shrugged. "He go."

"Was he a good friend? Was he special to you?"

There was a short lull before her face showed a moment of wistfulness but then as quickly hardened. "I like him, yes." Dex reckoned she must have been a stunner back then and no doubt Pepe would have been quick to spot her. But as a good Catholic girl back then, would they have been lovers? Did good Catholic girls work in casinos?

As he debated whether to ask the next question, he wished that he had no need. Had he successfully accessed Beth's data, all the answers were there—assuming she *had* questioned Tavio before he was silenced. "Did Pepe have a scar," he ran his finger down his cheek, "just here?" Dex looked at each of the family in turn and knew at once that he had touched a toxic tripwire. Immediately, every face showed hostility. "Did he maybe get injured here? Was he attacked here?"

"Señor, we end now." This time Maria-Elena rubbed one hand against the other in a dismissive fashion. She signalled to the brother sitting across the table to let Dex out. "We say nothing. Go now."

"Maybe I can explain more about Tavio," Dex suggested forlornly, hoping to restore a better platform. That failed. He found his arm being tugged to get him out. He stood up, left thirty dollars on the table, and with a resigned look shuffled sideways out of the booth. As he bowed slightly to the woman, there was no reaction from her, not even the hint of a smile of goodbye. He said *adios* but nobody said a word. The atmosphere, which had started to warm up when the food had arrived, had sunk to fifty degrees below. His question about the scar had touched a wound that was still raw over twenty years later.

He tried a feeble smile to them all and then walked out, almost at once realising that one knee was stiffening up and his back was aching from the scuffle. As he limped back toward his hotel, his mind was racing much faster than his feet. Had she been in contact with Pepe? On balance, he believed her denial. What had happened involving the scar? He had never found out. The discussion had turned into a gold-plated disaster. He had discovered little except that Pepe had been working in Panama.. And that made getting into Beth's database all the more urgent.

*But on the bright side, he had never provided his real name. Like with Mike Glenn.*

*Small consolation.*

*None really, if she tried to contact Carmino now.*

*Or had already done so.*

He ignored the second invite into the strip club and spent the ten-minute walk back agonising over why all three had looked shocked at the mention of the scar. It had been a conversation-killer. Once in his room, he eased the pain in his back and joints in a piping hot bath and then sat in a toweling bathrobe with a beer beside him, confronted again by his laptop. He forced Maria-Elena to the back of his mind, staring now at the username and password. He was reminded of the expression in the article Tiffany had scanned through. *Think out of the box.* Uncertain what had been wrong with *breadth of vision* or even *lateral thinking* and fortified by a second beer and a whisky chaser from the minibar, he decided to leap as far from the box as possible. He looked at the mumbo-jumbo yet again—*GADECH714538* and *ZAYBXCWB*.

He decided to order a cold plate like the one left behind at *El Cuervo* and opened a packet of cheesy dippers to keep him going as he settled down in front of the screen. He had to try something very different. On his scribbling pad, courtesy of the hotel, he wrote the alphabet across the page.

*There!*

*That was out of the box.*

Then beneath every letter, he entered every number up to twenty-six. That was when the fog that had surrounded him started to clear. Fired up now, he wrote down GADECH and beneath each letter, its number. Momentarily forgetting the throbbing pain in his lower back, he leaped into the air and wished he had not. But then he looked again at his jottings—GADECH was a perfect match of *714538*.

Room service had still not arrived and so he took his beer out to the wraparound terrace, his heart pounding with excitement. The night air was still pleasingly warm and once again, after midnight, the city had come to life, the traffic jamming the dual carriageway in both directions. The night owls of Panama were certainly out hunting now—for food, drinks, dancing, partying or gambling.

He wandered round the corner of the terrace to look across the Bay of Panama. The inky black emptiness was littered with the reds and greens of the countless vessels moving maybe a mile or two offshore. Above, there were only a few stars visible due to the city lights and hazy clouds. He leaned against the rail and stared at the black horizon, sipping the beer appreciatively.

*Perfect symmetry.*

*I've got the correct username.*

*So what gives with the password?*

Impatiently, he drained his glass and hurried back inside just as the cold platter was being delivered. But suddenly, he wasn't hungry. Or at least his eagerness to crack the password now seemed more important. He sensed a breakthrough coming on and sat down at the desk. *ZAYBXCWB.* Once again, he wrote down their corresponding numbers from the alphabet—26, 1, 25, 2, 24, 3, 23, 2. The figures danced in front of his eyes as he tried to penetrate the logic. Then everything fell into perfect focus.

He kicked himself for not spotting it before. Again, there was perfect symmetry except for the final letter B. He changed the B to a D and that made the last number a 4. The letters zigzagged from one end of the alphabet to the other. With shaking fingers and pulse racing, he typed in *714538 for the user name* and then the password *ZAYBXCWD* after switching the B for a D.

He had misheard the D for a B. *Why didn't I spot this before?* The vein in his forehead pulsing with excitement, he waited for the sound of the computer opening.

*Nothing.*

*Access denied.*

For a moment, he just stared in disbelief, his disappointment stopping any coherent thought. He knew he was almost right, so close now to the answer, his nerve ends alive with anticipation. Apply logic.

That was what computers bred on. So too had Beth. He looked at the letters again and saw Plan B staring at him. He entered the username as before but this time for the password entered the numbers 26 1 25 2 24 3 23 4 instead of the letters.

*Glory be!*

*Thinking outside the box really works.*

This time the innards started to whirr and the dreaded *access denied* words did not appear. Instead, within a few seconds he was connected to Beth's backup system stored somewhere in the clouds.

*Close to her.*

He opened Word and then looked at her list of recent documents. Typically, there was nothing called Tavio or Vegas. He clicked on Recent and was immediately rewarded. There it was—Tavio's statement, the last words she had ever typed.

What he read made him flick through the pages quicker and quicker. The sweat on his hands needed wiping and he found that after the tenth and final page, his fingers were trembling and he felt drained, utterly exhausted by the horror. He knew now why Maria had ended the discussion. He checked the recent documents again and found a PDF version of the interview, this one actually signed by Tavio.

*Dynamite.*

*Certainly enough to kill for.*

*RIP Tavio.*

*You never deserved that ending.*


While Dex had been sleeping off his paella lunch, darkness had fallen over north London. The last chatter of thousands of starlings had died away. The tall chestnut trees were swaying gently in the evening breeze. At just after ten and with all quiet, Mick Glenn locked his front door and set the alarm.

He was looking forward to the confrontation with *that bastard Carmino.* There was a spring in his stride as he hurried across the gravel to his yellow Porsche and zapped open the locked door. He was wearing jeans, a black shirt with a red-and-white-striped tie under a black velvet jacket. He wanted to look good, to feel good. He had again selected his Cuban boots with the highest heels to emphasize his height.

He settled into the bucket seat of the 911 Carrera and fired the engine. Immediately, Elton John's "Crocodile Rock" resonated from six speakers. On the passenger seat he saw his agent's briefing note about tomorrow morning's visit to the sick kids in Great Ormond Street Hospital. He always looked forward to hospital trips. Seeing a famous footballer meant so much to the desperately ill youngsters and he always promised the older ones match tickets for *when you're better*.

Every visit had a sobering effect. They helped him get some perspective on what a lucky sod he was to be earning so much and to be in good health. From the doctors or nurses, he knew that some of the kids would never make it any further from the ward than the morgue, their short lives snuffed out almost before they had begun.

Sixty metres away and out of sight down the curved tree and bush-lined drive were the large security gates. He pressed the zapper to have them open by the time he reached them. With some scuffing of gravel, he pulled away, the Porsche's throaty roar splitting the silence.

*Pepe Carmino—you was so out of order.*

He licked his lips in anticipation of the confrontation.

In Dukes, Pepe Carmino was doing paperwork in his office, the cool, jazzy tones of Diana Krall playing from the Bose system. He checked his watch and then phoned down to FB. "I thought you said Mick Glenn was due in around ten? He here yet?"

"No sign. Shall I call him?"

Pepe thought for a moment, tapping his fingers in time to the rhythm. "Forget it. He's either running late or chickened out. My money's on the latter. He's just a big mouth. Are the security guys still here?"

"Two of them."

"Keep them till 12:30. Just in case." Carmino ended the call with a smile of satisfaction. He stretched out his arm and reached for his Padron cigar and Baron Otard.

# CHAPTER TWENTY

During the night flight back from Panama, sleep had not come easily. Long after starting the second leg from Miami, he kept seeing the words *hornets' nest* flashing through his overworked brain. They were the very last words that Beth had ever typed and ended her conclusions on her evidence. About two hours out from Florida, after the meal had been cleared, he thought through Beth's handiwork yet again.

According to Tavio, Pepe had worked in the Casino Sienna alongside Maria-Elena and a passionate relationship had developed. Using card-sharping skills learned in a shady dealing school on Maryland Parkway just east of the Vegas Strip, Pepe's role had been to cheat drunken sailors and inexperienced tourists.

With his ability to deal seconds and to shuffle up to the house advantage, the management had valued him highly and rewarded him generously. Over an eighteen-month period, he had saved them thousands of dollars by screwing the players.

Dex stretched out on the sleeper bed and angled the light before opening his laptop to read Tavio's statement again. No wonder Maria-Elena had been hostile to his final question. But it was more than hostility—her reaction had gone even beyond fear into terror. Where was the original signed statement? Had it been burned in the wreck? Probably. Father apart, hardly anything had survived. He started to read the statement again.

"In this statement, I call the dealer in question Pepe Carmino. I now know that is his real name as I explain below. I recognise his picture. However, at the Casino Sienna twenty-two years ago, we knew him as Rick Hensfleet, a young Brit with Vegas training. But my sister, who was very close to him, knew his real name—Pepe Carmino—and she told me. Maria had seen his real name on his passport.

"The scar on his cheek—I know how he got it. It was early afternoon. The casino was almost empty. I had one player at my roulette table.

Maria was standing at an empty blackjack table waiting for players. The only other player was a young sailor called Pancho. Maybe his family name was Torres. He was a big guy for a Mexican. Maria watched him lose several hands and a large amount of money playing blackjack. Carmino was dealing. It turned nasty, noisy, shouting. The Mexican said that the dealer was cheating. I expect he was.

"He angrily accused Pepe, banging the table with his fist. Maria, who was working at the table next to Pepe, saw and heard this. Punters often lose their cool when their bets go wrong, so to me whatever noise there was not so unusual. I too was close enough to see what happened once the action started. Maria saw the sailor foolishly lean across the baize and grab Pepe's arms, pulling him across the table. There was a scuffle. Carmino broke free and pulled a large knife, I think it is called a Bowie, from a sheath inside his jacket and tried to stab the youngster. Maria told me later he always carried it *for self-defence*. Carmino was shouting in Spanish that he was no cheat, but of course, we knew differently. He had shown some of his tricks to us.

"He struck out and I saw the knife stab the Mexican in his chest. Blood spurted out. The Mexican should have run but instead, to save himself, he smashed a glass ashtray on the corner of the table and struck Carmino down his right cheek with the jagged edge. Carmino went berserk as blood gushed down his face. The pit boss, an inspector, and me, we tried to pull Carmino off the Mexican. Impossible! The guy was crazed, snarling like a dog. He delivered many blows with the knife. It was all over in seconds.

"Maria was deeply upset, shocked and screaming because she had been his lover. Later, she called him crazy, a psychopath. From what I saw, I agree. He repeatedly stabbed the Mexican in the eyes, neck and chest, long after he must have been dead. Nobody could have stopped Carmino without risking their own life. Carmino really enjoyed killing the guy. He was laughing when he got up saying the fucker had deserved it. He never showed any remorse. It was hard to count with blood spurting everywhere, but I'd say there were over twenty stab wounds.

"Management captured everything from the cameras and from about six of us as witnesses. They wanted to protect the licence. They needed no scandal. The casino was then emptied and closed. The player at my table was taken away by security. I guess he was murdered and dumped in the jungle far from the city.

"Back then in Panama, maybe still, money talked. Friends of the casino owners, the top brass in the police, were all bought. Me, Maria, and several other employees were each given one thousand bucks. This was for our lifetime silence. We all had to sign statements that we had seen the Mexican produce the knife and try to kill the dealer—*after Pepe Carmino had caught him cheating.*

"Our statements said the dealer had tried to defend himself but had been wrestled to the carpet. In the fight, the dealer had bravely tried to pin down the player but the Mexican had escaped, brandishing the knife.

"In truth, on orders from management, two security guards, wrapped the Mexican in some blood-stained carpet and took the corpse into a back room. I never saw it again. The knife disappeared too. Management brought in the police and we all gave false statements. Pepe was taken to hospital about the deep cut on his cheek, where he signed his false statement. Maria said his name was recorded as something like van Zandt, a South African.

"As far as the police were concerned, there was no murder, just an attack on a dealer who was so scared he had decided to quit. They 'accepted' our signed statements that the Mexican had left the premises unharmed. This was supported by more witness statements confirming a sighting of him later in the day, apparently very drunk while drinking beer in *El Cuervo.*

"From that day, Rick Hensfleet never existed, and certainly not Pepe Carmino. His name was airbrushed. The boss later told Maria that Carmino had been smuggled over the border into Costa Rica, perhaps even that same night. He disappeared. We thought maybe he too had been murdered but perhaps because he had been so popular with the casino boss, that saved his life. We kept silent. It was safer that way.

"I quit Panama with my thousand bucks to start a new life. I trekked and bummed lifts up the Pan-American Highway. Eventually, I paid to be smuggled across the border from Mexico into Texas. I reached Vegas. Though I had no need I took a blackjack dealer's course to shut out my past in Panama. I said I was from San Juan, Puerto Rico. I then started work in a casino.

"Two months ago on TV, I saw Rick Hensfleet outside the Space City project. I saw the scar. I checked him out and discovered this was Pepe Carmino. Along with a local guy called Enzo Letizione, they were the bosses of this new casino. We were expecting our second child. I needed more money. I reckoned I was due for promotion, but where I was working, the mean bastards, they said no. Space City was hiring, so I approached the company, who said no more blackjack dealers needed.

"I was goddammed pissed at this. I was desperate to earn more. After a few tequilas, I stupidly boasted to another dealer, Diego Rodrigues, about knowing enough to convict Pepe Carmino. Diego had a big mouth and started loose talk. Then by chance one night I was playing poker and met Enzo. He seemed a regular guy. I told him I wanted a job and that I had stuff on Pepe Carmino from Panama. As soon as I said those words, I knew I'd made a big, big mistake. He became frightening. So I never told him the details—just that Pepe had murdered someone.

"Enzo became furious. He said it was crap and blackmail--but that guy was worried. He warned - one more loose word and I would end up in the desert. I did not get any job. As for Diego, I told him to say nothing but he or someone kept the story alive! Diego's loud mouth, led you to me. I only ever told Diego and Enzo.

"I am giving this statement now of my own free will. I am scared but am happy to record the full story. Pepe Carmino must be charged with murder."

Dex felt hot and tormented and then chilled and shivery. As the jet rumbled its way back east, the words *dangerous* and *psychopath* played on his mind. He poured sparkling water and called for more, forcing himself to resist sinking a few glasses of malt. No wonder Tavio had been silenced. Had Letizione or Carmino somehow known that Tavio and Beth had met up? If yes, then probably Beth had been silenced too.

That left Diego Rodrigues, the guy whose big mouth had led Beth to Tavio.

Dex sighed. The police investigating Beth's death were clam-like. There was still no news on the tachograph analysis. He wandered down the aisle and the stewardess gave him a day-old *Daily Telegraph*. He wanted to take his mind off Carmino but when he turned to the sports pages, there was a picture of Mick Glenn. Irritated, he immediately flipped over the pages to read about cricket, tennis, snooker and even women's fashion—anything to forget his impetuous phone call.

Tired and lightheaded after a barely an hour's sleep, Dex cleared Customs and Immigration and grabbed a welcome double espresso at Costa Coffee. There he switched on his phone and saw a text from Tiffany. "Where are you? Call me. Any time." It was timed at 8:05 a.m., just an hour ago. Any time? That sound intriguing. Or ominous.

"Hi, Dex! Are you still in Vienna?" Dex was puzzled at her directness. There had been no frilly niceties, just straight to the point.

"Just landed. Your message sounded a bit frantic. Not the usual Miss Cool. What's up?"

"You haven't heard the news? No, of course you haven't. How could you?"

# CHAPTER TWENTY-ONE

"What news?"

Dex heard both concern and excitement in Tiffany's voice. "My TV station is at the scene now. Mick Glenn was murdered yesterday evening, London time."

"My God!" Dex was stunned into silence as his tired mind assessed the implications. A stressed-out traveller leaned toward Dex from his nearby chair as if trying to listen in. Dex twisted around to keep his distance.

*Was that my doing?*

*Down to me?*

*Had Mick ignored what I said?*

*Unlikely.*

*Had Mick challenged Carmino? Maybe.*

*Maybe probably.*

*Had he landed me in it?*

*No.*

*He didn't have my name.*

"You still there, Dex?"

"Sorry. Yes. I'm just…I don't know."

"The reporter says he was shot outside his home. A neighbour heard two shots."

"Where was this?"

"On his driveway. The Bishop's Avenue. Behind a pair of high- security gates."

"This is just *too* awful.."

Tiffany was typically forthright. "I warned you." Her irritation crossed the miles, no problem. "Did he raise hell with Pepe or not? You'd better face up to that."

Dex's tired mind was ill-equipped to resist. "I told him to do nothing. I wanted to create a plan. But he flew off the planet. Ape-shit, so I ended the call. He never got my name."

"If he confronted Carmino, those cameras? Carmino will spot who might have seen something—including me." Tiffany sounded angered now. "I told you to go to Scotty Brannigan, not Mick."

"I'm sorry."

"If a big-mouth like Glenn had spotted something himself, all hell would have broken loose on the spot. Carmino will know that."

"All roads lead to Beth's brother, the new kid in the casino."

"And me being a journalist. He'll suspct me. We're not in a good place, Dex." Then Tiffany's voice brightened. "But our sports editor says the rumour mill is already in overdrive. Remember those four footballers arrested on match-fixing allegations. Y'know, for that Malaysian gang? Already there's gossip on Twitter suggesting Mick might have been a fixer. Several contributors point to an easy goal he missed. Others are speculating that it was the husband of some woman he had bedded."

"That's Twitter for you! Fiction can become fact too quickly." Dex lowered his voice. "But he was knocking around with Creole Henry's woman. Remember?" He tipped the small cup nearly vertical to get the last drops of caffeine into his system. "I'm heading back to the barge to clear out the last few bits. Tomorrow I'm moving into Porcupine House." Then he stopped. "Oh God, Tiffany, I'm sorry. I should have asked. How was former President Clinton?"

He was rewarded with a throaty chuckle. "That man has charisma in spades. He spoke for forty minutes without a note and I swear every person present thought he was talking just to them. It's something to do with his eye contact."

"And you got to speak to him?"

"We chatted for nearly five minutes. He approached me after I'd done my piece. First he looked me straight in the eye, boring into me in the best possible way. He oozed sincerity, of course. Then he clasped my arm like US politicians do and said *my book had done the world a great service*. My legs just turned to jelly."

"That is just so cool. After that type of praise, your book's going to number one." He fell silent as an image of Mick Glenn lying on a slab destroyed the pleasure of the moment. "Where are you?"

"Atlanta. I flew from DC this evening, my head so big they had to widen the door into the 737."

From somewhere, Dex managed a laugh. "Not your style. But get this. Thanks to your help, I cracked the code."

"You mean into Beth's…"

"Right on."

"And?"

"You just don't want to know."

"Try me."

"No. Trust me. You don't want to know. Enjoy your memories of meeting Bill Clinton. There's been enough bad news for one day."

For the next few hours, Dex could think of nothing else but whether Glenn had confronted Pepe Carmino.

*Probably not.*

*This was the work of Creole Henry.*

*Or the match-fixers.*

It was little comfort.

# CHAPTER TWENTY-TWO

Back at Porcupine House, Dex busied himself for his father's home-coming. On social networks, even in the tabloids, Glenn's womanising remained a constant theme. Names of ex-girlfriends and persons he had been seen dating had prompted over thirty names, speculating about angry husbands and even suggesting a quickie with the wife of an England teammate. Nobody had yet mentioned Dukes or Creole Henry—but give it time. Other missed goals fired the conspiracy theorists. Someone even wondered if he had gambling debts from betting on horses and roulette.

Between shifting his belongings to Porcupine House, somehow Dex had found time to track down Billy Evans—the blackjack specialist suggested by McKay—leading to a breakfast date twenty-four hours after his return. He had chosen Simpson's-in-the-Strand. Billy had brought along his small daughter. "My access day with her," he explained on sitting down in the very traditional surroundings. "I'm taking Emily to the zoo. Hope you didn't mind her being here."

Emily was like a china doll with delicate pink skin, an engaging smile with a gap where her two lower front teeth were missing. Her hair was like flax and tied in a ponytail at the back. The ponytail was the only similarity to her father. Meeting a stranger in a smart London restaurant seemed to come easily to Emily's open personality.

Emily pulled off a tartan poncho and sat in the corner of the booth in a pair of red dungarees over a white jumper. To Dex, she truly had the face of an angel, round and smiling with large eyes that beamed across the table. Yet she bore no resemblance to Billy Evans, who was somewhere the wrong side of gaunt, his eyes tired and his cheeks prematurely lined. He looked to have slept rough with the winos on a park bench. Her mum must have been the looker in that setup.

"Hello, Emily. I'm Dex. Did you bring something to read or play with?"

She nodded and from a Barbie box, she produced a faded but

obviously loved Winnie-the-Pooh and a small book. "These are my favourites," she said proudly. "Pooh goes everywhere with me."

"Pooh will love the zoo. That's if he's not scared of lions, tigers, and hissy snakes."

"*My* Pooh is very brave and very hungry. He needs some honey."

"He'll get honey here—the very best. You're a big girl, aren't you? Tell me how old you are."

"I'm five. Soon, I'll be six, won't I daddy?" She waited for his proud agreement and then beamed, her face radiating excitement.

"Well, Emily, us grown-ups, we're going to be talking about very boring things. But when we've finished, perhaps we can play I-Spy or Connections."

"Teach me Connections, Mr. Dex. I don't like I-Spy."

"I will. Now let's all order." He turned to Emily's father, hoping his concern at Evans' appearance wasn't apparent. "I'm going for the Simpson's special—the Ten Deadly Sins. What about you?"

As he was speaking, he took in Billy's strange appearance. The man could do with a square meal…or ten. The way his blue-and–white-striped seersucker jacket hung, it looked as if he had lost a hundred pounds on a crash diet overnight. The tired and bloodshot eyes were sunken with purple rings beneath them. For his age, his skin was too pallid and scrawny. His age? Thirty? Forty-two? It was impossible to know. He looked such a wreck.

Billy's accent and somewhat flat vowels suggested an upbringing in the Midlands. "Sorry to keep you waiting. I didn't leave the casino until late. Then I had to collect Emily. We're having pizza and ice cream at the zoo, aren't we?" He was rewarded with a hug and then a nuzzle from Pooh. Billy's eyes were furtive, such a contrast to the openness of his daughter. "I'll share the Deadly Sins with Emily. Coffee for me, hot chocolate for her."

Dex poured orange juice from a large pitcher as he appraised the shabby figure in front of him. The prospect of getting help from Billy wasn't obviously appealing. He wondered what McKay would now make of the man he had rated the best blackjack player he had even come across. "Do you work locally?"

"Computer Programmer in Eastcheap. It passes the time until I get back to the tables." He wiped his hand under his nose and moments later did it again. He glanced at Emily who was pretend reading the menu to Pooh. "Let me tell you at once—I'm not an addict. I did have a problem but it's behind me now."

Dex raised an eyebrow, unsure whether to believe him. Shutting any addiction into a locked box was a tall order. It *was* possible but he knew that Billy would always be struggling. *Just as I was, just as I am with the booze.*

"Gussie McKay will have told you about," Billy looked at Emily, who was busily playing, "the white stuff. Cost me my marriage. Sandie and me—we're separated, not divorced." He spoke softly. "I'm not after sympathy. It was my fault and I'm trying to get her back. But beating an addiction?" He shook his head. "My life became a mess. My only friends were coke dealers and casino bartenders."

"Any casinos after you for counting?"

"Not in London. I never did it here."

"In America?"

"I was never caught. That's why Gussie respects me. Together, we toured the USA—played Atlantic City, Mississippi, the Gulf Coast, Vegas, Indian Reservations in California."

"That," Dex grinned hugely "is just what I want." Dex explained in a few brushstrokes that he needed someone to count cards but never to play as a counter would. "I want you to be the typical better-than-average punter who plays Basic Strategy well and who may win or lose."

"But still counting? I don't get it."

"I need to know if the decks are fixed."

"You mean some tens and aces removed?" He saw Dex nod a yes. "It happens in less-regulated countries. And they slip in a few extra 4s and 5s. But in London? I'd be amazed."

"Prepare to be amazed!"

"That's cool with me."

Dex noticed that Billy's hands were unsteady. He had chewed the fingernails almost to nothing. His bloodshot eyes were dull, dead even and lurked between prominent cheekbones. Except at the back, his hair was cropped to a shadowy black, exaggerating a rather pointed skull. The black ponytail looked as if it had been glued onto the almost bare scalp. In one ear was a stud, and the wide blue tie hung a full inch below the collar of his shirt. *That* was overdue for a car-boot sale in a poorer part of town. The eyebrows needed a trim and the nose was a mess.

"I can tell you're looking at me and thinking, my God, he's a bloody wreck. You're right." He looked down, making his face seem even more forlorn. "Counting cards reduced me to this." Billy shook his head in self-disgust. "The risk of being caught. Pushed me down the wrong track. For months, I couldn't live without it, the white stuff that is. I didn't eat properly. Couldn't afford to. My money went up my nose." He shook his head. "Then when I got back from the USA, Sandie locked me out." He shrugged at the position. "I don't blame her."

"But Gus McKay?"

"Some while back, we toured the USA off and on for nearly eighteen months, never playing at the same table but often watching each other. He was a canny old sod."

"But then?"

"He got caught."

"His gorilla moment?"

Billy's eyes managed a flicker of life. "That scared me. Seeing him dragged away between those two guys." He glanced at Emily, who was now looking at her book. "Vicious circle, then. No counting equals no big wins equals more white powder equals cash crisis equals marriage meltdown. The big wins stopped." He cut up some bacon for Emily. "This is a real treat, isn't it, Emily. I told you we'd have a fun day out."

"Thank you, Daddy. Thank you, Mr. Dex." The little girl wriggled along the bench seat to be closer to the father she so obviously loved.

"You have no idea what it's like—card-counting, I mean." He twiddled his fork. "Playing blackjack badly isn't difficult. Just like Happy Families or Snap. You may win, but you'll probably lose over time. But card-counting's different."

"Go on!" Dex wanted to test McKay's comments and advice.

"Tallying the high-low count is a no-brainer. I could do that while playing with myself." His face looked even longer as he exhaled a deep sigh. "But these casinos are not charities. No way! They just pretend they like winners—that's good marketing. Deep down they want every last penny and your balls as well. They're always updating wizard technology, real Big Brother stuff, like image-recognition software to trap counters who try disguises. They've even built devices into the shoe from which the cards are dealt to permit player-tracking. For card-counters, that's the end. Kaput. Stone dead gone. Face-recognition, player tracking and automatic continuous shufflers kill off anyone using card-counting skills."

"But counting cards isn't illegal."

Billy laid down his cutlery and chewed thoughtfully, patting Emily on the head at the same time. "No, but if you're caught like Gussie, you get blacklisted everywhere. That's the problem—concealing you're a counter." He stabbed into the fried bread with an angry movement. "You live on your nerves, become paranoid."

They fell silent, each weighing up the implications and putting away bits of kidney and mushrooms. Dex's initial concern about the man's appearance had eased. This train-wreck of a figure was not a known counter. He was off the drugs—so he said. Billy's role would be stress-free. He needed money to rebuild his life. "Here's the story. I'm gathering evidence against a casino. I'll fund your membership fee of £25,000. There's strings attached, mind. You'll join via a friend of mine. I'll bankroll you and pay for your time. I want you to test the count over two or three weeks."

"I think I get you but explain."

"One member was griping that he rarely wins. Reckons there aren't enough tens and aces in the shoe."

"You said this was in London?" Billy stopped his fork in mid-air. "Dukes."

Billy ran his finger under his misshapen nostrils. "You surprise me. But I could prove it. By counting through enough shoes, I'd spot whether they were spooking the decks." He watched Emily finishing the last of her breakfast. "A clean plate, Emily. Well done!" He smiled for the first time. "That must be your good influence, Dex."

Dex waited while Billy wiped egg off the girl's cheek. "Here's the deal." For the next few minutes, they fixed the small print of what was needed. "Your cover is you've met a good friend of mine and you're teaching him how to play Basic Strategy. His name is Adam Yarbury." Dex paused, slightly embarrassed about what he wanted to say. "Adam is old-fashioned. One of the chaps."

Billy pushed aside the remains of his toast. "You mean you want me to smarten up?"

"Get rid of the stud, the ponytail. Look conventional. Without a makeover, nobody would believe Adam would ever have spoken to you. Oh, and get some new shirts, ties, jackets. I'll pay."

"You're turning my clock right back." Billy did not seem offended.

"You known in Dukes?"

"No. Far too posh."

Dex was pleased at the denial. "Let's meet after the zoo. I'll give you the money and enough cash to kit yourself out. Oh, and I'll fix a meeting with Adam. He's away on a wine-tasting jolly in France. Adam will introduce you as a new member." Dex waved his knife in emphasis. "You don't know me if you see me. Got it? Not till Adam introduces you to me. Understood?" Dex waited for the firm nod.

Billy checked his watch. "Time to go, Emily."

"But Mr Dex is going to teach me Connections."

"Next time. We must hurry to the zoo." He grabbed her arm, her poncho and toys.

Dex patted her head. "That's right, Emily. Next time. That's a promise."

"The bears will get you if you don't keep promises," she warned, suddenly all stern.

"I wouldn't want that."

Emily looked across at Dex with sad eyes. "Goodbye, Mr. Dex."

"You'll have a lovely day." Dex then turned to Billy and gave him the address of Porcupine House, which he slipped into a slim-line wallet. "I'll be here later today. It's not far from the zoo. Come over by taxi whenever."

The euphoria he had felt on receiving a giant hug from Emily vanished as he stepped out into the noisy bustle of the Strand. The air was filled with the noise and smell of diesel from the steady flow of buses and taxis. Motorcycle couriers raced by as if practising for the Isle of Man T.T. He had an hour to get to the consulting rooms in Harley Street, and he thought of what lay ahead as he crossed over by Charing Cross Station.

Dr Wilfred Grierson, MBChB, MRCPsch. Psychiatrist.

Miserable. Mean.

Obsessed with prescribing pills or potions to be inserted into *every* orifice. And a mad-keen Morris dancer. With the emphasis on the *mad*.

# CHAPTER TWENTY-THREE

It was just after 10:30 a.m. and Dex was in plenty of time to meet Grierson in Harley Street so, despite the muggy fumes, he walked through Trafalgar Square, Piccadilly Circus and up the long curve of Regent Street with its mix of touristy memento shops and designer stores. Everyone seemed to be a tourist. He was stopped twice by hopelessly lost foreigners asking for directions to Buckingham Palace and Downing Street.

He didn't mind helping but each interruption broke his endless shuffling of facts and priorities. He needed to get Adam Yarbury onside about Billy while still debating what to do about Mick Glenn. *Should I go the cops? And if I do? Say what? That Mick was dating Creole Henry's squeeze?*

*Tonight.* He shivered despite the muggy heat. Tonight would be high risk territory—secretly filming in Dukes. From the espionage shop near Park Lane, he had bought a camera disguised in a tiepin and had another installed in a cufflink. *Do I play Reverse Labouchère or just make random bets? Do I watch One-Eye? Or maybe Andy? Or flit from table to table? How do I conceal I am not up to something?*

Impulsively, he broke off the jumble of thoughts to pop into Hamleys to buy a cuddly panda for Emily. He had just exited and turned right to continue his walk when he had an idea on how to win big at roulette. At first it seemed wild, impractical and fanciful, but every step he took convinced him that just maybe it could be a masterstroke. To succeed, there would be three problems to overcome. The second one looked insuperable. As he approached the top of Regent Street, he tucked the idea away for later, concentrating instead on the arrival of the Aussie nurse and his father.

After entering the crisscrossing streets north of Oxford Circus, he saw the length of Harley Street stretching out ahead of him. Both sides of the legendary street brimmed with every type of medical consultant.

Dex had harboured a jaundiced view of shrinks from long before he ever had the indignity of being referred to one after his breakdown.

Dex thought back to a story told by his former neighbour, a Queen's Counsel. Apparently, this top lawyer had dismissed a psychiatrist's evidence with the mocking jibe to the judge that "in giving his evidence, you may think this expert's feet very rarely touched the ground, and when they did, they moved in singularly unattractive directions."

The QC had also warned Dex that too many Harley Street consultants were better at extracting cash from patients' wallets than extracting a grumbling appendix. Still smiling at the thought, he spotted Grierson's brass plate. It was his sixteenth visit. The specialist's consulting room was shared on a hot-desking basis for his two mornings a week. Dex reckoned Grierson probably made enough in those few hours to indulge his passion for Morris Dancing.

After he had browsed through a well-thumbed *Country Life* magazine, he was called in. Grierson was sipping from a bone china cup in a room that might once have seated thirty Victorian gentry for a very long lunch. The cup's contents smelled smoky enough to be Lapsang Souchong but Dex was offered nothing. Presumably the consultation fee of one-thousand pounds was insufficient to cover such extravagance.

"How are you feeling?"

Grierson was late fifties and meticulously groomed. The Scottish accent and the tweed jacket suggested the man probably owned a salmon beat in the Border Country. Or a whole river, come to that. Unless he spent all his spare time Morris Dancing and wearing a daft hat, jingling his bells and waving hankies. Grierson looked at the panda, a question mark on his face.

"I sleep with eight or nine friends like this every night," Dex impulsively invented, trying not to laugh as the psychiatrist frowned as he noted this new quirk on his pad. As Dex replied, he was already rolling up his sleeve to have his blood pressure checked. He knew the drill sixteen times over. As the gadget tightened on his upper left arm, he confirmed he was feeling a damned sight better since he had flung the pills into the Thames.

There was a long silence as Grierson watched the deflating arm band and then grunted. "No pills, eh? Since when?" The man's gruff voice always made him sound as if he had an anger problem of his own to contest.

"I forget," Dex prevaricated, "but long enough to know they weren't doing me a damned bit of good."

"You think so?"

"I know so."

Grierson fell silent again as he sniffed his tea and then sipped thoughtfully. *That silence has probably cost me at least thirty quid,* Dex thought as he waited for a response. At last after much flexing of fingers and examination of his nails, it came. "How?"

Dex reckoned that single word had probably cost another fifty quid at least. "Not a single nightmare since I fed them to the fishes. On the other hand, the perch and roach downstream are having nightmares about ending up on a dinner-plate and being sprinkled with vinegar."

Grierson gave an expensive grunt. Humour had always passed him by. He leaned across the antique desk and picked up his Mont Blanc pen and made a laboriously slow note. Dex imagined it confirmed that *this patient still presents as unstable. Collection of fluffy toys suggests lack of breastfeeding as a baby.* The doctor then tilted his gold-rimmed spectacles further up his nose before looking over them to stare at his patient. "Your blood pressure…"

"You never treated me for that, did you?"

"When you were on your, eh, med-ic-ation for stress and anxiety disorders," he spoke the words so slowly Dex reckoned he was dreaming of his fee again, "your blood pressure was 112 over 77."

Dex knew that was good. "Is that bad?"

Grierson ignored the comment. His lips narrowed. "And today it is 155 over 109." He shook his head very slowly, like everything else he did.

Dex understood the figures were high. "Well, thank God for that. Higher, eh! I'm getting better." Dex rubbed his hands. "The figures are going up at last." He enjoyed winding up the miserable bastard and getting more of the man's time for the fee.

"When you were on that med-ic-ation and following my advice to relax, you were coming along nicely, really well."

"Really well, give or take nightmares twice a week that scared the shit out of every young wench who happened to enjoy my company in bed."

"Really well. Aye, really, really well." He gazed at a nineteenth-century painting of a clipper sailing defiant in a storm. "Are you relaxing like I advised? You're not nearly ready for life in the wider world yet."

"No stress in my life at all." Dex grinned disarmingly as moments from the previous few weeks flashed by—the smell of the burning car; identifying his sister in the morgue; visits to his father; moving homes; the murder of Mick Glenn; taking on a psychopath; running for his life down a Panama back street; secretly filming in Dukes tonight. "No, Doc, nothing stressful, nothing out of the ordinary."

"No alcohol still?"

Dex waved a long arm airily. "Oh no, Doc. Strictly and absolutely off-limits."

Grierson was unimpressed and leaned forward. "I don't *believe* you. Something is pushing up your blood pressure." He looked Dex up and down. "You're lean, fit-looking. Something is doing this. We must start a fresh course of er, eh—med-ic-ation—something to reduce the blood pressure. An ACE inhibitor."

Dex shook his head. "*We* are starting nothing."

Grierson ignored this instruction. "And besides taking something for the blood pressure, I want you back on the pills you discarded so foolishly."

"I bet you do, Doc, but I've swallowed enough pills to make me rattle." He stood up rather abruptly from his chair. "Pills? Thanks but no thanks. I'll heal myself." He started to head for the door. "And now that I've got this consultation and the shock of your fees off my chest, I'll be a stress-free zone. I bet my blood pressure will be just fine again. Ticketyboo, as you medical professionals would say."

"You're not consulting me again?" Grierson sounded shocked and looked close to despair at the prospect of losing many thousands of easy money. "That blood pressure is a ticking time bomb. Be warned." He barely paused. "And remember, I don't take AMEX."

"Yeah! I got the message." Dex nodded thoughtfully before stretching out to shake hands in farewell, but Grierson had already turned away to study the notes for his next patient.

Dex let himself out and offered his AMEX card to the receptionist, who told him Dr Grierson did not accept it. Dex gave the young woman a big smile and a friendly wink.

"You're new here, aren't you? I always use it," Dex insisted. "He just doesn't like AMEX taking their cut. Tough. I've no cash with me." He watched the receptionist hesitate. Then she smiled sheepishly before pulling out the card-reader from a drawer.

"Thanks, darling."

Dex left with a broad grin, enjoying his moment of minor triumph.

# CHAPTER TWENTY-FOUR

As he sat in his office, the door shut against the noise and dust of ongoing finishing touches to Space City, Enzo Letizione should have felt happier than he did. The union reps were at last supportive, so that plans for the Grand Opening were almost ready. The finishing touches by the after-trades were dovetailing. Even the dickhead at the bank was docile, with big cash coming through from London. Better still, the Caribbean nest eggs for himself and Pepe were being generously topped up.

Because they were casino profits being moved within a group structure, the transfers from London to Vegas had passed the smell test for money laundering. Sometimes it would be three million, but often it was seven or eight depending on which of the Swiss lawyer's high rollers had visited Dukes for special treatment.

But Letizione still had a nagging problem—one that had started with a small item in this morning's *Las Vegas Review Journal*. A man had gone missing while boating on Lake Mead about fifteen miles outside town, but no body had been found and neither had the victim been named.

As a Vegas story, it was unremarkable. Countless times, Letizione had read of drownings on the vast expanse of water. Over weekends, hundreds and often thousands of Vegas folk took to the water in small boats to fish, to booze or to poodle around. Accidents happened. Usually they involved alcohol and a loss of balance or perhaps a drunken argument ending in a fight. But Letizione's memory dated back to days when the mob might invite a victim for a day on the water. The tickets were one-way only, and always ended with a concrete jacket and boots.

Now, just moments ago, Channel 13 Action News had named the victim. Diego Rodrigues! The name had hit him like a kick in the gut. He sat thoughtful for a few moments, his anger growing. The chiming wallclock confirmed it was just turning 3 p.m., so 11 p.m. in London. He clicked open Skype, wanting to see Pepe's face during the conversation. This was often a good time to catch him, as he had usually finished dinner and the biggest Asian high rollers might not be arriving till after midnight. The call was quickly answered.

"Yeah. It's all good at Space City. And you?"

"Going well. No problems." Pepe's eyes narrowed as he spoke, something not lost on the American. Then he smiled disarmingly. "Well, that's not quite right."

"Go on!"

"We're keeping a close watch on one of our new members. He acts a bit strange, like a detective—always hanging out round the tables and watching."

"You think he's a cop? Or maybe snooping for the Gambling Commission?"

"No. Definitely not. I know his background from one of our elder statesmen members."

"So he's just suspicious?"

"Says he's learning. Maybe he has spotted something. But like I say, we're watching him."

"Twenty-four-seven?"

"Yes and no. The cameras here follow him constantly." Pepe faltered, unsure whether to go on. "Okay. Let me explain. Remember I mentioned an Aussie woman? Bit of a looker?" Pepe waited for the nod before continuing. "I've only got her planted in the guy's home. Cool, eh?"

"I guess." The American was bothered by the need for such an extreme step. "Gonna explain why?"

"Just wanting her to take a mosey round."

"Sure but why? What are you looking for?"

Letizione noticed the pupils shrink as Pepe responded. "To see what his game is, if anything. To see what he's got on us, if anything. To check out if he might bring in the cops. Anyway, Jude's drop-dead gorgeous. She'll get him talking."

"Pillow talk, huh?"

"Whatever." No way was he going to admit that part of Jude's brief was to check Dex's passport for evidence of a Panama visit. No way was he mentioning that the target was dead Beth's brother. "She's just starting as a carer for the guy's sick dad."

"And she's not a hooker?"

"For the right guys, I reckon she does tricks for free. But get this: Arnie's mate forged some great references. Fooled the guy a treat." Pepe looked smug at his ploy.

"Hey, Pepe! There's a story over here. Guy drowned out at Lake Mead. Name was Diego Rodrigues. Mean anything?"

Pepe looked away and then pursed his lips in a tightly shut no as he shook his head. To the American, the frown seemed exaggerated. "How, why should I know this Diego?"

"He used to hang out with Tavio Sanches—remember, the guy was shot outside his apartment."

"You mentioned him before. But the names mean nothing."

"Want to know more?"

As he crossed his arms defensively, Pepe was unsure what to answer. "Well, I suppose you're going to tell me anyway, so make it quick."

"Diego also reckoned you worked in Panama. Two guys, same story. Both dead." The speaker watched for a guilt reaction but was disappointed as Pepe swatted away the jibe with aplomb.

"Don't you get it?" The Englishman's tone was sharp. "I've said before, I've never been in Panama. Listen: is someone trying to screw us over our license? Is that the story? Getting these Latinos to spread crap around the city?"

"Not so I've noticed. But heh, something else—what's with all this shit I'm reading about Dukes and a guy called Mick Glenn?"

"Reached Vegas, has it?" Pepe looked genuinely surprised. "Glenn was a member, came in occasionally with a racing driver. He was shagging a Jamaican thug's woman. Big mistake. Ended up with a couple of bullets. What's your problem? Someone bad-mouthing us?"

"Uh-uh. No. Just chat about him and gambling at Dukes. Nobody suggested Dukes was involved in the murder."

"I'd have had our lawyer onto it if they had!" Pepe laughed at the prospect and reached for his espresso. "We're not part of the story. Mick had the sex life of a prize stallion. My guess, he upset this mobster, Creole Henry."

The listener stroked his chin thoughtfully. "That's good, because I mean you lost that member, that woman, in the car wreck. Now there's Glenn and there's these two dealers. That's four—all dead. All within a few weeks." Letizione paused for emphasis. "And each knew you or claimed to know you."

"Nothing to do with me, us, or Dukes. I'm telling you. These two over in Vegas? Never been on my radar." Pepe's voice had risen, his angry eyes dominating the screen. "I'm due downstairs, right now. Keep me posted about the opening night."

The American settled his hands across the spread of his stomach and fought to keep his voice calm. "Just remember, Pepe—I warned you, no whacking."

Pepe's face hardened but as quickly broke into a disarming smile. He waved his arms airily to match the wide-eyed innocent that he was portraying. "Relax, Enzo. You stick to getting the joint ready on time. When we started this thing, we rode a tandem, both working like fuck. Recently, I've been the only one pedalling—raising the money, taking the risks. And that, my friend, is because of your fuckwit control of the project.

"So get this," Pepe waved the stub of his cigar as he spoke in rapid fire. "I'm covering your butt, not kicking it as I should. Never forget that!" He spoke even slower again as he continued. "You deliver that great opening night, we'll sell our stakes, maybe after five years, maybe sooner. Become stinking rich. So don't go getting humpty with me over some moronic conspiracy theory. Got it?" Pedro clicked the red button.

Enzo stared at the blank screen. Slowly he got up and paced his office, looking at a photo of him with the mayor and another with a senator outside the Capitol in Washington. He thought of the skimmed money, drip-feeding his secret account. Pepe was right. He was gonna be okay, either way. And they were in too deep to back off. Each needed the other.

"But you're still a lying lump of crap. This is for you, Pepe."

He hurled his cup against a picture of Pepe at the topping-out ceremony. Both broke with a resounding crash.

He felt better for it.

# CHAPTER TWENTY-FIVE

As he heard Jude enter the room, Dex swung round from his laptop in Father's study. He was seated at the generous proportions of the enormous desk. Much as he had disliked the idea of returning to Porcupine House, he relished the extra space. "Are you settled in up there?"

"Yeah! No sweat."

He gave her a welcoming smile and a longer look as he took in the change of clothes. She had arrived in faded blue jeans, a grey sweatshirt and a baseball cap with a fishbone logo. The cap, so she explained, was to remind her of Doyles restaurant at Watson Bay in Sydney. Now, however, her copper-coloured hair dropped down over her shoulders and across the top of a clinging gold-coloured catsuit, a type of figure-hugging onesie with sex written large into the design. Jude approached, sliding across the thick grey carpet with feline grace to match her outfit.

She looked round the room with obvious approval. Dex had turned the spacious study into his own work area with the roulette wheel and layout permanently set up on a mahogany side table. Previously, Father had used it to spread out his OS maps and architects' plans for his projects—including, Dex thought sourly, the ones for redevelopment of his company's autospares site. Even now, the room still smelled of the Erinmore pipe tobacco that the old man had favoured. Of other memorabilia, there was no sign. Dex had dumped photos of completed projects and other industry trophies in the cellar downstairs.

"Don't think it will always be this easy," Dex commented. "But once you've got Father's room ready for tomorrow, you can bunk off—watch TV here or see your mates in Earl's Court."

Jude shrugged *whatever*, a movement that seemed to waft the scent of a subtle perfume closer to him. "What are your plans?"

Dex sensed an invitation to chase her round the house - with her not exactly hurrying. "I'm going to a casino in Mayfair."

"You're obviously pretty damned expert," she prompted, nodding at the wheel.

"Hardly." Dex stretched his clasped hands behind his neck and leaned back in the expensively upholstered chair. "I'm a novice. But I'll be a bad loser, so I'm practising."

"Roulette's a tough game. In casinos, here's the rule: think like a winner; play like a winner; be a winner. Trust me. I used to play at the casino in Sydney."

"At roulette? You must have lost."

"Same as my virginity. Just once, long ago and best forgotten. Nah! Losing's for wimps. After that I switched to Punto Banco."

"Which is?"

"Strewth! You are a novice! It's cards. Best odds in the house. Or maybe you call it baccarat." She adopted a very upper-crust English accent to say the word.

He shook his head, showing she was talking way over his head. "You ever play in London, Jude?"

"Occasionally. I've had city friends take me to Aspinalls."

"Dukes?"

"Dukes?" She thought for a moment. "Is that in Mount Street?" She saw Dex agree. "Sure. Just once maybe but after a gutful of vodka martinis I sometimes forget." They both laughed at the image as she leaned her shapely thighs against the roulette layout. "Mind, at Dukes, I was bankrolled by a broker. He lost his New Year bonus playing blackjack. I won a few quid playing Punto Banco."

Dex thought for a moment and then plunged in. "Well, if you're not doing anything, come along tonight?"

"Gamble? On what you're paying me?" Her laugh this time was coarsely raucous.

"I'll bankroll you. You win at Punto Banco; I lose at roulette. Your win will balance my loss."

"I don't keep *all* my winnings? You kidding me?"

"Christ! You Aussies! But dinner's on me."

Jude seemed ready to jump at the chance, but then a frown flickered over her tanned face. "I'll take a rain check. Tomorrow's going to be busy."

Dex fought to conceal his disappointment. "Okay. Another time?"

"You got a deal, Dex. I love gambling." She paused. "Dukes? I was thinking. Did I meet Pepe someone there?"

"Pepe Carmino."

"What a charmer, eh! Pepe joined us in the bar. He has some stories, that guy!"

Dex could have added one or two that Pepe would not have told her but let it pass. "I'll remember that." He checked the time. "So if you'll excuse me. I want to finish here and then I'll be off."

"I'll get everything ready for Sir Charles. Hey? Is that what I call him?"

Dex was floored. "I don't think Father's in any condition to complain if you don't—but on the other hand, why not?"

She left the room and he heard her go up the creaking stairs. He had learned as a teenager that he could move about the house silently by keeping to the very edge of the stairs. Walking in the middle could awaken the house. Sometimes when his father was at his drunken worst, this knowledge had proved useful.

He ended typing the email and then, as he now invariably did, he checked the web for news from Vegas. The main stories were about the rifts between big-name casino moguls who were either for or against eGaming, but when he scrolled down, he saw another headline—*Missing Dealer Named*. Not having been aware of the story, he clicked on it and paused after just a couple of lines. The name Diego Rodrigues jumped out. His fingers trembled as his eyes stared unseeingly at the story.

Heart pounding uncomfortably, he was reminded of Grierson's blood pressure warning but was in no mood to take heed. Not yet awhile. He read on. Drowning was presumed. Rodrigues had set off, apparently alone, in a twenty-foot craft with a small cabin. It had been found empty and there were no witnesses. The person who had spotted the empty boat had seen several empty beer cans and a near-empty bottle of tequila. No distress call had been received.

*Two dealers.*

*Both fingering Pepe.*

*Both dead.*

*Coincidence?*

He closed the study door and Skyped Tiffany. Had she picked up more fast-track on Mick Glenn? Or from the police about the accident?

She was offline. He needed her. He needed somebody to *trust*. Maybe Jude? Perhaps he could confide in her? Reminded of McKay's words about loose talk, he decided not to rush that though Jude ... yes, she might be ideal down in Dukes.

Eager to finish his notes and hit the tables, he typed up the latest developments and then shut down his now password-protected Sony. Lid shut, it lay on his desk beside a scattering of cheap gel pens, a stapler, a calculator, his empty coffee cup and some crumbs from a raisin cookie. With no shredder, he had debated whether to bin all his scribbles but instead took them across the room to the heavy safe that stood in the corner.

He shut them inside alongside Father's cheque books, share certificates and years of old annual accounts that would never be read by the old man again. He slammed shut the heavy door with a sigh and set the combination lock.

# CHAPTER TWENTY-SIX

Pepe Carmino swivelled the screen on his desk so that Nigel Forster-Brown could see it. Carmino was in his comfy chair, the picture of relaxation, whereas his deputy stood nervously, eyes looking at the carpet rather than the screen. His restless hands looked even whiter than usual. Carmino knew there was no point in yet another inquest into what had happened when Mick Glenn had made his threats but he enjoyed watching his manager's discomfort.

Suddenly on screen, Forster-Brown joined the footballer. Moments later, Pepe laughed, knowing what was coming: "Listen, you bald-headed bunny. You tell that ponce Pepe: I'm not leavin' next time without all me money back—all £210,000 of it, or I'm goin' to Scotland bleedin' Yard. I know the fuckin' works on you lot. An' I'm goin' to tell every fuckin' member the way it is. Got it, you carrot cruncher? I'll be in next Thursday evening. 10:30. You tell him."

Carmino let the recording continue until Glenn had bounded up the stairs toward the exit. "So, FB—you finished that check yet?"

FB handed over a typed list with nine names on it. "My take, boss. Glenn saw nothing, otherwise he would take no shit. Scotty Brannigan? Less volatile, but he too would also have said something. That guy knows enough from living in Vegas. He gives no quarter. Wouldn't have been world champion if he did. You can discount the two bimbos. That leaves the German, Gerhard Hoge, Virat Khan, Zaheer Ashwin, Ajit Badani, Tiffany Richmond, and Finlay Dexter."

"Any of them friendly with Mick Glenn?"

Eyes locked on the carpet and feet shuffling, Forster-Brown said he had overheard banter between Hoge and Mick Glenn about penalty shootouts but other than that, nobody on the list had ever associated with the footballer. "Mick Glenn might have invented it?" He finished unconvinced even himself.

Pepe glared at his manager and for a fleeting moment caught his eye. "Get real, you bald-headed bunny—One-Eye *was* cheating them.

You know that." Pepe enjoyed seeing Forster-Brown wince at the insult. "So it's pretty damned likely that somebody saw something. Someone sharp enough to spot what One-Eye was doing."

FB kept his anger to himself, and as he often did when Pepe was insulting, reminded himself of the juicy pension on retirement. Carmino looked at the list again. "Those three Indians?"

Forster-Brown hesitated, wary about putting his head above the parapet again. "The cricketers? They seemed pretty much wrapped up in each other and anyway they scarcely spent any time at the roulette whilst Mick was playing. But they might have known how to make contact, you know—being fellow sportsmen—but there was no sign they knew him."

He saw Pepe nod and heard him grunt which was some encouragement, so he carried on. "Tiffany is a smart journalist. She might have an enquiring mind. She would know how to contact Glenn. Dexter is a novice. I can't believe he would have spotted anything. But Tiffany? An unknown quantity. So my money is on her."

"Just suppose you're right. Who brought her in? Answer—Finlay Dexter." Pepe lit his cigar. He had no interest in a daft law that said he had to sit on the steps outside if he wanted to smoke. "Dexter may have brought her in as an investigative journalist. Possible."

"So your instructions?"

"One-Eye continues. Business as usual. But keep One-Eye away from Dexter if he plays or if his woman comes in. Move One-Eye if Dex seems to be watching him. Same for Andy. And tell Jeb Miller to keep an eye on Dexter. Anything suspicious, let me know at once."

"Dexter arrived about forty minutes ago. I'll get back down there."

As FB turned away, one of Pepe's two mobile phones vibrated on his desk, a signal for him to shoo FB out of the room even faster. When he heard the voice, his face broke into one of his most charming smiles and his voice oozed ersatz friendliness. "I'm so glad you called. Settled in?"

He listened for a few moments.

"Yes, you're fine. Plenty more time. He's downstairs." He clicked a switch. "Yes. I can see him in the bar. What's that? A roulette wheel? Interesting. You say he practices? And documents?" Again he listened to Jude's report. "So pretty careful, you would say? No passport in his desk? Hmm! Try his bedroom, briefcase."

He was then silent for rather longer as he listened, his face growing increasingly solemn. "Password protected? I know someone who can beat that. One for me to think about…but a modern safe? Short of a skilled safecracker, I'm stumped."

As Jude continued, Pepe suddenly laughed.

"He did, did he?" He adjusted the angle of his desk lamp thoughtfully. "Bring him down here for a long evening. I'll have someone pay Porcupine House a visit. You have your own key?" He was pleased at her answer and then scribbled down a number on his pad. "That's the alarm, is it? I'll read it back. 19293900. Correct? And where is the control box? Beside the kitchen door? That's down one side. Okay."

He had heard enough, and suddenly sounding impatient, he thanked her.

"Yes, I enjoyed our afternoon together too. Of course. We must. As soon as Dexter's old man is settled in and you can get away. My place again, of course."


Dex had deliberately not gone to the wheel where One-Eye was spinning. He settled in next to a cheerful middle-aged German who introduced himself as Gerhard Hoge. The dealer's name was Jasmine. Hoge only played the outside bets and so Dex asked if he would mind if he followed him, as he seemed to be winning. "Ja! Please bring me more of this luck," Hoge replied in good English. "For sure, I'm not always winning like tonight."

"Is that because of Jasmine or are you wearing your lucky underpants?"

"Ha! I guess the guy I shook hands with earlier was a chimney sweep." Hoge saw Dex look puzzled. "For us Germans, that is the best way to get good luck."

"And a black, sooty hand," laughed Dex, pushing a stack of chips to back even numbers. He was happy to be talking. It took his mind off his secretive cameras that would be catching the action. Forty minutes later, Hoge said he had won enough—just over twenty-nine thousand pounds—and so Dex eased back his chair and coloured up his chips and found Hoge's good run had won him nearly eight thousand pounds. But if anything hokie had been going on, he had spotted nothing.

The German rose to his beanpole height. "So, my friend. Maybe we play again together."

"Maybe I can be your honorary chimney sweep."

"Any time. See you." With that the German headed for the bar while Dex strolled to the Punto Banco where he rapidly decided the game was totally beyond him. He stopped by the blackjack and watched a few hands before squeezing himself into a corner seat at One-Eye's roulette table, where he was paying out over forty thousand to an Indian in a purple turban.

During the evening, Pepe Carmino had done a meet-and-greet tour and disappeared. FB had been strolling around, but then, he always did. *Am I paranoid, or is FB following me like a hungry mongrel?*

That apart, there was nothing out of the ordinary, no sign that he was a marked man, so he placed his wrist on the table close to number 34 and aimed his tie toward One-Eye, hoping to catch some sleight of hand on one or both cameras. He was disappointed. Not only was the Indian paid out exactly right but One-Eye was moved on after the next spin. Nothing unusual about that either. Dealers were often moved, sometimes every twenty minutes, sometimes after rather longer.

For the next hour, Dex played the outside bets but still not testing Reverse Labouchère. Instead, he played the same way as Gerhard Hoge but with less good luck. "That's me done," he volunteered to the dealer after he had lost most of his winnings.

In the taxi back to St John's Wood, he was disappointed. He had no hard evidence against Dukes. Worse still, FB had told him that Space City would soon be opening. Thank God Adam was flying back tonight! He desperately needed Billy Evans monitoring the blackjack tables. When the taxi purred to a halt outside his imposing home, Dex saw a light from Jude's room on the top floor. He checked the time. It was 2:20 a.m. Not quite the early night she had suggested.

He went into Father's study and opened his laptop to Skype Tiffany but she was offline so he left a message. He was just about to switch off when he noticed the second drawer down on the desk was slightly ajar. Though he was not obsessively tidy, one thing he always did was to close all drawers tightly shut.

It was a silly habit that had started on a school trip to Sri Lanka. They had been briefed that, in the hostel where they were staying, there could be cobras and always to keep drawers tightly shut. Despite the risk of a cobra getting into a drawer in St John's Wood being nil, the old habit had never died.

With an angry shake of the head and a sense of shock, he pushed the drawer shut before checking out the rest of the room. He spotted nothing else unusual. If there were a bug, it was well hidden, but having the place swept when Jude was out was essential.

Nothing seemed to be missing, and at least Jude could not have accessed his laptop or the safe. Even so, it was with slow footsteps and deep in thought that he mounted the stairs. By the time he reached his bedroom on the first floor, he was philosophical. At least he knew he had a prowler living in the house.

# CHAPTER TWENTY-SEVEN

Two days later, Dex headed up to see his father, reflecting that during the previous forty-eight hours the pace had quickened. The police intended charging the truck driver with causing death by dangerous driving. First though, they had to find him and decide who he really was. The sergeant would not tell him what the tachograph had revealed or whether it had been tampered with.

Yesterday afternoon, after meeting Adam and Billy in the morning, he had watched Mick Glenn's funeral on TV. Speculation continued about the murderer and once again the police were tight-lipped, revealing only that they were following "a number of lines of enquiry."

Breakfast with Adam Yarbury had been in his penthouse apartment overlooking the Millennium Bridge. The elderly maid called Ursula, dressed in a black uniform with a white frilly headband, was from a bygone era. She served them fluffy scrambled eggs, smoked bacon, and grilled tomatoes as they sat on the sun deck taking in the dramatic shapes of the London skyline and the murky brown of the Thames far below. In the warm morning air, the entire conversation had been somewhat surreal as far as Dex was concerned—but that was the beauty of dealing with someone like Adam.

"I see that fella, the footballer, was murdered whilst I was away. I never much liked the cut of his jib but he didn't deserve that. Or perhaps he did. Perhaps he *was* a bit of a cad—what we called a poodle-faker."

Dex laughed at the outmoded vocabulary but quickly became serious. "I spoke to him. Not long before he died."

"My dear old thing! Good gracious me! Whatever were you doing talking to him?"

Dex rapidly explained what he had seen when Mick Glenn and Scotty Brannigan had been cheated. As he spoke, Dex could see that although Adam was listening, he was also marshalling his own train of thought. At first, Adam was tapping his teeth thoughtfully. Then a frown developed and he scratched his ear as if somehow this would clarify whatever was in his mind.

"Dex, my boy. I wish we had shared this conversation sooner."

"Oh! Why would that be?" Dex put down his coffee cup and placed his elbows on the table to lean forward to emphasise intensity.

"It all makes sense now. Not at the time, of course. It was all mumbo-jumbo to me. Jail and all that stuff." Adam was really talking to himself more than to Dex, who was trying to curb his impatience. Adam stood up and leaned against the parapet with its spread of summer flowers lining the top. Across the river the mighty dome of St Paul's Cathedral was the backdrop. Then he nodded his head in recollection. "The game's up, mate. You're all goin' to jail."

"Adam! Come on! What do you mean?"

"I was there. Coming down the stairs in Dukes when Mick Glenn rushed past me going up. That's what he shouted down to Nigel Forster-Brown."

It was not what Dex wanted to hear. Now he knew that Glenn had raised hell in Dukes. "And now he's dead." Dex pushed aside the crust of wheat toast. Suddenly, he was no longer hungry. "Along with Beth and two dealers in Vegas who big-mouthed about Pepe being in Panama."

"He told you he had never been there."

"He lied." Dex grinned. "So did I. I never did make Vienna. I went to Panama. Pepe murdered a blackjack player there. Beth got the signed statement off one of the Vegas dealers."

Adam looked as if his bowels were about to drop several floors—and explosively too, such was his pained expression. His normally benign bonhomie was unable to cope with what he was hearing. He turned toward the river and stood facing it for over a minute. "This is beyond my comfort zone. Not the way chaps behave, Lord Lucan apart." He turned, adjusted his city tie and suggested it was time to head for his office where Billy Evans was due in thirty minutes. "You had better go to the police too."

"I will. But not yet. Remember my promise to Beth?" He waited for the resigned nod of the head. "You, Adam, are pivotal to what happens next. Let me tell you about your new friend Billy Evans." They left the decking and crossed the galleried room, thanked Ursula for breakfast and went to the private elevator. "And prepare to be shocked." Dex gave the listener's arm a friendly punch. "But you must do it—for Beth."

Dex need not have worried. The brisk walk across the Millennium Bridge seemed to bring out the bulldog breed in Adam. "Undercover stuff, eh? Like that movie—*The Third Man*. Spiffing stuff."

Twenty-five floors up above Fenchurch Street, in Adam's office, Dex introduced Billy and an unlikely rapport seemed to be struck. Billy's makeover in Selfridge's had been transformational. His style was casual but understated. In a lightweight grey suit, dark burgundy shirt, and no tie, he looked like someone that Adam could have met in the Grandstand at Ascot racecourse. The ponytail had gone—along with the ear stud and the stubbled look.

Dex had known from a while back that Adam regarded the half-shaved fashion *as neither fish nor fowl, dear boy.* "Makes them all look like Abel Magwitch in *Great Expectations*—thugs and villains."

For his part, Adam, after complaining that you can't teach old dogs new tricks, gradually became enthusiastic about learning Basic Strategy. Dex left them at noon, satisfied that each understood their precise role. Unlike most London casinos, Dukes had made it a positive that they did not open twenty-four hours a day, preferring to close at 8 a.m. with a hearty breakfast for those who wanted it and reopening the gaming tables at 2 p.m. Billy thought that closing at all was unusual. "But mainly," he explained in his flat-vowelled accent, "for their high rollers, mornings will be when they sleep or buy Ferraris or check out their racehorses."

When Adam later reported back, Dex was in the study, satisfied by the experts that no bugs had been placed. Adam had enthused that it had "all been rather jolly" losing less than usual using Basic Strategy. Seemingly, nobody at Dukes had shown any suspicion. "I introduced Billy to FB and told him I was being taught Basic Strategy." He laughed. "And I warned him I would no longer be one of his biggest losers. FB smiled a little and wished me a pleasant afternoon."

"Any opinion from Billy on fixed decks?"

"He refused to say."

Now, as Dex paused on his way up to Father's room, he replayed a plan he had been fermenting since learning Jude was a snooper. From one floor up, he could hear Jude's voice as her rasping Aussie accent carried down the top flight of stairs. He was pleased she was working on stimulation, though he had no idea what techniques specialists like her used.

Her behaviour had given him other food for thought. As expected, Jude had proved to be quite a character and when they had eaten together, Eggs Benedict at lunchtime, the atmosphere had been openly flirtatious—on her part. The previous evening, short of leaping into his bed, she could not have made her availability much more obvious.

She had tested him with the briefest of mini-kilts and a white tank top with nothing underneath so that, as she had sat beside his father, her image was more like a character about to strip off in a cheap porn movie. To add to the image, whenever he entered Father's room, she always seemed to be bending over to pick up something, on one occasion revealing a black thong and on the other some skimpy tiger-themed briefs.

In different circumstances, her fun personality, her stunningly haughty appearance and obvious availability would have been irresistible. Resisting had not been easy but every time she flirted by word or with a glance, he reminded himself of the slightly open drawer. Was she just nosy? Or was there more to it? As he reached the top landing, his pulse was racing as he anticipated what he planned to do.

Dex breezed in. "How's it going? Any improvement?"

Today was no different. Jude was already standing, and now she bent to grab a tissue from her handbag, revealing tanned thighs and scarlet panties beneath her micro-skirt. The hunched and feeble figure of his father was just beside her, his eyes staring at nothing and his shoulders drooping forward in his high-backed armchair. Despite the air fresheners, the room, close to Sir Charles, still smelled faintly of rotting cabbage.

From Jude's iPad came the heavy beat of *Men at Work*, the volume low. He sat down on a low stool to be on a level with his father while Jude resumed her seat opposite on a matching black stool, her legs now firmly apart.

"Too soon to say," Jude responded. "Occasionally, there's a flicker of reaction but my guess, these are nervous ticks rather than actual responses." She crossed her legs extravagantly and was pleased to see that her boss had copped an eyeful. "It's early days."

Dex respected the assured response. She certainly seemed to know the jargon consistent with her references from Westmead Hospital and one of the consultants.

Dex looked at the man he had hated for so long that he could not remember ever liking him. But God! It tore him apart to see him now; short of a miracle, the old boy was beyond all hope. Yet he was aware. *Aware.* That was the worst bit. And short of pneumonia, he could live another twenty years like this. It was an indignity and a punishment that nobody should have to endure.

"Jude, we're out of milk and cookies. I'd like to sit with Father for a while to see if my voice helps him. Can you pop round to the corner shop?" As he spoke, he handed over a ten-pound note and suggested she use the change for something for herself. She nodded and rose inelegantly from her padded stool, pointedly brushing past Dex, her fragrance almost overpowering.

Dex held his breath as he waited for what would happen next. Would she grab her iPad or leave it? She usually carried it everywhere and was forever tapping and sliding her fingers on-screen. He was lucky. It was being charged. Her instinctive grab for it changed to a spin around and a cheery exit.

Dex had no qualms about snooping. He waited till he saw her exit onto the street. Then he was instantly tapping the screen, looking through her Apps until he found her Calendar. With luck, he had four minutes, four vital minutes to get into the real world of Jude Tuson.

Feverishly, he scanned through each recent month, stopping only at pages with a dot denoting an entry. There were many—in fact, most pages had entries. Some made him grin, others made him laugh outright as he skimmed page after page, working backward till suddenly, nine days earlier, he spotted something that made him shudder. He let out a low whistle and raced on for more, finding seven key entries in the past month.

*Is this worse than I feared, or better than I had expected?*

He was unsure.

It was certainly dynamite, even forgetting the flowery references to bondage and studded leather. He wanted to go back further, but in truth he had seen enough. Any more would have been pure voyeurism—but highly entertaining too. He wondered who Mr. Littlun was and if the reinsurance broker, knew her nickname for him.

Rapidly, he cleared the search history and restored the music channel. By the time she slammed the side door returning with coffee, cookies, and muffins, Dex was busily reading aloud from a book about travel in Europe, something his father had always enjoyed. But if he were receptive to the description of the Roman remains at Arles in Southern France, you would never have known.

Not for the first time, but the first time as a serious rational possibility, Dex thought of taking his father to Digitas, a one-way trip to Switzerland. He was uncertain but guessed that assisted suicide was still illegal in England, and on his return he could be prosecuted. But it was the kindest answer. He decided to flag the thought with Jude but here and now was not the place for that.

# CHAPTER TWENTY-EIGHT

Later that day, when Jude was upstairs tending to Sir Charles, Dex shut the study door and Skyped Tiffany. There were just ten days till Space City opened—ten days to destroy the rotten empire.

"Is it better to know or not know?" Tiffany was musing over Dex's question. "My take? Suspicion is draining, debilitating. It leads to paranoia, so yes, you did the right thing. Good on you for finding out. And if I were you, I'd check out her references too."

"I will. Knowing this changes everything."

"Like how?"

"Like everything. By keeping stumm, I can set her up as a double agent."

"That I like." Tiffany's face sent a devious and uncharacteristic grin across the Atlantic. "You going to share with me?"

"Not yet but it involves a tethered goat." Dex was rewarded with a long silence and he saw Tiffany's cheeks being sucked in.

"And the goat would be?"

"One guess."

"Just as well I'm returning at the weekend. You need someone to… get you to *butt out* of crazy, dangerous schemes." They both laughed at the pun but beneath the surface, Dex knew Tiffany was right. If it worked, then great. If it went haywire, then God help him if Carmino was wielding a Bowie knife.

"Any new gossip about Mick?"

"The sports editor has spent hours watching match after match to see if Mick missed too many sitters."

"And the answer?"

"No. Which only leaves Creole Henry, or some other cuckold. One of our braver journalists door-stepped Creole. He denied everything. Said he was at a boxing match in Manchester. Probably true—but then, guys like him don't always do their own dirty work."

"We now know Mick had threatened Dukes." He paused to look

over his shoulder to make sure he was still alone. "According to Adam, Pepe has now told the police that Glenn was due in the evening he was murdered."

"But I bet he said nothing of the jail threat," she laughed. Then she checked her watch. "Almost eleven. Time to go. I'm doing a signing in Santa Monica. The limo is due. Look, Dex. You take care. I mean it." Then for the first time ever, there was a touch of emotion. "Anything happened, I would miss you."

Dex couldn't stop himself from responding. "And I need you. Back here."


It was twenty-four hours later that the relief nurse arrived to look after Sir Charles so that Dex could take Jude to Dukes for dinner. Dex was keen to keep everything seeming normal between them even though he now knew that the references were bogus. They had been a *scan, cut and paste* job, done well but not well enough to withstand enquiries made down under in Sydney.

He had also done some errands in the West End before hurrying back. Just as he had hoped, a scrap of paper left on his desk with flight numbers to Zurich had been moved—not much, but enough to be sure that Jude had been sniffing around again.

"Forget the money. Only results matter, and I'm running out of time."

He had hurried back mid-afternoon from McKay's bookshop. Just as he had hoped, a scrap of paper he had left on his desk with some flight numbers to Zurich had been moved—not much, but enough to be sure that Jude had been sniffing around again.

Just after eight, Dex called up the stairs and Jude appeared in a slinky and strapless aquamarine outfit with her flowing hair beautifully coiffured. "You look just great," he enthused like a guy on a first date. No doubt she expected to be bedded on their return, after a romantic dinner and some laughter-filled hours in the casino. Knowing she was more of a Judas than a Jude, he was going to disappoint her.

After signing Jude in as a guest, FB appeared and greeted them with his usual embarrassed charm. He led them straight to the restaurant, Dex suggesting they should eat at once to allow more time at the tables. The maître 'd showed them to a circular corner table with a pink cloth, a small table lamp, heavy silverware, and the finest Riedel wineglasses. "Great table." Dex smiled encouragingly at Jude.

"Flirty too, tucked away where nobody can hear us."

"Yeah, lot's to talk about." Dex threw in a wink as he forced himself not to laugh at the image of Carmino somewhere in the building, listening to every word. After a half bottle of Krug had been poured and glasses chinked, Dex got straight to the point. "Jude, this isn't going to be easy. I'll come straight to the point." She put down her glass, looking uneasy. "Since we planned to come here on your night off, things have changed—at least, my thinking has changed. And please don't take this the wrong way. This is nothing to do with you. You're doing a great job but…" He hesitated. "It's about…well, me and Father."

"Go on. Tell me I'm fired."

"I wouldn't put it like that. I think the Americans put it rather better—yes…*I'm letting you go.*"

"Why?" There was no anger in the question, but no easy acceptance either.

"I've agonised about keeping Father alive. I can't take seeing him suffer a moment longer. Tomorrow, he's off to a residential unit in Northampton while I go to Switzerland to check out Dignitas. I think a dignified end is kinder."

"No worries, mate." She paused. "Jeez, and I thought I was getting through better to him today."

"Maybe you were but I'll be blunt. Right now, let's say he's 100 percent useless. Is it kind to improve him to 98 percent, or even to 90? So he drools rather slower?" He topped up their glasses. "I don't think so."

"So he's going to this unit."

"While I'm meeting the Dignitas team at Forch. It's near Zurich. I'm discussing a humane end for him."

"Did Sir Charles ever express a wish for this if his health ended up this way? A living will or whatever."

"No. Father no doubt considered himself invincible." Dex saw her weigh up that answer.

"Your call, Dex. Poor you."

"I consulted a solicitor. He warned I could be prosecuted. Well, so be it." He was sure that her sharp brain would be racing.

Jude's reaction surprised Dex. She leaned across and clasped his hand. "Dex, that's brave. I'll survive and despite my nursing instincts, I agree with you. The law is a load of shite." She squeezed his hand tighter.

"Do you have somewhere to move back to?"

Dex noticed the slight hesitation before she replied. "No sweat, mate. I'll land on my feet quickly enough."

"Thanks! I suggest you leave before my flight to Zurich."

"Whatever. Tomorrow's cool with me."

"Let's order and you explain Punto Banco. Roulette seems far easier."

"Easier to lose too." They both laughed as Dex imagined Reverse Labouchère delivering a win to make Carmino's eyes water. A huge win without even playing would be better, but that depended on the goat and the predator.

"I could slaughter a lobster, followed by a rare T-bone?" Jude's voice cut short the dreams that were taking him far ahead of himself.

"Good choice."

Having been alerted by FB, through the bug in the table lamp Carmino could hear every word. As the conversation changed to food, he had already decided that he would use Jude once again in a different capacity.

He chewed a delicately cut smoked salmon sandwich on brown as he weighed it up. Dex kept anything significant locked away or password-protected, so unless she got pillow talk tonight after giving him a right old dicking, she wasn't doing much good there anyway. And so far, in her words, she reckoned *he had the sex drive of a castrated monk.*

As he listened to her explaining Punto Banco, he played with the figures in front of him. These showed the secret profits being siphoned off from the hot money. Most nights, he had one and sometimes up to five different high rollers playing in the casino, always assisted and signed in by a friendly casino hostess. Each hostess was great eye candy for the generally older men, a role he had agreed with Jude until Dex's job offer seemed a better opportunity.

These new players had made their wealth from tax fraud and political or corporate corruption, mainly in Brussels. Their bribes and dirty deals had led to hidden money in banks in Switzerland, Austria, Liechtenstein, or Campione d'Italia. These undisclosed bank accounts were now under constant threat of exposure and most of the powerful figures were desperate to launder the money without discovery.

With false IDs provided for entry as guests and using its second set of books, Dukes could work this a little longer till Space City became a cash cow. Carmino had no illusions; even with the blind eye from corrupted officers from the UK's Gambling Commission, this was no long-term game.

For now, the risk had to be taken due to Letizione's bad management, but in under two weeks, every Space City slot would seat an excited gambler, the roulette wheels would be spinning and the craps tables would be crammed with noisy drunken optimists. The twelve bars, seven restaurants, three nightclubs, two stage shows and the huge conference rooms would all be thronged. The cash would flow and he could close down the scams, become legitimate once again.

He looked in the safe and from under a wad of fifty thousand US dollar bills he pulled out his own trio of false passports, credit cards and driving licences. He flicked through them, reviewing yet again whether he could disappear if he had to. In his own hidden accounts, there was now enough to spend a million a year for life and still have change.

*So long as you're not in jail, my old son.*

*Yeah! Right on!*

He knew that the Gambling Commission worked on a risk-assessment formula. On that basis, he reckoned a blue-chip casino like Dukes was below their daily radar on one count but above it on another. Cheating, under-age, or inebriated gamblers were the playthings of the smaller grind casinos and in the UK, they were pretty much kosher. But London casinos, like Dukes, handled such big money that the Commission assessed them as ripe for money laundering.

Under the deal with the Swiss lawyer, every client playing at Dukes was leaving with 85% of the cash he had arrived with—his casino loss of 15% a small price to pay for a cheque, seemingly from blue-chip Dukes—a nice freshly laundered casino cheque that he could present to carefully identified banks in Limassol, Dubai, the Seychelles and even one in London where no questions would be asked.

But none of the cash introduced by these players would feature other than in the parallel bank account, the profits of which were being disbursed to him, to the Swiss lawyer, the Vegas bankers, and grudgingly to Enzo Letizione. His own share passed through a Caymans bank in the name of a Belize corporation using nominee shareholders and directors linked with a Panamanian foundation. It was then automatically transferred to an account in Dubai in the name of a Mauritius corporation in which his name appeared nowhere.

During the height of the Dubai property market crash, another anonymous corporation had bought a penthouse apartment for his use not far from the Burj Khalifa, the world's tallest building. The throbbing and ever-changing expat business community in Dubai presented the ideal location in which to disappear and reappear with a new identity for a new life of pleasure and luxury.

Pepe finished totting up the figures with a satisfying murmur of *good, excellent.* But running parallel accounts and grabbing every chance to cheat the regulars was a short-term play only. An overzealous bean-counter or an arsehole like Mick Glenn shouting the odds with no evidence could destroy everything.

Under Duke's licence from the Gambling Commission, with cash sums like ten million pounds constantly arriving, the casino was obliged to send Suspicious Activity Reports to the National Crime Agency. But with his cashier in the cage fixed to channel the hot money outside the Profit & Loss account and off–Balance Sheet, Carmino reckoned to avoid making any SARS.

For just a while, a short while, longer.

He locked the passports and figures away while in the background, he could hear Jude trying to explain Punto Banco. He poured himself a glass of chilled Chablis and finished his sandwich as he planned what to say when he went downstairs. Then, as he adjusted his bow tie and slipped on his DJ, he realised he had been humming *The Gambler.* That was pleasing too.

Dex spotted Carmino enter the restaurant, slithering over the thick carpeting. He stopped at every table for either a quick word, a friendly squeeze of an arm or a shared moment of laughter. You had to give it to the man, he certainly knew how to work a room, schmoozing the men and charming the women with suggestive nods or smiles. When he reached their table, he insisted that Dex remained seated as he addressed Jude.

"It's Jude, isn't it? You've been in before." He stroked his chin thoughtfully as he tried to recall. "Yes. With that Spanish insurance broker, wasn't it?" Dex suppressed a smile at the thought of Mr Littlun. Jude confirmed the recollection.

"Didn't we talk about you helping Dukes to look after our members and guests?"

"Right on!" Jude sounded astounded at his recollection. "I remember now."

"Well, that offer stands but I expect you've found a job since then. Nursing, wasn't it?"

"Care support, yes, but…" She paused. "Well, mattrafact, I've been looking after Dex's father."

Dex caught Pepe's eye. "You know, the crash that killed…"

"Yes, yes. Of course." Pepe was quick to intervene. "So how is your father?"

"He needs twenty-four-seven care in a special home—at least for now."

"I see," murmured Pepe, looking his most sympathetic, his eyes oozing sincerity.

"And," chipped in Jude, "that leaves me looking for a job."

"Well, if you want a break from using care skills, let me know. Think about it. But the hours are demanding."

"Look, Mr. Carmino, I mean, can we talk about this? Like seriously? "The details? We don't want to bore Dex with this."

Dex looked at Jude and then up at Carmino. "Carry on. I'll play roulette. The way I've treated you, I'd feel better if you landed a job."

Jude leaned across and patted his wrist. "Nah, no worries, don't blame yourself. Look, Mr. Carmino, I'm as full as a goog, so why not talk now?"

Dex watched them head for the bar, chatting comfortably with each other. He declined port or brandy and instead sat quietly. Playing dumb during their charade had been difficult as he relived Jude's mentions of someone called PC in her calendar. She had lunched with PC at The Ivy the day after visiting Dukes with the Spaniard.

After that, they had lunched together often, but she had also spent several afternoons and nights at his home in Holland Park, studded leather and all. Several of the entries were punctuated with three or even four exclamation marks. On two occasions, he had spotted his own initials, FD—the timing consistent with her job application having been prompted by Carmino.

Though being civil to the casino boss had left him feeling unclean, despite everything, he still liked the carefree zaniness that was Jude. As he headed for the roulette, his conclusions were that she was an okay person—just a young kid on the make who had fallen for Carmino's charms.

It was over an hour before Jude reappeared and excitedly tapped Dex on the shoulder. He waited till the ball landed in number 10 black, a win for him, before looking over his shoulder.

"Get this! I got the job. I start tomorrow."

"That's great. When I finish playing, tell me all about it. You joining me? Or will it be Punto Banco?"

"Punto Banco for me. When you've lost everything here, come and watch me win," she laughed.

"You might have a long wait," Dex grinned. "I'm up over £17,000. Beat that if you can!" He watched her turn away and saw a number of other men's eyes follow her as she strutted with self-confidence beyond her years to the Punto Banco. Dex played a few more spins, the good run continuing and when £40,000 ahead, he quit.

But he was not happy.

Yet again his secret filming would confirm nothing. Almost as soon as he had sat down at the table, One-Eye had been moved away, never to return. Not once had he seen Ned, a young Cockney dealer, play any tricks at all. Having stuffed his cash chips into his jacket pockets, he spotted One-Eye and Jeb Miller at a table where the minimum bets were £10,000 on the outside or a total of £50,000 on the layout.

Playing at the table where a couple of older men that Dex had never seen before. Each was accompanied by a young woman, dressed to kill and in both cases a good twenty-five years younger. *Perhaps this is what Carmino had in mind for Jude.*

Dex sat down at the table, impressed that the next spin was worth well over a million to the winners. Feeling excited at having the chance to film One-Eye stealing the occasional chip from these high-rolling players, he settled in, his cufflink filming across the table and the tiepin aimed toward One-Eye. Stealing even one of these high-value chips would be mega for the casino.

The two men, both Russians, seemed more interested in keeping their shot glasses filled than the action on the table. It was the young women, both English, who placed the huge bets. Dex spotted that there had not been a red number for eight spins. He put a £10,000 cash chip backing red.

"Getting more confident, are we, Mr. D?" Jeb Miller leaned forward and sounded friendly.

"I had a good win on the other table. Hopefully, my luck will last."

It did not, as more black numbers hit, but one of the Russians had a 20-high stack of £5000 chips backing 33 Black, a win worth £3.5 million. Making sure that his twin cameras were perfectly positioned, Dex was sure One-Eye would cheat the winner, who was noisily nibbling the brunette's ear. But nothing happened. One-Eye paid out the correct amount, a huge win, which the stocky brick-faced Russian barely seemed to notice.

Dex won the next four spins and quit over £55,000 ahead but not once had a player been cheated and neither had One-Eye been moved on. It was puzzling. Hand in pocket, he strolled toward the Punto Banco, wondering whether Mick Glenn's outburst had stopped the casino from cheating. Or perhaps a different scam was in operation.

Deep in thought, he never noticed Adam Yarbury, who was seated at the blackjack table with Billy Evans. "Dex! What a pleasure!" Shocked out of his thoughts, Dex turned to Adam and smiled.

"Come on, Adam! I'm celebrating my first big win. Want to join me?" There was a pause before Adam responded with a shake of the head.

"Hit it, Adam," said Billy. "Remember what I said. You've got sixteen. The dealer has a king as his up-card. You've got to take another card."

"But I'll go bust."

"Just assume that the dealer's hole card, that's the one you can't see, is a 10. He'll have twenty, so…you'll lose anyway. Go on, Adam."

Dex watched as Adam, reluctantly and with a grimace at Dex, signalled for another card, which was a 5 giving him a great hand at 21. The dealer then flipped his hole card, which was indeed a 10. Realising he had won, Adam's face looked as if a magician had produced a brace of rabbits from a hat.

"Dex, let me introduce Billy Evans. He is teaching me some damnably clever thing called Basic Strategy. Seems more like kamikaze to me but blow me down, it seems to work!"

"Hello, Billy! You'll have your work cut out changing Adam's habits of a lifetime."

Billy laughed. "Tell me about it!" He returned his attention to the table almost at once.

Dex was about to head for the bar when he remembered the Punto Banco. He stood behind Jude and saw that the £10,000 float he had provided was now depleted.

"Struggling?"

"I'm just playing for Tied Hands now. This is the 61st hand of the shoe without a tie. Ridiculous. Typically by now there would've been three, maybe four, and sometimes seven."

Dex nodded as if he understood as he watched her place £300 cash chips in a box marked *Tie*. Bank won the next hand 7 over 1, and again he saw Jude backing the tie, this time with £500 of his money. Out came the cards, a total of 8 for both Player and Bank. There was a loud whoop from Jude. "Tied Hand!" She turned to him and held his arm. "See—I'm paid out at 8 to 1. That's £4,000 smackeroos."

Dex looked at her chips. "That puts you ahead! Fancy a drink?"

She shook her head. "Ties may repeat! I learned that in Sydney. No logic, but it often happens." She bet £2000 and they watched as the Player's cards totalled the perfect hand of 9. It did not look promising when the first card to the Bank was a 3, but with a flourish, the dealer turned over the final card. It was a 6—a tie on 9.

This time Jude half-stood and rewarded him with a hug as if it were his doing. The dealer pushed across £16,000 as winnings. "Quit now and I'll split the winnings with you."

"You're on!" Jude collected her chips and they cashed in at the cage. "Winning always makes me thirsty…and horny." She gave him a nudge in the ribs and a peck on the cheek.

As they settled in the bar, Dex restricted himself to a Spitfire beer whilst Jude downed a couple of Moscow Mules. She was trying to explain why sometimes there were three cards dealt to each hand in Punto Banco when her phone beeped that she had a text message arriving. She glanced at it, completely unfazed at Pepe's question about keys. She replied confirming that she had already made a duplicate set for him. "That's Mr. Carmino. Wants me here by 6 p.m. tomorrow."

*It was time to tether the goat.*

"So you use an iPad and a regular phone?" He tried to sound casual as he asked the loaded question.

"Yeah. Covers all bases for me. And you?"

It was just the response Dex wanted. "I used to take my laptop everywhere. I mean, like my entire life is on there but since I bought a smartphone, well, now I just take that on short journeys, like over-nighting to Zurich. I'll synch the new stuff up to the laptop when I get back."

*Got that, Jude?*

*Got that, Pepe?*

"Makes sense." Jude called for another drink just as the two Russians departed, looking very chirpy for men with three chins and cheeks flabby enough to lose a tongue in.

She downed the third Moscow Mule pretty smartish, so he sank his beer and suggested it was time to leave, but with her coming on so strong, he had to plan for what lay ahead. It was not going to be easy.

*What was it she had wanted to find out?*

*What had she been looking for?*

*Had she found it?*

*Unlikely.*

*Something that Carmino wanted to know.*

*Not the length of my dick when aroused, that's for sure.*

# CHAPTER TWENTY-NINE

The limo collected Jude shortly before 11 a.m., even before the private ambulance had arrived for Sir Charles. By then, Dex had been working discreetly on the phone and internet. He placed her three suitcases and several totebags into the back of the BMW. After giving her a hug, quite a lingering one, the vehicle moved away. He saw her smile, sad and wistful as she blew him a kiss.

Inside the house, it felt empty without her. Her personality seemed to linger, her raucous laugh still seeming to resonate down the stairs and from room to room. Life played curious tricks, he decided, as he toasted some cheese and brewed some English Breakfast tea.

Tiffany, who he fancied something rotten, had played a standoffish game, while with Jude there had been role reversal. In the taxi returning from Dukes, she had come on pretty strong, smooching up to him with her wandering left hand making her intentions very plain.

No sooner had they entered the kitchen and the alarm had been deactivated than she had flung her arms around his neck and kissed him firmly on the mouth, thrusting her hips toward him. No question, as she writhed against his lean body, his own reaction was immediate, and when she felt the hardening, she pushed against him even more forcibly, whimpering and simpering into his ear.

Dex knew that he was close to the tipping point. Never in a situation like this had he ever backed off, but then, typically he was the instigator. Now, his testosterone charged instincts were being tested almost beyond endurance, as she eased back gasping and moaning for him to *come on, come on.*

But he didn't.

Instead, he pulled away, gradually releasing himself from her grip, forcing himself to think of her in bed with Pepe Carmino, an image sufficient to make his erection shrivel to Condition Docile. In the half-light, she looked at him questioningly. "What's the matter, Dex? Don't you fancy a hot Aussie girl?"

"You felt the evidence." He saw her eyes flash understanding. "There's someone else?"

Dex saw the escape route. "Yes—but right now, she's in the USA."

"Jeez! I'm not telling if you're not. Come on!"

But he didn't.

"I promised I'd Skype her." He grasped Jude's hand and led her through the hall and stopped at the foot of the stairs by the study. "I'll regret this because, believe me, in different circumstances, we might have become an item. I'm sorry, really sorry." He gave her an affectionate hug that turned into a long moment before Jude pulled away.

"And I shall miss you." Her sincerity shone through in the darkened hallway. Her voice even had a slight emotional croak as she continued. "Dex—there's not many around like you. Loyal, strong, sexy to a fault. Maybe if things don't work out with this American girl, you'll remember me." For a moment, Dex saw tears in her eyes before she turned away to conceal her emotion as she climbed the stairs, two at a time.

After she had gone to her room and replaced the relief carer, it took Dex several minutes before he could bring himself to call Tiffany. To her, he was just a friend. To him, she was…? He was unsure. Was he starstruck, especially now that she was big-time? Or was it lust and the heat of the chase? Did he just want to prove a point—that he could succeed with her? Or was there something deeper? Ten minutes later, he was no nearer any conclusion. He booted up the laptop and Tiffany appeared, her eyes looking tired from her travels and time zone differences.

Tiffany's big news was unsettling. "I've been offered a three-book contract and an American TV network want a series on my work in Africa. I'll be over here a great deal."

He hoped his disappointment did not show. "Terrific! If I can help in Africa, I will. And not just with money."

"The tethered goat?"

"The stake's in the ground. Besides which, long story, Jude's leaving and Father's going to a special unit."

"Interesting but listen, Dex—I've been thinking. You've got the evidence from Panama. There is your evidence of cheating. Perhaps this Billy will prove more at blackjack. Even Adam thinks something strange is going on —all the new faces turning up with big money.

You've got Adam's evidence of Mick's threat. You've got the evidence that Beth was scared for her life. You've got two dead dealers in Las Vegas, the missing truck driver. Surely there's enough for the police without you playing the goat? Hell, don't they normally slit the throat of a sacrificial goat?" She paused for effect. "And Carmino is a psychopath, for God's sake."

Dex drummed his fingers on the desktop as he looked at the pleading half-smile on Tiffany's face. He knew she was right but his promise to Beth nagged like toothache. "Trust the police? After the house fire and their failure to find the murderers? Letting this truck driver slip through their fingers? Can't do it." There was a long silence and Tiffany looked unconvinced, so he continued. "I want to deliver a dossier to the FBI. They don't pussyfoot."

"A man's gotta do—you know the rest." With an irritated shake of the head, Tiffany trotted out the unfinished cliché. "You think the tethered goat will make Carmino bleat?" Tiffany's narrowed lips showed her scorn. For a moment, Dex was angered until he realised this was not the journalist speaking. This was a caring friend fighting tears.

"Tiffany, whatever the danger from Carmino, this could be the clincher."

For the second time in less than thirty minutes, he saw a woman shedding tears. She produced a small hankie and dabbed at her cheeks. "Dex," she faltered with more dabbing of her eyes. "Since we've been apart, I've realised what you mean to me. The goat was the clincher."

"Jealous of my goat? There's no need. It's not even a pretty one." He laughed and it seemed to do the trick because he saw her face respond with a watery smile.

Gradually, her helpless look changed to reproachful and then to reluctant admiration. "Dex, you're impossible!" She put the hankie aside but still spoke falteringly, her voice breaking. "So when is all this happening?"

"UK time, tomorrow night. When Jude thinks I'm in Switzerland."

"Switzerland? What's that about?"

Dex ignored the details. "Jude thinks the house will be empty. She also knows that my laptop will be here."

"Carmino might break in?"

"I'll forget to collect Jude's keys. Carmino needs to know whether

I went to Panama, what Beth had uncovered and whether I spoke to Glenn."

"And your plan?"

He smiled. "You don't want to know. See you on Saturday. I'll meet your flight. No kidding."

Tiffany laughed for a flickering moment at the silly pun. "Stay safe." Once again, her eyes started to fill with tears as she cut the connection.


When the private ambulance arrived, Dex had expected to travel, but the two paramedics discouraged him. He used the time to prepare for Carmino. *If he took the bait.* He was interrupted by the private eye who had been watching Carmino's penthouse in Clarendon Road, Holland Park. "The target arrived. Moved in, I'd say. Yes. Carmino is there too."

In the afternoon, he met Gus McKay who was almost invisible between the stacks of books, parceled and ready to go. In tartan trews and yellow waistcoat, he added colour to the brown of the endless wrapping paper and the grey of the walls. It was a brief meeting, very much to the point.

"A private eye in Vegas?" McKay's tic went ballistic as he racked his memory. "This guy will know one. He's an attorney, as sharp as they come. In Vegas that's saying something. Mention my name or he'll bill you a thousand bucks just for answering the phone."

"My second request is trickier." Dex ran through what he needed and why.

There was a long silence as McKay absentmindedly spun a roulette wheel in his back office. Only as the ball slowed and dropped onto number 17 did the Scot speak. "17—a lucky number." He looked Dex straight in the eye. "I was wrong. I underestimated you when we first met. You're an evil bastard, aren't you?"

"I'll take that as a compliment, not a question." Dex was rewarded with a widening smile. As if reluctant to say anything out loud, the Scot wrote down a name and details.

"Use me as the introducer only. My name or not, he'll skin you alive. Greed is his creed. He's as mean as hell."

"Money is not an issue."

"He's a perfectionist. He'll do the business."

Still fired up by the meeting and running on a double espresso, Dex headed for Lillywhites, the sports suppliers at Piccadilly Circus. Then it was a quick race to the spyware supplier just behind Park Lane and on to an ocean supplies store beside Charing Cross Station. He then found what he needed at an office equipment specialist in the Strand.

The final essential was trickier. Trying to look unconcerned, he went into the *Naughty Nocterne* sex shop on Archer Street in Soho. Going in was bad enough but even worse was buying what he needed. *Should have worn a long and dirty raincoat*, he told himself as he rummaged through the weird accessories that obviously helped some customers to get their rocks off. The bored-looking woman at the cash-desk had seen all human depravity before and never gave him a second look as she accepted his money. At least she stashed the purchases in a plain bag.

He hailed a taxi and after dropping everything off at Porcupine House, was just in time to dash to the Sherlock Holmes pub off Trafalgar Square. He was due to meet Billy Evans.

It was then that an unwelcome thought struck him.

*Had Carmino had him tailed?*

*Today's shopping, even the visit to the sex shop, was no problem.*

*But Billy Evans?*

*It was not a comfortable thought.*

*Top, top confidential.*

As the taxi headed toward the famous pub, he was passing the long and weathered brick wall of Lord's Cricket Ground. For the first time today, he glanced behind him. A mile further on, he did it again and then checked after the taxi took a left, right and left through some back-doubles. He saw nothing suspicious but he varied the instructions.

"Forget the Sherlock Holmes. Take me to the River Entrance of the Savoy Hotel."

When he got out, he immediately entered Embankment Gardens opposite the hotel. There were still quite a few people about in the late afternoon but he reckoned that if he were being followed, he would spot somebody, as concealment was impossible in the open spaces between there and Charing Cross. He walked with no great speed for about 150 yards and then took a seat outside the café and immediately looked back.

He saw the usual mix of Londoners—office workers, tourists, mothers pushing prams and lovers arm in arm. Was there a private eye among them? Every person seemed very much in place. Nobody suddenly paused to tie a shoelace or stopped to look at the view.

After a couple of moments, he moved on until he reached the magnificent statue of Robert Burns, the Scottish poet. He stopped suddenly to look back but there were no familiar faces, nobody suspicious at all. He hurried up Villiers Street, took the steep flight of steps into Charing Cross station and out through the other exit. Even then he did not head for the pub, instead doubling back through the crowded concourse, looking out for anybody he had seen more than once.

As satisfied as he could be that nobody was trailing him, he cornered Trafalgar Square and entered the pub. Billy Evans was already there.

*Oh God!*

*Had Carmino been suspicious of Billy? Had him followed?*

Dex looked around the cosy half-light of the atmospheric bar. If he had, there was nobody obviously interested in them as he joined Billy who was looking at the evening paper. Billy declined a drink, saying he was sticking to water. Dex ordered an orange and lemonade for himself and felt pretty virtuous as he did so. Memorabilia of Holmes and Watson were everywhere. Plaster casts of the hound's footprints and Holmes' pipe in a glass case set the tone.

Though Billy still looked transformed, his face was a train wreck and his hands were shaking. *Was Billy a risk too far?* He didn't need another Mick Glenn disaster.

The opening chitchat went well enough but the occasional body twitch kept stoking unease. When Billy mentioned little Emily, Dex felt a sense of responsibility to her. She and her mum were so helpless and dependent on Billy's money.

*Not your problem.*

*You owe Billy nothing.*

But he couldn't get to convince himself of that.

Images of Emily sitting with Pooh Bear played on his mind, her laughter reminding him of of baby Jamie who should now be running round the house playing with scooters and hitting balls.

He glanced up at the life-sized head of the Hound of the Baskervilles fixed to the wall. Its huge eyes flashed insanity almost like the figure sitting opposite. To the left was a portrait of the great detective. The contrast was remarkable. The shrewd beakiness of Sherlock Holmes' face was so calm, so unhurried. The watchful eyes looked into the distance with measured disdain. Sherlock's look seemed to be reproving Dex about his choice of associate. *Elementary, my dear Dex. Compassion, yes. But involvement, no.*

"Billy, before we get into detail, I want a straight answer. Are you back on the white stuff? Are you struggling? Your hands are shaking. You need to shape up."

It was an age before Billy responded. He looked crestfallen. "It's been hard. Much harder than I thought. Cold turkey, that is. If you want to end this, I can't blame you." It was an incomplete answer and Dex knew it.

"Did you get to bed last night? It looks as if the Gaderene swine have just crapped in your eyeballs. You're no use to me like this."

"Late night after I left Dukes."

"Cocaine? Something worse?"

Billy shook his head. "Booze. Buckets of it. At my digs, I couldn't sleep. I never made it to the day job."

"When did you last eat?"

"A quick bite yesterday evening with Adam in a Thai restaurant on Piccadilly."

"How about steak pie and chips now? Soak up the alcohol?" Dex stared hard trying to get across both irritation and sympathy.

"You reckon?"

"I'll order for you. Meantime, buy a razor and shaving cream. Spruce up in the Gents'. You owe it to Adam for this evening."

When he returned, Billy looked better for his shave and sluice down. "So let's cut to the quick. Is the blackjack fixed?"

Billy paused,his fork filled with pastry in midair. "I'd say but I can't prove it. Not credibly. I need to play longer and at different tables."

"So how do they do it?"

Billy popped a chip into his mouth using his fingers and finished chewing. "I have a theory. Adam couldn't be there this afternoon. He was watching cricket at the Oval. Otherwise we could have road- tested my theory. Or at least," he laughed, "I could. Adam has not the slightest idea what is going on."

He dipped a chip in his ketchup, examined it for a moment, and then chewed hungrily. "Don't get me wrong. Adam's a real gent. He's intelligent too but at the blackjack tables, his brain is never in gear. I expect he's been cheated for years."

"Why the afternoon and not the evening?"

"I'd rather not speculate. Not yet."

"In a couple of days? That would give you two afternoons. How long do you need?"

"See, Dex, it's like this. Firstly I got to play enough hands, enough shoes to prove that statistically the games are bent."

"By rigging the number of good and bad cards?"

"Exactly. So, if you want me to give a statement that will hold up with the Gambling Commission, I need to know how, in a regulated environment, they can fix the decks. That's where the afternoons come in. Trust me."

"Don't get me wrong, Billy. I trust your expertise, no sweat. It's your demons that worry me." Dex rose to leave. "You okay for money? A taxi to Dukes?" Just a quick glance and Billy's face gave him the answer. "Here's two hundred to keep you going for a couple of days. Don't piss it against the wall or shove it up your nose." He gave Billy a friendly smile. "And remember, stay in character when you're with Adam." As he left, he found he was chewing his lip in frustration.

Billy was a walking time-bomb.

But essential.

# CHAPTER THIRTY

Jude stretched her arms as she lay in the black silk sheets of Pepe Carmino's bed. It was late afternoon. She heard the front door shut as Pepe headed for Dukes. She was alone, free to do nothing except relax before luxuriating in the Jacuzzi bath. Later, she planned to dress in a sheer navy-blue off-the shoulder while hosting some rich Croatian who Pepe wanted her to meet in his hotel suite. He needed his false ID delivered and, if need be, she was *to help him relax* before going through the charade of gambling at Andy or One-Eye's table.

On Pepe's side of the king-sized bed lay his black mask designed to cover his eyes and nose. She knew well enough that Pepe's erection turned on creating pain, fear, and domination. On the floor were his studded leather vest and a jock-thong, also in leather with studs back and front. Her thighs were still sore from when he had pounced before ripping the damned thing off.

In Saudi Arabia, she had occasionally refused weirder requests involving mirrors and panes of glass, but generally she had played along with fantasists and dressing-up games. The casino boss, though, was pushing her to the outer edges. Forcing her to wear a spider gag had been a step or ten too far. The device had held her jaws wide apart while her wrists and ankles were restrained.

As she lay there, her jaw still aching and her mouth tasting foul, her thoughts turned to Dex. Men rarely refused her invitations but he had been different—old-fashioned really, staying faithful to some American. *Face it, girl. You liked him. Enjoyed flirting and teasing. Hated spying on him and pretending to look after his father.*

At first, Pepe's suggestion of nursing the old man had excited her but the better she had got to know Dex, the more she resented what Pepe wanted done. Maybe they might meet soon at Dukes and then maybe, just maybe, she could set up the chance to show him what he had missed. So long as Pepe did not find out.

Apart from his perverted pleasures, Pepe had treated her well so that accepting his offer to move in had been simple enough, especially with his promise of *you and me* private jet trips to exotic places. Yet listening to him barking and growling on the phone, she had no illusions: he was someone not to be crossed. One afternoon a few weeks back, she had heard him shouting abuse at the cleaner who had dropped by unexpectedly. She understood what casual acquaintances never did: his charm was barely skin deep.

Restless now, she got up and hung her clothes in the walk-in closet that lined one side of the huge and pastel-shaded bedroom. When she had done, she was intrigued to look inside the end where Pepe kept all his suits and leather paraphernalia. Besides spider gags, what else lay ahead to turn him on?

She slid back the treble length louvred door and saw everything neatly arranged, from casual through to blazers to suits to DJs and then an evening suit. Beyond that was the leather—singlets, Y-fronts, bracelets, wrist-grips, and on a series of shelves were all types of butt plugs, cock rings, and giant black dildos that he had yet to try on her. On the floor lay his whip and a large paddle-slapper, which he had promised for *a special treat*.

*Not for me, it isn't*, she had thought - but said nothing.

Out of curiosity, as she rummaged in an eye-level shelf she spotted another gadget that she had never seen before. Seemingly designed for a contortionist or as a challenge for Houdini, she pulled at the thick leather straps and metallic rings to get it out. It was heavy and fell with a clatter to the floor. She pushed it this way and that, trying to understand just how she would be immersed within it. Then on the shelf she saw the instructions and a padlock and key.

She pulled out the leaflet and her mouth dropped open as she studied the diagram. Her hand trembled at the prospect of being strapped into an extreme position with no ability to move whatsoever, her neck strapped to her knees.

She was about to replace the gadget and instructions when she spotted something else, tucked away at the very back. She pulled at a belt and out followed a sheath, and in it a knife, a huge knife such as she had never before seen except in movies. The blade measured at least nine inches, with a tip so sharp that it could instantly draw blood. Feeling very shaky now, she shoved the knife back into the sheath and returned everything to where it had originally been. For a moment, she sat on the bed, but then hurried through to the drinks cabinet and poured herself a very large neat bourbon.

She felt no better for it and poured another.

# CHAPTER THIRTY-ONE

Dex was restless as he perched uncomfortably. As far as Jude and Pepe knew, he had taken the early evening flight and would now be in Zurich, ready to visit Dignitas in the morning. Instead, he was alone in Porcupine House, a tethered goat. As the minutes ticked by toward darkness, he had become intensely aware of the high risk he was running. Several times, he had to force himself to stay in his hiding place, telling himself that he owed it to Beth not to chicken out now.

Tiffany's words rang in his ear. *Stay safe.* Risking an encounter with a psychopath after dark was far removed from *staying safe.* Of course, Carmino might not take the bait but planting Jude showed his desperation to probe whatever Dex was doing. Surely the empty house and a key for entry would be irresistible.

*Oh my God!*

*There's a thought!*

Perhaps he would not come alone! He had not planned for that. He shivered and grabbed a biscuit for comfort. From top to toe now, Dex was dressed in black, awaiting something that might never even happen. Did he now still want it to happen? Or did he secretly hope that he would spend the night in Father's study undisturbed?

As he shifted position to kneel uncomfortably in the darkened room, his face and hands blackened, he liked the reassurance of the baseball bat that he had bought in Lillywhites. He hoped a single swipe would be enough. He was positioned behind the study door, where a large artificial plant provided additional cover. He swigged from a bottle of water and nibbled on a tuna sandwich, shaking as once again he swapped positions.

Two hours earlier, Jude had briefed Pepe on the geography of Porcupine House. He had taken Jude's keys and memorised the code for the burglar alarm. While Jude finished her tea, scones, and strawberry jam, he was dressing, as he always did, in smart-casual for his office work in Dukes. He hovered by his closet, debating whether to take his Bowie. *The place was going to be empty. But then…I might be disturbed by a nosey neighbour. Play safe and take it.*

After kissing Jude goodbye and telling her he would catch up with her much later, he set off in his Aston Martin for the short commute from Holland Park along the Bayswater Road. The journey at this time of day was rarely more than twelve minutes and as he drove beside the trees beside Hyde Park, he always had just about enough time to plan the evening ahead. Today was no exception. By the time he reached Marble Arch, an idea was developing, *a very good idea.* He kicked himself for not thinking of it before.

Jude knew what Pepe had planned for the evening but she was still unclear *why* he was so obsessed with Dex. All he had explained was that he had been tipped off that Dex had been planning a major heist to rob or cheat the casino—maybe at roulette. She doubted whether she had the full story though the roulette wheel at Porcupine House *had* pointed to something a bit unusual. "Tell the cops, then," she had volunteered.

"Look, if Space City had not been one almighty snafu and I wasn't bailing it out with hot money, I'd be down to Scotland Yard straight off. But I can't afford coppers or anyone sniffing round the place, not for a while yet. But if I can find out what the hell Dex is up to, I can take care of it—in my own way."

Those chilling words coming so soon after spotting the Bowie knife the previous day made her go through to the bedroom to check that it was still there.

It was not.

For a moment she was rooted to the spot, staring at where the knife had been.

*Panic over!*

*Dex is in Zurich.*

She flounced through to the bathroom and threw aside her negligée and ran the shower. Tonight she was looking after a Belgian industrialist who had made his money in the illicit arms business. Her role was to reassure him as she laundered over fourteen million at roulette. She hoped he smelled rather better down below than the Croatian; the stale fishy odour as he had mounted her had lingered in her nose and played on her mind for hours after he had finished his staccato performance.

It was gone 11 p.m. now. Porcupine House felt chill and Dex noticed the smell of damp rising from the cellar beneath him. Everywhere was blackness, every light was off, every curtain drawn. He passed the time by planning his visit to see Father in Northampton, *assuming I'm alive.*

He checked his watch again, stood up, yawned and stretched to avoid his legs going numb. He could not even move around the room for fear of triggering the alarm. Except for a rustle from the trees and the house showing its age, there was silence. He was alone and surrounded only by the ghosts of old memories—of Mother shouting in fear as Father kicked and beat her; of him and Beth playing hide and seek for hours; of Beth calling out, "Ready or not, I'm coming to get you."

Only tonight it was not Beth who was coming.

He hated the creaks, groans, and sighs as the house cooled, wishing he could set U2 to full blast to drown the sounds. He opened and closed his hands and wriggled his toes, did a few stretches.

Another hour disappeared. Still there was silence. Until.

*Hello?*

*Was that a scratching sound?*

*Yeah—just branches rubbing on a gutter.*

*Nothing to worry about.*

*A click.*

*Fuck!*

*No question.*

*A key had unlocked the kitchen door.*

He heard the sound of night air moving. Dex recognized the familiar noise of the dark blue kitchen door moving uneasily on its hinges. There was a creak, followed by another. The alarm system started buzz. The intruder had thirty seconds to kill it. He guessed Jude had briefed Carmino well.

*What a dumb-fuck game this is!*

*What in hell's name got into me?*
*Poking sticks at psychopaths.*
*But he's expecting an empty house.*
*You're in Zurich, remember?*
*He'll be unarmed.*
*You have surprise on your side.*
*That and a baseball bat.*
*But was Carmino alone?*
The buzzing stopped and the kitchen door was gently closed.

# CHAPTER THIRTY-TWO

Between Dex and the kitchen was the square hall with parquet flooring. After the kitchen door closed, the sound of the giant horse chestnut's waving branches was again muted. The intruder was now within thirty feet. Dex felt his stomach gripe and his bowels inch closer to free fall. His heart was pounding, his mouth now dry, his breathing short and strangulated. His limbs had turned to water. He felt weak, helpless against mounting panic.

*Fight it.*

*Ignore it.*

He dug his nails into his palms and by a slight contortion, twisted enough to peer through the crack above the lower hinge of the study door.

*Nothing.*

*Just blackness.*

*Then distant breathing.*

Then nothing again. The intruder seemed to hesitate, unsure of his bearings.

*He must be by the door from the kitchen into the hall. Waiting for his eyes to adjust?*

*Debating whether to turn on a light, perhaps?*

*Moving about was never easy in the dark.*

The darkness was absolute.

He heard a few slow, steady footsteps. Eye close to the crack, Dex scarcely dared to breathe as he waited for the first sighting at the entrance to the hall. Suddenly from the blackness, a face appeared but nothing else. Disembodied, it was fearful—only visible were Zulu warrior green and white luminous stripes moving toward him. Of the body beneath there was no sign.

He fought down a scream, his sphincter control fighting on the cusp of failure. Again, he dug his nails into his palms and tried not to cry out at the pain.

*F'God's sake, Dex.*

*It's just a kid's mask.*

He heard a grunt of satisfaction. A flashlight clicked on, its beam searching around the hall, its holder invisible. The beam steadied and concentrated on the open study doorway. Barely ten feet separated them now. He wondered if the sounds and smell of his own fear were a giveaway as the torch advanced across the hall.

*Nightmarish.*

*Sub-human.*

For a second he was back in the Sherlock Holmes pub, the ferocious Hound's head just above him.

*Relax, Dex.*

*Be rational.*

*Like Sherlock.*

*It's just a man.*

*Nothing more.*

*A man with a kid's Halloween mask.*

*Just Carmino.*

*A psychopath.*

The footsteps moved unseen now, just the thickness of the door away as Carmino entered the study, the beam pointing ahead at the computer on the desk. "Ah!" It was the sound of satisfaction on seeing the laptop where it should have been. Then the torch flashed around the outside walls revealing that all windows were hidden behind floor-to-ceiling drapes.

Satisfied, Carmino switched on the desk lamp. Dex peered from behind the green fronds of the King Sago. Carmino was wearing thin gloves, trainers, jeans and a black roll-neck. He switched off the torch, put down his bag and seated himself at the desk with his back toward Dex. Then he eased up the mask till it perched across the top of his black beret.

Deliberately, Dex had left the laptop running. Plan A was for Carmino to search it on the spot rather than *borrowing* it for some geek to look at. Plan B assumed a take-away-and-return job, in which case he planned to club Carmino from the rear as he left, laptop in his possession. Either way, the laptop on the desk was not his trusted Sony that

Jude had found to be password-protected. He had bought an identical one yesterday and had transferred mountains of useless old data onto it. Everything sensitive about Dukes remained on the original, now stashed away in a carry-on bag at Waterloo Station Left-Luggage.

Carmino opened Firefox, having linked his own laptop with a short blue cable. He was going to copy across anything interesting. Would he realise this was a different laptop? Dex reckoned he would not.

The intruder flicked from screen to screen, searching the programmes and then exploring the contents. From Firefox, he saw that Dex had been looking at Dignitas, British Airways flights to Zurich and at online shops selling fishing tackle, Dex then saw Word opening. Scarcely daring to breathe, he knew this was the moment. The two most recent folders were called *Obsession* and *Onisac*. Both appeared at the top of the drop-down list under *Recent*.

From his crouched and aching position, Dex had a partial view of the screen, obscured only slightly by Carmino's right shoulder. As he looked at him, hunched forward now, he heard a grunt of satisfaction at seeing these two files with intriguing names. He clicked to open *Obsession*. Dex watched as he skim-read but after about four pages, he saw the reader's shoulders sag in disappointment. With an angry and dismissive movement, Carmino clicked and transferred the folder to his own laptop.

Dex watched as the next folder was opened. "Onisac? Onisac?" Dex heard the muttered question. Carmino clicked on the mouse and the page appeared. There was a relieved laugh as the word ONISAC appeared typed large across the page.

"Ah! Casino." The words were accompanied by a derisive laugh.

Dex was puzzled.

*Those words? That snorted laugh.*

*This was not Pepe Carmino.*

*This was his poodle.*

*Nigel Forster-Brown.*

*The computer boffin.*

*This was FB in a ridiculous kid's mask.*

*And probably terrified.*

*No Bowie knife.*

*Just the errand boy counting the days to retirement.*

Dex felt his chest muscles relax. His heart that had been pumping as if turbocharged started to slow.

*It's just FB, thinking he's alone and on a home run.*

He thought rapidly, reassessing how to use the unexpected situation. Not netting Carmino was a setback but FB would be easier. Everything now turned on a single mouse-click. Dex saw ONISAC on screen, with the introductory words beneath. He could not read them but could recite the hand-picked words as easily as The Lord's Prayer.

"This folder and the sub-folder are strictly confidential and relate to crimes I and my dead sister have uncovered at Dukes Casino. In the event of my sudden death, my solicitor holds one copy of everything and will draw the obvious conclusion. The sub-folder is listed under SEKUD."

The wait as FB read the introduction seemed endless but in truth was only seconds.

*Would he?*

*Won't he click the mouse?*

*This is the moment.*

# CHAPTER THIRTY-THREE

*Click.*

FB opened the sub-folder SEKUD, mumbling *ludicrous anagram* as he did so.

A new page appeared. Light-headed with relief, Dex fought back a laugh and then a snigger that threatened to ruin everything. FB scrolled down the page and then paused and started to reread. He enjoyed FB's discomfort as he tapped his fingers and then scratched his ear, Then he shifted uneasily and Dex could imagine cold sweat dripping down the foot of his back.

The page had been written to shock.

*Would Carmino have reacted like this?*

*Hopefully.*

As if being manipulated by a puppet master, FB slowly turned to look uneasily over his left shoulder toward the far corner of the room. Then, he looked above his head and directly in front of him. From the profile, Dex glimpsed fear, confusion and bewilderment on FB's face before he scrolled through the screen again.

> Hello, Pepe! I hope you enjoy my joke. I have caught everything on camera, a bit like you with members. You have been filmed entering my home. Look over your left shoulder. Top corner. There! See that camera? Perfect mug shot. Look up in front of you, above the desk. See another camera? Get the picture? Well, if you haven't, don't worry, because I have…if you don't mind another little joke.
>
> The microphones under the desk have captured anything said too.
>
> Entering the house triggered an armed response team to surround the building. Escape is impossible.
>
> These heavies will be taking you away for a chat. Well, they'll start by, shall we say, *encouraging* you to talk. But you

are dispensable. Like you dispensed with Beth and Tavio. Know what I mean? If you don't cooperate, they will have some fun, a few laughs, with your body parts until you do. Maybe you won't see the fun side at all. But I do think that after their *probing*, you will be eager to return all Beth's winnings you stole.

The charges, if you survive the interrogation, will include murder, conspiracy to murder, accessory to murder, keeping fraudulent records, money laundering, conspiring to defraud members by rigging casino games, and of course theft and burglary. Your gaming license will be revoked. Nobody at Dukes can be regarded as *fit and proper persons* to operate casinos ever again. Space City will never open. You, Pepe, will die in jail - assuming the guys surrounding you even bother with the police.

Your choice.

Fun,eh?

You can surrender, if you prefer.

If you are armed—say with your Bowie or gun—place them on the desk now. Turn off any lights in the study. You will then walk empty-handed to the French windows. You will find them to your left, about nineteen paces. You will stand beside them, open the left-hand curtain, and tap on the glass three times. You will then face the window with your arms high up, legs apart, palms against the glass until someone opens the door in front of you. Sorry I can't be with you to see this, especially if the boys get to use the electric cattle prods.

**FINLAY DEXTER**


PS: If you have simply stolen the laptop without opening this folder, you will know too late that my team was waiting outside. If by any chance you somehow gave them the slip, my boys will be dropping by Dukes and your home in Holland Park.

But it won't be for a cup tea and slab of cake. You're
dead meat!

Dex watched FB now sitting as if frozen stiff—lifeless. Dex guessed
he was staring at the screen but seeing nothing, hands gripping the
edge of the desk. Perhaps this seemed safer than tapping on the window for armed thugs to take him away. Dex's brain was now on fire,
recalibrating the plan. Everything needed to be changed. Holding
Carmino until he signed a confession and had ten million transferred
from Dukes was now junked. Would Carmino pay for FB's release and
a no-police deal? Doubtful. Calling in the Old Bill would get Carmino
jailed. Probably. But he'd pay not a dime in recompense.

There had to be another way.

"Fuck you, Pepe Carmino! Fuck you." FB's sudden exclamation was
spat out and full of venom. It brought Dex back to FB seated just feet
away, confused and transfixed.

*What would FB do?*

# CHAPTER THIRTY-FOUR

Dex watched as FB fumbled above his beret. He was replacing the mask.
*Don't make me laugh!*

Reluctantly, FB rose from the chair and stood staring at the instructions on the screen. Slowly, he removed the mask and dumped it on the desk. He extinguished the light and counting aloud up to nineteen, he walked hesitantly to the distant corner of the room. Out of vision now, Dex eased himself from his niche and heard three sharp raps on the glass.

Despite the blackness, Dex could just make out the shape of FB standing with his hands above his head, palms on the glass, legs apart. Unlike FB, who had moved slowly as if on autopilot to the hangman, Dex was seeing and thinking in 3-D and glorious Technicolor, everything now vivid. Of all the options that had opened, one now stood out.

He tightened his grip on the baseball bat and started to cross the carpet with soft and silent steps. All the while he watched for the slightest sign that FB had heard anything, his baseball bat poised ready to strike a fearsome blow to the shoulder if needed. But FB never flinched, his hands firmly on the window and expecting action from in front of him, his eyes peering into the blackness.

Dex crept to within three paces before he roared—roared louder than he had ever roared. The sound came from deep down and bounced off the walls, the windows and resonated through the house. In the study it sounded as if the hounds of hell and the lions of Longleat had all been unleashed right behind FB.

In the darkened room, it scared the hell out of the terrified figure. He did not even look behind him as he pressed even harder against the window. Then he screamed, realising he was trapped and unable to run, to escape, to go anywhere.

"Turn round." The command was shouted.

In the shadowy light from the night sky, Dex saw that the roar had been even more effective than he had dared to hope. FB turned to face him. The guy had lost it. His face was gaunt, his eyes saucer-wide with fear. Judging too by the hangdog look, Dex wondered if he had crapped himself big time.

Dex saw a man pleading to crawl back into his mother's womb. If the Baskerville Hound had been bounding toward him, he could not have been more distraught. But his path was blocked.

"One move, FB, and I'll club out your brains. You won't wake until morning and you won't like where you find yourself." Dex switched on the corner table lamp. "Back against the glass. Put your hands out in front of you." He stepped forward and in a swift movement, courtesy of *Naughty Nocturne*, had handcuffed the obedient figure. Then he roped FB's legs at knees and ankles and pushed him roughly to the floor, back against the wall. Dex turned to the window and rapped on it four times—in two bursts of two.

"You due back in Dukes?"

Silence.

"I said are you due back in Dukes? Answer me." He rapped out the command as FB nodded his head, yes. Dex then acted on his father's advice when demanding attention. *Speak slowly and to the point.* "You will tell me everything. If not, you will be taken to Dalston by the boys. In the end," he leaned down to drive home his point, "you will be beaten to pulp. You won't *survive* the experience."

He grinned, his confidence soaring now. "You *will* talk first. You're scarcely James Bond material, are you?" Dex laughed. "Don't answer that." Dex paused. "But I'm giving you a chance. I expected your boss." He prodded FB in the chest. " Decision time, FB - cooperate or it's the electric cattle probes and fingernail treatment—for starters." He saw FB flinch at the thought. "Then electrodes attached to your scrotum. I'm told it hurts. Shockingly." He alone laughed at his joke. "But they tell me most folk talk after the third fingernail."

Dex waited for the terrified man to look toward him.

"FB, Carmino is not going to tell the cops you're missing. Buried in the Epping Forest, you won't be discovered any time soon. Some they bury alive. Maybe you'll be lucky."

He heard FB whimper and reckoned if the cowering shit could have put a thumb in his mouth for comfort he might have done so.

"To Carmino, you are dispensable." He spat out the words and broke down *dis-pens-ible* to make the point. FB stared at the carpet but said nothing, his chest still heaving from the shock of the roar. Dex now crouched down so that his face was inches from FB's. "Carmino did not realise who he was messing with. Big mistake! *Nobody* fucks with me."

He saw FB shudder again. Dex pushed even closer so that FB tried unsuccessfully to retreat.

"So. Where was I? Oh yes. Buried alive or dead." He was so close now he smelled FB's aftershave and garlic. "FB, you are entering the *last hour* of your life." He prodded his captive again. "Sad thought though,—you being so beautifully *dispensable*."

Dex enjoyed the contempt he had injected into the word. He leaned across to the window and signalled, five raps and then another five. "There, FB. You have ten seconds. Help me or it's Dalston."

Without hesitation, FB spoke, but his words croaked out like an old man's death rattle. "Call them off. I'll talk."

"Full cooperation. At Dukes, from now on, you take orders from me." He gimlet-eyed FB again. "Yes or no?" He barked the words for effect. Dex waited for a few long seconds and then moved to open the French window. "Last chance."

FB's eyes drooped toward his mouth like a weary bloodhound. "Stop! Stop! I'll talk. But Carmino," he faltered. "That bastard. He scares me."

Dex said nothing. He gave four bangs, two and two on the window. "When is Carmino expecting you back?"

"Soon."

Dex thought fast; this was no hostage situation. His mind turned again to Reverse Labouchère and the missing link in his plan. Gus McKay had given him the pointer, but exploiting FB from the inside was *fuck me* good.

"Talk fast into this voice recorder. Tell me everything. But if you give me just one wrong fact, Carmino gets the recording and will know who squealed on him." He smiled in a disturbing way that made the listener look away hurriedly. "Me? I'd rather jump under a train than let him near me with a *Master* Bowie knife."

FB's voice croaked again and he cleared his throat as he glanced up. "I hate the man. Dukes used to be kosher. I was never involved in this, never wanted to be. But there was a blackmail moment." His eyes were furtive and Dex sensed there was a story here. "Plus then I spotted Jeb Miller and One-Eye working a flanker—I thought for themselves."

"Go on."

"I told the boss. The bastard laughed and said cheating the fuckwits was company policy." He looked away again. "All I wanted was a quiet life till retirement." His tone was wheedling like a small child defending the indefensible. "I had to stay stumm but got sucked in deeper."

"You knew about Panama, of course?" Dex was sure FB knew nothing of the kind. "Well, let me read you this." From the safe, he took out Tavio's witness statement. Quickly, he read the most brutal extract of the murderous attack. "That was Pepe Carmino. A rock and a hard place. That's where you are. My thugs or Carmino. Or me." He pointed to each finger in turn. "Carmino's days are numbered. He is going to the electric chair. I'll see to that. Believe me. Space City will never open."

"What do you want?" FB was close to meltdown, his voice weak and pleading. "Carmino doesn't tell me much."

"Don't give me that crap! Tell me the scams, the cheating. The laundering. About these big players all appearing."

"And Carmino?"

"I'll tell you what I want you to do. If you agree, Carmino will never hear about this—until too late."

FB's simpering and whimpering were getting on Dex's tits, but he had no intention of loosening the leash.

FB raised his frightened eyes, some dribble slipping over his lower lip. "And what do I tell the bastard when I go back tonight?"

Dex needed time to think that through. "I've thought of that. You start spilling first." There were a couple of questions he wanted answered at once. "On a typical day, how much cash is in the cage?"

FB shrugged as best he could when handcuffed, his hands clamped together now beneath his knees. "That depends. Recently, between fifteen to twenty million in a mix of sterling, US dollars, and euros. But if you're thinking of stealing it, forget it. From 8 a.m when we close until the security team take it to the bank, the strong room needs iris recognition, plus another staff member changes the daily code before the safe opens."

"But when you open again at 2 p.m., you have cash available?"

"In the past, maybe five hundred thou. Recently, with these whales playing, never less than ten million will be deposited by them—but big payouts are usually by cheque."

"And the daily code? Who knows that?"

The answer suited Dex very well. "Usually me."

"And Pepe? What time does he start?"

FB looked shifty as he answered, but the response made sense. "Most days, he arrives between 5 p.m. and 8 p.m. He either eats in his office or joins a member in the restaurant."

"And you?"

"Normally I arrive by twelve noon. Officially I end at 10 p.m. but," he muttered, "these days he makes me stay till much later."

"Okay. The frauds. Who is involved? How does it all work? Give."


As the hands on his watch nudged toward four, Carmino was standing close to the cage, chatting to a Lebanese regular called Doumany. He tried to appear interested in the guy's views on British culture. As he nodded politely, murmuring the odd *of course* and *couldn't agree more*, his thoughts were only on what had kept FB. He had expected him back by three.

There were only about a couple of dozen members and guests still at the tables. He could see Jude at the roulette with one of the rich guests, probably the Belgian judging by the loud checked-cloth of his suit. Then from the management relaxation room, FB appeared in his working gear of black tie and dinner jacket.

"Ah, FB! Good of you to come back. How is your brother?"

"Doing a little better, thank you."

"Remind me to send fruit and a card. No, better still, come on up to my office and I'll arrange it now. I wanted to show you some figures anyway. Goodnight, Mr Doumany."

The charade over, the two men went up to Carmino's spacious office and took their seats. It smelled of Mediterranean flower spray struggling against stale cigar smoke. As he crossed toward his desk, Carmino started talking. "Before you report, we did well here tonight. One-Eye rolled over that fat Swede for 2.3 million. Of course, the slob was as drunk as a skunk. A bottle of vodka behind each eyeball." He rubbed his hands cheerfully. "Anyway—you? Strike gold?"

FB looked at the ashtray on the corner of the desk, his eyes no more evasive than usual. Then he shook his head. "No."

"You left no clues?"

"Gloves on all the time. When I left, I double-checked. Everything looked undisturbed. I reset the alarm."

"Good. And?"

"You could have gone, like you first planned. My expertise wasn't needed. Dexter had forgotten to switch off the laptop. I didn't even have to crack the password. The bad news is, I found nothing! If he's up to something, you'd never know from the computer." FB's eyes looked at the carpet and then gazed toward the colourful Lassen original on the far wall.

"You were so long, I was hoping...." Carmino could not ask if Dex had been checking out Panama.

FB shook his head and played nervously with his fingers. "Knowing you were convinced the shit was onto something, I didn't give up. After checking the laptop, I took my time—searched every drawer, shelf, bookcase, cupboard, from the top rooms to the bottom. If he's got anything on us, it must be in the safe. In a drawer by his bed, I found some rambling notes about hating his father because of some land deal. His web viewing history was a typical mix of a fishing tackle supplier, Dignitas—that's the place you go to die—flights to Zurich, Vienna. Nothing sinister." He glanced up briefly. "On the computer there was a folder called *Obsession*—that sounded interesting."

"No?"

"Was it hell! It's the name of a novel. Dex is writing a thriller about a student obsessed with beating the casino. That's probably why he has a roulette wheel in the study." He shook his head. "Looked like tripe to me. Unpublishable unless he sharpens up the long-winded drivel." He yawned into the back of his hand. "Can I go now? I'm feeling pretty bushed. Creeping round someone else's house like that."

"No emails between him and Mick Glenn? No links?"

"He uses Outlook. I checked it out. I ran a search. No. He emails that Tiffany woman, who is in the USA—nothing interesting. Just setting up Skype calls. She's back this weekend it seems."

"Anything about Jude Tuson?"

"Besides hiring her? Nothing. You were so sure there would be something, I even undid his last defrag to see if he'd hidden any old material. The Recycling Bin contained nothing of interest. His recent letters and emails are all about winding up the estate of his sister."

Carmino struck a match for another cigar. "Nothing concealed behind some other password-protected area?"

FB's snort of derision was response enough, but he also threw in an impressive *do-me-a-favour* look. "First thing I checked—looking for secret areas. That's what I was hoping for, something meaty. A bit of cryptography." FB then tapped his forehead as if he had remembered something. "Oh, yes! I copied his contact list—names, addresses. No Mick Glenn."

Carmino poured himself a Bushmills but offered nothing to FB. "I'm not sure whether I'm surprised or disappointed."

FB frowned. "Isn't it better that he's not onto us?"

"You'd think so. But I felt sure that Dex tipped off Mick Glenn. So who was it?"

"Boss, tonight did not prove you wrong. I just found nothing to prove you're right."

Pepe nodded as he absorbed the comment. He spoke slowly. "Yes, of course. That's right."

He turned away with no word of thanks or goodbye, so FB headed for the door. Once outside, he paused to take a deep breath. Somehow, he had come through unscathed. But what he had to do on command for Dex was already scaring him shitless.

# CHAPTER THIRTY-FIVE

Dex slept for barely an hour. The adrenaline was still pumping through him long after he had bundled a trembling FB into his Vauxhall parked on Circus Road. His immediate thought on waking was of meeting the management in Northampton.

He took the train from Euston and mentally ticked off the plus points from the night just passed. Having FB on the inside changed everything. On his smartphone, he checked where he was meeting Larry Jamous. Google maps identified Penarth Street, not far from Millwall FC—a tough part of southeast London. It was about five miles from Tower Bridge and looked like an anonymous back street.

More hub-cap thieves than designer shops, he told himself as he took in Google's street view of a light industrial area.

There was only yesterday's email from Tiffany warning him to watch out for the Ugly Troll. He had replied in the same vein, saying *no problem - this tethered goat eats Trolls, ugly or not.*

The jolt of the train slowing as it entered Northampton brought him back to visiting Bistbury Care Centre, a few minutes' walk from the station. It proved to be clean, modern and unsurprisingly smelled of boiled fish, floor polish and disinfectant. The director, Marty Baxter, rather surprisingly produced coffee in bone-china cups and a plate brimming with chocolate biscuits. He summoned the nurse who had been assigned to Sir Charles and Dex listened to their ongoing assessment process. He took in the now familiar jargon—*stimuli, reaction, responses, deficit, motor function*—and after twenty minutes of explanation knew that his worst fears were justified.

"This sounds hopeless."

"Please give us a month till we conclude all the tests and observations. The CT Scan shows minimal consciousness." Baxter, who was about thirty, shook his head sadly. "One thing though, we've seen enough to establish that the previous appraisal was right: your father has significant cognitive awareness."

On hearing those words again, Dex mentally slumped in the chair opposite the director's metal and glass desk. "And after a month?"

"You'll know what we think the future holds…whether there's any hope." Dex could tell by the way the man looked away that he was not expecting miracles.

As he rose to leave, Dex nearly said that in one month, Bistbury would be losing a patient. But he said nothing of his plans for Dignitas.


By 3 p.m., after a fifteen-minute cab ride among nondescript council blocks and repair shops built under railway arches, he reached Penarth Street. As he looked at the area, Dex kept imagining Del Boy Trotter appearing from Nelson Mandela House.

The taxi dropped him outside a low-rise brick-built building. It looked nineteenth-century and careworn. It was built around a small courtyard with a sign naming about eight different businesses. Meaningless graffiti had been spray-painted in lurid red. In the yard, he found Emporium Supplies (Global) Limited, where he asked the bored-looking receptionist for Mr Jamous. She put down a hefty sand-wich and dialled through to him.

Moments later, Jamous appeared using small, busy steps. He was a little man with a pencil-thin moustache and thick grey crinkly hair. He led Dex into a small office crammed with files, invoices, a calendar showing the wrong month and at least three coffee mugs gathering mould and dust. Dex shifted a box from a chair and after settling in by the ex-MOD metallic desk, told Jamous how but not why he was here."Recommended by that eccentric little Scotsman, was you?"

"Said you're the man."

"I might be. What do you want?"

Dex explained in a couple of brushstrokes what he needed and Jamous stayed poker-faced, his hands busily adjusting the clutter on his desk. "By when?" Jamous, who looked part English, part Egyptian, showed neither surprise nor interest in the instruction.

"Eight days max."

"Nah. We're busy, mate. Up to our bleedin' necks in work. Two months."

"Cash payment."

"Don't cut no ice, mate. We got stuff going out seven days a week already. I got my existing customers to worry about, not piss them off by giving you priority."

"How much for delivery in two months?"

"Forty thousand quid, twenty-five up front."

Dex knew from Gus McKay that Jamous would screw him. He didn't care. "Look, Larry, here's the deal. Sixty grand in cash tomorrow. Forty more on delivery in ten days or less." Dex rose to leave. "Gus McKay gave me another name. Max Horobin. Said he was a real craftsman." Dex was now by the door, hand on the frame. "Okay. Suit yourself. I'll visit him now. Morden, isn't it?"

"I'll do it…well, try to do it. What you want, mate, is a work of art. Bleedin' van Gogh wasn't pressurized like this."

"Van Gogh cut off his own ear. In your case, if you don't deliver on time, it won't be your ears I cut off. Get this straight. You will deliver on time."

Jamous flinched in his tubular chair. "You're a hard man, Mr… er?"

"Cornelius. Jake Cornelius. The courier will deliver the cash by ten tomorrow."

"How do I contact you?"

"You don't. I contact you."

# CHAPTER THIRTY-SIX

During the taxi ride back from Penarth Street, Dex received a text from Tiffany. "R U OK? Spk soon. Heading to LAX." He wanted to speak to her but contacting the Las Vegas attorney was more urgent, so he texted, assuring her he was just fine and would meet her at Heathrow. As he typed *Heathrow*, memories of Beth flooded back. He imagined her clearing Immigration, waiting at the carousel, before climbing into the limo for her final few minutes of life. Like Princess Di, stepping out of the back-door of the Ritz Hotel in Paris.

He could almost see again the giant truck pointing skywards on top of the limo. In his exhausted state, his emotions got the better of him. This morning, seeing his father slumped forwards and sideways with dribble slithering on his unshaven chin, had been bad enough. Now, reliving memories of Beth was even worse. He wiped away tears with a red-spotted hankie.

He had to compose himself for the vital call. He took a dozen or so deep breaths and then dialled the attorney.

Anders Thomassen was a partner in a firm in a Vegas high-rise office block on Howard Hughes Parkway, a prestigious address appropriate for a top-rated commercial lawyer. He did not enquire as to the target or why top sensitive data was needed. "Not my concern, buddy. But the guy you need, the best private eye bar none, operates from over in Summerlin in the northwest valley. His name's Otto Schneider. Tell him I recommended you. He hangs out below the radar, specialising in commercial espionage—but don't ask about his methods. Just whoop at the results. Give my best to Gus. We had some great nights in Binions."

Dex rang Schneider at once. The private eye sounded like an American Dutchman and assured Dex he could move quickly so long as the fee was immediately transferred to his bank at the Trails in Summerlin. "And the fee?" enquired Dex.

"Three hundred dollars an hour. Minimum billing of fifty hours. Your account must be evergreen at this figure."

Dex swallowed hard. "Give me the bank details. You will receive $15,000 today." After scribbling down the routing number and account, for the next fifteen minutes he explained precisely what he needed. No sooner had he put the phone down than it rang again.

He heard the familiar Wolverhampton accent of the policeman in charge of the accident investigation. "The tachograph had not been tampered with, sir. I am not permitted to tell you the details. There's no evidence of murder."

"But no driver? A false address." Dex felt his blood pressure rising. This was the same negativity he had encountered after Carole and Jamie had been murdered.

The gloomy voice, with its strong nasal overlay, continued. "That, sir, is the best pointer to something suspicious. But it's circumstantial. He might be an illegal immigrant. As I told you before, he reckoned he was blinded by the morning sun. If we find him, that is no defence to a criminal driving charge." The soulless accent made the negativity even more depressing.

"Lack of evidence, story of my life."

"I'm sorry, sir? I don't understand."

"No matter. Let me know when you find the driver. I'm not holding my breath."


Adam Yarbury had suggested that the three of them meet up in the Bulgari Hotel in Knightsbridge. Dex was dropped off close, but not too close, in Sloane Street. At least now, he could be officially back from Zurich but all day, he had been checking whether he had been followed. There had been no sign during his trip to Peckham but meeting Billy was particularly sensitive.

Taking no chances, he bought a Tube ticket and entered the system at Sloane Street. He dropped deep down to the Piccadilly line platform, walked its length and then resurfaced at the western exit.Satisfied now that he had no pursuers, he rounded the corner and entered the boutique hotel.

The lobby and sitting area were crowded. Dex heard Arabic, Russian, broken English and American accents as he strolled towards the bar. He was a few minutes late, his watch showing just after 6 p.m. It was his first visit to a hotel much favoured by international dealmakers. He took in the burnished copper curve of the bar and the clever blend of colours in the decor. It was obvious why it was beloved by oil tycoons and the many Russian oligarchs who lived nearby.

He saw Adam and Billy seated on the far side and waved on his approach. Adam offered him a champagne cocktail but after a day of roller-coaster emotions and with exhaustion kicking in, he went for a spicy tomato juice. He appraised Billy. "You're looking better than last time. How's Emily? And your wife—Sandie, isn't it?"

Billy down-turned his mouth. "I'm not back with her yet." Then he brightened. "Emily's just had a new bike for her sixth birthday. Pooh goes everywhere in the little basket."

Dex wished he could help but marriage counselling was not his forte. "You keep away from card-counting, cocaine and booze, hopefully she'll come round. Your boss still okay about your flexi-hours?"

"Yeah. It's a zero-hours contract, so they're pretty cool about what or when I work."

"Good!" Dex then looked at each of them in turn. "Productive afternoon?"

"You tell him," prompted Adam, looking at Billy.

"As planned, Adam and I hit the tables, soon as they opened. at two."

"Anyone less likely than Adam to *hit the tables* at any time, I've yet to meet."

"I've never done that," explained Adam. "Normally," he explained with a chortle in his voice "I would be in the restaurant with the chaps till well-gone three. Limbering up for the racing with a schooner of port ... or twain."

"You had the camera going?" Dex had lent Billy the cufflinks, but Adam had declined to risk the tiepin. He saw Billy nod and then grin, very much a cat that got the cream. "I know how they could fix the decks."

"Could?" Dex look puzzled and wanted an explanation. "Or do?"

"Look—when the tables open, the joint is empty. Unlike most London casinos, which are twenty-four-seven, Dukes is just coming to life at 2pm."

"Most of the chaps, the regulars like me that is, are still lunching," explained Adam.

Billy took up the story. "But there's a woman, early thirties, all alone at one of the blackjack tables. She must have been there waiting. When we joined her, the cards were already in the shoe."

"This popsy looks just like Charlotte Rampling back in the seventies." Adam's tone was lyrical. "Penetrating eyes and a proud, almost supercilious look. Stunning gal." He sighed. "If I were thirty years younger! She's often in the bar of an evening. Too damned familiar with Pepe. All touchy-feely. Less so these days, mind. Sometimes she plays the tables with older men. But never with me." He looked disappointed.

"Showing your age there, Adam but I get the picture. Go on, Billy—explain."

"At the start of play or whenever the cards in the shoe are changed, typically perhaps six new cellophane-wrapped decks are opened. Then all the cards should be semi-circled on the table, face up, so that all fifty-two cards from each pack are checked. The dealer then shuffles up. A player then cuts the cards. Only after that are they put in the shoe."

"So this had been done by this woman before you arrived?"

"Or not, as the case may be."

"Anyway," Adam leaned forward as if someone might overhear them, "as soon as we sat down, she played one more hand and moved to the next table beside us and had that one opened up."

Billy continued the explanation. "We could scarcely switch tables to check what she was doing. That would have looked very odd. The dealer certainly spread out the cards before shuffling."

Dex now understood. "But if she were on Pepe's payroll, missing tens and aces wouldn't bother her." He saw both Billy and Adam agree. "She played three or four hands on her own and then moved to another table and opened that. I heard her saying something about needing better luck."

Dex whistled quietly. "That bloody simple! So when genuine players arrive later, all the shoes are ready. Decks with some tens and aces removed have already been opened. Players arriving assume other players have already checked."

"The cameras?"

"If checked? They might show it but not if done quickly by a skilled sharp."

Adam's tone of voice was incredulous. "I can see why I found it so hard to win."

Dex laughed. "No, Adam. You kept losing because you played like a trout." He saw Billy enjoy a quiet smile.

Adam looked severe for a moment but then laughed too. "Oh, alright! I lost *even quicker* because of fraud."

"Agreed on that."

Adam's voice still showed his indignation that Dukes had been cheating him for so long. "She opened four tables in all. The fifth one never opens until late evening anyway."

"We're nearly there," Billy confirmed.

Dex waved his hands calmingly. "Let's not get ahead of ourselves. Billy, how many shoes have you played?"

"After tomorrow afternoon, I will have played 100 shoes. Nice round number for the stats. But based on the 80 played, I'd say they're rigging the decks." Billy helped himself to a smoked salmon tartlet. "Every time the count tells me that the remaining cards are stuffed with tens and aces and so great for the player, they sure as hell are not. Every time!" He looked at each listener to add force. "Different tables. Different shoes, different dealers—same result."

Dex nodded for Billy to continue. "Any card-counter would expect a good run of hands later in *every* shoe at Dukes." Billy saw Dex look puzzled and went on to explain. "The early cards prove a shitload of tens and aces should still be in the shoe. Except they're not. Too many 4s and 5s, I'd say."

"But not all the aces and tens." Dex repeated the words slowly, letting them sink in.

Billy opened his BlackBerry. "My notes and calculations." He read from the screen. "The count is haywire, madness. At least five aces and maybe a dozen tens and face cards are missing. Instead they've slipped in a few extra fours and fives."

"Sensational! Don't go tomorrow. Not with what you've proved."

Billy ran his hand over his head thoughtfully. "No. I disagree. Firstly, I want to reach one hundred shoes played. Secondly, I want to see if this woman opens the tables again and thirdly, I want to beat her to the first table and open it myself. That way, I'll know every deck is kosher."

"Reckon they have complete packs if troublemakers like you open the table?" Dex saw Billy nod in agreement. Then he looked at Adam, his hesitation showing. Billy's reasons were convincing but there was something about the way Billy's tongue flicked in and out that made him unsure.

Adam looked at Billy and then at Dex. "If Billy could play the remaining twenty shoes where the decks aren't rigged, the contrast will show up." He looked back to Billy for confirmation. "Isn't that what they call a double whammy?" Adam seemed proud to have picked up some modern jargon.

Dex grinned as he thought about it but not for long. The logic was impeccable. "Go ahead and somehow film a table being opened without a proper card check." As Dex said it, Billy adjusted his bottle-green blazer so that the pastel green shirt cuff appeared. He rubbed the lens centred in the patterned cufflink. Dex ordered another round of drinks. "You'll be there with Billy tomorrow?"

Adam finished a blini before explaining that he had a committee meeting in Cannon Street with a spot of lunch. Dex looked round at the patterned grey walls and the array of bottles neatly centred in the bar. "Not once have I ever filmed any roulette cheating. It would be great if you filmed rigged blackjack decks."

FB's recorded admission, taken under extreme duress, might not stand up in court but it supported what Billy was saying. Not that he could tell them that. "Fortunately, but don't ask me how, I think I can still prove roulette and blackjack are fixed."

It was Adam's turn to look puzzled as he chinked glasses with Billy. "Sorry, old chap! Am I missing something?"

"Something fell into my lap. Anyway, I want belt and braces."

"We must be just about there, aren't we?"

"I want to bring down Space City, remember? I've got to persuade the Feds. That's why I've kickstarted enquiries in Vegas. But I've still got to win at Reverse Labouchère. I'm going up there now, just tootling around. I'm still not ready to take them on. Any takers for dinner there?"

There were not. Billy was heading for Thames Ditton for a quick pizza with Sandie and to kiss Emily goodnight. Afterward, he would return to his bedsit in Clapham. Dex turned to Adam, who explained he would be dining at Le Gavroche but adding that he *might just toddle over to Dukes afterward.*

After Adam left, Dex leaned across to Billy. "Look—tell me straight. Are you still off the drugs? Because if you are not, no way can I trust you. I won't blame you. But I will not trust you to continue."

"No, Dex. I'm still clean. Honest!"

Dex felt unconvinced. There was just sufficient hesitation to cause alarm. He watched Billy amble toward the exit while he waited to pay for the drinks. He hoped Billy was not lying his arse off about drugs.

He took no notice of the two men and one woman seated at the entrance to the bar, drinking sparkling water as he paid in cash.

# CHAPTER THIRTY-SEVEN

"I may be off to Vegas shortly." Pepe Carmino threw in the casual remark as he dusted his black loafers.

Jude's face lit up at the thought of a few days chilling out on the Strip. "When do we leave?"

"Not this trip, sorry. Busy, busy, busy. Anyway, I need you here, looking after these old geezers." He came over and kissed her on the cheek. "Once Space City is flying, then we'll be hitting the hotspots. Your choice. Promise."

Jude pouted as she sat at the dressing table. Perhaps Pepe was all bullshit, empty promises, and she would be cast aside when it suited him. The previous evening, she had chatted to Irenke at the bar. Perhaps too many vermouths had loosened the Hungarian's tongue. She too had been promised a great future by Pepe but had been dumped. In a slurred voice with a harsh accent, she had explained she was now a shill playing blackjack in the afternoons and *helping* new members in the evening.

*Sounds like a warning to me*, Jude thought as she checked her eyeliner. "Will you be away long, Pepe?"

"One night, maybe two. Depends if Enzo Letizione is still fucking up."

"Get rid of him."

"After the launch, I'm going to…" He was interrupted by the old-style American ringtone on his phone, . "Arnie! What's news?" He took the phone into the corridor outside the bedroom but Jude could still hear Pepe. "Good job! Good job. Yeah, that's all I need for now." He returned to the bedroom, punching the air. In a few jubilant strides, he stood behind Jude and cupped his hands under her generous breasts and kissed the top of her head.

Jude looked in the mirror and gave Pepe a questioning look. "What was that all about?"

"Arnie? An old schoolmate. He's had a team following this new friend in Adam Yarbury's life—Billy Evans. I thought there was something odd about him. Arnie copped a photo of him buying crack cocaine from a street dealer on the edge of Chinatown."

"He takes drugs. What's the big deal?"

"Finlay Dexter was in Knightsbridge with Adam Yarbury and Billy."

"That's no crime. Dex didn't do drugs. I asked him."

"Dexter's up to something. Planning a heist. Something. The floor staff and guys watching the monitors were suspicious about some of his body movements."

"Tight trousers and huge tackle, Pepe," Jude joked as he kissed the nape of her neck.

"The way Dexter holds his left arm and sometimes twists his body. They reckon he's almost certainly been filming. They suspect either a tiepin or his ornate cufflinks."

"And?"

"Billy was wearing the same cufflinks today at the tables. And guess what? He too held his left arm in a similar way. He was followed to the Bulgari Hotel, where he rubbed the cufflink."

"Cleaning a lens?"

"You betcha."

"What are you going to do?"

"Maybe cut him a bit of slack before pouncing. I'm not sure."

"But," Jude hesitated, her open-looking face puckered into a slight frown. "Don't take this wrong, but Dex seemed a regular guy. What's your problem? That he's friendly with Billy? We know he's friendly with that old guy, Adam."

"Face it. Billy's not the type Adam Yarbury would normally notice, let alone talk to." He saw Jude nod in agreement. "So when you're there tonight, if either Dexter or Evans is in, keep an eye on them. But this Greek politician takes priority. Make sure every last drachma, euro, pound or whatever is squeezed from him. He's top, top loaded."

"Who is he?"

"Vasilis Eliades, a former prime minister, his pockets stuffed full of untaxed wealth and bribes. A right slippery bastard."

"Not, please not, a bedroom job?"

"He's about seventy-eight. Who knows? Do what it takes." He gathered his jacket, watch, wallet, keys and small change while she finished the last of her makeup. "Ready? I'll drop you off at the Westbury. Eliades has the best suite."

"Well, I hope I don't see much of it." She twirled round in her new red halter-neck midi dress by Balmain. "These dirty old guys are all the same now. I blame Viagra."

"Whatever it takes, Jude, whatever it takes. I'm paying you very well."

Jude could not disagree as he grasped her hand and led her toward the garage.

"I'll be home by dawn. Make it a date. I've some different gadgets to try out. I think you'll enjoy them."

Jude forced a smile at that unpleasant prospect. "You, Pepe, are a lusciously evil bastard. I mean, must we wait till then?" She kissed him full on the mouth, forcing him to hesitate.

"Duty calls. Be back by dawn, deal?"


It was a fine summer evening and with the large crowd leaving Lord's cricket ground after a One-Day International, Dex decided to walk to Mount Street. A taxi would scarcely move in the gridlock. Instead, he joined the twenty thousand fans, most of whom were looking dispirited at a defeat by India. On the way, Dex tried phoning Tiffany but she was not answering, though her flight wouldn't be leaving for hours yet, California time.

Thoughts of how the relationship might blossom kept him oblivious to the drab surroundings on the Edgware Road. Truth to tell, he was uncertain of his feelings about her, maybe because he was uncertain how she felt about him.

He crossed Oxford Street and a few minutes later greeted Tom the doorman, who asked if he knew who had won the cricket. Dex told him and he looked overly pleased. "Glad we lost, Tom? Surely not?"

"Patriotic, that's me but we'll get some of the Indian players in later and they tip well."

After snacking in the bar on a Wagyu burger with a glass of Fixin, Dex was about to start playing when Jude appeared, looking ravishing with her copper hair piled on top of her head and the Balmain dress, emphasising her curves. She sat down beside him and air-kissed his cheek. Earlier, she had been clasping the hand of an ageing man who was slightly stooped and who walked with a limp.

"I saw you with that coffin-dodger. You're not fussy, then?" Dex laughed.

"I'm helping him play roulette."

"Holding his hand, then? But not just metaphorically."

She gave a coarse laugh, deep and throaty. "Sugar daddies can be generous."

"Nursing him, are you?"

"He's a randy old goat. Erection like a broom handle." Dex could see she was joking before she turned serious. "And Dignitas?"

Dex had read enough of the place to bluff his way through. "Northampton has one month. If they're not progressing, Dignitas is impressive."

"Tough call. I'm sorry for you."

"And you? You okay?"

"For now, I'm staying with a good mate. You playing tonight?" Dex spotted that she was keen to change the subject. She was saved by Vasilis Eliades peering into the bar to look for her.

"You take care, Jude. Mind you don't kill him off."

Dex watched her escort the doddery figure toward the gaming tables. He followed shortly after. He was excited to be trying Reverse Labouchère for real but his clammy palms warned him it was not going to be easy. He withdrew £100,000 in plaques from the casino cage and eased into a chair beside Gerhard Hoge.

The dealer, called Angie, smiled a welcome which was not lost on Carmino as he watched every move down below. Meantime, he could watch Jude at One-Eye's table across the room as she laundered the Greek's millions, stolen from the European Union budget.

Carmino hoped to spot Dex filming. He settled in to watch, a garlic-laden Moules Marinière and a chilled Chablis in front of him. At the roulette table, he picked up the flippant banter with the German while Dex played a few hands, betting on both red and black. "Dex, my friend. You can't win backing red and black together. That is crazy—even if you shake hands with ten chimney sweeps."

Dex grinned. "That depends on the way you stake your bets. Sure, if you bet the same amount each time on both, you'll be bust and ragged-arsed in no time."

Dex watched Gerhard shrug. "So, you did not like my system? But for sure, you won?"

Dex leaned out to place £20,000 on black and £10,000 on red. "Gerhard, my friend, I *loved* your system. But this is Reverse Labouchère. Your system? I agree—you'll win most times but never mega. My system can bring life-changing winnings."

"And this Labouchère? Was it named after some weird French professor who majored in Mad Maths?" Gerhard guffawed. "Has he been locked up as a crazy man?" He patted Dex on the back as if to console him.

Dex was defensive. "Mostly you lose. But when it goes well…" He waved his arms expansively.

Gerhard shrugged again. "To me, you are insane." He tapped the side of his head in emphasis.

Dex winced as zero came in—the worst possible number—and both bets lost. He adjusted his stakes and continued backing both red and black for the next thirty minutes until his last chips had been lost. Meantime, Gerhard kept pulling in his winnings with a smug look, as if he had just scored the winning goal against England at Wembley.

"So, Dex. You lost £100,000." Again came the booming guffaw, accompanied this time by the German slapping his thighs. "Remind me. Whenever I want real pain, I try your system. It is better than having your bottom spanked, *ja?*"

Dex laughed. "Not a good advert today. It can work, believe me but if red and black numbers alternate with the occasional zero, I'm stuffed." He grinned ruefully. "If, say, three reds, a black, and then five reds and a black and then another four or five reds hit, I'd win mega, especially if red goes on even longer."

Gerhard looked bemused, his bushy eyebrows knitting in a frown. "*Viel Glück!* Good luck. For sure, I must arrange for you to meet *every* chimney sweep in London before you try again."

"Mind you, I really need a helper playing black while I play red." Dex paused but then jumped in with an idea. "If I explained the staking system, would you do this? I could cut you in."

"For sure, my friend! If we play only with your money." Gerhard slapped Dex on the back, almost knocking the wind out of him. "Tomorrow I start a ten-week cruise to New Zealand. But when I return? Of course."

Dex was disappointed. "Deal!" He could not explain that he planned for Dukes to be dead and buried within days. "Enjoy the cruise."

Two floors up, as he poured a generous Taylor's port with some Camembert, Carmino watched with satisfaction as Dex stopped off at the cage to top up his account.Of filming, there had been no sign, no strange body movements at all.

Dex checked the receipt, wondering who might play with him. *Billy? Adam maybe?* Someone had to be trusted and trained to calculate every bet correctly. There was no room for errors.

He saw Jude quitting the roulette, clinging to her pockmarked Greek with his liver-spotted hands. *If only she were not shacked up with Pepe, she would be ideal.*

*Could he turn her?*

*Could he trust her?*

# CHAPTER THIRTY-EIGHT

Dex was surprised how edgy he felt as he waited at Terminal 5. As Tiffany appeared, she was also looking out for him and although she could not wave, the excited smile said it all. When she had cleared the mix of various nationalities pacing through from Customs, she put down her wheelie suitcase and carry-on and stretched out her arms to wrap around him. Her face buried into his neck. Straight into his ear, Dex heard her whisper, "Thank God you're safe!" He could feel her trembling with emotion. For a few moments they were oblivious to their surroundings, hugging each other.

"Come on," Dex said at last. "I gambled on the short-term parking." He led her to his open-top Audi and once inside, flipped back the roof. "It's a beautiful day. It's now 11:30. Wouldn't it be great to have lunch somewhere away from it all? Unless you want to get back home?"

"Absolutely not. I want to see, oh, so many things, including Porcupine House. Being with you, I'm on a high. Going humdrum doesn't do it for me." She leaned across and kissed him gently on the mouth. "An escape after the whirlwind tour sounds really cool."

"I know just the place." He looked deep into her eyes before kissing her again. "The Sir Charles Napier at Chinnor. About thirty minutes."

She leaned back, stretching her hands in front of her. "No phones. No flights or speeches to make. I could go on. No PR team telling me it's time to go and no more hands to shake. But I loved it."

"And no journalists asking the same questions over and over again."

Tiffany laughed her yes as she switched off her phone, and on seeing her do this, Dex did the same. "This is *us time*. You and me but mainly you. These past weeks," her sigh turned into a yawn, "have been too much about me."

Dex fired the engine, and after leaving the airport took the M25 and then the M40 west.

The gastropub was secreted away in the middle of leafy Buckinghamshire but worth the effort. The garden was an abundance of trees, lawn and a mix of blues and purples with abundant lilac shrubs and plants. As they settled in under the spreading branches of a huge tree, the air was filled with birdsong and the buzz of bees. Summer scents surrounded them.

Tiffany leaned across the table and held his hand. "I couldn't have dreamed of somewhere better. Barely more than a dozen hours ago I was in the fumes of La Cienega Boulevard." She yawned, stretching her arms above her head, emphasising her shapely figure. Her bare arms were tanned and her face radiated a glow that belied her long flight.

"And no job to come back to. A good feeling?"

"More USA, Africa and more writing? What's not to like? But after we've ordered, this is about you. Tell me all."

Dex took well over an hour to explain everything, glossing over Laurence Jamous in Penarth Street and fighting off Jude's advances. He doubted Tiffany was ready to know about that now—if ever. As they chatted about the interesting black sculptures that were scattered around the grounds, they enjoyed the haddock soufflé and fresh turbot. And by the time Tiffany enquired about what he was planning for Space City, they were starting on strawberry Eton Mess.

"I may leave for Vegas tomorrow. It all depends on what Otto Schneider digs up."

"When does Space City open?"

"Never." Dex laughed. "But they think in five days." Dex lowered his fork. "You never did a signing in Vegas on your tour, did you?"

"My book would never sell there. Too many long words and not enough four-letter ones. Why?"

Dex had been waiting for the moment to tell her. "I want you to come with me. I have a plan to nail Enzo Letizione and I need your help. Hear me out." He saw the dubious upturned eyebrow. "Please?" She managed a quizzical smile of encouragement. "I know you're a convent girl but have you ever done anything really naughty? And I don't mean sex."

Dex was rewarded with a laugh while she stroked his hand. "As a journalist? Absolutely. You have to be brass-necked or tell the occasional porkie."

"Yeah, yeah! Like door-stepping a funeral."

"But me? When I'm not a journalist?" She looked at him with an impish grin that dimpled her cheeks. "Goody two-shoes, that's me! Oh! We did creep out of the dorm one night to smoke ciggies when I was fourteen. We felt very naughty doing that."

Dex leaned back, hands clasped behind his head. "A perfect CV. It's the journalist in you I need. Let me explain."

# CHAPTER THIRTY-NINE

It was nearly three o'clock when they reluctantly left the shaded warmth of the garden to drive back to London. Tiffany was in no mood to switch on her phone but Dex wanted to discover if Billy had struck gold yet. As they sat in the car park about to leave, he listened with mounting concern to the three voicemail messages from FB, each of them increasingly panicky. Dex looked at Tiffany, his eyes narrowed. "All the good work gone in a flash."

"Big problems?" Tiffany's prompting was unnecessary, as she had seen Dex chewing his lip as he listened.

"Billy was bounced from Dukes. A security guy challenged him about filming. He made a run for it and got away but dropped his Blackberry and never stopped to pick it up. Just kept running."

"Ring FB."

"He said not to phone. Carmino was due to leave for Vegas but has postponed."

"What's on the BlackBerry?"

Dex thought for a few seconds. "God knows! Plenty enough, like his notes on fixed decks for starters. There'll be emails and texts we exchanged. Carmino could never link us before this. Now he knows I'm after him."

"Then go to the police. Now."

Dex recognised the solid advice. "Let's talk and think while I drive. I don't like this. I don't like this at all. Think of Mick Glenn. Think of Tavio and that other big-mouthed dealer that drowned."

"Diego Rodrigues?"

"Good memory. And add Beth to the list—whatever the cops think. They don't know what she discovered from Tavio. Think of Carmino desperate enough to burgle Porcupine House after planting Jude Tuson as the carer."

"Your point?"

"We're in danger. Me and Billy especially. Even Adam. But anybody who gets in Carmino's way."

"But he wouldn't get away with it, not if he murdered…"

Five minutes later, they were on the M40 and cruising at 70 mph toward West London. "That's not the point. Look at the way he butchered the Mexican. For a guy who acts like that, this is about revenge and bloodlust." Dex left the thought hanging long enough for Tiffany to get the message.

But she was not buying it. "Why are you so stubborn? Go to the police." Tiffany's voice was tetchy. "You've enough to bring down Carmino and Dukes. The Feds will move in and Space City won't open."

"What have the police ever done for me?" Dex continued driving in an uncomfortable silence for several miles. It was only when they were approaching Hanger Lane that Dex had marshalled his thoughts. "Firstly, Billy is in danger. Carmino will know where he lives from his membership form. I've got to protect him."

"And he knows where you live too."

Dex ignored the comment. "Secondly, Otto Schneider's report should be ready tomorrow. Thirdly, Billy didn't finish his evidence. Fourthly, I want to win big at roulette and give it to your charity. Only then will I have met my promise to Beth. Lastly, I want to nail Enzo Letizione. Y'know, what we discussed at lunch."

Tiffany could see from the set of his jaw and the way he gripped the wheel that he was not to be deflected. "And so?"

"If Pepe Carmino is staying in London, this is not where we should be."

"We? Meaning, including me?"

"Carmino is a cornered rat. You, a journalist, were there the night I caught One-Eye cheating Glenn." He let that uncomfortable fact sink in. "*Anybody* in his way is a target." Deftly, he swung off the end of the elevated section, turning north toward St John's Wood. "I'm collecting my passport, laptop, some cash from the safe. We fly to Vegas today."

"Count me out. I'm bushed, sick of travelling. He wouldn't attack me, or I can hide up somewhere for a while—Blakeney or Polperro."

"Tiffany, please. I need you to nail Letizione. You agreed over lunch. Nothing's changed except we're flying sooner and hopefully with Billy and Adam." Dex looked up and down the road beside Porcupine House before pulling into the drive. There was no sign anybody was watching. Dex gave her a peck on the cheek. "Plus, I want you around."

"Obsessions can be dangerous." She gave him a weak smile as a sign of surrender. "Are you going to phone Billy?"

"He has to phone me. My only contact is his Blackberry."

Dex hopped out of the car and she followed his rapid strides to the back door. "If Billy's like most of us, he won't remember your number. His BlackBerry does that for him."

Dex turned and looked at her. It was obvious she was right. "Then we must get to his Clapham bedsit." They entered the house. Dex was satisfied that nothing had been disturbed during the day. "Book a big car to pick us up. Find a jet charter company from Stansted."

"Private jet? That'll cost…"

"Forget the cost. Remember, I'm on the Rich List. Have it on standby for this evening. I'll pay en route to the airport. I'll ring Adam and throw a few things together."

Within twenty minutes, they were ready. Moments later a large black Mercedes pulled up. Dex again looked up and down the street. If anybody was watching, it was not obvious and no other car pulled away after they did. "We're not being followed."

"Adam?" Tiffany enquired.

"Shocked but excited. He was actually *toddling along* to Dukes when I phoned. We pick him up in South Kensington on the way to Clapham."

"And if Billy is not at home?"

"We wait for a while. If that fails, I leave a message for him to disappear. He should have enough of my cash to hole up in Brighton for a few days."

"I've a better idea," Tiffany volunteered as she rummaged in her handbag.


Dex had not been the only one enjoying fine dining at lunchtime. Pepe Carmino had taken Jude to the intimacy of Julie's Restaurant in Holland Park, not far from his home. Based on Arnie's report, he had fixed that if Billy Evans appeared, he should be challenged about filming and then quizzed. After arranging that, he planned to fly to Vegas, allowing time for a leisurely lunch followed by an hour or two in bed with Jude before heading off.

The plans had not quite worked out. It was FB who telephoned shortly after 2 p.m. The call interrupted their enjoyment of the selection of cheeses. "Evans arrived. Malky Fuller from security then challenged him about filming illegally and carrying narcotics in contravention of the club rules. He *suggested* Evans join him for a chat but Evans bolted for the stairs. Malky was too slow to catch him and he got away."

"I'll deal with Fuller later." The look on Carmino's face scared Jude as she prodded a lump of goat's cheese.

"Better news," FB continued, his voice sounding flaky. "Evans dropped his BlackBerry. I have it."

"I'll come in. I'll delay Vegas." His irritation at being interrupted and by the runt escaping was only partly counterbalanced by what the BlackBerry might reveal.

They hurried back to Clarendon Road. After a dark and violent session that matched his mood, he left the paddle-slapper on the bed beside a naked and still quivering Jude.

"I may not leave for Vegas until tomorrow or even the next day. This may change everything."

Jude tried to sound excited that he wasn't going after all. She lay on her front, her taut buttocks a flaming red from the beating. As she vaguely listened to an American comedy on the TV, she concluded there was something deeply sinister about Pepe. Ever since finding his knife, she had grown increasingly uneasy. Not for the first time, she wondered why he had taken it the other evening. Had he used it?

Still in pain from the beating, she padded through to the bathroom and ran the Jacuzzi, eager to ease the pain and wash away the smell of his sweat. As the hot water bubbled and splashed, her thoughts were confused. Did she really believe that Dex would rob the casino? Why would Billy Evans be filming? What had that got to do with orders to find and check every page of his passport? Why had he wanted to get inside Porcupine House?

As she dried herself, she still had no answers. Except that Pepe Carmino was not to be trusted. Her life would be better without him.

If only Dex would…

# CHAPTER FORTY

Arnie Fisher had been summoned to meet Carmino in his office. "Bang to rights," he concluded after reading some of the messages passing between Billy Evans and Dexter. "What now?"

Carmino tapped his scar before circling his office as he thought about Dexter. "He's a real danger. How much he knows, we can only guess but certainly too much. So? Do I ban him from membership?"

He returned to his desk and sat down opposite the weasel face of his old school friend. "No. If he comes here, so much the better." He helped himself to a biscuit and pushed the plate nearer to the agent. "But get someone watching Porcupine House and Billy Evans' place in Clapham. I want to know where they are twenty-four-seven."

"Time for another accident?" The narrow face contorted into a sly grin.

"Or they disappear. Best of all—get Dexter in a room. Find out what he knows. Then he must be silenced. While he holds evidence, he's a menace."

Fisher looked doubtful. "Won't he go to the cops?"

"Arnie, I'm banking on you. Use your bent copper contacts. If Dexter tells Scotland Yard, I want you to be first in the know. I can disappear just like that." He clicked his fingers. Then he fell silent. "This god-dammed mess is down to Enzo. He's screwed up. He'll pay for this, I'm telling you."

Arnie rose. "I'll get the tails fixed now."

"PDQ, Arnie. And keep me posted."


The Mercedes was parked along the street from Billy's bedsit in Lavender Gardens SW11. They sat watching street activity for a few minutes. There was nothing unusual—a mother with two kids, a few civil-servant types returning from work. "I'll chance it," Dex said as he opened the rear door.

"Got the notes?"

Dex nodded yes to Tiffany. He saw no watchers in any other vehicles as he approached the three-storey building. He knew Billy had the garret room, but there was no sign of any light or life from the small window. He rang the bell. No response. He checked the time. It was just gone 6:30 p.m.

*How long should I wait?*
*Billy could be with Emily.*
*He could be pissed out of his brains.*
*Snorting cocaine.*
*He could be anywhere.*

He decided to head for Clapham Junction station and check the pubs along the way. As he walked, he called Tiffany to explain what he was doing and to let him know if Billy appeared. He entered the Waggoners. Even a quick glance in both bars revealed no Billy. The next two were also fruitless .He was just about to enter the Drum and Whistle when he saw Billy emerge from the station into St John's Hill.

He did not see Dex who stepped in behind him to observe. Billy was walking briskly, much more so than usual, his short steps busy and his arms swinging. If he had been drinking, it did not show.

"Billy." At the sound of his name, Evans jumped, nerves suddenly evident. He turned his head and was poised to bolt until he saw it was Dex. Relief flooded his face.

"I couldn't phone you. Long story."

Dex hailed a taxi and bundled him in. "I want you packed with passport. Ten minutes turnaround?"

Evans looked confused. "I'm seeing Emily tomorrow."

"You stay here, there may be no tomorrow." Dex saw that the message had got home.

"You know about…?"

"The BlackBerry? Yes."

Billy scurried into his home while Dex thumbs-upped to Tiffany and Adam. Then he pulled out the blu-tack and two notes from his jacket pocket. Now that Billy had appeared, one was redundant but the second he folded and stuck above the bell marked *Top Floor*. Tiffany's idea just might work—it might buy them time. Like an anxious father waiting in Maternity, he stood outside tapping his feet and looking up and down Lavender Gardens for any sign of hostility. He checked his watch. 7:22 p.m.

*Come on, Billy!*
*Come on!*
*For fuck's sake!*


In a Ford Focus on Battersea Rise, the driver and passenger were mouthing abuse as they waited at the traffic lights. When Arnie Fisher had called, the two men had been settling down for a pizza in Borough High Street. Leaving it behind, they had used their back-double experience to race to Clapham but the roadworks for the new cycle lane were screwing everything up.

Arnie's instructions had been clear. *If he's there, keep him till I arrive. If not, wait for him. As long as it takes.*

Across London, a Ford Taurus had left a council tower block in Shepherd's Bush heading for Porcupine House. The instructions had been the same. The third vehicle, a Mini Cooper, had already reached Adam Yarbury's home and reported there was nobody home.

It was 7:31 p.m. when Jack, the Ford Focus driver, phoned Arnie. "We're gonna wait. He's not here but the geezer's coming."

"Give!"

"Only found a bleedin' note pinned to his bell, didn't we? Here, get a load of this."

# CHAPTER FORTY-ONE

Even in the powerful Mercedes, it was slow progress through east London heading for Stansted Airport. There the Gulfstream had a 10:30 p.m. departure slot. They stopped at a drive-through Burger King and picked up burgers, fries and Cokes. "Really rather good," said Adam, sounding surprised. "My first ever burger." The three listeners laughed at the revelation. It was the first lighter moment on the journey.

Everyone had been tense following the earlier exchanges. "Billy, you told me, even yesterday, that you were clean. That was a lie." Even Tiffany looked shocked at what Dex knew. "Don't ask me how I know but I do. A dealer on a street corner in Chinatown."

Billy flinched at the word Chinatown. He said nothing though his head drooped in shame.

"Billy, you lied to me. And I don't deserve that." Dex turned, resting his arm on the seatback so that he could face Billy directly. "I want the truth." The words were barked out, filling the passenger zone and reminding Dex of the shock tactic on FB. "Firstly, can I rely on you? Was the blackjack fixed?"

"I swear. But I've no evidence. Carmino has it, not me."

Dex gripped Billy by the shoulder. "You've blown our cover. You've buggered everything. Because of you, we're now running for our lives."

There was an embarrassed silence until Billy perked up, for the first time looking more confident. "No. Wait. I've got it. On my laptop. I copied it across."

"Thank God for small mercies." Dex lowered his voice slightly. "Billy, what you said at the Bulgari was bollocks, wasn't it?" Dex was backing a hunch. "You went there today to card-count and *to play the count* because there was no Adam beside you." He paused for emphasis and wagged his finger close to Billy's pale face. "You wanted to win cash. You wanted cash to spend with pushers on street-corners."

He watched Billy's face twist one way and then the other as he wiped his hand under his nostrils. "That's right, isn't it?" Dex snapped out the last words, a technique he had picked up from watching a barrister at the inquest into the fire deaths. It had proved effective then and again now.

Billy looked at the three occupants in turn and started to sob, his shoulders heaving. "I'm sorry. I needed a big win. You don't. You can't understand how, how…" His voice trailed away and his whole body trembled.

"How hard it is to kick the stuff? Assume I can. But if you hadn't lied, we would not be in this mess." He pointed to Adam. "Thanks to you, Adam now faces the prospect of Carmino inserting a Bowie knife into his jacksie."

Tiffany, who had tried a smile of encouragement to Billy, recoiled at the choice of phrase.

Dex had no intention of taking his foot off Billy's throat now. "Because of you, we're running away like dogs in the night or maybe more like scaredy-cats. I don't trust Pepe Carmino to take prisoners." He moved closer to Billy and made a sudden jabbing move with his right hand. "I never told you this before but the poor sod Carmino murdered in Panama had over twenty knife wounds. *That* is the guy we are now facing."

"I'm sorry. I…I was desperate."

"You're not carrying any drugs now, are you?" It was Tiffany chipping in. "Because the US use sniffer dogs at the airports. If your bag contains the slightest trace, you are in the slammer."

"Trust me," he muttered as he started to calm down. "I finished the last line before heading into Dukes."

"What else was on the BlackBerry?" Dex took up the interrogation.

"Besides e-mails and text messages? Photos. My Contact List— y'know, names, addresses, and phone numbers. Music, apps, the usual."

"Think carefully, Billy. Is there anything suggesting I'm after Space City?"

"You never told me that."

Dex changed position, relaxing his posture. He turned to Tiffany. "We implement the plan on Letizione. I'll phone Otto from the airport." He thought back to the recorded confession from FB. " My take is Letizione will know nothing of Carmino's London problems. Carmino is not the type to admit weakness."

"Or," Adam intervened for the first time, "Carmino might vanish, leaving this Lavazione or whatever his name is to catch the doodah."

It was then that Dex had spotted the Burger King. "I'm famished." He patted Billy on the shoulder. "We are where we are. From now on, we need to be smarter than we've been. After we get back, I'm sending you to a great clinic in Wiltshire. They'll help get rid of your demons." He tapped on the smoked-glass screen that divided the rear seats from the chauffeur in his black suit and cap. "The drive-through, please."


Jack was standing by the Ford Focus as he reported to Arnie Fisher.

"Yeah. The note's timed at 5:40 p.m. It says, *Where are you? Tried calling but someone else answered. Pickup was 5 p.m. Meet us in the hotel. Train it from the Junction. The hotel is a short taxi journey along the seafront. We fly early to Monte Carlo.*"

"Monte Carlo?" Arnie was quick to react. "Must be a gambling jolly."

"The note ends: *We hit the casino tomorrow night. Need you there. If need be take Easyjet from Gatwick.*" Jack tucked the note into his pocket. "It's signed *Adam.*"

"Must be Yarbury and Dexter off to France, then." Arnie tried to weigh up what he had heard. "Sounds like they plan to take the casino for big money, but God knows how. Wait there and grab Billy-boy when he appears."


At Stansted, after clearing Security, Dex distanced himself from the others in the Departure Lounge. There were no messages from FB and no way could he phone him, so he phoned Vegas. "Otto. I'm arriving at the Wynn at around 2 a.m. your time. Will you have what I need?"

Otto was cryptic and to the point. "No. One more shoe to fall. But mid-morning, say eleven, how about we meet in your hotel—the Parasols Up bar beside the main gaming floor?"

"See you there." He rejoined the group, sensing an uneasy silence without him there providing the glue. "Let's go."

Dex felt exhilarated at the prospect of boarding a chartered jet, a new experience. Sure, his bank balance had taken an £80,000 hit, but if a problem could be cured by money, then spend it.

Being one step ahead of Pepe Carmino was worth every last penny.

As they followed a hostess in a gold tunic across the tarmac to the Gulfstream G650, Dex relished the moment. It was his first ever taste of what unlimited wealth could buy. "Better than flying to Malaga crammed in with two hundred others," he enthused as they stood at the aircraft's steps. The pilot welcomed them. Moments later, the whine of the engines turned to a roar as the jet accelerated away westward and soared up into the night sky.

Adam and Billy were in seats across the wide aisle from each other. Billy was almost instantly asleep while Adam was reading *Wine Spectator* magazine. Dex looked across the aisle at Tiffany.

"Hard to believe you only flew in this morning?"

In her leather chair, Tiffany stretched her legs, her eyelids drooping. "I'm not even sure what time zone I'm working on!" She looked around at the calming décor—all muted shades of greys and blue. Just ahead was the dining area, the rectangular table carved from the finest light oak. It was ready to seat four when they wanted to eat. "First class was pretty special, but this is pampering. I could get used to this." They fell silent as Tiffany's eyes closed and Dex opened a scribbling pad. He had to get his thoughts into focus.

About an hour after takeoff, supper was served at the table. Tiffany had chosen the menu on the phone. The hostess laid out pasta, cheeses, cold meats, and a selection of smoked fish. It arrived on fine china with a bamboo-leaf motif. Adam also assured them that the red and white wines were from renowned vintages and enhanced by the stylish simplicity of the glassware.

After the plates were all cleared away, Billy and Adam returned to their reclined seats and fell asleep almost immediately. Looking at her, Dex sensed unspoken resentment from Tiffany. He was keen to build bridges and restore the magic they had shared in the pub garden. It was not going to be easy.

"Dex, let me tell you straight. I don't agree with all this. You should have told the police, even though you don't trust them." She reached out for his hand. "That apart, considering you're meant to be a stress-free zone, you're handling this well. After all…"

"Don't remind me of Grierson! My blood pressure would blow his gadget apart."

Tiffany laughed. "You mean the sphygmomanometer? Try saying that without your teeth in!" She helped herself to a Belgian chocolate and then squeezed his fingers tighter. "Actually, I was more thinking of the booze. Despite the stress of all this," she waved her hand airily toward Billy, "you seem under control."

"Dumping the pills changed everything. As the saying goes, *they was doing me head in.* But I need you. Desperately. That note left at Billy's—bloody marvellous idea."

"We'll never know if it fooled them."

"Oh, we might. From FB. He may text or even phone if he picks up some vibes from Carmino. Hopefully we've bought twenty-four hours. That's enough to set up Enzo Letizione."

"Or Lavazione, as Adam calls him." They both laughed. "Is he a mafiosa type?"

"Otto says no but he's tough. That's why he won't crack if I use normal methods."

"But he knows what's been going on?"

Dex nodded more confidently than he felt. "Let's see what Otto delivers. Time for some kip. Tomorrow is going to be busy."

For the first time since the pub garden, Tiffany looked deeply into his eyes and clasped both his hands. She motioned to Adam and Billy. "Pity we have company. The six-mile high club would have been a great first."

"They're asleep. Way, way gone. I'm up for it."

She shook her head. "Let's wait for the right moment. I want it to be special." Dex saw her tilt her head to the side and run her fingers through her hair in a way he found almost irresistible. "Dex, when I was haring round America, I realised you really are different to the rest of the pack." She stood up before easing her arms around his neck, and for the first time gave him a deep and meaningful kiss. "Not always in a good way. But different. Goodnight, Dex."

# CHAPTER FORTY-TWO

After a restless few hours in which he had ignored Jude's attempts to chat, Pepe Carmino had surprised the cleaners and morning staff by arriving early at the casino. For him to arrive before 5 p.m. was rare. To be there at breakfast time, when the cashiers were still balancing the books, was so rare as to set tongues wagging. He had coffee, V8 and toast delivered and then phoned Enzo. It was shortly before 2 a.m. in Vegas when he ended the discussion.

As he cut the call, assuring the American that everything was just fine, Pepe was irritated because Letizione had said nothing to get angry about. He needed someone to be the punchbag, someone to feel the heat of his simmering fury. Somehow though, everything in Vegas was now running smoothly. Even when he had tried to nitpick, Letizione had an answer.

He pushed aside the remains of his breakfast and sat doodling at his desk, desperate for a strategy. He took some deep breaths, forcing himself to be calm. It was a time for straight thinking. He could grab his false IDs and live a new life between Montevideo and Dubai. Every small detail was in place. The entire Dukes empire would collapse like a soufflé, leaving the bank with nil chance of recovering the loans.

*Shed no tears for bankers!*

*Jude?*

*Surplus baggage.*

*Finlay Dexter wins. Am I ready for that?*

*Has he called in the cops?*

*Why go to Monte Carlo if he's told the cops?*

*So he hasn't.*

*Why go there at all?*

*Have I got this all wrong?*

*No.*

*Dexter plans to destroy me.*

He called Arnie. "Yes, come at once. And bring that note too." He returned to jotting ideas—lots of underlining, plenty of scratching out between the meaningless shapes and curved or straight arrows.

By the time Arnie arrived twenty-five minutes later, the jumble of thoughts had morphed into Plans A and B. Arnie was clutching a takeaway coffee and a bacon bap in a brown bag.

In clipped terms, Carmino outlined the alternatives. "Is this the end, Arnie? Time to cash in the chips and fuck off into obscurity? Or can we fix that shit and survive?"

Pepe picked up the note and read it over and over. The words Monte Carlo seemed to ebb and flow before his eyes. It made no sense. He put it down and raised an eyebrow toward Arnie.

"So? Plan A or B?"

"Plan A sucks. You just can't do that—it's…" He fought for the right word. "…it's grotesque." Arnie screwed up the brown bag and dismissively chucked it into a bin. "But I'm not buying Plan B either. I'm not ready to quit London."

"I set everything up. Of course you're ready."

"Yeah, right. New ID, a place in South Africa, blah-di-blah. But I like London. And I've got my new bit of stuff up down in Sutton."

"Tough." Pepe was enjoying the chance to let rip. "There is no Plan C."

Arnie wriggled uncomfortably. He knew Pepe Carmino better than anybody and sensed the ugliness in his mood. Someone was going to suffer.

Arnie had helped his school friend for over twenty-five years now. He had seen his many moods. This one scared him. Like this, Pepe was the guy who had strangled a pet rabbit *just for a laugh* and who had swerved to drive over a King Charles spaniel.

*Someone* was going to pay for Pepe's mood. He squirmed on his chair knowing he would have to deliver. Like this, friendship counted for nothing. He had recognised the mounting menace in Pepe's voice and had heard his knuckles cracking the way they had done before the order to murder Mick Glenn.

Pepe stood up and leaned across the desk, his already dark features looking even darker, the brown eyes boring deep into Arnie. Then he edged even closer and thumped his fist on the desk. "You're right, Arnie. I'm not ready to surrender. Not while there's a chance. I've decided. We go for Plan A." His lip twisted into a snarl. "Do it."

# CHAPTER FORTY-THREE

Over breakfast at the Terrace Pointe Café in the Wynn Hotel, Dex fixed for Billy and Adam to go on a helicopter trip to the Grand Canyon. After they had cheerily left the table, he briefed Tiffany on what he wanted her to do while he was seeing Otto Schneider. In her matching pink T-shirt and shorts, she looked very much at home in Vegas.

"You really think this could work?" Tiffany's brow was unusually furrowed as she spoke. She sounded doubtful – and was.

"You can do it. As the Americans say, we attack Letizione from left field." He checked his watch. "Time to meet Otto. If he's delivered, we press the button." He gave her a fleeting kiss. "I'll come to your room when I'm done."

Otto Schneider had no photo on his website, presumably deliberately for someone operating in his shady field, but Dex spotted him as the guy sitting alone with a slim leather briefcase. After pleasantries and a couple of coffees ordered, Dex looked enquiringly.

Schneider was aged well into his sixties, with greying wild eyebrows in need of a trim. His eyes were deep-set, his forehead and cheeks crinkled and his nose aquiline. His mane of silvery hair was swept back into a duck's arse. Overall, he oozed an aura of street-smart.

Dex could tell that thirty years before he would have been a handful in a fight. Now, he looked bettter suited to industrial espionage. Schneider opened the briefcase and produced a sheaf of perhaps eighteen sheets of paper tucked into a Perspex folder. "I guess this is what you wanted?"

The coffees were delivered as Dex read with unusual care. After the third page, he looked up. "Amazing." He read to the end while Schneider browsed a copy of the *Review Journal*. "I cannot believe you obtained this. It is authentic? No chance we've been set up?"

"Nix. I know my sources here and in the Caribbean."

"I've another job. I guess I'm still in credit by a country mile."

Schneider's face showed no reaction. "Tell me what it is. You may be."

After the explanation, Dex ended the meeting and dashed to the forty-eighth floor. His room was on the forty-ninth, looking over the Strip. Tiffany let him in. The room was identical except that she looked east over the golf course. "My room has a much better view, especially at night," he suggested and was rewarded with a tap on the nose telling him not to get ahead of himself. They sat down on the sofa by the picture window while she skimmed through the documents. She exhaled a long whistle and shook her head in astonishment.

"And your research?" Dex asked as he looked down at the tiny figures on the fairway far below.

"I found just the place. But Dex, are you really sure about this?"

"With this stuff from Otto? Absolutely. But I need Carmino here—when I'm ready. He must be coming for the Grand Opening."

"Why here? We left England to be safe."

"Because the Feds will nail him for crimes we never even knew existed. Jail sentences topping a hundred years." His smile was grim but carried a message of just how determined he was. "Plus the death penalty if the murder raps stick." Dex watched her check out her notes and then reluctantly stand before reaching for the phone by the bed. "You can do it. Just remember, you're a journalist." He sat back on the sofa, swinging one leg along its length.

"Is that Mr Letizione's PA? Ah, good! My name is Shani Sharp of Alacrity TV Productions. I'm over here doing background on the opening of Space City. The editor wants me to interview Mr Letizione at Haldeman Facilities on South Rainbow."

Dex watched as Tiffany listened to the PA, her face impassive.

"Of course, I understand he's busy. But believe me, he'll really appreciate this opportunity. You must know how many Europeans visit Vegas every year. With our audience reach, we'll be profiling Space City in over thirty countries. If Mr Letizione declines, my editor will spike the entire piece."

Dex tried to catch Tiffany's eye but she was looking firmly in the other direction. All he saw was the side of her shoulder and the shapely curves underneath her shorts. "7 p.m.? Fifteen mins? That'll work. He knows Haldeman? He's been there before? Ah! Excellent! He should ask for me, Shani. I'll be doing the interview."

"Brilliant!" Dex commented when she put the phone down. "Otto has three men on standby. I'll firm that up as we go to Haldeman to make the arrangements."

For a moment or two, they stood by the window, she with her hand round his waist. They watched as a helicopter flitted across the clear blue sky. "Perhaps that's Adam and Billy," she suggested. "You're not keeping them in the loop?"

Dex shook his head. "You've seen how Billy was this morning. He's struggling. The sooner he's in a clinic, the better. He needs help." He turned away and headed for the door. "You know, I wasn't joking. My room has a much better view."

Tiffany rocked her head back. "You must know better chat-up lines than that. One ceiling looks much like the next. I'll meet you downstairs in twenty minutes."

Back in his room, Dex phoned Jamous, imagining him surrounded by the clutter and chaos in Penarth Street. It was nearly noon and way down below, the traffic on Las Vegas Boulevard was starting to back up as the city gradually awoke from its usual late night. "Jake Cornelius here. How's it going? I assume you've finished."

# CHAPTER FORTY-FOUR

Haldeman Facilities was a twenty-minute journey by taxi from the hotel. South Rainbow lay several miles west and parallel to the Strip. It proved to be significantly unpleasant, crammed with six lanes of traffic speeding in each direction. It was a mix of commercial premises, showrooms, endless fast food joints and waste ground. The fumes of thousands of semi-trailers, trucks, four-by-fours, and speeding Japanese cars left the air hazy and polluted as the desert sun beat down on the tarmac.

A digital sign showed that the temperature was now 108°. As the taxi travelled south, the road ahead was littered with overhead cables, huge advertising hoardings for Firestone, Subway, and Wendy's. Countless gas-stations and small trading corporations made everything pig-ugly. Haldeman Facilities proved to be just one small doorway of several in a two-storey block about a hundred metres long.

After telling the driver to wait, they went in, telling the receptionist they had an appointment. As the boss, Mel Willmer, showed them round, Tiffany was impressed. She looked at the lighting rigs, the camera positions, the microphones and video monitors that circled the studio floor. "I'm getting a real buzz from being back in a studio. I shall miss this way of life," she sighed as they checked seating arrangements and camera positions. "And I want to see the control-room, please."

As they followed a few steps behind Willmer, she whispered that this would be where Dex would be positioned. Once behind the glass-screened zone, she showed him where he would be seated, what he would see, and which controls he would need.

Forty minutes later, the driver took them further from the Strip to Marché Bacchus, a French-style bistro overlooking a lake some ten miles from the Wynn Hotel. The contrast to the nastiness of Rainbow Boulevard was absolute. The restaurant had been recommended by Otto Schneider as a great place to enjoy the ducks, moorhens, and swans. For a second, Dex was reminded of sheltering from the elements watching similar wildlife beside the Thameside lake, waiting for a carp's powerful tug. The similarity ended there.

They sat on the shady terrace, cooled by a misting system, and looked across the translucent blue of the lake. For the next two hours, over a bottle of chilled Sauvignon Blanc and grilled salmon, they flirted, joked, and scripted the evening ahead, the fine spray cooling them while a small turtle occasionally broke the surface as a backdrop.

At about the same time but eight hours ahead, Pepe Carmino had dropped off Jude at the Ritz Hotel on Piccadilly, where she was meeting the widow of a former Lebanese president. Later, she would bring her for an evening in Dukes. As soon as the car was empty, he called Arnie. "Plan A? Are you taking the piss or what?"

"I'm on the case. Trust me. Okay, I don't like it. But I agreed, so I'll do it. But easy it ain't. Okay? So stop pissing me off. I'll deliver when I can."

Carmino changed the subject. "That Monte Carlo note. It's bollocks."

"Meaning?"

"Adam Yarbury never wrote that. I compared it with the membership forms he signed for Dexter and Billy Evans. Whoever wrote that was not Adam." He made a left and then a right turn as he fought the one-way system toward Mount Street. "And that means Monte Carlo is bollocks too. It never made sense anyway."

"None of them have been home. Where are they?"

"That, Arnie," snapped Pepe, "is for you to find out. Dexter's been pulling my plonker for too long. Plan A. That'll fix the odious shit." He cruised to a halt at the foot of the steps up to the grand entrance to Dukes. "Action. Now."

"No chance tonight. Tomorrow morning."

One of the car jockeys appeared and took the keys. At the top of the steps, he passed a couple of flippant remarks with Tom before going inside and up to his office.

As 7 p.m. approached with the sun outside on South Rainbow still relentless, Dex, Tiffany and Mel Willmer were prepared for Letizione's arrival. Tucked away out of sight were Otto's trio, all briefed on what to do and when. A solitary cameraman and a sound and lighting technician were making last-minute adjustments. Using a legal precedent that Dex had found through Google, the technicians had been paid $2,000 each to sign a confidentiality agreement with unlimited damages liability for any loose word. Everybody else had been paid for an evening off.

"The power of money," Dex had enthused to Tiffany over lunch. "Willmer doesn't know the details but I'm paying him way over the odds. Short of us trashing the place, he'll put up with anything."

# CHAPTER FORTY-FIVE

Enzo Letizione's stretch limo pulled up a minute after 7 p.m. On both sides was the Space City logo of a golden spacecraft, ringed by the words SPACE CITY. He was feeling ebullient, having just chaired the final meeting of the executive board. They had been purring after hearing his final and upbeat report for the opening in less than seventy-two hours. It was therefore with a confident stride that he came down the corridor to be greeted by Mel Willmer

Seconds later, Dex, watching from the control-room, saw the bulky figure of Letizione for the first time as he came under the glare of the lights to be greeted by Tiffany. He was wearing a lightweight suit, expensively cut to conceal his spreading stomach. The shirt was pale lemon but the tie was overstated and multi-patterned.

Tiffany stood, a clipboard with notes in her hand, and greeted him. "Hi! I'm Shani. Thanks for sparing the time, Mr Letizione."

"My pleasure, Shani. Call me Enzo."

As Willmer positioned him on a dark blue chair with generous armrests, Dex felt the tension mounting in the dry air. It showed in his throat, which he had to clear more than once.

What Tiffany had first described as a wild idea and *way outside the box*, was now hard reality and about to commence. As he looked at her, the very model of a cool professional and so at ease, he had no doubts about how she would cope. Letizione, though, was different, unpredictable.

The high-risk game was about to start. The trap was about to be sprung. He swallowed hard, wondering how he would handle his own role. In the control-room, Dex could hear every word from the studio floor. By pressing a rocker-switch, he could make himself heard. He watched as the microphone was clipped to Letizione's tie. Willmer returned to join him in the high-tech control-room as the cameraman moved in for his head-to-foot opening shot of them both. "Can we do a sound test, please? Get the levels."

"Hi," said Tiffany. "My name is Shani Sharp and I'm about to interview Enzo Letizione about the Space City opening."

"And I'm Enzo Letizione." All around, his strong but heavy features were on display on the monitors.

Willmer's voice came from the speakers. "We're good to roll."

Tiffany checked her clipboard. "Mr Letizione, as CEO and president of US Operations at Space City, I bet you're pretty excited about what's going to hit the Strip."

"We've invested nearly five billion dollars. Space City's gonna be the hottest hangout on the Vegas Strip. So, sure! I'm excited. *All Vegas* is excited. You can feel the buzz. Everybody's talking Space City."

"So what makes it so special?"

"The gaming room atmosphere will be terrific. The shows, the outer-space experience, the mockup of a space shuttle. Awesome! Mind-blowing! Space City'll will be uber-cool, the best bar none. But bars we have! And then some!" He rocked back and laughed at his scripted joke. "And how!"

"And when is the Grand Opening?"

"This Saturday. Y'know, despite the challenging global economy, we're booked solid. Every room has been sold out for weeks. We're booking through Christmas and New Year, months away."

Dex clenched his palms, knowing what was coming next. His heart had been racing earlier. Now it was pounding, thudding as if trying to escape from his ribcage. Despite sipping water, his throat was parched, his eyes wide open as he stared through the glass at the two people on the studio floor just below him. He saw Tiffany shift in her seat, almost imperceptibly, so that she could lean rather more toward him.

"So not opening this weekend, that would be a huge disappointment."

Letizione's time-weathered face showed puzzlement rather than concern. "Excuse me? I'm not following your comment. We're good to go—and right on time."

"I mean, if the Feds closed you down. Arrested you for RICO offences, for fraud."

Dex enjoyed watching puzzlement become concern and then confusion bordering on panic. Letizione's swarthy face seemed to darken and age in seconds. "What in hell you talking about? What is this? I'm out of here."

As he saw the American start to fiddle with his microphone, Dex knew this was his moment. Volume turned up, Dex flicked the rocker-switch. "Sit down, Mr Letizione. You're going nowhere."

The voice boomed out from the wraparound sound-system, filling the studio floor. The sharpness of tone caused Letizione another moment of doubt. Dex enjoyed watching a frown etch across his brow as he looked in every direction to spot the speaker.

"Let me introduce myself. I'm Dex—Finlay Dexter from London, brother of Beth Dexter." Dex paused to watch the reaction and, satisfied, continued. "Beth Dexter, *deceased.* I can see you know my name and who Beth was. As you should."

Letizione crossed one leg over the other and then as quickly uncrossed them

"I'm here to talk about your conspiracy with Pepe Carmino. Money laundering. The Racketeer Influenced Corrupt Organizations Act. RICO to you and me." His chuckle reverberated round the compact studio. "Though it is more pertinent to you." Dex laughed, suddenly finding he was enjoying himself. "Fraud. The murder of Mick Glenn. The gunning down of Tavio Sanchez. The death of Diego Rodrigues in Lake Mead. The murder of my sister."

Still with the microphone clipped to him, trance-like, Letizione stood up again."I'm outta here."

"Mr Letizione, until I say so, *you* are going nowhere." At that moment, Otto Schneider's three bruisers appeared and circled him. "Pepe Carmino will go to Death Row. You may be joining him. Whatever, you'll spend the rest of your days in a federal penitentiary. The other prisoners will just love the CEO and president of a casino group that cheats and robs gamblers." He paused to make his point. "Gang-rape and sodomy, wouldn't you agree?"

Dex watched the beads of perspiration forming on the lined forehead. No doubt the heat from the lights did not help but he knew that he was now deep under the man's skin. The lemon shirt looked as if it was soaking up nervous sweat as the wearer tugged it away from his chest.

The American stared toward the camera and tried to sound defiant. "Quit dreaming. This is garbage. Utter bullshit."

Dex spoke slowly to articulate every word. He glanced to his right and saw Willmer's jaw almost drop to the floor as he continued. "Bullshit, you reckon? Here, I'll help you. Laundering money through banks in Montserrat, Panama and the Cayman Islands." Dex read from the notes in front of him. "Caymans Account XCEHZY6398401."

He saw shock and panic once again flood Letizione's face.

"You think I'm bullshitting you now?" Dex saw Enzo Letizione run a finger around the collar of his shirt as the perspiration broke out across his entire face. His cheeks had turned ashen. "Want to hear something else? How about the felony of concealing from the Nevada Gaming Board that your colleague and CEO in London, Pepe Carmino, murdered someone playing blackjack in Panama? You knew, didn't you? Tavio and his pal Rodrigues had to be silenced. Both murdered."

Letizione pulled a handkerchief from his pocket and started mopping his face with jabbing movements. From above and all round him, the unrelenting glare and heat from the studio lights added to his discomfort. "I knew nothing of this. Nothing to do with me.

Dex ignored the denial. "The death penalty. Nevada still has the death penalty." He stopped to let silence hang heavily across the studio-floor. "Mr Letizione, you are in line for it."

"Not me. Pepe never told me."

"That's for the Feds. Wait one! There's more – like conspiracy to fund Space City with laundered money?" Again, Dex paused to enjoy the meltdown as Letizione looked around, trying to spot where the interrogation was coming from. In contrast, Tiffany was expressionless. She looked unruffled as she sat motionless, transfixed by the discomfort just a few feet from her. "These jail sentences are racking up against you."

Letizione tried to speak, but his voice was croaky from the dry air and the tension. He grabbed for a bottle of water. When he did speak, the confident baritone voice had gone, replaced by a nasal whine. "Whaddya want?"

"I want Pepe Carmino here, tomorrow. I'm offering a deal—for you both. I want you to phone him now."

"It's 3:30 a.m. in London."

"I don't need you to tell me the time of day, Mr Letizione. Give me his direct dial number. We can all join in the call. When he answers, you speak, introducing me."

Letizione pulled out his phone, checked the number and read it off. Dex dialled from the phone in the control-room. Mel Willmer switched it to loudspeaker so that everyone could hear.

Moments later, Carmino's falsely cultured voice came on the line. "Hi, Enzo. Board meeting go well?"

"Pepe. I have someone with me wants to speak to you."

"It's Finlay Dexter here. I've been chatting with Mr Letizione. In particular about murder, money laundering, and bank accounts. No doubt the number LMKPZB407993 is familiar."

"No."

"Cut the crap. That is your personal account in George Town, Grand Cayman. You thought it was hidden under the corporate name of Dykeside Global Inc. The present balance is seventy-one million dollars."

Even as he read out the details, Dex quickly switched to watching Letizione. The sweaty unease now showed a flash of anger as he heard how much more had been siphoned off to the Brit.

"Here's the deal, Mr Carmino. Meet me at the Galleria Bar, Caesar's Palace, at 4 p.m. tomorrow. Mr Letizione will join us. He and you will prove a transfer of twenty million dollars to my account. And I will want cash handed over. Mr Letizione will have the details."

"In return," the disembodied voice explained, "you receive the originals of everything I got in Panama concerning the murder of the Mexican at the Casino Sienna. I will also include the signed statement of Tavio Sanches taken by Beth plus the statement made by Diego Rodrigues before he was dumped in Lake Mead." He enjoyed the bluff and decided to continue. "I will hand over all films proving cheating at blackjack and roulette. Finally, you can have my report on money-laundering through Dukes."

"Pepe, you gotta go for this. We got the opening on Saturday," prompted Letizione. From Carmino, there was just silence as he inwardly cursed Arnie for not delivering on Plan A.

Dex let the American's plea linger before going on. "My security guys will take the cash from the Galleria Bar. We can then discuss the future of Space City and Dukes. By then, I will have Mr Letizione's signed confession. You can write yours on the flight over. Both confessions will be kept by a Las Vegas attorney to be released only if any harm ever comes to me or anybody known to me. Understood?"

Before Carmino could reply, it was Letizione who spoke. "Pepe, the guy's got the nuts. It's our only chance. You gotta get here or I'm going to the slammer. If I go, sure as hell, you are joining me. I'll see to that."

# CHAPTER FORTY-SIX

"I'll be there. Enzo—fix that transfer. See you at 4 p.m. Caesar's Palace." Carmino's heavy breathing could be heard around the control-room and studio floor. Dex ended the call.

For the next eighty minutes, Dex worked on the confession, Letizione denying involvement in the murders. Tiffany sat opposite the sweaty figure, chipping in with questions. Throughout the Q&A session, Dex did not appear. Everything was controlled by the hidden voice probing and prodding toward the truth. After every paragraph, Dex read back the details, asking Letizione to agree to their accuracy.

Even after the confession was complete and Willmer had taken it down to Letizione for signing, the camera was still running, the recording continuing. Only after the sullen and unsmiling figure had been escorted off the premises did Mel Willmer end the session. Dex thanked him warmly.

"Shit fucking hot." Willmer breathed the words as he shook his head in wonderment. "It's all…so goddammed unreal."

Tiffany arrived, her cheeks glowing with excitement. She grinned at Dex. "As the Americans would say, *like, I mean, wow.*" She gave him a hug. "Brilliant."

Dex gave her a huge boyish grin before hugging her. "You were just great but for now, *omerta* rules." He turned to Willmer. "I want you and your guys each to sign this statement confirming you were here and heard this. Also, you must both confirm on the recording that you heard every word."

Formalities completed, Dex handed over cash for use of the facilities plus $4,000 to the technicians. He took duplicate copies of the recording, leaving nothing behind. "A Mr. Otto Schneider will inform you when you are free to speak. Till then—absolute confidentiality."

Moments later, they exited into the evening air. Darkness had fallen but the ugliness of the surroundings was still obvious. though the fumes were less obnoxious with the lighter traffic. "The Forum

Shops, Caesar's Palace," Dex instructed their limo driver. "I want to double-check the Galleria Bar and then how about dinner in Spago."

"Billy and Adam?"

"Billy texted me earlier on his new phone. They were going to a magic show somewhere. The MGM, I think. But anyway, tonight's about the two of us. Or am I wrong?"

For an answer, he felt her reach for and hold his hand. As they cruised sedately down West Flamingo, Tiffany turned to him, their shoulders close. "You won't hand over the evidence, will you?"

In the darkness, Tiffany did not see the sly look. "If he brings my two million cash and twenty million is transferred to my bank, sure, I'll hand over the evidence."

Tiffany looked puzzled. "You would do that? Let that swine off the hook?"

"I didn't quite say that. I never agreed to hand over Mel Willmer's evidence, everything now recorded in the studio."

"You, Finlay Dexter, are a devious bastard." She breathed the words, heavy with admiration. "Every base covered. But I can sense there's more." She prodded him playfully in the ribs. "Come on, Dex, what am I missing?"

"I said *if* Carmino comes. He won't."

Tiffany turned sharply. "He won't?"

"Carmino despises Letizione. Would he risk a Nevada death penalty? Would he risk his skin just to save Letizione? Or put it round the other way, would Letizione truly expect Carmino to save him?" He draped his arm over her shoulder. "No way. They won't come to the Galleria Bar, neither of them."

"In which case," commented Tiffany, "what does Letizione do? Cut a deal with you?"

"I bet those two are on the phone right now. Carmino will say, no way you make any transfer. Letizione will then be shit-scared for himself." Dex looked up at the multicoloured Rio Casino towers. "What would you do in his position?"

Tiffany looked out of the limo window at the Rio's giant marquee. "Look after number-one. Dump Pepe. Make a run."

"Right. He'll be scared shitless of Carmino coming here. Besides wanting my balls on a plate, Pepe would crucify Letizione."

"Unless for some reason, he needs him for now."

"Possible. We can only guess."

"Might Letizione cut a deal with you?" She did not sound her usual confident self. There was hesitation before each word. She sensed rather than saw Dex shake his head. "Okay. Tell me—what would you do?"

"If I were Letizione? I would not transfer twenty million. I would not appear at the Galleria Bar. PDQ, I'd shift my money from the Caymans to some other account." The limo entered the underpass to the destination. "And I'd get out of here. Vamoose. Grab and go—before the Feds arrive."

Tiffany paused, ready to exit as the limo slowed. "Game, set, and match. Space City would not open. But Carmino?"

"He'll be of two minds. He could agree that *we have the nuts*. He'd then run, disappear. Start a new life with his seventy million bucks."

"Or what? Surrender?"

The limo pulled up under the sweeping curve of the entrance, fountains, water and statues everywhere. "Carmino? Surrender?" Dex sounded dismissive. He looked across the darkened interior and then eased Tiffany out of the limo. "He is now more dangerous than ever." He put his arm around Tiffany's shoulder and led her into the cool of the air-conditioned foyer. "He'll run, but not before he's finished."

Tiffany shuddered as she realised the implications. "Finished? What will he do?"

"If he doesn't run?" Dex shrugged his shoulders. "What's another murder now? He'll want to kill me before he disappears. Or he'll run but vow to get me someday, sometime."

# CHAPTER FORTY-SEVEN

In the Galleria Bar, they took a seat in a distant corner close to the high-rollers' room. It was dimly lit and slightly raised above the main gaming floor with a scattering of comfy chairs and low tables. The chairs were deep, large and relaxing—well-enough set apart for private discussions. They sank a couple of large gins.

"Otto was right." Dex clinked glasses with a rather sombre Tiffany. The euphoria that had filled the control-room had not lasted. "Cameras everywhere, casino security. Otto's team. If Carmino does show, it would be lunacy to commit a murder here." He pointed to the sprawling casino-floor, packed with noisy gamblers playing craps, roulette and blackjack. "Then, after the deal, protected by Otto's security guys, I can disappear in so many different directions."

Tiffany lowered her goblet to the table. "*Lunacy*? Dex, the guy's a psycho. He murdered the Mexican in front of the casino staff. They couldn't pull him off. Remember?" She leaned over to grip his wrist, her frustration at his obstinacy showing.

Dex sipped thoughtfully, his eyes fixed on the ceiling. "He *won't* show. Trust me, Tiffany. If he is going to get me, it won't be here." He managed a watery smile. "The timing is his to choose."

"Condemned men are unpredictable."

"Then we must be smarter. You, me. Our joint intellects." He stroked her cheek. "Come on, let's hit Spago." He stood up and when she followed, their steps were slow, heads bowed in thought. They paused briefly between the crowded tables where a throng surrounded the craps. Further on, after watching Rod Stewart, a stream of people swarmed around them before they approached the entrance to the Forum Shops.

Dex noticed the intensity of her grip on his arm. No question. She was shaking. Tiffany, the cool TV journalist and best-selling writer was shivering. She was scared. Terrified. For him. And though he could not admit it, that made him feel the same. He needed a drink.

Not one
Not two.
Several.
Large ones at that.
But he had to fight that urge.
For Beth.


Unpleasant reality lingered throughout their pasta dinner and Barolo. "Assuming they are a no-show tomorrow," continued Tiffany, "promise me, you dump everything on the Feds and the Met Police."

"No promises but that's my intention." His answer seemed to satisfy her though she sensed he was still determined to skin Dukes and claw back Beth's losses and more.

"Don't let your promise to Beth become an obsession. You've done brilliantly. You have their empire right here." She slowly ground her thumb on the table. As Dex settled the bill, she could see he had no answer to her logic yet his silence confirmed that he was not yet ready to abandon his promises to Beth.

Heading back to the Wynn, they window-shopped between the designer stores of the Forum and then out onto the Strip. Night had truly fallen, only to be lit by the dazzling array of flashing neon from every direction. In the packed street, noisy revellers were dawdling in both directions—either toward the junction at Flamingo or to take in the volcano eruption at the Mirage.

Tiffany paused to look at him beside a small fountain. "This must be how a US president feels."

"When everyone is a potential assassin?" Dex agreed and pulled her head closer to his. "The best security can't protect you from someone prepared to die for his cause." He kissed her on the mouth, just lightly. "Carmino's too cunning to want to die. Anyway, *carpe diem*. Live every moment for what you have."

They continued toward the Fashion Show Mall. They had barely gone a few paces when Tiffany stopped him in mid-stride. "Was that a subtle message to me?" She kissed him full on the mouth for a lingering moment before they headed up the walkway over the Strip.

Still shaken from his visit to Haldeman Facilities, Enzo Letizione returned to his desk and sat sinking Jack Daniel's while looking both dazed and confused. By 1 a.m, he had still made no decision and had not heard from Carmino, something he decided was an ugly sign.

In London, where it was 9 a.m., Pepe Carmino was fighting exhaustion after a night without sleep. Arnie Fisher had not delivered on Plan A. And Dexter? His worst fears had been proved right. F'Christ's sake! The bastard had been so well informed! Who had been leaking? One-Eye? Jed Miller? Someone in the cage? FB? Jude? Or had Enzo Letizione just squealed under pressure?

It made no sense. Jude knew about the hot money but nothing involving the banks. FB knew of the frauds but nothing of the Caymans. O'Keefe knew of the laundering *and* the secret accounts in the Caymans. Were these two working together? That didn't hang together. Not easily.

He checked the time. He could charter the Dassault executive jet if he had to or the Virgin flight would land at 2 p.m., plenty early enough to meet Enzo.

*But why go to Vegas at all?*

He sipped his third espresso since dawn, oscillating between salvation and revenge. Could Dukes and Space City be saved? Could he trust Dexter? Would he hand over the evidence? Did he really have hard evidence, or was he bluffing? For over $20 million, would he keep stumm? No way! He crossed the Wilton carpet and helped himself to a ridiculously large Baron Otard.

*Should I go?*
*Or should I stay?*
*Letizione deserves a trip to the desert.*
*But I don't need to be in Vegas for that. Except for the pleasure.*
*Dexter needs silencing.*
*But where?*

The questions were still troubling him when the phone rang. It was Arnie. It was 9:45 a.m.

"Plan A might be today or definitely tomorrow."

Carmino knew then what he was going to do.

# CHAPTER FORTY-EIGHT

"I'm scared. For you," said Tiffany as they entered the elevator to whisk them high up the Wynn. "I had a scary nightmare last night. Carmino was waving this huge knife and we were running, running but he was catching us."

Dex paused to see if she would expand on what happned next but she did not, so he laughed with a scoff and put his arm around her. As the elevator soared upward he hugged her close to him, aware of her trembling. "Don't worry. Just a bad dream. Like I said—*let's love the moment.*"

"I don't want to be alone. Not after that dream. Can you prove your room has a better view?" Tiffany spoke softly into his ear.

Dex smiled though Tiffany never saw it. "The ceilings are identical."

She managed a laugh but it was unconvincing. "I want to stay close. I'll see you in a minute."

It was several minutes later when she joined him, dressed now in an American Flag onesie. She was carrying a tiny vanity bag. "What do you think? I picked it up in Santa Monica."

Dex, who had changed into a fresh red sports shirt and white shorts, nodded approvingly. "We should play the *Star Spangled Banner* and place our arms across our chests."

"Hold me, hold me tight," she commanded after she had reached the floor-to-ceiling window. Dex felt ripples still running through her. "I need you close, closer than you've ever been." She kissed him, their bodies touching from top to toe like never before.

Dex sensed her urgency came from fear. It was as if she thought this night together might be the last. He responded, trying to calm her, stroking away her worries, running his hands gently up and down her spine, stroking her, reaching the tight curve of her buttocks.

"I can't bear that this might end." Her voice was cracking with emotion. "Carmino is going to kill you. And you're too stubborn to see it."

All her pent-up feelings were unleashed as she sobbed into his shoulder. And the more she sobbed, the tears dripping onto Dex's neck and shirt, the more protective he felt. He clasped her even tighter, as if doing that would squeeze out the panic that shuddered through her.

"I'll be okay. Trust me," he said, with more confidence than he felt. "We need to be strong, united. Together, we can see this through."

Tiffany leaned back, her cheeks soaked and her round eyes still moist. "You think so?" She wanted to be convinced. and forced herself free from him, the room lights bouncing her reflection off the window. She arched her back and stood tall, forcing herself to be defiant.

For a moment, this was the Tiffany he had first encountered—strong and determined. Her eyes flashed pleading yet compassion as she tried to reason with him. "He's a killer. You're not. Not even close. You won't win. Your intellect, our intellect, won't cut it. Not with him, Dex. This is major league. You've beaten him. Quit now." She threw herself at him, as if to prevent him escaping. "This mustn't end badly. We can walk away. Forget Dukes, Space City, Carmino. We can…get a life. Do great things in Africa." Tears once again rolled down her cheeks.

"Carmino can never break us." Gently, he led her to the bed and stretched her out, his steadfast gaze and clenched jaw revealing the strength of his determination. Then he lay down beside her and held her closely, her back nestling tightly into his chest. "Tiffany, my sweet, let's live for this moment." He kissed her neck and he felt her pushing back, responding to his urgency.

He unzipped the front of her onesie as he rolled to lie facing her. Tiffany wriggled her way out of the onesie, revealing she wore nothing underneath. For a moment he feasted on her trim and shapely body. In the half-lit room, she lowered his shorts and pulled him closer so that bare midriffs touched, at first gently and then more powerfully. Her eyes though were still delivering mixed messages of lust and longing, sadness and fear.

He stroked the smooth warm skin of her stomach for the first time, savouring also the mounting swell of her breasts as she unbuttoned his shirt. "Dex, darling, you sweet, luscious and crazy man—make me forget the nightmare. Make the night never end." Her voice was raw with emotion and her words were throaty.

The night did end but not till they awoke at 9 a.m. after pleasuring each other into an exhausted sleep, bodies still entwined. As Tiffany pressed the wall-rocker and the curtains swished open, reality and bright sunlight flooded the room. Las Vegas already looked hot, dusty and arid, ready for another day.

Dex had to catch up with Adam. "Enjoy yesterday?"

"Brilliant. Unbelievable show," said Adam. "And we won at blackjack. What's not to like?"

"Adam, you're sounding more American by the minute. You'll be saying *cool dude* and high-fiving if we don't get you back to London. We're jetting off at five thirty. I want you, Billy and Tiffany to meet me at the airport."

"And Pepe? Is he here?"

"Long story."

"He'll have to be here for the opening."

"There'll be no opening." He heard the sharp intake of breath at the other end of the line. "But he might have reason to be here. Breakfast in twenty minutes. Get Billy there."

Tiffany, still lying on the bed, had pulled the pure white sheet over her head to shut out her fear. Dex returned to her and eased it back to kiss her on the mouth.

"Tiffany, darling - be strong for me. Please. I'm going to be well protected. If I don't make the flight, take the duplicate set of evidence to London. Go to the cops. Otto will look after this end. I can't risk us being here with everything." He kissed he again. "If he doesn't show, we blow them all out of the water." He wavd his arms demonstrating a huge eruption and was rewarded with a watery smile and hug.


Dex took a selfie seated in the Galleria Bar with his watch showing 4 p.m. He sent it and a text to Carmino. "No show. No money transferred. Meet me in the lobby of the London Hilton, Park Lane, at 7 p.m. Unless twenty-two million is transferred before then, you've blown your last chance."

Twenty-five minutes later, there had been no response when he joined the others at McCarran's Executive Jet Terminal. Tiffany dashed toward him and hugged him with relief as he appeared at the entrance.

"No show. If the money is transferred first, I've offered to meet

Carmino tomorrow." He checked his watch. "That's today, London time. It's nearly one in the morning there now."

"You think he'll pay up? Show up?"

"No to both. I'm second-guessing he won't be in London. The opening has not been cancelled. It's all business as usual here. Maybe I was wrong and Letizione is toughing it out."

"Could be like the swan – gliding along, all smooth on the surface but frantic effort out of sight."

"Whatever." He could see that Adam and Billy wanted explanations but he ignored the enquiring glances. On the pretext of buying a mango juice, he moved away and broke the rules by phoning FB. Forster-Brown was almost whimpering like a toddler at receiving the call.

FB's voice was a whisper. "I said never phone."

"Too urgent. You alone?"

"On the casino floor. He's in the building."

"Is he flying to Vegas?"

"Unclear."

"I play Reverse Labouchère tomorrow afternoon. Be there. Understood?"

Dex ended the call, hoping that Carmino had not spotted FB looking furtive on camera. A few moments later, the smiling hostess escorted them across the shimmering tarmac to the plane, its spanking white fuselage glinting under the crushing peak heat of the afternoon sun. After settling around a table laid out with finger food and their choice of drinks, Dex turned to Billy who looked exhausted, still fighting demons. "I know you're going through hell. You'll get the best treatment once this is over."

Billy's dull, sunken eyes showed a glimmer of enthusiasm. "I've let you down something rotten. All this mess…because of me." He waved a limp arm vaguely across the table at nothing.

With a surge of thrust, the Gulfstream accelerated along the runway and then lifted off. Dex enjoyed the sound of the wheels being raised with a satisfying clunk. "When we're back, we'll sort that clinic." Dex patted Billy's knee reassuringly. I'll take care of Sandie and Emily."

Dex then produced a notebook and tore out blank pages for Tiffany and himself. "Billy, Adam—watch if you want. I'm going to teach Tiffany the Reverse Labouchère staking system. We're taking on Dukes."

Tiffany's brow furrowed. "Not happy, Dex. Poking bears with sticks?"

"I've squeezed their bollocks. Not enough. Tomorrow it's the jugular."

"So you've given up hope he'll surrender?" Listening to her, Dex realised Tiffany was desperate to find an escape while not letting him down.

"We'll know by the time we hit Dukes. For now, we assume he's whistling in the dark."

"You banking on Carmino not being down there when you play?" It was now Adam, sounding concerned.

"Afternoons he rarely is. Anyway, he ought to be headed here."

"Unless he's already bolted. But you? You're bringing in the law? Like you promised?" Tiffany sounded cheated.

"I phoned Otto. His men have Letizione under surveillance. He'll call in the Feds if Letizione seems to be running for the border. Or if Carmino arrives, he'll know."

"On what you're paying him, he should be doing a jig along Las Vegas Boulevard." Tiffany sounded more relaxed than any time that day.

"Sound chap this American, is he? You trusted him with the evidence?" Adam sounded disapproving as he poured himself a generous glass of chilled Chablis.

"I'd say so." It was Tiffany who chipped in as Dex looked grateful.

"Simultaneous raids by London police and the Feds," suggested Adam. "The sooner the better."

Dex nodded thoughtfully, still not sharing his innermost thoughts and now turning to Reverse Labouchère. "This is the staking system. Tiffany, you only bet on black numbers. I always back red. Simple, eh? One of them may dominate, hit significantly more than the other. Our staking system is geared to that happening. Don't be scared about huge bets. I can afford it. If either colour dominates, then we win back everything they stole from Beth and loads more."

"And if you lose?"

Dex looked away. "I'm overdue a big win," he replied, convincing nobody.

"And otherwise, you lose your shirt?" It was Billy who chipped in, surprising everybody. He had said what everyone was thinking.

Dex steadied his glass of Santenay as the plane struck a small patch of turbulence, climbing through 18,000 feet on the way to its cruising height. "Our starting bets will be £20,000, but hopefully we'll get to stake much, much more. I owe it to Beth—one final chance before Dukes is raided and shut forever."

"Did I see you buying a rabbit's foot charm?" Tiffany's good humour seemed to have returned.

"My real name is Warren." The plane lurched sharply and the copilot came through on the intercom to say that they would soon be above the turbulence caused by the mountains below. "So here's what you do." He handed Tiffany a sheet of paper. "Across the top, you write 10, 10, 10, 10. Each one represents £10,000. Your first bet is the total of the two outside numbers—10 plus 10 equals 20, equals £20,000. My first bet is identical, because on the top of my page are the same numbers. "Red wins. I add 20 to my line so it reads 10, 10, 10, 10, 20. Because you lost, you strike out the first and the last 10s. You have the two middle ones remaining." He watched whilst she struck out the two numbers.

"I'm with you."

"We now bet the total of our outside numbers. So I bet 10 plus 20 equals 30, equals £30,000."

"But I bet only 10 plus 10 equals 20, equals £20,000." Tiffany showed she had picked up the idea.

"The next number is also red. I win again. I add 30 to my line so it becomes 10, 10, 10, 10, 20, 30."

"So I can see that you will then bet 30 plus 10 equals £40,000. But me?"

"You strike out the final middle 10s. That line is complete and you start over, writing 10, 10, 10, 10."

Billy nodded his head in understanding, whilst Adam looked thoroughly confused. "So although Tiffany is down £40,000, you are up £50,000 so far."

"If red goes on winning, my bets keep increasing, whilst Tiffany keeps betting the same basic bet of 10 plus 10 equals £20,000. Let's take it much further, with all red numbers. Your line would still be 10, 10, 10, 10, but mine might be 10, 10, 10, 10, 20, 30, 40, 50, 60, 70, 80,

90, 100, 110. If I win again, I pocket £120,000 on that one spin and you still only lose £20,000."

Tiffany looked at him suspiciously. "Okay, suppose your rabbit foot fails and black wins. What then?"

"I cross out my two outside numbers, which are 10 and 110. My next bet is my outside numbers of 10 and 100 equals £110,000."

"So my next bet is10 plus 20 equals £30,000."

"Trust me, I've checked this time and again. If either colour dominates for an hour or so, we win big. These figures crank up hugely. A bet of £500,000 is perfectly possible. Of course, you could never bet like that in smaller casinos because of the table limits but Dukes accept outside bets up to £1 million." He grinned as if the money had already been won. "And even higher stakes by special arrangement."

"I get it," Billy exclaimed, suddenly perking up. "You're using winnings—casino money to bet bigger. Not chasing losing bets." He looked at Dex admiringly, but then his tone changed. "But red or black dominating? That's a crapshoot."

Adam seemed to have caught on too. "Even I could win big if my cards totalled 21 every hand." He put a fatherly arm over Dex's shoulder. "Dear boy, casino life is not like that."

The hostess in her gold tunic and shimmering stockings took their orders for dinner. Whilst they waited, Adam read the *Wall Street Journal*. Billy was hunched over a game on his iPad and Tiffany was playing around with the figures for Reverse Labouchère.

Dex did little except top up his glass and gaze into it, his thoughts on what lay ahead. Occasionally, he reached out to clasp Tiffany's hand or to smile reassuringly at her. More often though, he was deep in thought, gazing out of the small window as the jet cut through the night sky toward Canadian airspace and Hudson Bay.

After the remains of dinner had been cleared, each of them went to their own separate recliner, Billy and Tiffany watching movies, Adam dozing and Dex agonising on how the hell to survive the next twenty-four hours if Carmino was still in London.

After kissing Tiffany goodnight, Dex fell into an uneasy sleep. Tiffany switched off the movie and lay back, her eyes closed but her mind in turmoil. She had a troubled night, more awake than asleep and still haunted by her nightmare images of Carmino in hot pursuit,brandishing his knife.


As the Gulfstream was crossing into Irish airspace, Carmino was in his home-office at Clarendon Road. After showering, he had taken his phone there to ring Arnie but instead had found a text delivered a few minutes before. He read it quickly and for a flickering moment, looked pleased. "Forty-eight hours too late," he muttered.

On landing at Stansted, it was approaching noon. Dex switched on his phone immediately to see if there were any messages. There was one from Carmino.

"Hilton Hotel unsuitable for serious discussion. The chairman's company apartment is available at 7 p.m. He's travelling."

Dex knew Cadogan Square well enough. Being close to Knightsbridge, it was certainly a likely address for a company chairman. But that was not the point.

Tiffany was watching and sensed Dex was concerned. "Not good. Carmino wants to meet me in the chairman's flat."

Tiffany shook her head. "Say no deal, Dex. Alone in a flat with Carmino? Did he say the money had been transferred?" She saw his negative response. "Forget the money you wanted. Go to the police."

Dex knew she was right. "I'll reply from the car. We need to hurry to get to Dukes first though."

They exited the executive terminal where car and driver were waiting. Dex spotted Adam with his hand over Bill's shoulder. Billy was almost epileptic in his movements, arms flailing. As they drew close they both heard his fearful groan. "Oh my God! Oh no. Not that. Never!"

# CHAPTER FORTY-NINE

Billy's hands were trembling. If it were possible, his face was even paler than ever. He flourished the iPad bought in Vegas. "It's Emily. She's gone. Been taken! A man seized her while she was riding her new bike close to home."

"No, surely not," said Adam, a silly remark which he regretted at once.

The journalist in Tiffany got straight to the point. "When was this?"

"If Sky News is correct, just before nine this morning. Her friend was not touched. First reports say…" Billy's head slumped and he started to howl uncontrollably. Dex helped to ease him into the rear of the limo. No sooner were they moving than Tiffany was on the phone to her TV station whilst Dex did his best to console Billy.

"I'm sorry," he said. "It can't be coincidence." As he took in the tormented face, Dex flashed back to the little girl clutching her bear. "It must be Carmino, and that means…it's all my fault. I'm to blame. Oh God! Dear, poor Emily."

There was silence while Tiffany clung to her phone. Then Billy looked up, his gaunt face looking even thinner than usual. "No. No, Dex. You helped me, gave me a chance. It was me who screwed up. Me and my addiction. But Emily, what do we do? What do we do?" His voice rose with the repetition. He started to wail again, almost drowning out the conversation that Tiffany was now having with the news-desk.

She ended the call. "I can't add much more." She leaned across the seat to clasp Billy's hand. "But Billy, my take…it could be much worse. This was not a lone pervert enticing a child into a car. First reports suggest there were two men. It looks like a kidnapping. Much better than a pervert."

Dex glanced at Tiffany. "That makes one decision easier."

Tiffany's attention turned back to Dex. "If you mean you'll go to Cadogan Square, no way. This changes everything."

Dex thought for a split second. "Carmino wants me there. He wants my evidence. He wants me dead. He can't imagine he'll buy my silence—unless there's a deal over Emily." He fingered his phone, poised to respond to Carmino. "I'll do any deal to get Emily back."

"Then the cops must be there too."

"If I tell the cops, well …" He let the conclusion as to Emily's fate hang before going on. "Anyway, I'd be dead before the cops would even know. Arresting Pepe with me on a slab, somehow doesn't do it for me. There has to be something better." He ended with a nervous laugh.

Adam showed his concern with meaningless platitudes but his stiff-upper-lip instincts were ill-suited to proving real comfort. He fixed Dex with a steady gaze. "Refuse to go. Just take the evidence to the boys in blue and get the FBI moving. You don't *have* to see him."

Dex rubbed his chin thoughtfully. "No can do. The game has changed. This is only about Emily and a deal to get her back. Nothing else. I must see him and no cops." He looked at Adam and Tiffany while Billy wrapped his head in his arms, sobbing uncontrollably. Tiffany muttered soothing words but her eyes and narrowed lips showed Dex her fury at him. That made up his mind.

Quickly, Dex texted, *Confirmed. Meet Cadogan.*

Almost instantly came a reply. "Wise move. I have the nuts. No law. Or else…" Dex showed Adam and Tiffany the response before turning to Billy. "You must get home. Sandie needs you. Imagine how she's feeling. Adam will go there with you. Phone her."

"That makes sense," commented Adam. "Billy, Emily won't be harmed. Dex will do a deal this evening."

"Corrrect. This kidnap is pathetic. It can't achieve business-as-usual. Dukes is finished. This is revenge and desperation. He should have done a runner after Haldeman."

"Billy, Emily will be fine. It's Dex he wants." Adam's consoling words seemed to do little for Billy but they hit Dex with sledgehammer force. Adam nodded to Dex. "Pepe is a beaten man. This can't achieve anything."

Tiffany nearly retorted that logic played no part with a psychopath. "So you conclude, Adam?"

"He'll murder Dex because that's the man we now know he is. He'll then run if he can. He succeeded for twenty odd years after Panama,. He's no fool. He'll know Dukes is doomed."

"Nicely put, Adam. Thanks a bunch!" Dex tried to sound flippant but failed. He looked sideways at Tiffany and then at Adam. "So I take my chance." He was thinking aloud now. "Just maybe he won't harm me in case the cops are there. He'll pick me off…some other time." He forced a grin. "Well, that's made my day."

"Perhaps Pepe's actions will depend on what's happened in Vegas. Any news?" Tiffany looked less angry now that Dex had taken responsibility.

Dex shook his head. "Otto would have told me if Letizione had bolted." Dex sent another text. *C U at 7 p.m. Both alone. We each have what the other wants. Fair exchange.*

Adam turned to Billy. "Come on, old chap. You really must ring home."

Dex looked through the window as the Mercedes cruised past Euston Station. Outside, it was just another London day—people of all colours and nationalities dashing about their business, unaware of the life-or-death drama now being lived out so close to them. "Billy, you'll be home in under an hour from here. I'd join you, but Tiffany and I…"

"Dex, no! Emily changes everything. No way are we going to go into Dukes."

"We are." Dex's tone was adamant. "He's not there afternoons. If he is, then we don't go in. If we win big it's another bargaining chip for Emily's return."

After emotional goodbyes all round, Dex instructed the limo to drop them in Berkeley Square. Dex was close to tears as he saw Billy huddled on the backseat, hopelessly ill-equipped to cope with the burden. "Ring Sandie. You really must, Billy."

The limo pulled away into the traffic after he and Tiffany had removed their luggage, including her grip with the American evidence. In his solicitor's office, the receptionist recognised him at once. She fetched the envelope with Tavio's original witness statement and his own signed statement detailing how One-Eye had cheated Mick Glenn. Everything was placed in Tiffany's carry-on.

"We'll be back for our things late afternoon."

"We're open till 6:30 p.m.," the receptionist confirmed.

"Perfect." Dex forced a smile, thinking that thirty minutes after 6:30 p.m., he was likely to be slashed to death with a Bowie.

He led Tiffany outside, turning almost at once into Mount Street. Ahead of them, down the street on the right, he saw the familiar steps leading to the black door of Dukes. Beside the door was Tom, standing tall and upright. As ever, it all looked so establishment, so permanent. Nothing gave a hint of the turmoil behind the walls that rose high above and below the steps to the lower ground floor.

"Beautiful day, Tom."

"Going to rain later. Might be thundery tonight, sir."

"Pepe arrived yet, has he?"

The doorman shook his head. "He was in earlier. Left an hour ago."

It was exactly 2 p.m. Once inside and standing at the top of the stairs, Dex kissed Tiffany and then clasped her hand. "Think like a winner, be a winner."

# CHAPTER FIFTY

After signing in at front desk, Dex led Tiffany between the tables, almost all still empty. Nobody was even opening the blackjack, a sign that Carmino must have stopped the trick that Billy had spotted. From the bar and restaurant came laughter and the aroma of rare beef on the trolley. The familiar sights, sounds, and smells welcomed him back. Despite his brave words upstairs, Dex fought to control his breathing, anxious to hide his mounting fears from Tiffany. Dr Grierson would be charging double if he could check the blood pressure.

He headed for the cage for the last time. Everything seemed so mundane, so normal. He spotted FB hovering close to the empty baccarat table. "Mr D! Oh, yes and it's Ms Richmond, isn't it? I hope you are well. So good to see you."

"Not in Vegas for the opening?"

"Sadly not. But the Cinderella role suits me just fine. Las Vegas is so vulgar, like Southend only bigger. Will you have some lunch first?"

"We've come to play roulette. Remember I once discussed Reverse Labouchère? We want to try it today."

For a brief moment, FB raised his eyes from the carpet. "Take care, Reverse Labouchère can bite." He led them toward the tables. "We've a table open but if you're serious about having *real fun* at our expense," he coughed into the back of his hand, "we'll open up a high-stakes table for you. What stakes did you have in mind?"

"Twenty thousand minimum. Right up to the maximum."

"I see. In that case, yes, of course. I'll get a table open."

"And if Jeb Miller and One-Eye are on duty, I'd like them dealing. I want to kill the jinx. Especially One-Eye. Those two put the yips on me."

"As you wish." FB smirked discreetly. He slipped away to the house phone and by the time Dex was ready to sit down, Jeb Miller's fat bottom was already sagging over the end of his high stool. One-Eye was setting out the chips.

Dex nodded to Miller. "Table limit of two million max on outside bets, right?"

"No, Mr D." Miller's brown-toothed smile was both disarming and obnoxious. "Today, the spread is twenty thousand to one million."

"Christ! No wonder you casinos make money. That maximum is ridiculous. Who decided that?" Dex looked and sounded aggressive. "Get FB over here."

"I'm sorry, Mr D. It was FB that instructed me."

"Mr Carmino, then?"

Jeb Miller enjoyed playing his trump card. "Is not here yet."

Dex looked irritated as he turned to Tiffany. "Stuffed as usual. Let's just get on, then." Now that he was at the table, he found that his palms were no longer sweating and his breathing was settling down to something like normal. He smiled at Tiffany who was looking thoughtful but otherwise relaxed.

He called for two glasses of orange juice as he and Tiffany settled down. In front of them were their chips and their sheets of paper, both showing 10, 10, 10, 10. Dex had yellow chips, each bought in at £10,000. Tiffany's were blue at the same value. Beside them were plaques from the cage, each worth £100,000.

"Let's go for it!" Dex smiled at Tiffany and admired the confident way she pushed out her chips to back black. One-Eye spun the wheel with a deft flick of the wrist, the small white ball speeding round under the rim.

"Labouchère?" One-Eye questioned Dex.

"Much better. Reverse Labouchère." Dex watched the ball bouncing around the wheel. The fuse was lit and he was now seeing everything in slow motion, even though his pulse was racing. As he looked around, it seemed unreal to think this room, this whole building, was doomed. Jeb Miller, One-Eye, Andy, O'Keefe, and probably several more would soon be arrested and headed for jail. But would he be the last big winner? The thought quickened his pulse as the ball trickled to a stop.

"8. Black. Even."

Tiffany swooped on her winnings and added 20 to her line of 10, 10, 10, 10. "Start as we mean to carry on." Despite nagging feelings of distress about Emily and the 7 p.m. meeting, her face showed shock at winning twenty thousand pounds after just a few seconds. "I can get to like this. Plenty more black numbers, please."

"We haven't actually won at all yet." His words were smiled at Tiffany who looked puzzled for a moment before laughing her agreement. Dex turned to Miller. "I told Tiffany, my stars said my luck was in today. So far, it looks more like business as usual." He crossed off the two outside tens.

"Perhaps the luck is in having me here." Tiffany raised a quizzical eyebrow.

Dex looked unconvinced. "So long as one of us keeps winning, I suppose you're right." Seeing her like this helped him relax as he saw the confident way in which she placed her next bet, staking £30,000.

"I'm on a roll, Dex. I can feel it."

"Swallows and summers," retorted Dex but his reference to Aesop was lost. Tiffany was now focused solely on the hiss and clatter of the slowing ball.

"32. Red. Even."

"Hmmh! That didn't last long then." She crossed off the outside 20 and 10 from her line. "I'm losing now."

Dex turned and gave her a gentle kiss on the cheek. "We're *both* losing. A zigzag. Red then black. Last thing we want." He ran his finger across his throat but the next four numbers were all red. "Hey!" Tiffany protested. "I'm well down, just busy crossing off lines."

Dex pointed to his chips. "But we're winning, between us."

"I liked that winning feeling—pity it lasted just one spin."

Dex looked at One-Eye. "A few repeat numbers would be good." He saw the dealer shrug without interest. "Yeah, yeah, yeah. You don't have to say it, One-Eye! *You can't control the ball. The wheel has no memory.*" Dex shook his head. "Don't give me that stuff. An experienced dealer like you can make the ball do anything you want. Make it land anywhere."

"On just reds or just blacks? Dream on, Mr Dex-tah!" The dealer's small dark eyes met Dex's stare. His moon-like face was inscrutable, his sallow features revealing nothing beneath the mop of jet-black hair.

"He can, can't he, Mr Miller?" The inspector did not reply beyond shaking his head, as if Dex's suggestion were mad. One-Eye spun a red number again—and then again. "Don't pay me in yellows now. Cash chips, big ones please."

Tiffany looked uneasy and she shifted on her chair as if ready to quit. "You've won a bundle. Let's quit while we're ahead."

"Not yet. I'm on a roll." He turned to the dealer. "One-Eye, I can see you're trying to help me. Keep those reds coming."

Miller made a dry kissing noise used by casino staff to attract attention. A swarthy Maltese pit boss, his skin a deep olive, came across and Miller whispered to him—something that Dex strained to hear.

The pit boss left the table and spoke to a bulky, severe-looking man in his fifties, who would have looked more comfortable in a wrestler's leopard-skin than a DJ that barely contained him. Dexter had never spoken to the man but guessed he was a floor manager, perhaps one below FB. He seemed to pride himself on being a man of few words with even less charm. His half-shaved appearance barely concealed a pockmarked face. The *en brosse* hairstyle added a *don't mess with me* image. After listening to the pit boss, he disappeared but returned a few moments later to stand behind Dex.

Dex whispered to Tiffany so that he could be overheard. "Casinos *pretend* they like winners—until you start winning. This guy standing behind me—we're getting what they call *giving us heat*. They want to make us uncomfortable. Ignore it."

Moments later, FB himself appeared with a worried frown.

# CHAPTER FIFTY-ONE

Jude Tuson sat in an armchair, seated crossways in a white T-shirt and torn jeans, her legs dangling. It had been an unpleasant start to the day and the way it was shaping up was not much better.

Her mind was in turmoil, wondering and worrying about what to do as she gazed at a rerun of *Fawlty Towers*. Ever since Pepe had mentioned that Dex and a guy called Billy Evans had been out to screw Dukes, he had been distant and uncommunicative, more or less ignoring her. And it had been getting worse since he had not gone to Vegas.

She did not know Billy and had never linked him to Dex. He had seemed harmless enough, playing blackjack next to an older and rather distinguished-looking gentleman called Adam somebody. At first, she had taken Pepe's story at face value. Yet there was something unreal about it. Dex was rich anyway with a sick father and a dead sister. Would he really be planning a heist on Dukes? Or was Dex a threat? Had he got suspicious of money laundering? Now *that* was possible.

This morning, while Pepe was showering, his phone had been beside the bed with his wallet, keys, and small change. She had heard the bleep of an incoming text. Interested at what he was up to, she had taken a peek. "Plan A success. Emily at my place. Speak soon. Arnie."

She had got out of bed and wrapped a crimson dressing-gown around her. Frowning, she padded through to the kitchen to make a cup of coffee. The names meant nothing. As for Plan A, Pepe had never mentioned anything but the words sounded sinister and secretive, in keeping with the way he had been behaving.

She heated a croissant and loaded it with butter and marmalade. Reluctantly, she decided to do the same for him, carrying a tray with breakfast through to the bedroom. He came out of the bathroom in a towelling robe, his hair wild and still damp. He grabbed his phone and went into his office.

When he returned, he helped himself to the croissant without thanks, pacing around the room as he ate, his mind elsewhere. At first, he said nothing but then he glared at her. "You didn't tell me a message came while I was showering."

"What message, darling? In case you didn't notice, I've been getting your breakfast." She took in his dismissive shake of the head as he stood in front of the mirror, fingering his scar. "Pepe, pretty please, let me come with you to Vegas? I'd love to see Space City." She was sprawling on the chaise longue. Her dressing gown was untied and her long legs were apart. She moved slightly so that a nipple appeared and she licked marmalade off her fingers, the invitation obvious.

Pepe continued pacing, showing no interest in the golden mound of pubic hair and the protruding nipple. "No. You're too important here with the high rollers." His tone was as abrupt as his aggressive movements as he finished drying his hair.

Jude crossed her legs and gathered the gown back around her, very keen to make her point. "When that's finished, we'll travel? Like you promised?"

"That's what I said." Pepe looked and sounded disinterested as he slipped into some tailored trousers and a navy-blue polo top. "I need time alone. I have some important calls to make." He left the room and she heard him shut the door of his bijou office, which lay off the sitting-room.

What he said in there, she had no idea. She too showered and then dressed and when she had finished, he was still behind the closed office door. She settled down in front of the TV with a second coffee, waiting for him to come out. When he did so, he barely acknowledged her, going straight into the bedroom, grabbing a sports-coat and his essentials, before returning to the sitting-room.

"I'm going to Dukes and the bank. I may fly to Vegas tonight."

"Fancy a leisurely lunch?"

"No. See you after two, I expect."

Moments later, as she stood by the window, she saw his Aston Martin exit the underground garage and cruise toward Holland Park Avenue. She was unsure whether she wanted to be around when he returned, so she debated whether to wander down to Kensington Church Street or through Notting Hill. She could take in the antique shops, stopping off somewhere for brunch—perhaps with one of her mates in from Sydney.

It seemed a good plan but that was for later. She switched TV channels and grabbed the two morning papers that had just been delivered. A jingle for Sky News came on in the background and then she watched a reporter standing in the rain outside Scotland Yard, followed moments later by another reporter, rather more fortunate, who was reporting a story from Bermuda. She skimmed the pages, looking for items about fashion, Australia, or exotic destinations.

She put down the *Daily Mail* when she realised that her mind had been more on Pepe than what she was reading. *Did she really want to travel with him? Come to that, did she really want to continue the relationship? Did she really care about him? Did he really care about her? Ha! That was the easiest to answer.* She knew that was a big and definite no. *Was jetting everywhere worth putting up with his moods and weird demands? If it ever happened.*

He was an enigma…oozing charm when it suited him but devoid of any loving instincts. To him, generosity was an affection substitute. She doubted he had ever loved anyone except himself. He was secretive, hated being asked anything and was impossible to get close to. For him sex was no two-way thing. She was his plaything; a blow-up doll to be abused in the nastiest ways. She shivered.

Her downturned mouth showed her distaste and she reached out for an expensive Swiss chocolate for comfort. Her thoughts drifted to Dex. He too was an enigma—a tad mysterious but funny, kind and intriguing. Maybe she should make another pitch for him. No harm. He could only say no—and politely, knowing him.

Imagining Dex's friendly and genuine smile, she was just starting to get some aching feelings that needed satisfying when the change of tone from the TV caught her attention. "We have some breaking news. A six-year-old girl has been snatched and dragged into a car. Emily Evans had been with a friend, riding a bike near her home in Thames Ditton, Surrey. The vehicle may have been a small red saloon. First reports suggest two men were involved. Our reporter is now heading for the scene in Sugden Road, southwest of London."

The word *Emily* jarred. Emily in Arnie's message? *Emily Evans? The time matched the text message. Could she be? Billy Evans's daughter? Surely not? But why not? Had Plan A been orders from Pepe to snatch Emily? Why would he do that? Because of something Billy had done at Dukes? So who was Arnie? Nobody Pepe had ever mentioned.*

Any idea of window-shopping was blown aside. Instead, after putting the chain across the front door, she decided to check out this Arnie guy. She went into Pepe's cubbyhole office. Unless he came back early, there was plenty of time. She had peeped through the door a couple of times but never been in. The air stunk of cigars, and one was stubbed out on an onyx ashtray on his small desk. There was a well-padded chair and a small rear-view window. It was almost empty of clutter, which, given its size, was no surprise.

A large monitor, a keyboard, a pad of paper, a mouse and mat almost filled the desk. The computer tower on the floor was switched off. She knew how to switch it on but was scared to do so for fear of being caught out in some way.

After deciding it would be password-protected anyway, she turned her attention to the three-drawer filing cabinet. The top drawer was marked *Dukes* and was locked with no sign of any key. She hurried to the bedside but his keys had gone. Her attention then turned to the lower two drawers. One was labelled *Space City and International.* It too was locked, but the bottom one, marked *Sundry*, opened at once.

It contained about a dozen or so green folders, each labelled and filed alphabetically. She riffled through them quickly, hoping for something magical like the name Arnie to jump out. It did not. There were files for *Accountants, Car Tax, Cleaner, Council, Electrics, Insurance, Neighbour Dispute, Oil, Old Blenkinsoppians, Solicitors* and *Water.*

She quickly dismissed most of them as irrelevant and so started with the accountants but nobody on the notepaper or in any document was called Arnie or Arnold. The solicitors' folder was bulky and took a while to study. It too proved useless, as did the file for the *Cleaner.*

*Neighbour Dispute* did not sound too promising, so she tried what she assumed was his old school association. The folder contained a printout of association members, the document being fronted by a blue crest and the address of a school near Chelmsford. She flicked through the list of names to *Carmino* and there he was—*Carmino (Pepe Rolando) (1986-1991).* His email address was given and a mobile phone number.

Quickly, she decided to search for anybody called Arnie or Arnold from the same era. There were over sixty pages, but she found she could skim down the years quickly and then cross-check to the name. And then she found one: Arnold Harold Fisher (1986—1991). There was no email address but there was a London area phone number, which she entered into her smartphone.

She hurried on, one eye on the clock, even though there seemed no reason to worry. By the time she reached the final entry for Edward Zachariah, there had been no other Arnold. She returned the file and almost ignored the one marked *Neighbour Dispute*. Then, for completeness' sake, she decided to take a quick look.

Within seconds, she could see that Pepe had been having trouble with an Indian family next door. He had been irritated by the constant smell of curry that wafted across his roof terrace but had been even more pissed off by the constant, repetitive Indian music, played too often and too loud. The Council had done nothing about his complaint.

She turned to the next letter. It was addressed to Arnold Fisher, and it read, "Dear Arnie. Copy self-explanatory correspondence herewith. Fix this. Free rein. Just do it. Whatever."

She tapped Arnold Fisher's address into her smartphone—*37 Pinesta Crescent, Pimlico, London SW1*. There was no sign in the file of what Arnie had done but she had never heard Indian music nor smelled curry, like even now with the sitting-room window open.

She returned the folder, closed the drawer, double-checked that there was no sign of her visit and unchained the front door. Having grabbed some Ryvitas, cream cheese and poured a large glass of New Zealand Pinot Noir, she sat at the table and ran a search on Google for 37 Pinesta Crescent.

Up came the name Arnold Fisher Limited, so she checked again with Google Maps. She soon saw that the crescent was about a half mile from Victoria Station in a confusing mass of small residential streets known as Pimlico. She turned to Google's street view and took in the details before honing in on number 37. This was it, then. Not an office block.

Pinesta Crescent was a quiet residential street and seemingly, Arnie Fisher ran his business from home. Her fingers flying over the keys, she looked up Arnold Fisher Limited. There was very little about the business. It was not on LinkedIn, Facebook, or any London business directory. It had no website.

Over a second glass, she was still pondering what next to do when Sky News at 2 p.m. came on. Emily Evans was the lead story. A sad-faced journalist in a fawn Burberry was standing outside a suburban three-up and two-down semi-detached property. It had a small unkempt garden and there was a policeman at the gate.

The reporter pointed down the road to where there was considerable police activity. "That is where Emily was seized just around five hours ago. Forensics are at the scene and door-to-door enquiries have been made as police seek witnesses. About ten minutes ago, Emily's father arrived in a large black limo, refusing to say anything except to confirm who he was. He entered the house with another gentleman who would not give his name. He had the appearance of a family solicitor but that is pure speculation."

The screen filled with a shot of a limo pulling up, and instantly Jude recognised both Billy Evans and the distinguished gentleman from the casino.

After a moment or two, she decided to switch to an entertainment channel so as not to give Pepe any sign that she even knew of this horrible crime. It seemed better. *But what to do? Go to the police? Would Pepe discover who had told them? What would he do? Would he be arrested and jailed till his trial? Or would he deny, deny and be bailed? And what then?* Could he wipe the text from Arnie and get away with that? She rather thought not. She thought of his vicious-looking knife and shuddered. *Why did he have that?* She swung her legs to and fro over the chair arm as she tried to decide.

That poor kid!

Maybe she should text Dex. Jude switched channels again to a quiz show as she picked up her phone To hell with the consequences—she had to do what was right. But at that moment, the key sounded in the lock and the front door opened. Her chance had gone. She quickly put down her phone before Pepe breezed in, looking no more relaxed than when he had left.

"Hi, darling! So, do you know yet? Are you going to Vegas?"

He barely smiled, replying over his shoulder as he headed to the bedroom. "I'll decide later. For now, come to bed. Then, I've still got things to arrange,." Reluctantly, she swung her legs down and stood up, knowing that it was *fun-for-one* time.

*In the meantime, while I'm being screwed by a child-snatching bastard, little Emily is a prisoner in Pimlico.*

*Assuming she is still alive.*

# CHAPTER FIFTY-TWO

A few uncharacteristically brisk strides brought FB to the table. He looked at the number display board showing that red numbers 7, 3, 34, 16, 16, and 27 had all hit. Dex turned round and saw FB take the shift manager's arm The duo walked a step or two further away but just in Dex's line of vision. He enjoyed watching them engage in an intense debate. He heard One-Eye's name more than once but the context was unclear.

"What a buzz, eh? Better than a legal high." He looked at both the dealer and the inspector. "Plenty more reds are there, One-Eye?" Dex checked his sheet of paper. "We've only had nineteen spins." He checked the stack of cash chips that were mounting beside the yellows. "That's over a million ahead. Come on, One-Eye, keep it going! Spin that wheel! You and me, together we can really clean up. Just keep spinning reds and I'll leave a good tip. And stop slipping in the occasional black."

One-Eye scowled at him, something Dex relished. Occasionally he thought of Emily but there was nothing he could do for her just yet. Meantime, he knew he had to play the cocky winner role. That was the plan and though Tiffany was hating his bumptious drivel, he had to lay it on thick. As he had planned on the flight, he started humming Dire Straits' big hit, *Money for nothing and your chicks for free.*

Surprisingly, this did make Tiffany smile despite herself. Then she pointed to her chips. "I'm losing like a drunken sailor."

She saw Dex's face twist slightly in apparent disdain. "Tough! Look at my line: 30, 40, 50, 60, 70, 80, 100, 120, 150, 180. My next bet is £210,000." Dex turned to Miller. "What's the longest run you've seen of all reds or blacks?"

Miller coughed into the back of his hand before responding. "Me personally, I've seen twenty-seven. Just the once, mind."

"See, Tiffany. And today, we've been nowhere near a run of all reds without a black."

The ball landed in 9 red odd. Dex leaned toward Tiffany as he swept in the big win.

"I told you, One-Eye. You the man! Keep helping me!" This time, he actually broke into the lyrics. "*Money for nothing and your chicks for free.*"

The shift-manager changed position so that he could now glare at Dex and watch One-Eye more closely. Dex saw the penetrating look as he pushed out £240,000 for his next bet. He nodded toward the dealer but addressed the Maltese pit boss and shift-manager.

"He's some guy, this dealer—aren't you, One-Eye?" He hummed more of the Dire Straits hit to add to their irritation and loved being rewarded with a Maltese scowl. Miller too was now watching One-Eye more closely, just what Dex was hoping for.

"34, red, even," said One-Eye, looking slightly uncomfortable as he pushed across nearly a quarter of a million pounds. As on each win, Dex made a big point of checking he had been paid out correctly. The next three numbers were also red but then came a black and another four reds.

"Let's quit," said Tiffany. "You've won enough."

"Against a casino? You can never win enough. Keep them coming, One-Eye!" He turned to Jeb Miller. "Can you order us some Earl Grey tea and smoked salmon sandwiches, please? And if there are any French pastries? Thanks! We shall be here for a while."


In Clarendon Road, Holland Park, Jude eased herself from the bed, her arms and legs aching from the contorted position in which she had been bonded for the last *God knows* how long. Pepe had now dressed in smart-casual and had started packing a small suitcase. She glanced at him and on seeing he was engrossed in sorting his washing-kit, she hurried into the bathroom. She felt soiled and abused.

As soon as he heard the thunderous water from the shower, Carmino laid out a change of clothes, three false passports, three wigs, three different pairs of tinted contact lenses, hair dye, a false moustache, cheek padding, two different pairs of glasses and some charcoal pills. Then he added facial makeup to mask the scar or to age his face to suit the image. The foreign money he would still have to collect from his safe in Dukes.

As he gathered everything for his permanent departure, his mind was on Dex. Using the garrotte on the bastard would be less pleasurable but very effective. Job done, he could exit the building looking a different person. With five apartments served from the front entrance, there was always plenty of coming and going. He reckoned the disguise of an older man with a limp would fool the cops, even if Dex had set them up.

But the kid?

The delay in the kidnap had scotched his original idea. No way did he trust Dex now to stay stumm, not when someone had been leaking. The kid's only value now was getting Dex to Cadogan Square. After that? She was redundant. So? Release her?

Or?

He looked at the garrotte and nodded in satisfaction. That would teach Billy Evans.

*How in hell had Dex been so well informed? Who was leaking?* For the hundredth time, he went through the possibilities. The guys in the cage? O'Keefe? Unlikely. FB? That wimp would never speak out of turn. *Christ! For fuck's sake, Dex had even got the bank account numbers from the Caymans and Montserrat.*

For a moment he smiled. *Big mistake mentioning that, Dex.* This morning, every last dollar had been electronically transferred to dormant accounts in Dubai and Hong Kong. *But that was not the point. Who knew about the hot money from Switzerland? Who had the chance to tell Dex?*

The sound of Jude exiting the shower set him thinking.

My God! She knew of the hot money…and she was cosy with him. Had probably shagged him, if the truth were known. *But had she tipped him off? Could she have found his banking details? Possible. If she had been into his office. But I keep the drawer locked. Had I ever left the keys lying about?*

*Possible.*

*Who else could it be?*

He felt mounting dryness in his throat, a sensation he always got when this inner urge started to grip him. Feverishly, he scurried round the bedroom looking for her phone. Nowhere. He raced into the sitting-room. Nowhere. Kitchen. Nowhere. Then he spotted her cavernous handbag lying beside the chair she had been using. In a violent move, he unzipped every pocket and shook out every last item—tissues, make-up, eye-liner, hair lacquer, credit-cards, small change, a wad of notes, a couple of matching pens, a notepad, a pack of condoms. But no phone.

He hurried back to the bedroom, his fury and certainty mounting in equal measure. She was now beside the bed and staring at the flight reservation for Singapore. His suitcase had been flipped open. "You're not going to Las Vegas." It was not a question but Pepe ignored it anyway. His mind and his eyes were on the phone in her hand.

"You devious bitch! Been using your phone in the bathroom, were you? Ringing your pal Dex?"

"Dex? Why would I ring him?" She stood fiercely defiant, hands on her waist. "You filthy sod! You've been lying to me. You're dumping me, not coming back." She pointed to the passports. "Mr Ralph Dawkins. First Class ticket to Singapore. You're doing a runner, you bastard."

He stared at her cocky face, her eyes flashing anger. His throat was now parched, his breathing coming faster. His hatred was mounting. Inside, he had that familiar feeling, like a time-bomb about to explode. He had to check her phone. Plus she had seen his ticket and passports.

He said nothing.

At times like this, his pupils always started to widen, his nostrils always flared, and an irresistible passion consumed him. The lump in his throat swelled so that speaking could not now come easily. He turned away and went to the built-in wardrobe by the bathroom. Seconds later, he had unsheathed the Bowie's nine-inch blade.

At first, as Jude stared at the wigs in the small case, she did not notice the knife. Even when she saw it in his hand, she seemed not to understand. There was confusion on her face. For a second or two, she stood mesmerised, her puzzled look remaining before her hand flew to her mouth and her eyes showed panic.

"Give me your phone." Pepe somehow forced out the order but there was a dry rattling throatiness to each word. She saw the tip of the knife now pointing toward her. She screamed, backing away as he advanced from about ten feet. "The phone, I said. Give it to me, you snooping bitch. You've been playing me off against Dexter, telling him…"

"No. No. Pepe, you've got it wrong. I've said nothing about the Swiss money. Nothing. And I know nothing else." The words tumbled out in a torrent as the knife drew closer. Jude saw the lips, narrowed and mean. "Leave me alone. Please. Please, Pepe. I've done nothing wrong." Seeing the animal ferocity in the snarling look, she realised that further pleading would be useless. She needed to retreat, to get away. But where to run?

His unflinching eyes now reminded her of a cobra that she had encountered in Morocco, the intense and unflinching blackness an unmistakable warning. She tried to think straight as disbelief changed to stark reality. He was blocking her path to the bathroom, where she might have locked the door.

Her only chance was through the sitting room to the front door. Still in her bare feet and with only a towel wrapped around her, she turned and ran, defying the pain from their sexual contortions. She had a dozen or so metres, nearly forty feet, to cover. As she sped beyond the dining-table and between the settee and an armchair, she hurled her phone through the open window to crash onto the pavement far below.

Inwardly, Pepe was calling her every foul word from his repertoire. In the compact hallway, as she wrestled with the lock on the front door, he reached her. Had it been unlocked, she might have bolted down the stairs. With the door double-locked, he was onto her.

Mustering all his force, he jabbed his arm forward so that the vicious knifepoint savagely entered Jude's throat from the side, penetrating deep and beyond her windpipe. Her scream died, to be replaced by a gurgling sound as the blood pumped out, dribbling from her mouth. He jerked the knife upward to ensure certain death. Jude's knees buckled and she slumped against the wall before collapsing onto the carpet.

His eyes even wilder with excited satisfaction, Carmino withdrew the knife and stabbed her again, this time in the chest, then once in the stomach. Breathing heavily with satisfaction, he looked at the lifeless body. With a snarl that came from deep inside his stomach, he grasped her hair to tilt her head. Using a vicious horizontal cut, he ripped open her neck, nearly severing her head. Satisfied, he stood over her before giving her inert body several vicious kicks, grunting each time with primeval pleasure.

He looked around the tiny space. For a moment, as the knife had plunged deep, he had been back in Panama sorting out the Mexican. There was blood on the walls and grey carpet. Her towel lay bloodied and sodden beside her. His own clothes were ruined. With a laugh and a toss of his head, he returned to the sitting room, leaving a trail of bloody footprints.

At the window, his short, excited breathing returned to normal. Far below, he saw what was probably her phone lying in the road. Whether it would have survived from three floors up he had no idea. Looking like he did, with her blood on his face, arms, hands and clothes, he could not go outside. *Anyway*, he decided, jettisoning her phone had proved it.

He had been right.

She *had* tipped off Dex about money laundering.

For a few anxious moments, he wondered if anybody would react to her scream. Unlikely. The Indian neighbours had sold up nearly a month before. Their home was still empty. The couple on the ground floor were never at home during the day. There was no sign of activity in the street.

He showered quickly and dressed in clean clothes. Having wiped clean his knife, he changed his mind and decided the chance to slit Dex's throat was irresistible. He strapped the belt around his waist, folded another change of clothes into his carry-on and was ready to go. On leaving, he avoided the front entrance and instead exited using the kitchen door leading to the communal corridor and emergency stairs.

Before driving away, he checked for Jude's phone. It had gone. A passer-by must have spotted it. *Inconvenient*, but no point worrying about that. Inside the Aston-Martin, he saw the time. *Perfect—empty the office safe, visit Arnie, sort the kid, and be at Cadogan Square well before 7 p.m.* And then the *10 pm flight to Singapore.*

He was looking forward to the rest of the day.

One down, two to go.

# CHAPTER FIFTY-THREE

Another forty minutes passed. The Earl Grey tea, the sandwiches and strawberry tartlets had been and gone. And despite six interspersed black numbers, red still dominated, hitting a further twenty-two times with just a solitary zero. By now, Dex had moved on to the Beatles and was irritating Tiffany every time he pulled in his winnings by singing, "Now give me money, *that's* what I want."

Loving putting on the show to distract the watching casino staff as they hovered around him, his winnings were stacked high in front of him. Rapidly, he counted his chips and deducted Tiffany's losses.

"We're just over nine million ahead. Let's make it ten." He changed to Abba and, while grinning at the poker-faced shift-manager, he broke into *money, money, money, always sunny in a rich man's world.* He enjoyed hearing the stifled snort, so he decided to wind the guy up even more. "You're right! Not everybody likes Abba." He watched the ball nestle into 25 red and waited while the huge win was pushed across the green baize. "How about Liza Minnelli in Cabaret? *Money makes the world go around, the world go around.*"

His brows knitted together in a furious scowl, the man could take no more of Dex's deliberate cockiness,. He turned away as if he had been summoned to elsewhere. Instead, he just strolled around the table, keeping out of Dex's eyeline and further away from the strains of money making the world go round.

Jeb Miller nodded toward Dex. "Funny old game, roulette. It can change suddenly. Don't go losing it all!"

"I didn't know you cared, Jeb. But with my pal One-Eye helping me like this, I'm good to keep this rolling." Dex gave the dealer an unsubtle wink. As he had hoped, One-Eye looked embarrassed, his narrow eyes flicking left and right as attention once again turned to him.

Dex was just about to place his next bet with a tower of chips when he felt his phone vibrating in his pocket. He took it out to check the message. He was shocked to see there was not just one message. There were three. In the heat of the action, he had missed the first ones.

"Move away from the table please, Mr D. No phones." Miller's tone was polite but firm.

Dex took a few steps away to read them quickly. The most urgent was from FB. Carmino was heading for Dukes. "Tiffany—time to quit. That's Father's nursing home. He's sinking fast. I'll have to get to Northampton." He turned to One-Eye. Cash us out, please."

To Dex, the payout process seemed to take an age. By the time he and Tiffany had somehow scooped up the winnings from the table, FB had appeared and was talking to the shift-manager. His agitation was obvious. All his actions were full of energy his left hand repeatedly brushing against the silvery bristle of his hair.

Dex interrupted. "I'm in a hurry. My father may not survive the day, and I must dash to Northampton. Cash me out into US dollars, sterling, and euros. Big denominations, please. Oh, and FB. Remember I joked that one day I'd need a suitcase?" He saw FB shake his head, his face grim. "Today's the day, so have the guys in the cage fill one up." As an afterthought, Dex tugged FB on the sleeve. "And please sign a letter addressed to me certifying these are casino winnings."

It was nearly nine minutes before the cash mountain had been counted and cross-checked. Then FB appeared with a rollalong suitcase and the letter. "I'll bring it back," Dex grinned cheerily as he grasped the handle. "Empty, though."

He was struggling to keep calm—but it was not the excitement of winning but rather from knowing that Pepe Carmino might even now be in the building. Dex lugged the heavy suitcase up the stairs, Tiffany a couple of strides ahead of him.

Tom was not there, but Dex stopped a passing taxi almost at once. "Hello! Berkeley Square, and then the Goring Hotel in Victoria. Thanks."

"The Goring?" Tiffany was all at sea. The size of the win, the panic over Dex's father and the suitcase of cash between them had left her dazed.

"We're taking the suite where Kate Middleton spent the night before she married her prince, though I doubt we can afford it," he joked nodding at the suitcase. He allowed himself a grin before his deliberate bravado and cockiness evaporated. "We need a base for the money and must make some urgent calls."

Even as the taxi pulled away, he saw an Aston-Martin appear behind them and slowly glide to a halt. Pepe Carmino was talking intensely on his phone and never noticed the departing members.

"God, Dex! You were so bloody annoying in there."

"I know. It was deliberate." He tapped the suitcase. "It worked too. I wanted *heat*. And I got it. Explanations later." He kissed the side of her flushed cheek as he changed the subject. "Forget Dukes. Now it's Emily. Then maybe meeting Carmino."

"But Northampton? Your father?"

"Ah! Yes. I was coming to that."

He pulled her as close as the seatbelt allowed and his eyes told her that something was afoot. At that moment, the taxi pulled up outside the solicitors' offices and Dex was gone, running to the large brown doors.


No sooner had FB finished confirming the payout than he was back on the casino floor, where he was joined by the Maltese pit boss and the shift-manager. "I saw almost every spin," said the shift-manager. "Dexter seemed too damned familiar with One-Eye. Even winked at him."

FB wrapped his hands around each other. "Winked twice. And Dexter *asked* for One-Eye to be the dealer." He saw he had their attention. "I did not like that. He was so damned cocky. You'd have thought he knew he was going to win. But with One-Eye? Do we trust him? He was one of the team." The listeners were not drawing any instant conclusion, so FB continued, occasionally glancing at the motionless wheel. "One-Eye has been a star. Okay, we know he can land the ball damned close to any number he wants. But nobody's going to convince me he can mainly pick reds—or blacks. Not possible."

The shift-manager agreed. "Impossible. But then, he didn't. He hit a good few blacks but just not enough of them. We've seen these big imbalances before."

FB looked up sharply. "What about the wheel? Could it be faulty? Or gaffed?"

The Maltese shook his head. "To me? Dexter got lucky. This was nothing like a record run of all reds. Shit happens. Today was that day." He spun the wheel in a sudden, irritated move. "One-Eye was spinning sometimes slow, sometimes quicker. I can't see how he's to blame."

FB grasped his chin for a moment. "If it's not One-Eye, I'm having the wheel checked. I'm sending it away for examination and testing. What spooks me is this: the first time that Dexter plays really big, he cleans up."

"Yeah! Send it to TCS John Huxley."

FB nodded. "Ideal. We need a quick opinion from a top manufacturer. If we do nothing, the boss will go berserk."

The listeners both agreed. "If that wheel is gaffed, those Huxley folk will be onto it in a trice," the shift-manager agreed as he scratched his backside.

FB shook his head in bewilderment. "I'll get our security guys to take it now." He was about to move away when he gave each of the two listeners a meaningful stare. "And I want to see One-Eye in my office in fifteen minutes. Then I'd better put on a tin-hat and tell the boss."

"Rather you than me."

# CHAPTER FIFTY-FOUR

Dex googled *Police Belgravia* on his smartphone and found there was a police station on Buckingham Palace Road, just a quarter of a mile from Pinesta Crescent. He tapped on the glass behind the driver's head and slid open the partition. "Change of plans. Take us to 202 Buckingham Palace Road, the police station."

"Ain't so comfy as the Goring, mate," the driver laughed.

"Cheaper, though." Dex slid the partition shut. "Jude sent a text suggesting Emily is at 37 Pinesta Crescent. Belongs to someone called Arnie Fisher. Whoever he is."

Tiffany puckered her pink lips. "How does she know?"

Dex had to admit there was no explanation. "That's all I know."

"Surely she'd dial 999, not tell you. You can't trust her. That's why you got rid of her. This could be a trap."

Dex tilted his head left and right as if weighing the balance. "It's the only lead we've got. In Sydney, she really did do some kids' nursing. Perhaps she loved kids." He looked down at the bag with the evidence. "Anyway, we'll dump the evidence with the cops and get them to Pinesta Crescent."

His flow was interrupted by the taxi braking sharply to avoid a motorbike courier as they swung into Grosvenor Place. "Why would she want to trap me when I'm meeting Carmino at seven?" Progress seemed painful on the stop-go busy road. His tone brightened. "At least with Carmino in Dukes counting his losses, Emily should be safe."

"It's pretty flimsy. You'll have to be at your most persuasive with the cops."

"They'll have nothing better." The cab waited at the junction of Buckingham Palace Road with Bressenden Place. Dex fell silent as he rehearsed a brief but convincing story for the cops. Then his thoughts were interrupted by a text. "Shit!" he exclaimed. "Shit, shit, shit." He saw Tiffany trying to read the message. "It's from FB. Pepe was only at Dukes for a few minutes."

"Any reason?"

"No." Dex thought rapidly. "He may be going to Pinesta Crescent. You talk to the police. As a well-known reporter, you're credible. I'm going to number 37. I can't risk Pepe getting there before me. If I see him arriving, I won't let him enter. If I'm there first, oh, I just don't know…"

"This Arnie, he won't let you in. Not if Emily's there." Tiffany grasped Dex's hand and gripped it tight. "Leave it to the police."

Dex shook his head. "No time. I can't risk anyone harming her. Her kidnap was my fault. I couldn't live with myself if…"

"Take care," she said, a phrase which was the converse of what Dex had in mind. Tiffany saw the steadfast determination on Dex's face. It stayed there until she piled out of the taxi with all the suitcases, the winnings, and the evidence. Dex waved back as she blew a kiss goodbye.

"Be quick."

Dex told the driver to take him to Winchester Street, just around the corner from Pinesta Crescent. After juggling with the one-way system, the driver pulled up a few minutes later. "There you are, guv."

Dex paid him off and got his bearings. Pinesta Crescent ran off to his right and the corner house was numbered 93. He hesitated at the junction. If Carmino came by car, he would have to enter from the far end because of the one-way system. He checked the phone number Jude had sent him and then dialled. Putting a hankie over the mouthpiece, he spoke from a distance when it was answered.

"Arnie. Bad line. Can you hear me? Be with you in two minutes. Traffic's been a right pig." He ended the call, hoping he had done enough to be admitted.

He looked down the crescent, which had cars parked on both sides. There was a nanny pushing a pram, a black couple with bags of shopping and two young kids running in the other direction carrying a football. Cycling toward him was a man in royal-blue lycra. Otherwise, the street was quiet and no cars were moving. There was no Aston-Martin.

He walked briskly and looked at number 37. All curtains were closed and if any lights were on, it was not apparent. The property was mid-terrace, about nineteenth century and looked to be either two or three-up and two-down, the sort of design with a sitting-room fronting onto the street and the kitchen somewhere to the rear.

He looked at the solid white front door with a large brass dolphin for a knocker. It was well kept, even prosperous-looking. There was no security camera covering the frontage that he could see and no spyhole.

He was about to rap on the door when a nasty thought struck him. *Will Arnie be alone?* Two men had handled the kidnap. He hovered uncertainly, torn between immediate action and waiting for the police to come roaring into the street.

*Unlikely, but could Carmino have got here first?*
*Would he really want her dead?*
*Who knows?*
*Is he in there now?*
*Maybe even killing her?*
*While I'm waiting outside.*
*Or is Carmino going to move her to Cadogan Square?*
*Can I get her out before Carmino arrives?*
*And then no meeting in Cadogan Square.*
*Would the police arrive mob-handed?*
*Discreetly?*
*How soon could they arrive?*
*Not sooner than Carmino.*

He banged the knocker twice and after a slightly longer wait than he had expected, the door opened. Dex had tucked himself out of sight, flat against the wall to the side of the door. For a moment, Dex saw nobody but then a slim, short, and thin-faced man took a step outside. Dex pounced, grasping the man in a bear-hug and twisting him so that his back was pinned to Dex's chest. He shoved the man back into the house and used his own backside to shut the self-locking door, something he instantly regretted.

It was not pitch black but it was gloomy enough in the small entrance area with no lights on. The air smelled of cooking fats. His captive's grey sweatshirt was stale and damp with nervous sweat. *Was this the gofer who had fixed Beth's accident? Had executed Mick Glenn?* His anger mounting, he tightened his grip.

The door to the front room was slightly open, giving what little light there was. It revealed that Dex was in more of a corridor than a hall. Directly ahead was a straight set of stairs with a handrail on the left and wrought-iron bannisters with a wooden rail to the right. If Jude was to be believed, then somewhere in here was Emily. But where? Dex guessed at a bedroom though there was no sound of any other occupant besides the man who was wriggling and kicking with no chance of escape. To the right of the stairs was an unlit narrow corridor leading to what Dex assumed was the kitchen.

"Where's the girl? I want her freed now." Dex shook the man and snapped out the words but got no answer. He then yelled. "Emily! Emily! It's Mister Dex. We played with Winnie-the-Pooh. Remember? Where are you?" There was no response. No real surprise. She would be gagged. "I'm here to save you from the wicked men."

Still not a sound from upstairs. Instead, the front room door silently swung open, revealing Pepe Carmino, his Master Bowie in his right hand. In the half-light, his olive skin seemed even darker and his cheeks looked sucked in and locked in a moment of triumph. The sliver of light grew so that the menacing point of the Bowie flashed and glinted for a fraction of a second. It was enough for Dex to flinch as recollections of the murdered Mexican filled his mind.

"Mr Dexter! Thanks for phoning. Very helpful—though of course our meeting was not until seven."

Dex looked at Carmino, who was now holding the knife in whitened knuckles, blade pointed down just a few feet from him. He wondered what the hell the police were doing and how Carmino had reached here so quickly. He must have known the one-way system better than the taxi driver. His second thought, immediately dismissed, was to retreat through the front door.

*No way.*

*Not with Emily here.*

Anyway, he could not open it without releasing his captive.

At least for now, the lightweight man was something of a shield for as long as Dex could hold him. He felt his legs being kicked as the man's shoe heels hacked back into his shins. He fought to ignore the pain and tightened his grip, desperate to keep the prisoner's arms pinned to his side.

As before, Carmino spoke slowly but with a bite in each word. "Let Arnie go or I'm going up to take care of the girl."

*So Emily is upstairs.*

*And this is definitely Arnie.*

Dex looked at the gap between him and the bottom step of the stairs. Carmino could only reach the staircase by getting much closer to him and Arnie and then squeezing through the narrow space between them and the bottom step.

*If only I knew which room Emily was in.*

*If I could get to it.*

*If I can stop Carmino mounting the stairs.*

The plan had gone wrong, horribly wrong. Carmino arriving first had not been in the script. Now, he was facing down a psychopath, who every so often jabbed the knife towards them so that the point seemed perilously close. What Carmino would do if given the chance was unthinkable.

*Would he carry out his threat to the poor kid?*

*Probably.*

*Certainly.*

*I need time. Buy time.*

*Do anything to buy time.*

*Wait for the cavalry.*

*Give the cavalry a chance.*

He edged closer to the foot of the stairs, narrowing the gap to make it even harder for Carmino to get past. For now, with Arnie Fisher between the Bowie and Dex, a standoff seemed the best he could achieve. Dex yelled again, even louder this time.

"Emily! Emily! It's your friend Mister Dex. We're going to play Connections soon with Mummy and Daddy. Where are you? Make a noise, any noise."

For a few agonising seconds, there was no response. Then came a loud crashing sound from upstairs, at the rear of the house. Dex leaned back and flicked the light switch by the front door with his head. The whole area was suddenly illuminated. He could see Carmino's hatred, his eyes as cold as the knife. He was inching toward Arnie, hoping to get close enough to lunge around him and slash into Dex's side.

*Still no sirens, no thundering feet, no battering-ram enforcer break-ing down the door.*

*Nothing.*

Just the laboured breathing of Arnie as he panted a strong smell of lunchtime curry, his clamped chest heaving beneath Dex's strong arms. Carmino had now advanced again and was close to striking distance, the knife being flourished or jabbed with increasing frequency with only Arnue as his saviour. *It was decision time.*

*Where the hell was the cavalry?*

# CHAPTER FIFTY-FIVE

Had Tiffany not been a familiar face to the duty sergeant at the police station, she might not have received the supportive reaction she did. In a few pithy sentences, she captured his attention and was quickly seated in an interview room with two experienced detectives appearing almost at once. Det-Supt Bob Wylie took control and a chain of command was established. Calls were made to Scotland Yard and to the local team in Surrey.

But instant action cannot be instant. Procedures had to be followed. Officers trained in weaponry had to be summoned. The ambulance service had to be alerted. The surrounding houses had to be cleared and the street cordoned off. Someone contacted a Child Support Unit.

Tiffany gave them a description of Dex in his navy blazer, blue shirt, chinos and loafers. A detective-sergeant was deputed to get ID on Arnie Fisher and Pepe Carmino. "When you get there," she briefed them, "if Dex is not outside, ring this number. If there's no answer, he's inside and could be in big trouble. Oh…and watch out for a powder-blue Aston-Martin. The number is DUK something. That belongs to Pepe Carmino, so you'll know he's there."

After that, Tiffany was not privy to the detailed planning of the operation or to the lively debate about whether to force entry or to use a loud-hailer to get the occupants to surrender. Bob Wylie had taken on board that time could be short yet with a kid's life at stake, some things could not be rushed. Safeguarding his officers when facing someone reputed to be an armed psychopath also had to be considered.

A few minutes later, she heard the commotion as over twenty heavily protected officers gathered to leave, with more coming from across the river. Wylie refused to take Tiffany but nothing was going to stop her from being there. Having ensured that their belongings were safely stored, she set off on foot, knowing she would never make it beyond the police line at the end of the crescent. As she drew close, her heart stopped. Parked in the next street to Pinesta Crescent was Carmino's Aston-Martin. She rang Dex.

There was no reply.

The standoff had gone on too long—certainly the muscles in his arms were complaining at maintaining the stranglehold on Arnie Fisher. His legs were still taking a beating as Fisher kicked, though less fiercely now. Occasionally, Dex pivoted so that Arnie's body moved about, making a lunge by Carmino more risky. That apart, he had to do something. He knew he could not keep his grip on Fisher much longer.

*Do something!*

In a swift but effective move, he shifted his arms from the wraparound to gripping Arnie's elbows. At the same moment, he kneed him in the back and flung both arms forward, sending the small figure hurtling to slam straight into Carmino. The blade ripped into Arnie's forearm and he howled but he was fortunate not to be stabbed full-on in the chest.

Arnie's weight was too slight to topple Carmino, who stumbled backward as their bodies collided. But Dex had his chance and he seized it, leaping onto the bottom step and bounding up the stairs. As he did so, his phone started to ring. He recalled his instructions to Tiffany: *If I'm not outside the house or if I don't answer the phone, I'm in deep shit.*

*And I am.*

At the top of the stairs was a tiny landing giving straight onto the rear bedroom. There was a bathroom and seemingly two other bedrooms away to his right. He heard Carmino scrabbling somewhere behind him and then imagined him leaping up the stairs just a short distance behind him. The door straight ahead had a keyhole but no sign of a key, a mixed blessing. He could not risk discovering too late that the door was locked. By that time he would be cornered and Carmino's knife would be plunging deep into his back.

Impulsively, he spun round at the top step and saw his attacker was still about seven steps beneath him. Dex's unexpected move made Carmino falter but only just for a moment. "Arnie. Get your gun." Carmino's calm authority had not been shaken.

"My sodding arm's bleeding to buggery."

"The gun. Get it."

"The bullets is out the back." Dex heard Arnie's response in a rough London accent. "I'll fetch them."

Dex waited for a second, knowing now what to do. He had to let Carmino get closer. He waited as Carmino took another step up, his eyes fixed on Dex. Dex knew he had to give no clue of his plan as he stood, arms by his side. Carmino took another step closer.

Dex stood his ground, waiting for Carmino to get closer, danger-ously close as he mounted the stairs, one step at a time. *Now*! In a swift move, Dex gripped the banister with his left hand and the handrail with his right. Immediately, he swung himself horizontal, pivoting on his arms.

Both legs slammed into Carmino's chest with surprising force just as Carmino lashed out with a vicious upward swipe. The massive impact was decisive, like a kick from a mule. Carmino rocked momentarily before tumbling head-first, thud, thud, thud down the stairs. Dex heard an impressive cry of pain on impact at the foot of the seventeen steps.

Dex wanted to enjoy the sight of the slumped figure but had no time for that luxury. He turned and tried the bedroom door. It was unlocked! In a trice, he was inside the darkened room. He slammed the door shut and switched on the light. To his relief, he saw that in the lock was an old-style iron key.

He turned it easily enough and for a moment knew that he had bought time. But once the door had been smashed in, Dex knew that short of a miracle, he and Emily were trapped and defenceless. The door was wooden, painted white and designed with two lightweight panels centred within the frame. They would be poor resistance to a sustained attack. A few shoulder barges would probably smash the lock from the door-frame.

On the floor was Emily, bound and gagged, where she had bumped herself off the bed. Dex saw her tear-stained cheeks. The tiny helpless little girl looked terrified, her blue eyes wide with fear. On recognising Dex, her look changed to one of relief. A white sock was rammed into her mouth but there was no time to remove it. Her wrists and ankles were bound with cheap blue rope. He looked around and found he was standing in a single bedroom with a small dressing-table, a cheap violet and blue patterned carpet and a solitary chair. The full-length brown curtains were drawn. He had no interest in hiding in the empty wardrobe. A coffin smelling of mothballs and a sprig of lavender was not on the agenda.

"Hello, Emily, I'll free you in a minute. Everything's going to be just fine." He hated the certainty but it seemed better than saying that a murderous psychopath was about to kill them both. "Now listen," he said. "Do what I say and we'll fix the bad men."

As he spoke, he was dragging her away from the cheap bed with its tubular steel headboard. He pushed her into the far right corner and pulled the thin mattress and an old army blanket off the bed.

"Don't move. Be as quiet as a little mouse. Just think of dear old Winnie having breakfast with us. We're playing hide and seek from the bad men." He stroked her cheek as he covered her over in an ambiguous-looking heap. With a noisy crash, he then tipped the bed so that it was standing on its end and straddling the other corner straight ahead of the door. With its solid base, for people behind it, it looked like suitable protection.

He heard shouting but what was being said was muffled. The phone rang again but he did nothing to answer. At that moment too, the door shook with a mighty impact. The noise reverberated round the small room and Emily jumped in fear. "Stay still, Emily. I'm here, but the bad man is trying to break down the door."

The door bulged as it was struck again.

*That shouting!*

*Perhaps the cavalry had arrived.*

Dex looked around the simple room. He saw an ornament, a cheap-looking vase in multicolours with the word Benidorm on it.

*Perfect!*

*I can crack Carmino over the skull with this.*

He picked it up, and to his horror found it was made of *papier-mâché* and had no weight at all. A glance around the rest of the room showed no other weapon. He then looked behind the curtains for ornaments on the window ledge.

*Nothing.*

Then he saw that hanging from a hook at either end of the curtains were ornate tie-backs in maroon and gold cord. Each was knotted in a loop about eighteen inches long. He ripped one from its hook and hurried to the solitary forty-watt bulb set in a dusty pink shade that hung from the ceiling.

He saw the door bulge again as it was blasted with another shoulder-barge. Ignoring the searing pain from the heat, he removed the bulb and the room was instantly blackened. Then he got into position, bulb in one hand and the cord in the other. He removed his shoes and stood in his stockinged feet. From Emily there came not even a whimper.

Two, three, four more times the door was buffeted before the wood around the lock started to splinter and give way. Dex heard the splitting and knew that in just a few seconds, Carmino would be into the room. But where would Arnie be? Next to him with a gun? Guarding the stairs? There was no way of knowing.

*And where were the cops?*

From his position beside the door's hinges, Dex waited for the *coup de grâce*. It came with the next impact, the door bursting open with a shudder. Some distant light from the hall downstairs still left the bedroom darkened. Dex heard the click of the light switch and Carmino's muttered curse.

Before Carmino's eyes adjusted to the gloom, Dex hurled the lightbulb, 10-pin bowling style, skimming it a few inches above the floor toward the upturned bed. It crashed into the wall and exploded. Now he could see Carmino's back, because he had taken a couple of steps into the room. The noise stopped him dead.

Instead of looking around the room, his attention was instantly focussed on the source of the noise and the shadowy shape of the upturned bed. Carmino remained motionless for another moment, staring toward it. Then with a slight nod of satisfaction, he took another step away from Dex's concealed position and toward the bed. Dex tried to see if Carmino was still clutching the knife in his right hand, but in the half-light he could not be sure.

*Assume the worst.*

*It was now or never.*

*Carmino must not see behind the bed.*

In his stockinged feet, he took a silent pace forward, positioning himself very slightly to the left of the shadowy figure's back, wanting to keep as far as possible from Carmino's right hand. Carmino was much bigger than Arnie—a little taller than Dex but of slim build. Dex reckoned they were a match for each other except that Carmino had the knife while he had only the cord and surprise on his side.

Dex raised his crossed-over arms above head height, both outstretched. In each hand, he gripped the tie-back cord. Before Carmino had any idea of the imminent attack from behind, the cord had looped around his neck. Dex viciously yanked his arms apart, the cord instantly biting around the throat and the lumpy knot digging deep.

For a fleeting moment there was no reaction. Then came a short jabbing move from Carmino's left hand. Dex felt the sharp, searing pain of a knife driving into his left thigh.

*Shit!*

*He had switched hands.*

*Must have injured his right hand when he fell.*

He yelped at the searing pain and fought to ignore the sensation of blood gushing from the wound, Dex shifted his position, moving his body to the right and away from the blade. "Drop the knife."

Carmino did not, one leg kicking back, left arm swinging again, desperately seeking another strike. Dex reckoned he needed to gain more traction on Carmino's neck. There was only one way of doing it. He twisted and pulled so that they both moved backward in tandem, Carmino being dragged by the neck.

After one more huge effort, Dex was there, his back now braced against a wall for support. He forced his left knee upward, pushing it into the small of Carmino's spine.

*Success!*

He had the needed traction and was able to yank Carmino's head back further while pushing his spine forward. The smell of shampoo filled Dex's nostrils as he listened to the gasps from the strangulated throat. He needed Carmino unconscious. He could not keep this going for long, standing on his one good one leg. His left one could now take no weight and felt wobbly as the blood pumped out freely.

"I said drop the knife."

Dex felt a more feeble response from Carmino's left hand this time, as the strangulation took effect. Whether a deliberate decision or not, Dex heard the clatter of the knife as it fell to the floor. He was starting to feel lightheaded and his balance was unsteady. If only he could keep up the tension, Carmino would lose consciousness but as he wobbled again, he knew holding on would be impossible. The room was starting to spin and his left leg was almost useless.

*Where was Arnie?*

*Had he got the bullets?*

*Where were the police?*

As Carmino started to go limp, Dex heard Arnie's rasping accent. "Peps! I'm coming up, mate." Then he heard noise from the street. At last! The police! It sounded as if they were shouting *armed police*. From downstairs came a sudden boom as the front door was battered. But with Arnie drawing close, doing nothing was still not an option. He could be dead before they had beaten down the door.

Dex removed his knee from Carmino's back, and with a supreme effort, his left leg howling with pain, he heaved Carmino outside the bedroom to the top of the stairs. There he saw Arnie over halfway up. Instantly, there was a flash and the crack of a 9mm Beretta, the bullet missing them both and embedding in the ceiling. Instantly, Dex jettisoned the casino owner with a hefty shove toward Arnie, who was confronted with Carmino's near two hundred pounds crashing down toward him.

Whether accidently or in panic and confusion was unclear but there was another loud retort as the gun fired again. The two men crashed down together in a confused series of bumps and yells, ending up motionless in a heap by the front entrance. For a moment, Dex stood transfixed at the sight of the inert bodies.

*Emily!*

*I must get to her.*

*The knife! The knife!*

*I must get the knife.*

*Need a weapon to defend us.*

Dex turned to the bedroom. But as he reached the broken door, his knees buckled and he crumpled to the floor, his head spinning and delirious.

*Must stop the blood.*

*Thigh wound.*

*Femoral artery.*

*Not good.*

As the room spun around him, he saw bagpipers marching on the ceiling. *Was that Gus McKay with them?* For a second he blamed the medicaments from Dr Grierson, a wild thought as he tried feebly to scrabble over the bloodied carpet toward the knife and Emily.

The shouting seemed very distant now.

*The cops have given up.*

*It's just the bagpipers now!*

Again the swirling kilts danced in front of his eyes and the room did cartwheels as his fingers clawed feebly for grip. He was still six feet from Emily when he felt himself slipping, slipping more deeply away. He could hear no sound, not even a single bagpiper.

It was so very quiet now.

Nothing.

# EPILOGUE

*I found it strange being back at Bladon Church so soon after burying Beth but I guess I should have expected that father was always susceptible to dying from pneumonia. It had been comforting to hear the familiar baritone voice of Reverend Hillyer as the service came to an end. But it was a surprise that Father's Will had stipulated a funeral at Bladon— not the pomp and ceremony of a grand occasion in London that I had always expected.*

*"And now," continued the vicar, "we turn to Finlay Charles Dexter, a young man whom I have known from childbirth as Dex. Many of you will know that father and son had a difficult relationship, only to become reconciled after the death of Beth on that summer day such a short time ago. Tragic though it is to be gathered here again today, to me it is so very satisfying for them to be united in death, and for me to officiate at this double service and burial here in our quiet Oxfordshire church."*

*Double service?*

*Finlay Dexter?*

*But that's me.*

*There's been some mistake. This is not my funeral. I'm here to bury Father; to watch him join Beth, dear Carole, and baby Jamie. Fascinated and content just to listen, I decided not to tell them this was just one huge mistake.*

*"And so," continued Hillyer, "though we mourn the passing of a brave young man who gave his life to save young Emily Evans, we celebrate his courage, and his many other fine qualities."*

*I wished I could agree, but courage never came into it. Like so much else these past few weeks, I was never driven by courage. Duty?*

*Yes…that would be more appropriate. But for me and my obsessive behaviour, Emily would never have been kidnapped at all.*

*Craning my neck, I looked down the church. Sure enough, there was Adam Yarbury, come to pay his respects to Father. He was seated beside*

*Billy Evans, his face still looking tired and drawn. On Billy's other side was Emily, clutching Winnie-the-Pooh.*

*Billy, who seemed grief-stricken, was dabbing his cheeks with a blue hankie. But why was he taking Father's death so badly? And that woman next to him? Sandie—his wife, maybe? Oh, I hope so. I hope they are reconciled. Perhaps some good came from the kidnap after all. I looked at Emily again as she wiped a tear from Pooh's eyes.*

*I really must play Connections with her.*

*No. I've no plans for tomorrow.*

*We can play then.*

*"And now," continued Hillyer, "we welcome to our parish church Professor Margaret Tuson, who has flown from Sydney, Australia, to be here today because she wished to say a few words."*

*I was struggling to work out why Jude's mum would fly over for Father's funeral. I saw her come forward to stand close beside me and then turn to face the congregation. Mother looked more like a big sister to Jude, her features and figure so similar and her bronzed face not aged by time or events. I looked back to the lines of pews but among so many familiar faces Jude's was not there.*

*But why not?*

*After composing herself, Margaret Tuson started to speak, her voice cracking with emotion. "Many, many words have been written about Pepe Carmino and his corrupt and murderous empire. To the media, the world's press, this has been a story of epic and global proportions—and rightly so. But for those of us inadvertently caught up in Carmino's world, we see it all very differently.*

*"I never met Dex but like all of you I have read and heard so much about him. Jude told me she had grown very fond of him, respecting his decency as an employer. Her emails were full of his zest for life. But last week, as I expect you all know, we laid Jude to rest in Castlebrook Memorial Park in Sydney."*

*I could not believe what I was hearing. No, surely not. Not Jude, who had done more to save Emily than anybody? Yet I had to believe what Mother was saying. But why had nobody told me before now?*

*Oh God! Jude dead?*

*How? Why?*

*Carmino?*

*Oh God forbid, not another death down to me.*

*I looked across and saw Jude's mother in her black dress, head held high and looking defiant as she fought to carry on. At last, her voice still choking with emotion, she did so.*

*"Our Jude was a victim of Carmino's brutality, a price she paid to save young Emily. I have no doubt that Jude had discovered how dangerous Pepe Carmino really was. Tragically, she found out too late for herself… but thankfully soon enough to save Emily."*

*I saw Margaret Tuson give a watery smile in Emily's direction.*

*"It is a blessing for us all that Emily is here with us today. Jude did not die in vain. And as for Finlay Dexter, among the plaudits for his sacrifice, many harsh words have also been written. I want you to know that my husband Eric and I do not harbour any bitterness or resentment that so many have died in Dex's obsessive determination.*

*"Why? Because this fine young man was driven by the noblest of motives: he wanted truth and justice for his dead sister, a vow he had made to her even before she was cruelly killed in a road accident—an event we now know was another murder orchestrated by Pepe Carmino."*

*"And so I conclude by saying that, just as there were so many needless deaths in World Wars where Britain and Australia have stood together against evil, I am proud that our beloved Jude and Finlay Dexter died together in a noble cause…fighting unimaginable evil not of their making. Judge him not harshly. Thank you."*

*It would have been great to say that I agreed with her—to shout hear, hear, I'll drink to that! But I could say nothing because she was wrong— doubly wrong, and especially because I am not dead.*

*But Jude?*

*Murdered by Carmino?*

*Yes, I can believe that.*

*My fault.*

*Me, and my obsession.*

*Destroying other people's lives…only to survive myself.*

*I watched as the Reverend Hillyer appeared close to me, his rotund face so calm. As ever, the gold-rimmed half-glasses were low on his bulbous nose as he announced that Tiffany Richmond wanted to say a few words. That was a puzzle.*

*Why would she wish to say anything about my father?*

*I watched the elegant poise as she clattered up the aisle in her high heels, black pill-box hat and a tightly fitting black suit that just reached her knees. The colour suited her milk-and-honey complexion I had never seen her look so gorgeous, her head held erect and steady as she turned to face the congregation.*

*Maybe, just maybe, we were meant for each other.*

*Might get married.*

*Now, there's a thought!*

*I felt her closeness, and looked forward to spending more time with her now that the deep wound in my thigh was healed. Without a note in her hand, she looked the picture of composure as she stood so confident and erect. If she felt any deep emotion, it never showed in her face or voice.*

*"I knew Dex for less time than many of you gathered here today but I quickly came to recognise a steadfast determination and loyalty in everything he did. The catalogue of tragedies these past several weeks were neither of his will nor of his hand. He was never in this Greek tragedy for himself, least of all to achieve anything for himself. When I first met him, his sister and father had just been trapped in the flaming wreck of their car.*

*"I quickly discovered that Dex was a man of simple beliefs—someone who had been dealt severe blows throughout his life. He had lost his mother to another continent and his business and health to his father's relentless pursuit of the big deal. By then, Dex had a beautiful wife Carole and a twenty-month-old son, Jamie.*

*"It was to be Dex's cruel lot to witness them perish in front of his eyes in a flaming inferno where he was helpless to intervene." She paused for emphasis. "And history repeated itself that sunny morning on the A4 in Hammersmith."*

*She took a step or two sideways, so close that I could smell her fragrance above those of the flowers that lay all around.*

*"Dex so wanted to prove that the accident was much more than that. It saddens me that he never lived to know that Arnie Fisher confessed."*

*I wanted to sit up and punch my fist in the air but restrained myself, wondering what else I was going to hear.*

*"He wanted none of Beth's wild plan to destroy Dukes, yet his loyalty and promise to her were his undoing." Tiffany leaned across and nearly*

*touched me. "Dex was selfless. Nothing he did was for himself. For me, Dex had nothing to prove."*

*As I lay back, I felt uncomfortable hearing this insightful appraisal. Though I would never admit it, I found it hard to disagree. She rested her hand on the oak. "Some of you will have read what I wrote for a Sunday paper. Dex was no gambler. Nevertheless, through advice from Gus McKay, who I see in the congregation, he learned enough about roulette to take on Dukes and to win just short of ten million pounds—on the very day he died. That win was not for himself.*

*"As we flew into London that morning, he knew the huge risk he might be taking by confronting Pepe Carmino. He made a Will witnessed by Billy Evans and Adam Yarbury. In it, he pledged nearly all his substantial wealth to my African charity—including whatever he might win at Dukes. Yesterday morning, I applied to rename the charity as The Finlay Dexter Children's Foundation." Tiffany said nothing as the church was suddenly filled with applause.*

*I like that.*

*The Finlay Dexter Children's Foundation.*

*I thought back to the excitement in Dukes, when 85 percent of the numbers had been red. I recalled the books I had read, the pointers from Gus McKay and the brilliant craftsmanship of Lawrence Jamous. He had created a perfect replica of the wheel used in Dukes. Perfect except that every black pocket and zero were narrowed and shallower—not obvious to the naked eye yet sufficient to give red that advantage I so desperately needed to honour my promise to Beth.*

*Cheating?*

*Me? I prefer to call it poetic justice.*

*Dishonest?*

*Well, yes, I guess it was—but no more than Dukes deserved.*

*Fighting fire with fire, now that's an appropriate metaphor.*

*Sort of Robin Hood, giving to the poor.*

*FB had done well—switching the wheels whilst the casino was closed. And, because nobody had mentioned any furore, I guessed he had followed my instruction and sent the original wheel to Huxley for testing and the gaffed wheel back to Jamous. I needed to check with FB that the switch had worked as planned."*

*Of course, I can never admit this to Tiffany, although she's bound to ask again. When I die, that's a secret I'll take to the grave. Meantime, I knew now what I would say to her about her curiosity at the huge win.*

*"Tiffany, I once saw a pair of illusionists who ended up starring in Las Vegas. They were called Siegfried & Roy. They made an elephant disappear from right beside me. At first, I really, really wanted to know how they did it. But on second thoughts, I decided, isn't it better not to know?"*

*I wondered if Tiffany would buy that explanation when I told her perhaps over dinner somewhere quiet.*

*Oh, what's that she's saying now?*

*"With Pepe Carmino forever silenced by a gun fired by Arnie Fisher, some of the truth may never be known. But thanks to Dex, Arnie Fisher will stand trial for the murders of Beth Dexter, Sir Charles Dexter, Mick Glenn and the kidnap of Emily Evans. Today I heard that the FBI now believe Enzo Letizione, who was found executed in the desert just over the state boundary in Arizona, was also silenced on orders from Carmino. They also expect to link Carmino to the deaths of Tavio Sanches and Diego Rodriguez."*

*I saw Tiffany look down toward me, as if she were addressing me now rather than talking to the assembled congregation. She placed both hands just above my face, as close to me as she could get. I looked up, my gaze fixed upon her beauty.*

*No, surely not?*

*Not crying?*

*But yes. Tears are rolling down her cheeks.*

*"Dex, you fulfilled your promise to Beth. Sleep in peace."*

*I saw her dab her eyes with a small white hankie. "Even though you are now to be laid low, for me you will forever walk tall. Dex, I never told you this in life. But I loved you."*

*I liked the sentiment. I loved it.*

*She was right.*

*I will walk tall.*

*And tonight I will tell her my feelings about her.*

*I'll look forward to that.*

CPSIA information can be obtained at www.ICGtesting.com
Printed in the USA
LVOW08s0805270716

497502LV00004B/11/P